PENGUIN

Betrayal

Stewart Binns began his professional life as an academic. He passed selection for the SAS in 1980 and served for three years before settling into a career as a schoolteacher, specializing in English and history. Later in life he began a successful career in television. He has won a BAFTA, a Grierson, an RTS and a Peabody for his documentaries.

Stewart has written two highly acclaimed historical series. *Betrayal*, a standalone, is his seventh novel.

Betrayal

STEWART BINNS

PENGUIN BOOKS

PENGUIN BOOKS

UK | USA | Canada | Ireland | Australia
India | New Zealand | South Africa

Penguin Books is part of the Penguin Random House group of companies
whose addresses can be found at global.penguinrandomhouse.com.

First published 2017
001

Copyright © Stewart Binns, 2017

The moral right of the author has been asserted

Set in 12.5/14.75 pt Garamond MT Std
Typeset by Jouve (UK), Milton Keynes
Printed in Great Britain by Clays Ltd, St Ives plc

A CIP catalogue record for this book is available from the British Library

ISBN: 978-1-405-92705-5

To all the good people of Northern Ireland who struggled for decades to live with their past. Perhaps now they have finally found a future together.

Author's Note

Betrayal is a work of fiction. Although set during actual events and based on the author's service as a soldier, all names, characters, places and incidents either are the product of the author's imagination or are used entirely fictitiously.

Contents

1. Wheels Within Wheels

'Morning, sir.'

'Morning, Roger. Come in and sit down.'

'Cold today; autumn's here.'

'Never mind the bloody weather, I'm in no mood for pleasantries.'

'Sir?'

'I've just had the Secretary of State on the blower; he's not happy!'

'Gerry Adams's incendiary speech, I suppose?'

'No, we can't be blamed for that; that's the politicians' business. It's something much more worrying – and on our patch.'

Roger watches his boss go to the window and stare out across the London skyline.

'You're right, it does look like autumn's here.'

Roger takes the comment as a half-hearted apology for being snapped at. But then his superior swings round to face him. His look could melt stone.

'Listen, I don't like early-morning calls from skittish politicians. Prior's alright, but he's got Maggie on his back, and she's got problems again.'

'But we've just had the Falklands Victory Parade; she can do no wrong.'

'That's not the way she sees it: enemies around every

corner; fourteen per cent unemployed; discontent in the military and big business. She's picking fights again. The latest twitch is on your watch, Roger.'

'Other than the usual mayhem, DG, I don't think there's anything particularly untoward over the water.'

'That's not what Prior's been told.'

'By whom, sir.'

'Rumours, whispers; conversations in White's and the Carlton. Last night, some old Unionist backwoodsman collared him in the Commons and berated him about a recent op in Belfast that went belly-up. A couple of your people making a right fucking mess. Apparently, they got out, but the word is that they're a major liability.'

There's a long silence as Roger takes in the news.

'I'll look into it, sir.'

'Don't fob me off, Roger. Which op are they talking about?'

'I'm not sure. I need to go over the files and talk with my team.'

'Bollocks, Roger, it was only last year. I need straight answers.'

'Did Prior give you any more details?'

'No, he didn't. I think he assumed I'd know about any of our ops that have become a problem. And he's bloody well right!'

'You've caught me cold, sir; we're running dozens of ops over there. Let me get the boys together and go over everything.'

'Alright, tomorrow morning. But I'll have to open this to the whole department and the other agencies.

Smythson will have to be there and Special Branch; Prior insists.'

'Bloody hell! Isn't this making a mountain out of a molehill?'

'Come on, Roger, with Maggie rattling her sabre, every molehill's a fucking mountain.'

2. Cold Bath in Clapham

'Jim! Wake up; it's lunchtime! Jim!'

Despite the cries, I don't stir; nothing is registering. I can hear someone shouting at me, but it seems to be just another bad dream.

'Bloody hell, Jim, get up. You stink.'

I hear the shouts but I'm still numb to the world. Like many before me, my quest to bury painful memories is futile. I still have vivid, horrifyingly violent flashbacks. I never see myself in my dark visions, only people staring at me in fear and loathing. Their eyes burn into me. They know who I am, and I know them. They're not ghosts; they're real.

I hear rapid movement around me and finally realize that this isn't a dream. My visitor is darting around my flat. She's looking for the commodities of normal life: toothpaste, washing-up liquid, soap. She finds none.

I'm still barely conscious as I'm dragged from my sofa to the bathroom. She hauls me up and sits my dead weight on the side of the bath.

'You don't have any hot water, so this will wake you up, you drunken bastard!'

She tugs at my clothes and discards each item as if it's a soiled nappy. Suddenly, I'm drowning. I can hear splashing, feel cold water rushing over my face; my mouth and nose are assaulted by gurgling liquid. I gag as a torrent invades my throat. I'm fully conscious, lashing out.

'Whoa, Jim! It's Maureen . . . calm down; you're OK!'

I rub my eyes and shake my head, trying to come to my senses. Then I recognize who my assailant is.

'Fuck me, Mo! What are you doing here?'

'What does it look like? I'm giving you a bath. Have you looked at yourself in the mirror recently?'

'I know, I'm not a pretty sight.'

'How long have you been like this?'

'Not sure.'

I try to calculate in weeks, but give up.

'Months.'

I suddenly realize that there must be a purpose behind Maureen's unexpected visit.

'It's good to see you, Mo, but what's up?'

She looks at me like a casualty nurse dealing with a wino.

'We've got a problem.'

'Course we have; we've had a problem for ages.'

I notice that she's changed. It's obvious that she's also having a hard time; she looks haggard and has lost a lot of weight. Even so, she's still a fine sight: long, elegant limbs, and a lean but powerful frame; a firm jaw setting off a strong face, with dark brown eyes below an unruly mop of russet hair.

'Things have just got a lot worse.'

'Really? From where I am, that doesn't seem possible.'

'They have, believe me.'

Two hours later, I look vaguely normal. I feel like shit and I'm gagging for a drink, but I look better than I have in a long time. Maureen lets me have a beer, which is a relief.

She opens all the windows, washes up and brings a semblance of order to the kitchen. She goes to the corner shop and we devour a mountainous lunch washed down with a cheap bottle of red wine.

My old partner runs her fingers around the rim of a plain white mug that's serving as a wine glass.

'I've been drinking a lot too.'

'You're kidding me, Miss Goody Two-Shoes?'

'Don't be a sod; after what we've been through. I'm not made of stone.'

'You used to be.'

'Jim, please.'

Maureen's eyes fill with tears.

'Heh, I'm the one who's in a bad way. Remember your training.'

'I forgot all that, weeks ago . . .'

She pauses.

'Jim, we're in a right mess.'

'OK, you said things have got worse; how worse?'

Maureen pulls herself together and sets her jaw.

'Control asked to see me.'

She pauses again, looking very solemn.

'They're concerned about both of us, but mainly about you; your drinking. They think you're a lost cause and a major liability.'

'And they've sent you to sort me out.'

'Of course.'

'And if I don't want to be "sorted out"?'

'We'll both be on our own.'

'How come? They could still protect you.'

'Think about it, Jim; if you're a liability, so am I. They'll cut me adrift as well. We'll be described as "lone wolves", acting alone.'

'Fuckers!'

'They're pragmatists. It's what they're paid to do.'

'They're still fuckers!'

'Where's your pistol?'

'Why?'

'They want it back.'

'Like fuck! No way.'

She goes to the window and stares at the identical terraced houses of Victorian London. I hear kids running and screaming down the street. I go to check my watch, but I lost it ages ago – a nice stainless-steel Rolex, about my last prized possession. But the babble and jabber of young kids tells me it's four o'clock, the end of the school day.

Maureen stares at them.

'I miss the kids.'

'So do I.'

She turns to face me, looking stern.

'They want me to sort you out. One last chance.'

'Generous of them. I think I can get by without their help.'

'No, you can't, Jim. If you carry on like this, you'll be dead before the end of the year. Then it'll be my turn.'

I smile, trying to be mischievous, trying to win back some credibility with her.

'Best to go down fighting, then, Mo.'

'Look, if you're happy to sign your own death warrant, then more fool you. But I want to come out of this at the other end.'

'What, with a husband and two point four kids in the Home Counties?'

'Something like that.'

'Then you're as crazy as I am.'

'Jim, please. I need your help.'

A faint memory of my former life stirs in me. Maureen never needed anybody's help before, least of all mine.

'You've never asked for my help before.'

'Well, I'm asking now.'

3. Not a Belle Vue

After a dinner in the pub and enough booze to knock me out, Maureen, sleeping on my careworn sofa, stays the night. The next morning, we're off. Maureen has a plan.

I don't want to go wherever she's taking me. She talked about getting out of London, but I wasn't really listening. I want to retreat into the warmth of a boozer, where I'll find a sanctuary of convivial loneliness far removed from the world's woes and my own sad sorrows.

I'm trying to keep up with her loping strides. I feel like I'm a little lad again, being taken by my mum to Burnley Bus Station to catch a 'chara' to Blackpool. It's hard to keep up when you've only got little legs.

We cross the road towards the clock tower and the glass rotunda that is Clapham Common tube station. There's a scruffy pub on the opposite corner called the Belle Vue. My last chance? Bugger! It's not open yet.

Maureen's a yard in front of me and almost at the entrance to the station. As I take a final glance at the little part of South London that has become my home for the last few months, I catch sight of a moped racing towards us. It doesn't look right; it's going too fast, and the driver's only got one hand on the handlebars. Even though it's a dull, grey day, he's wearing sunglasses and has a baseball cap pulled down over his forehead.

A switch is thrown inside me. Is it the training or

9

instinct? It doesn't matter; everything slows down. I look at Maureen. She hasn't seen the moped. She's focused on getting me down the stairs to the tube.

'Mo! Get inside, move!'

My warning has hardly registered when, with a burst of acceleration, the moped bounces on to the pavement and heads straight for us. The rider puts his hand inside his jacket. I know what's coming next. I begin to freeze. Lassitude and alcohol have dulled my reactions and allowed fear to surface. I don't even reach for the pistol that Maureen rescued from under my bed. She's at the top of the steps that lead down into the station and has turned to see what's happening. Her reactions are better than mine. She's already reached into her bag and crouched down on one knee.

The stubby black outline of the silencer of a small pistol is now pointing right at my chest. Maureen raises her weapon, but she won't be able to aim and fire in time. I look into the black void of my assassin's sunglasses; shoot straight, you bastard!

My saviour is a baby's pushchair. Propelled by a young mother, the front wheels of a navy-blue pram emerge at the top of the steps, making the rider of the moped swerve wildly. In a cacophony of screeching tyres and crashing metal, my assailant topples off his saddle and rolls across the pavement, leaving his moped to smash against the wall of the station. I hear mother and baby screaming at the tops of their voices.

The bullet that was intended for me has left its muzzle but must have missed by a distance. The rider panics, gets to his feet and runs away without even glancing back.

Maureen has taken aim with her weapon, but not at the moped rider. She pulls at my arm and yanks me down behind her.

'Let's go, Jim! Come on, quickly! Three men in a Merc on the other side of the road. Move it.'

She fires three quick rounds as she pushes me down the steps. At the same time, a hail of bullets comes our way. We cower, several flights down the steps, as the bullets – at least a dozen – smash into the wall above us.

We're on the platform in seconds. Without appearing to run, we move as quickly as we can. When we reach the far end of the platform, God smiles on us for a second time; a northbound train careers into the station. When it stops, we step into the front carriage, but notice that, just as the doors close, three men wearing sunglasses, dark clothes and baseball caps manage to jump into the last carriage.

It's commuter time and our carriage is almost full. We have to stand by the doors. Several people are staring at us in our agitated state. I double-check that my weapon is well concealed in my belt and that Maureen's is out of sight. She's breathing heavily and her face is flushed as she peers down the carriage, checking for anyone suspicious.

It's a peculiar feeling, being on a tube with London's commuters at the beginning of an ordinary working day, knowing that three armed men, hell-bent on putting several rounds in you, are only a few carriages away. Trying to look normal, I smile at Maureen. She smiles back, but it's a thin, forced smile. It's obvious that at every stop our pursuers will move along the train to find us. They may even be trying to open the connecting doors between the carriages. We have to get off. Maureen looks anxious. She doesn't know the area as well as I do. She leans towards me and kisses my cheek. It's not a sign of affection, but an opportunity to whisper in my ear.

'What do we do?'

'Where are you taking me?'

'Kent.'

'That's Victoria. We get out at Clapham North, leg it to Stockwell and jump on the Victoria Line; assuming, of course, that we get past the three stooges at the back.'

It's only a couple of minutes to the next station, but it seems like an eternity. At Clapham North, we wait until the doors are about to close before jumping off the train. As we do so, we see that our shadows, pistols in hand and peering into every carriage, have covered half the length of the train. They're creating screams of panic with every step, and our hunters are between us and the platform exit.

Then they see us.

In an instant, they point their weapons towards us and open fire. The *crack*, *crack*, *crack* of several volleys echo around the confined space of the platform like thunderclaps. Fearing for their lives, a mass of terrified people rush towards us. I push Maureen to the ground. Several people fall. I hope that they've tripped rather than been hit. The crowd is another godsend.

'Down the tunnel, Mo!'

'Jesus! Are you serious?'

'No choice. Go!'

Seconds later, we jump on to the track by the driver's window. I glance at him; he's probably been driving for years. There's a look of abject horror on his face. The tunnel is in almost total darkness, illuminated only by an occasional grimy light bulb.

'Keep moving, Mo, and stay to the right; the live rail's the far one. The driver won't leave the station with us in the tunnel, and they'll soon switch off the power.'

'I hope you're right! What about the three fuckers behind us?'

'I don't think they'll risk following us. Given the commotion they've caused back there, they'll leg it, realizing that they'll likely be nabbed at the next station.'

'Same applies to us, doesn't it?'

'Not if we're quick.'

'How far is it?'

'Half a mile, perhaps a bit more. A piece of piss; four minutes.'

'Like buggery! Not in the dark, with a live rail right next to us.'

'Less talk, more speed. Come on!'

We move rhythmically; short, rapid steps.

We manage to get to Stockwell but alarm several travellers as we emerge, dirty, hot and bothered, from the bowels of the Northern Line. When we reach the street, all the buses are full and there are no taxis to be seen, so we decide to run to Victoria; it's only a couple of miles, and the run will help get rid of the adrenalin.

Several police cars and ambulances scream past us as we run across Vauxhall Bridge. Despite my diminished fitness, we're soon at Victoria Station, where Maureen buys tickets for Tunbridge Wells. We've a few minutes to wait for the train, so we sit down and order coffee and a cold drink.

My heart's racing and my hands are shaking. My weapon's digging into my flabby belly, which was once as hard as marble. It makes me all too aware of how I've let myself go over the past few months. Maureen takes several deep breaths. We both look around; all seems calm, but we can hear multiple sirens in the distance.

'Mo, let's take our drinks and get on the train. I reckon the bobbies will be here in a few minutes to close the station.'

Once we're seated, I feel better, especially when the train begins to pull away. A smile breaks across my face as we sit down in the carriage.

'The phones will be red-hot in Gower Street. It'll be pandemonium; the spooks will be running around like blue-arsed flies!'

Maureen also smiles at the thought of our lords and masters in a mad panic.

'Who do you think the shooters were?'

'An ASU?'

'A boy on a bike isn't their usual style, and neither is firing wildly into a crowd. Whoever it was, we got lucky; very lucky.

4. Pilgrim's Rest

I can't get my breath; my lungs are burning. Breathlessly, I call to Maureen, who's striding ahead with her usual gazelle-like lope.

'Is this a good idea? We're miles from anywhere and I'm shagged!'

'The Kent Weald's hardly "miles from anywhere".'

I persuade her to stop for a moment so that I can get my wind back. She'd hired a car at Tunbridge Wells, driven us deep into the forests of the Weald and insisted that we go for a tab as soon as we arrived. I've no idea where we are; Kent's an alien land for me.

'Fuck me, Mo, it's like the Scottish Highlands; we haven't seen a boozer for hours.'

'Fret not, there's one in the next village; we're staying there tonight.'

'Like the old days, boyfriend and girlfriend?'

'Of course.'

'I suppose I'm getting the sofa?'

'There isn't one.'

'Wow, has my luck changed?'

'It's a family room. I used to stay in it with my parents, years ago. You can have the single bed.'

'What a treat!'

We're both deep in thought as we resume our progress through the half-light of the dense Kentish woodland.

My chest struggles to cope with what my legs are asking it to do. I try to remember my training. I slow down to lessen the pain, trying to find a tolerable plateau. Maureen notices that I've slowed my pace.

'Keep up, we need to get fit, Jim.'

'I'm fine, just adjusting.'

'Let's step it up to a new, full-on regime, starting tomorrow.'

'If you say so, boss.'

Mercifully, Maureen suddenly pulls up, sits down on the fallen trunk of a large ash tree and gestures to me to join her. She gets her breath and looks at me closely.

'Why didn't you go to the Falklands?'

'Good question. I thought that's where I'd end up. I got the twenty-four-hour call-up papers, but then nothing.'

Maureen looks at me reflectively.

'It would've solved a few problems if you hadn't come back.'

'I know, I thought that as well. Who knows what was said between Gower Street and Stirling Lines. Anyway, I didn't go. Shame; a proper war, not like the bollocks we had to deal with in Belfast.'

'Do you think they were trying to keep you away from the other lads in the Regiment?'

'Never thought of that. Perhaps.'

'Do you know lots of blokes who went?'

'Yeah, of course. One in particular: my training officer, Malcolm Atkinson, Colour-Sergeant, G Squadron, Hereford.'

'Good bloke?'

'The best. Mind you, the bugger's probably responsible

for all this. If he hadn't sorted me one night in the Brecons, I'd have failed selection.'

I look up and catch a glimpse of a scowling autumn sky eddying above the canopy of soaring Kent oaks, ash and elms. The ominous sky reminds me of many similar days in the Brecon Beacons. I would finish work on Fridays, catch the tube to Sloane Square and take the short walk along the King's Road to the Duke of York's Barracks.

The Duke of York's is the home of 21st SAS, the Regiment's territorial reserve. The 21st is not 22 SAS, the regulars at Hereford, but the selection test's the same, the accolade just as compelling. Could I pass selection for the SAS? Looking back, it was a strange thing to do; a bit of machismo, I suppose. All my colleagues at work were going home to their wives and girlfriends, their families, weekend sport, a few beers and Sunday lunch. But I was voluntarily submitting myself to forty-eight hours of physical and mental punishment, which would prove to be unbearable for the vast majority of my fellow trainees. Then, if I got through it, I would go on camps for several weeks, where the testing would become more and more gruelling until a handful of us would earn our precious beige beret and winged-dagger badge.

It seems like a lifetime ago, but only two years have passed.

'It was the last tab before Long Drag, almost a white-out, middle of the night. I'd fallen behind schedule and, to keep on the move, I'd skipped a nosh and eaten too many dried apricots. So every time I took a glug of water, the dried fruit swelled up, making my belly feel like a pressure cooker about to explode. I was very uncomfortable and totally cream-crackered. I knew I shouldn't, but I had to sit down.'

Maureen looks at me with disdain.

'I know, I know, big mistake! The weight of my bergen dropped me into the snow up to my waist. Even though I soon felt the wet seeping through, it was such a relief to stop and rest.'

Maureen now offers me a compassionate smile. As a fellow soldier, she knows all about the rigours of a gruelling training regime.

'Looking back, I could have been a goner within minutes. You know that twilight zone, where the pain melts away and you start to feel like you're drifting into a cosy sleep.'

Although I try to stop it, I feel a tear forming in the corner of my eye. I really have gone soft! Maureen puts her arm across my shoulders, which only makes it worse. I feel like a little boy who's had his feelings hurt and needs his mum to soothe him. I take a deep breath and force back the emotion.

'Then, I feel my bergen being lifted off the ground and me with it, followed by a big size-twelve boot up my arse: *Get down that fuckin' path, you useless bastard! If I see you on the deck again, I'll kick the shit out of you all the way to the next RV!*

'It was Malcolm Atkinson, and when he said he'd kick the shit out of you, you believed it. I almost sprinted for two hundred yards, before stumbling into the RV. I was right on top of it; I'd had no idea. They told me the tab was canned; weather too bad, even for selection. Fifty yards away down the track, there was a brew and loads of scoff on the go at the back of a 4-tonner, a big pan of minced beef and veg. What a relief! Atkinson never said anything; if he had, they'd have jacked me on the spot. Weeks later, he told me that the reason he kept it quiet was because, when he found me, I still had hold of my weapon.'

'So he went to the Falklands?'

'Yeah, but he didn't come back. He was one of the eighteen good boys who went down in that helicopter. Wednesday, the nineteenth of May, 1982. I'll never forget the date for the rest of my life. He was the sort of bloke you thought was indestructible, without fear. But he was mortal – vulnerable, like the rest of us – and I bet, when that chopper filled with the icy water of the South Atlantic, he was scared shitless as he and the others fought one another to get out.'

Maureen squeezes me tightly. It's a wonderful comfort.

'Eighteen of the finest this country can muster; drowned like kittens in a sack. I cried like a baby when I heard. It happened at a bad time for me. It was as if whatever strength I had left died with them.'

Maureen is looking teary herself. She's fighting her own demons. She sees my weakness and she can't help revealing hers. She looks me in the eye.

'Have you ever thought of topping yourself?'

'Once or twice. It's a coward's way out, but it has crossed my mind.'

'Me too, but I haven't got the balls to do it.'

'Mo, you've got bigger cojones than anyone I've ever met – male or female.'

She smiles, but it soon fades and her face sags as she looks forlorn once more. It's my turn to offer succour.

'Come on, we can sort it.'

'We might have done, a year ago. But look at us now.'

'Then let's get our act together, back to basics.'

The all-but-extinguished embers of my training ignite into a tiny flicker of flame. I begin to think clearly.

'Who knows we're here?'

'No one. I'm sure we weren't followed.'

'How much money do we have?'

'Plenty. I borrowed loads of cash off my father; he's not short of a few quid. I also found loads of cash in your kecks drawer in Clapham and added it to my stash.'

'Good work. So we don't need any post office withdrawals, phone calls, any contact with anyone.'

Maureen's eyes brighten a little.

'We're in the clear, I think.'

'Then let's go to ground in this boozer you're taking me to, get strong and work out a plan.'

Maureen's face breaks into a smile again.

'We can only make it if you become as good as you used to be.'

She pauses and stares into my eyes as if she's peering into my soul, searching for anything of substance she can believe in.

'Can you manage that?'

'I can with your help.'

She puts her hand on my cheek. Perhaps she's seen a hint of the old me behind my eyes.

'Promise?'

'Promise.'

'Let's go and get the car.'
'What's the pub called?'
'The Pilgrim's Rest.'
'Perfect.'

5. Marital Bliss

Maureen and I have been trained to look 'normal' in almost any civilian setting. Don't stand out from the crowd; appear and act naturally. Be chameleons, blend in – whether you are in the Sloane Pony in Parsons Green or a republican club in West Belfast – that was the mantra drilled into us during our Det training.

Sitting enjoying dinner, we look like any other middle-class couple down from London to enjoy a few days of marital bliss. We've begun to relax a little in each other's company, and we share a smile at the report in the *Telegraph* that there's been a gangland shoot-out on the London Underground: three people with gunshot wounds. There's even an editorial which, predictably, bemoans the break-down of law and order on Britain's streets. I can almost hear the indignant tut-tuts echoing across this Garden of England. Maureen smiles at me. It is a smile full of memories.

'You know, when we met at the ferry terminal, I didn't think you were from the Regiment.'

'Too lightweight?'

'Don't get me wrong, but you did look a bit skinny.'

'A lot of people say the same about most SAS boys. I always reckon it's the marines, especially the SBS, who are the he-men; all that swimming and assault course bol-locks. We're all-rounders, but mostly we're stamina boys: long distance and long stay. Legs like quarter-milers, but not blessed with enough intelligence to get bored if we're stuck in a hide for days on end.'

'How did you find selection?'

'Tough as buggery. I told you about my night on the Brecons. There were other bad moments. Bloody hell, if I hadn't been as fit as a dog from sport, I wouldn't have got through the first weekend on the South Downs. We had two or three lads jack before lunch on the Saturday morning. One couldn't keep up with the first tab, another couldn't do more than ten press-ups, and the third got the hump because the DS kept shouting at him.'

Maureen nods knowingly.

'When I did my Det course, we had one poor girl, a sweet little thing – Cheltenham Ladies and all that – who wet her knickers the first time she got a bollocking from our DS. She literally pissed herself right in front of him. Talk about letting the girlies down!'

I smile, seeing the image all too vividly. I suddenly recall a bad memory of my own.

'When it came to the milling on P-Company, I got put in with the biggest, ugliest fucker you've ever seen. The big lummox, a Geordie with several front teeth missing, proceeded to knock seven shades of shit out of me for sixty seconds. I don't mind a scrap, but this lad murdered me. The other lads and all the members of the DS laughed their socks off when they saw my mush afterwards. My nose was bleeding all over my face, I had a big fat lip, and my left eye looked like a golf ball. What was the worst part for you, doing Det?'

'Being a woman, as simple as that; not that we couldn't hack it – the best of us could, just like the men. But it was the attitude, some of it really hostile. I really wanted to do SAS selection, but they wouldn't let me, so 14 Intelligence was the next best thing and in some ways tougher.'

'You reckon you could've passed selection for Hereford? The Fan Dance with a 55-pound bergen and all that?'

'What do you think?'

I look at Maureen's steely expression and remember our operational time together in Northern Ireland.

'OK, I concede you could've hacked it. I suppose you sailed through Det?'

'Not really. Physically, I was alright, even though it was the hardest thing I've ever done. I just about managed the interrogation routine, despite the humiliation of it with all those men around. It was pretty unpleasant; you know, the blindfold bit. I know you fellas are bollock naked, but they let us keep our bras and knickers on. And although I resent the concession on a point of principle, it was a relief, I can tell you. Then they brought in a big girl – at least she seemed big. I had this vision of a huge bulldyke with a mullet.'

'How did you know it was a girl?'

'Good question. I was desperate to know what was coming next and who from! But when she lifted me by the arms and pushed me across the room, I could feel her big tits in my back. She gave me an internal, front and back. I'm fairly sure it was behind a curtain – I could hear it being drawn – but the men were still in the room. What made it bearable was thinking how farcical it all was. If it had been for real in some squalid enemy prison camp, the internal wouldn't have been behind a curtain, it wouldn't have been given by a woman, and the "inspection" instrument wouldn't have been a finger in a rubber glove.'

I listen to Maureen with huge admiration. Properly brought up, demure in civvy life, she's a no-holds-barred, hard-headed soldier in her professional life; the sort you would definitely want on your side, when push came to shove.

My own interrogation 'humiliation' was a similar contrivance, but for the male of the species. After endless bullying and sensory deprivation, the white noise being the worst part, they drafted in a female officer, probably a senior Wren, or perhaps someone from 14 Intelligence DS. Christ, it could have been Mo. Perhaps it was!

'Mo, did you ever act as a female interrogator for SAS selection?'

'No, why?'

'Doesn't matter.'

I think back to my blindfolded encounter. They draft the woman in about two-thirds of the way through, when you're at a really low ebb. You've been shouted at relentlessly, threatened, cajoled, held in a stress position interminably and endured the white noise torment. Then you're sexually humiliated. They sneer at your John Thomas – which, thanks to the cold, has shrivelled to something no bigger than a walnut – and suggest it's about as much use to the female of the species as a broom handle up the Mersey Tunnel. But my female interrogator was a bad choice. They should've chosen someone who sounded like Rosa Klebb, but she sounded like Princess Anne, which definitely didn't have the intended effect.

Lost in my recollections, I suddenly remember that Maureen is in the middle of telling her story.

'Sorry, Mo, I am listening.'

'The worst of it was the relentless squalor. I know this sounds girly, but living in your sweat and filth for days on end – dirt under your fingernails, skin like sandpaper, hair like it's covered with chip fat, then having your period in the middle of it – it's not very nice when your entire life as a girl has been all about discretion and cleanliness.'

Listening to Maureen's blunt account, my mind drifts back to our first meeting; how prim she was, and how intimidating I found her.

'So you thought I was a skinny wimp when we met at the ferry?'

'I didn't say that.'

'You know what, I found you pretty formidable. I wanted you something rotten – like any man would – but I thought you were something to dream about, you would never be real.'

'Strange, after I got over how lean you were, I saw you as "Regiment": intellectually unimpressive, but good in a tough spot in the trenches.'

'Oh, thanks for nothing . . . God, Mo, it seems like a lifetime ago.'

'I know, but it's only been fourteen months.'

'I tell you what, for a while I was happy in our little flat. It was bloody scruffy, and definitely in the wrong part of town, but spending day after day being "normal" began to feel normal. The worst part was fancying you all the time.'

'Actually, I quite fancied you after a while.'

'Jesus, why didn't you say something or give me a sign?'

'Wouldn't have been professional, would it?'

'I suppose not, but it might have prevented what happened with Kathleen.'

In an instant, Maureen's face turns to stone; her tone switches from warm to ice cold.

'Not now, Jim, I don't want to talk about her. Let's change the subject.'

I had hoped Maureen might be ready to talk about Kathleen, but it's obviously too early. I do as I'm bid and change the subject.

'I began to warm to the kids we were teaching. They were hard work, tough little fuckers, and it was difficult to convince them that they could trust a Brit.'

Maureen softens again.

'But you did it?'

'Kind of. Football was the key. Turning out for the Hibernians won me lots of brownie points.'

'You're being modest. You know you were a bit of a local hero. All of my girls talked about you, said you were the Ardoyne's answer to Lenny Brady.'

'Liam Brady.'

'Yes, him.'

'Bloody hell, if I had ten per cent of Brady's talent, I would be ten times better than I really am. It also helped that I used to take the piss out of the bizarre practices of the Catholic Church. Only a real left-footer could do that. You know, incense, choirboys, holy grace, sins against the seventh commandment. That's the one you have to mention when you confess to the priest about wanking. The lads might have been good Catholic boys, but they knew it was all bollocks.'

Maureen nods.

'It was similar for me. Sport only worked for some girls. Sex and periods was the key for the rest. Many of the girls couldn't talk to their mothers or most of their teachers about intimate things. It didn't bother me, so they confided in me –'

Looking grave, Maureen suddenly stops herself. She stares upwards as if asking the Almighty for forgiveness. She then looks me in the eye, not accusingly, but with a woeful expression of guilt.

'We cheated on them, didn't we?'

I feel a sudden jolt of remorse and don't respond. Instead, I revert to the recent answer to all my anguish. I drain my glass of wine, then pour another one, filling it to the brim.

6. 140 Gower Street

It's a remarkably ordinary building. Built in the 1930s, its ground floor includes the entrance to Euston Square tube station. Twice a day it's a passing place for hordes of commuters, none of whom has any inkling of who occupies the six floors of the unimpressive grey monolith above them.

The top-floor office of the Director General of MI5 is full of section heads and anyone else involved in the anti-terrorism campaign against the Provisional IRA. It's a large room, but drab, not furnished as the spy movies suggest. There's a view to the north, but Euston Station and its surrounding blocks of nondescript architecture don't create one of London's more memorable vistas. However, the men in the room are the mirror image of their theatrical caricatures: navy-blue or grey pinstriped suits, regimental or Oxbridge ties and, above gleaming black brogues, the one tiny concession to individuality, loud socks in garish colours.

There is but one woman among them, 'S', who dresses as they do, except it's of the female ilk: black two-piece suit, a scalloped cream blouse and beige shoes with a modest heel. She also sports one hint of novelty: racy pencil-line stockings. Perhaps there's more to 'S' than meets the eye?

The DG, known as JJ to his friends, opens the meeting.

'The politicians have got the wind up. You all know what that means. Let's review the situation. We have John Smythson here today from our friends at Century House, and some new faces from SB. So we should outline the operation as it was planned from the beginning. Roger, the background, please.'

'Well, sir, Waddington, Gary and Townsend, Deborah, "Debs". Their cover names are Jim Dowd and Maureen O'Brien. Both have excellent training records. Townsend is by far the best female recruit 14 Intelligence has ever produced and one of the top half-dozen in recent years, male or female. She's very focused, highly intelligent – a Cambridge graduate – and sailed through interrogation without flinching. Although she has the manner of a successful lawyer or academic, she's as tough as old boots. Waddington's a rough diamond; although he's ex-21, a reservist, he's typical Hereford. The regulars liked him and he liked them. He spent a lot of time at Stirling Lines doing specialist training. He was one of the boys; good at most things, if a little wayward at times –'

The DG interrupts.

'Details?'

'A good athlete, first-class soldier; but a heavy drinker, violent when younger; womanizer, divorced; son of a single mother, long dead; got into a hell of a pickle when he had an affair with a girl he was teaching. She was nineteen and very mature; he was twenty-nine. The whole thing was covered up by the school and he resigned. He'd just passed selection with flying colours, so had come on to our radar, and we were assessing him. We knew all about him and the girl from our surveillance.'

The DG frowns over his half-moon reading glasses.

'He spun out of control a bit after the schoolgirl deba-cle and the divorce that followed. Drink, more girls, a couple of fist fights. Nevertheless, he was a good match for Townsend in the new venture we'd planned. We needed two quite specific individuals. She was perfect, he less so, but just about the only candidate available.'

The DG is still scowling.

'The only chap available is hardly a recommendation, Roger.'

'The only one in a very elite group. But, with hindsight, perhaps not ideal, sir.'

The DG's face remains thunderous.

'We had a few photographs of him with the young lady in question. When he came to see us, we suggested the operation we proposed was a way for him to get himself sorted out; that he'd got himself into a mess, and this was a way out of it.'

The DG smiles wryly.

'OK. Carry on, Roger.'

'As you know, all our Det operatives work out of secure bases in and around Belfast. By definition, they are iso-lated from the community. Given that the nationalist areas have become more and more tight-knit in recent years, we were finding it increasingly difficult to operate in the staunchest republican areas like the Lower Ormeau Road, New Lodge and the Ardoyne. So we wondered whether we could insert two people into the community and let them become assimilated. We thought it had promise.'

The newcomers to the operation's details look at one another. The Special Branch guest bristles.

'We weren't told?'

'No, the DG decided it was "need to know" only.'

'And we didn't need to know!'

The Director General comes to Roger's aid.

'We kept it in this room. We decided not to involve the RUC; we had a few concerns. Only a few in Det knew, plus OC-SAS and the Minister, of course.'

'And he sanctioned it?'

'Of course . . . and Downing Street.'

The Director General glares at the Special Branch man, making it obvious that further questions would be inappropriate.

'Continue, Roger.'

'Very good, sir. So, we needed a cover structure. We hit on teaching. Waddington is a qualified teacher; he was teaching when he did selection and up to the point of the impropriety with the young lady. Townsend is such a good athlete; it wasn't difficult to present her as an outstanding PE teacher. They both have excellent Irish and Catholic heritage and make a handsome couple. They walked into jobs in local schools. Townsend went in first; Waddington, a term later. They lived in the Ardoyne with almost zero contact with anyone outside the local community: army, SB, RUC. They then went off radar and began blending in. We gave them as long as necessary.'

He pauses, looks down at his notes and takes a deep breath.

'So far, so good. There was then a hitch, an unexpected development. Waddington's cover with Townsend remained platonic – I suppose we assumed it wouldn't, but it did – and his testosterone kicked in. He struck up a relationship with a fellow teacher, a local girl: Kathleen McKee, from a diehard republican family. We worried about it for a while, but then thought, a) it was a predictable consequence of the game we were playing, and b) it had potential advantages.'

Colonel Smythson from MI6, a beanpole of a man, an ex-Grenadier Guards officer, mutters under his breath.

'Sounds like a right cock-up to me; 5 playing spies.'

The DG wriggles in his chair.

'Thank you for that thoughtful contribution, John.'

7. A New Regime

Autumn is turning to winter in our Wealden hideaway and the harsher weather is helping us regain our condition. The ground is heavier, the air fresher, the temperature more demanding. We run progressive sprints before breakfast, do our DIY assault course and stamina exercises through the woods before lunch, and spend every afternoon on long tabs across the Weald until dusk.

We both know we're becoming fitter because our multiple blisters, aching joints and stiff muscles remind us every day. Our mental toughness is also improving. We don't cry on one another's shoulder so much. Most of our conversations focus on happier times, especially when we relax over dinner.

'You know your wines, Mo; this is excellent. How did you learn about wine?'

'My father – he's either an expert or a snob, depending which way you look at it.'

'What's he like?'

'Well, he's unusual for a man born in a tiny village in Galway Bay. He came to London when he was a teenager, started as a hod carrier and worked his way up the building trade. He set up his own business and became very successful. He managed to snare my mother, who's very Home Counties, but without much money. She knocked the rough edges off him and taught him, as she put it, "how to behave". Slowly, he lost most of his Irishness.'

'Was he ashamed of it?'

'A bit, especially when it all kicked off in the North. Although he's from the Republic and a good Catholic, he's very conservative – with a big "C" and a little one.'

'And that rubbed off on you?'

'Definitely. I was a real daddy's girl and worshipped the ground he walked on; still do. He could afford to send me to private school, where I became even more English than he is. Fortunately for both of us, he carries an English name. If he'd been called Paddy Murphy, it would have been a bloody sight more difficult to hide our Celtic roots.'

'I never did know your real name.'

Maureen smiles back cheekily.

'I'll tell you mine if you tell me yours.'

'Deal.'

'Deborah Townsend. I'm called "Debs", of course.'

'That wouldn't have gone down too well off the Crumlin Road!'

'God forbid! And yours?'

'Gary. Gary Waddington, very North Country and very English.'

'Very, a bit of a giveaway in the Ardoyne.'

'Shall we stick to Jim Dowd and Maureen O'Brien?'

'I think so, much safer!'

As the Pilgrim's Rest begins to empty, only four die-hard drinkers remain. They're talking politics, very loudly, mocking the Labour Party, especially Neil Kinnock, the party's rising star and shadow Education Secretary, one of Thatcher's greatest critics over her conduct of the Falklands War. The good people of affluent Kent talk about him as if he's a traitor and a coward.

My blood begins to boil.

'Little Englanders, bloody hell! Listening to that lot, you'd have thought Maggie was Joan of Arc.'

Maureen stiffens at my insult.

'She is, isn't she?'

'Fuck me! They've no idea about the Falklands. Jesus, we were within a whisker of losing it.'

'But we didn't.'

'More by luck than judgement: one more Exocet; one more HMS *Sheffield*.'

'I know, but it was boots on the ground that won it. Aren't you proud?'

'Course I am; I know lots of the guys who were in the "boots".'

I can't help thinking back. Our blood was up and, as usual, we sent the gunboats. I remember when my twenty-four-hour papers arrived. How close was I to copping it? One more major loss of life, one more ship sunk, and I could have been in that Sea King helicopter with Malcolm Atkinson.

'I'll grant you one thing, though, Mo. Despite the fact that she's a complete bitch, and regardless of the rights and wrongs of the invasion, if I'd been one of the boys yomping from San Carlos to Port Stanley in that snowstorm, I would've preferred Thatcher backing me up in Downing Street rather than Neil Kinnock. He's a nice bloke, but the last thing you need when lads are dying for their country is for politicians to get the wind up and start shitting themselves about whether what we're doing is right or wrong.'

Maureen looks sympathetic and seems impressed by

my bow to realism. Nevertheless, she can't resist claiming victory in our debate.

'Jim, you've made my case for me.'

'Have I? Thatcher's still a cow and her lovey-dovey tryst with Reagan makes me puke. The Falklands War saved her skin. Now she can do even more damage.'

'You really don't like her, do you?'

'No, I fuckin' don't! Look what she's doing to the country. There are no jobs. Lots of old industries are collapsing. We've had riots in Bristol, Brixton, Liverpool; the country's coming apart at the seams. And what does Maggie say? Let the free market rule, it'll come good in the end. That's bollocks. We elect governments to manage the economy, not to let it run riot at the expense of millions.'

'Well, well, Jim, quite a speech. You should go into politics.'

'Perhaps I will. Trouble is, I'd probably end up decking some Tory twat in the House of Commons.'

The four diehard drinkers eventually leave and the bar staff close the bar, but not before they serve us one more drink. The Pilgrim's Rest has become as quiet as the grave, the only distant sound the screech of a barn owl marking his territory. Maureen savours her malt and cups the tumbler in her hands as if she's making an offering.

'Were you always a leftie?'

'Yeah, from being a teenager. It was the sixties. Revolution; we were going to change the world. I managed to squeeze into university and became a proper "leftie".'

Maureen grins at me.

'And now look at you.'

'I know, I know. The revolution never happened. It's

37

all forgotten. Now we're older, but are we wiser? I don't think so.'

'And you ended up in the Regiment and went to Northern Ireland to do Thatcher's dirty work.'

'Yer, I'm a right hypocrite, aren't I?'

'No, Jim, you just grew up.'

8. Coffee with the DG

After Roger finishes his outline of the dilemma posed by
14 Intelligence operatives Waddington and Townsend,
the DG asks him to come to his office for a 'quiet word'.

'So, Roger, a bloody mess – and even more infuriating
that Smythson has to know about it. He'll be in Sir Colin's
office the moment he's back, and everyone at 6 will know
about it by the morning.'

'Yes, sir, a bit of a bugger.'

'A bit of a bugger? It's a bloody cock-up, that's what it is.'

'I think cock-up's a bit strong.'

'Do you? How about a right fucking cock-up! If this
isn't sorted quickly, I couldn't get you a transfer to the
post room. This has got Maggie herself rattled, and I
don't fancy standing in front of her ladyship to give her
the gory details if it gets any worse. Capiche?'

'Message received loud and clear, sir.'

The DG paces up and down, barely able to keep his
composure.

'I've two questions, and I want answers that you may
not have been prepared to give in the meeting. One: how
come their intel was flawed? And two: how come Waddington, who's clearly a ticking bomb, was put in there in
the first place?'

'We've no idea where the dubious intel originated. My
guess is, as usual, SB RUC.'

'Fucking hell, that place is a nightmare. We should've let them fight it out in 1922.'

The DG sits down by a small electric fire that is warming the room.

'I thought SB wasn't privy to the op?'

'Correct. But we think word filtered out in Belfast.'

'How?'

'We don't know.'

The DG gets up and starts pacing again, his red face betraying his fury.

'So why Waddington? A big mistake, Roger.'

'With hindsight, yes. But he was ideal in so many ways. Excellent report out of Hereford and in Det training.'

'Then there's something seriously wrong with our training regime. He should've been weeded out. Thank God for Townsend.'

'She's a rock, sir; I'm sure she'll sort him out.'

'She'd better.'

'And if she can't?'

'If he becomes a threat to the integrity of what we're doing, then the threat will have to be dealt with.'

'And Townsend?'

'She gets a choice; she must choose him or us. Make sure she understands.'

Roger nods.

The DG turns to him; his expression has softened. He adopts a more sympathetic tone.

'Her path to the top is blocked, but we can find her a sinecure somewhere.'

'As bad as that?'

'Yes, an MoD decision, out of my hands.'

'That's a shame. She's exceptional.'

'Was, Roger – very much past tense, I'm afraid. Where are they?'

'We're not sure. She went to dig him out of his hole in Clapham. She took him off somewhere, but we lost them after the incident on the tube.'

'What a bloody mess! Bullets flying around on the underground; three commuters hurt. An ASU, I suppose?'

'No, we don't think so.'

'Well, you need to find out, don't you? Not exactly covering yourself in glory on this, are you? You need to find those two, or the balloon will go up.'

'We're looking for them in some of the places where she may have taken him. Old haunts, family holidays. The bobbies have been briefed everywhere. Her file is pretty detailed, and we're monitoring her parents' home and phone.'

'Anything?'

'No, but I'm sure she'll bring him in soon.'

'I want to be there when she does.'

Roger makes for the door, but hesitates and turns to face his boss.

'There's something I should mention about the attempted hit in Clapham.'

'I'm all ears.'

'I think we might have some rogue elements on their tail.'

'Define "rogue elements".'

'I've had my suspicions for some time that those across the water not operating strictly under orders may be seen as sympathizers here as well.'

'By our people?'

'Possibly, but it might be members of SB or the Regiment gone freelance. I can't be sure.'

'And they were responsible for the attack in Clapham?'

'Almost certainly.'

'Jesus, can this get any worse! Do you realize how serious that could be if it's true?'

'I know.'

'Why wait until now to tell me?'

'Because I'm still not sure, but several things have happened that make me suspicious. And it's probably a factor with Waddington and Townsend.'

'How?'

'Because of the way they reacted at the end of the op.'

'Somebody thinks they've gone native?'

'Exactly.'

'Look, Roger, you're going to have to make these suspicions real or prove they're unfounded, and quickly. I have a decision to make about when to refer this upwards. Remember, Prior's been tipped off and he's on the warpath. And that means the PM has got her flak jacket on again.'

'OK, sir, this is what we know at the moment. As you are aware, there are strong signals of discontent from sources in the military. A growing number think the politicians are too soft. Their view is that we should let the dogs loose and clean out all the IRA nests, once and for all.'

'I know all that!'

'Yes, but that view may be spreading among some elements in our teams. There have been open expressions of frustration and anger.'

'Suspicions?'

'Not fair to mention them yet.'

'Bloody hell, man. When will it be "fair"?'

'Give me a few days. I've got Nigel and another couple of men I can rely on ferreting around.'

'You can have three days, Roger. I don't want any rotten apples in my barrel. Is that clear?'

'Crystal.'

Roger hesitates and takes a lungful of air.

'There's one more thing; more bad news, I'm afraid. We heard today that an ASU left Belfast last week and has already linked up with a cell on the mainland.'

The DG doesn't say anything for a while. His face is now a picture of resignation rather than anger.

'Any names for the ASU?'

'None.'

'The cell?'

'No names, we only know there is one.'

The DG marches to the door.

'Roger, for Christ's sake find Townsend and Waddington before somebody else does.'

9. Winter Bites

The first snow of the winter of 1982 falls early on the High Weald. It's only the second week of November, but a thick carpet of virginal snow covers the ground. The scene could be a picture postcard of England in winter, but it makes the tabbing Maureen and I are doing along Kent's forest paths difficult to navigate and very heavy-going. But it's doing us good.

We've been squelching along the wet ground for over an hour and are deep in Ashdown Forest, west of Crowborough, one of the most attractive parts of England. Sadly, we're paying little attention to the scenery; our focus is on the physical punishment we're imposing on ourselves.

We're covered in mud from the waist down, our hands and feet are numb with cold, and we're straining our lungs to the point of collapse. But our brutal regime is paying off: our once formidable levels of endurance are returning. Thankfully, we'll soon be back at the Pilgrim's Rest; another day done, another step taken on the road to recovery. At the landlord's insistence, we'll then have to endure hosing one another down with cold water in the pub's yard; but then a hot bath, a good dinner and a decent bottle of red await.

Maureen suddenly sprints ahead.

'About a mile to go, Jimmy boy. Last one back's a tosser and has to wash the kit.'

She does it all the time.

And always wins.

Yet again, the home-made food at the Pilgrim's is excellent. Maureen's in an effervescent mood.

'I think it's time we went to Gower Street and declared you no longer a basket case.'

This is a surprise. I'm anxious.

'Only if you think I'm ready.'

'I think you're fine now. They'll accept my judgement.'

'Sure?'

'Certain.'

'Then what?'

'They'll have to tell us what they're going to do with us.'

Apprehensive, I look out of the window and peer into the emptiness of the Wealden night.

'And what do we want them to do with us?'

Maureen smiles warmly.

'That's up to us. What do you want?'

I look back from the black window and stare at Maureen, realizing that I don't have an answer to such a penetrating question.

'I don't know.'

I pause, hoping for inspiration, take a gulp of wine, then grasp Maureen's hand. I feel closer to her than ever before and decide to go for broke.

'Can't we stay here together for a bit longer? I'm happier than I have been for a long time.'

'I'm happy, too, but it's not real. And, more importantly, we're not real either.'

Maureen's candour – searingly accurate, as always – is like a hammer blow, but I persevere.

'Let's make it real, let's make *us* real.'

'Oh, Jimmy! You big soft silly sod, that can't work.'

'We can make it work. I've always been able to find a way to make my dreams come true. Not like you, with God-given gifts, but with native cunning and stubborn determination.'

'Jim, I think we should get ourselves sorted before we do anything too rash. Let's just wait and keep sharp. We don't want to be distracted by one another while things are as they are.'

'You know what, Mo, you're as hard as nails. Do you ever let yourself go?'

'I try not to . . .'

Her face reddens and she pauses for a long time.

'Jim, you should know something.'

I sit back, sensing that Maureen needs me to detach myself from the story she is about to tell.

'I've been hurt very badly and vowed it would never happen again.'

I feel a sudden shiver. I'd always guessed that a lot of Maureen's attitude on the outside must hide a well of emotions on the inside. She takes a deep draught from her wine glass.

'He was called Tom, a marine. God, was he to die for! Every girl I knew fancied him. He was one of the DS on my Det course, CQB specialist. I fell for him big time. It went on from about halfway through the course until just before I was sent over the water. I thought he felt the same about me as I did about him. The strange thing is, as it developed, I thought I was the one gradually snaring him; little did I know.'

'Mo, you don't have to tell me.'

'I do, I want you to know ... no secrets ... I know yours, you need to know mine ... Tom was a con man, a sexual predator; a lying, two-timing bastard, with a nasty streak when crossed. He used women like an assault course; a challenge to be conquered by strength and stamina. Words like tenderness, warmth and love were for weaklings. I was so stupid.'

She pauses and takes another gulp of wine.

'By chance, I found out that he was already fucking one of the girls on the course after mine and that he'd had at least one of the girls on every course he took. He liked posh officers the most, he called them "Lady Ruperts", said he liked letting them know what real men are like. When I confronted him about the other girl, he couldn't understand what the problem was. He boasted he was easily able to make sure I got my fair share, so why not carry on with the status quo? A ménage à trois. What a prat! When I told him to fuck off and called him all the names he deserved, he went nuts. He knocked me about pretty badly.'

Maureen begins to cry.

'Then he raped me, pretty violently. He said it was to remind me of the good times. I was in so much pain; I didn't leave my room for three days. I pretended I was sick. Then I had to say that my bruises were from an accident in the gym. I thought of going to my CO, but realized that although Tom might get what he deserved, for me to reveal that I'd had an affair with one of the DS on my selection would have finished me.'

She lowers her head and begins to heave in anguish. God only knows how she kept it under control for all those months when we were together in Belfast. Everything about her suggests that, with her gifts and background, her life has been a stroll in the park. But it hasn't.

'The worst of it came later. When I went to Gower Street to be chosen for the op, they told me that they knew all about the affair with Tom and the assault. I've no idea how, but they did. So I'd kept shtum for nothing. I boiled with anger and shame; I nearly passed out on the spot.'

There's a long pause as she composes herself. Then she lifts her head and looks at me with one of those resolute looks I know so well.

'So I vowed that no one would ever hurt me again.'

I don't say anything; I can't, I just feel revulsion and anger that someone could've hurt her so much. So I just move over to the bench seat she's sitting on, put my arm around her shoulders and let her head fall on to my chest.

'Jimmy, it would be such a comfort if we became close, but it can't happen; not yet.'

'Mo, we are close.'

'I know, but that's not what I mean.'

'You mean lovers?'

'I suppose I do. Please let's wait until things are clearer. I couldn't survive being hurt again.'

'I would never hurt you, Mo.'

'I know. But somebody might hurt you, and I couldn't bear that.'

My heart is racing. She's made a commitment to me that I've always dreamed about. And I don't mind waiting as long as it takes. Now I have all the incentive I need to get us through the crisis we face.

10. A Sarcophagus of Spooks

As Maureen and I sit before our lords and masters on the top floor of Gower Street, I'm bored to despair by the relentless questioning, most of which Maureen is fielding, and find my mind wandering off to unhelpful places.

Inspired by the archetypes in front of me – neatly suited, very 'proper' chaps, singularly sanctimonious and self-important, and without a moral scruple between them – I'm trying to decide on the most appropriate collective noun for a group of spooks. I toy with 'tosspot' and 'shithole' but decide they're too crude. I've heard of 'nest', 'conspiracy' and 'intrigue' before, so – as they wouldn't be original – I discount them. I quite like 'subterfuge' for a while, then think I may have heard it before, so rule that out as well. Seeing them all in an orderly row, I quite like 'catacomb', but then their solemn faces, as if they're wearing their death masks in life, make me plump for 'sarcophagus'. I stare at the DG, who looks like a provincial undertaker, and the aptness of my choice is confirmed.

'Waddington, are you listening?'

I'm jolted back to reality. But I'm slow to respond to the question, making the DG furrow his brow and give me a withering look. I know what he's thinking: *Very much 'other ranks', that's why we're in this mess!*

'I said, are you following this?'

'Yes, sir.'

'Then try to keep up, man!'

Maureen had begun the meeting by outlining the skirmish on the tube. The topic made the already tense atmosphere very prickly, especially the mood of the officer in control of our op – the man who recruited me all those months ago, who I now know is called Roger. I'd christened him 'Wank' and still prefer it. His partner, 'Dank', is sitting next to him. As before, he says very little and his name has not been mentioned, so 'Dank' it remains. Both are now staring at me like disapproving schoolmasters. The DG is obviously the headmaster, so I christen him 'Spank' and imagine him taking the school cane to little boys' bottoms with bounding relish.

He then rounds on me as, sooner or later, I knew he would.

'So, Sergeant Waddington, Captain Townsend thinks your fitness levels are improving and that you're over your problems. What do you think?'

So Mo made Captain; that's impressive. We never disclosed one another's rank; it's against the rules. They made me a warrant officer when I passed Det selection, and gave a big hint about a commission after Belfast. But that's all history now.

'I think she's a shrewd judge, sir.'

'Do you want to tell us what derailed you so severely?'

'I think the facts are fairly well documented, sir. Besides, it's all water under the bridge now and I'd prefer not to go over the events again, if you don't mind.'

There's a long silence and some uneasy fidgeting in the room. Maureen looks concerned and obviously wants to answer for me, but knows I have to speak for myself. I stare at them all, feeling certain that not one of them has been at the sharp end like Maureen and I have. Then I think, perhaps they have and it hasn't affected them in the slightest. If so, they're even bigger bastards than I imagined.

It's obvious that the silence means the room doesn't want to accept no for an answer. I try to deflect the question.

'Sir, it's a long story and not one I care to talk about in a crowded room.'

Wank flashes a look of fury at me.

'Well, you're going to have to, like it or not!'

I feel my blood boiling. I want to leap across the table and rip his fucking head off.

The DG intervenes.

'Let's adjourn to another room and a smaller group. Roger, Nigel, "S", will you join us?'

As she's the only other woman there, I assume Spank wants 'S' there to support Maureen. She immediately does that by giving her a broad smile and gently guiding her out of the room with her arm.

So, Dank is called Nigel; typical, such a wet name! With Wank and Dank behind him like faithful ducklings, Spank leads the way to a new room, smaller and much more intimate than the meeting room.

This room is more like a spy movie. It does have real leather chairs and decent antique furniture. There is a deep-pile burgundy carpet and the walls hold a plethora of paintings illustrating Britain's imperial heritage. I assume there's a drinks cabinet and small refrigerator in one of the burr-walnut cupboards. I begin to wonder what bizarre and dangerous intrigues have been plotted within its four walls. Perhaps our little operation in the Ardoyne was dreamed up in this very room.

'So does this suit you better, Sergeant Waddington?'

'Yes, thank you, sir.'

I still don't want to tell him anything, but the walls are closing in on me, both literally and metaphorically. It's not a pleasant feeling. Maureen offers a reassuring smile as the DG gestures to me to sit.

'A glass of water, Sergeant?'

'I'd prefer a large malt, sir.'

Thinking my request unwise, Maureen turns her head away. There are disapproving glances between Dank and Wank. Spank ignores them.

'What's your poison?'

'Speyside, sir.'

'What about a Macallan?'

'Ten years, sir?'

'Of course.'

'Perfect, and perhaps a little jug of water?'

'You know your Scotch, then.'

'I should, sir. I drink enough of it.'

'Captain Townsend tells us that you have that particular demon under control.'

'I hope so, sir.'

Spank takes orders from the others and delves into his drinks cabinet. Like an efficient posh barman, he busies himself with alcohol, mixers, glasses and a jug of water, then puts a tray on the table in front of everyone and beckons to us to help ourselves.

'So, your demise, Sergeant; but, before you answer, let

me tell you that we're here to help. We want this to be resolved as much as you do, then we can all move on, especially in light of the events that now seem to be unfolding.'

He's playing the nice guy. If his paternal persona doesn't work – and it doesn't sit well on his craggy features – Wank will get out the thumbscrews. Don't they remember that they trained me in interrogation techniques? I look at Maureen. The expression on her face tells me that she knows what I know; that, right now, everything that has happened to us and everything that is going to happen to us hangs in the balance in this room, at this very moment.

I look at the calendar on the wall. It's Tuesday, 7 December 1982. A lot has happened in just a few months.

I start at the beginning.

11. Mona's Queen

It's the first week of January, 1981. Having left my small bachelor flat in London, I'm aboard the Isle of Man Steamship Company's *Mona's Queen* outbound from Fleetwood. After a couple of days of aimless sightseeing in Douglas, Isle of Man, I'm approaching Belfast, where my new adventure awaits.

There can't be anything more ordinary than the forty-vehicle car ferry I'm travelling on. A few elderly holidaymakers rub shoulders with commercial travellers and white van drivers, all of whom avoid several grubby students returning to their studies. I feel invigorated by what lies ahead; my sense of superiority is potent. I feel I'm very different from them, my purpose extraordinary.

Like so many before me, my crossed forearms are resting on the ship's passenger rail as I stare out across the pea-green murkiness of the Irish Sea. The folk song 'The Leaving of Liverpool' comes into the void in my head. I've no idea why – I don't like folk music, and I only know two lines of the lyrics – but it suddenly seems appropriate. I can hear The Dubliners singing it. I think of the countless poor emigrants who left Europe, decades ago, to find a better life in the New World. I feel that my voyage is similar; an opportunity to restore stability to my life, and the chance of a fresh, exhilarating career. But I quickly put an end to such optimism and remind myself that my future is a fabrication, a contrivance designed to serve Britain's political expediency.

As I stare at the rolling waves below me, I begin to think about what I'm about to get myself into. Northern Ireland is in the midst of, in all but name, a bloody civil war. Two bands of brigands are engaged in a vicious tribal conflict. In between them is the Royal Ulster Constabulary, within which the impartiality and virtue of many of its members are questionable. Supporting the RUC is the British Army, a national army of notable quality, but which lacks the training to deal with urban terror and whose officers and men would rather be anywhere else than fighting their fellow citizens on their own soil. Supporting the army is a muddle of security operations, including Special Branch and Military Intelligence in various guises, all of which are trying to come to terms with a political disaster born of decades of deprivation and oppression.

To add to the horror of it all, as is always the case when the tin lid is prised off civilized morality, there are many on both sides who are behaving way beyond the boundaries of human decency. And so, it is rumoured, are many within the paraphernalia of the British state, which is supposed to be protecting civilized society from those who would harm it.

The problem is that most people living east of the Irish Sea don't understand Ireland and its troubles, and never have. Behind the scenes, three governments are trying to pull the strings of the conflict and manipulate events in their own best interests. The Irish government in Dublin lends significant support to the Catholic republican cause.

The British government in London attempts to be impartial, but its traditional loyalty, especially within the ranks of the ruling Conservative Party, lies with the Protestant loyalists. There is also a dormant government in Belfast, the loyalist elite, which feels it has a God-given right to rule their precious Ulster. No one has any answers, except through the horrendous power of Semtex and the Armalite.

So what the fuck am I doing sailing towards this vortex of hate? I try not to think of an answer; it only confuses me.

Britain's new Prime Minister, Margaret Thatcher, is beginning to flex her substantial muscles. But unemployment and recession are growing. Many don't like her, but she has stood her ground against the steelworkers' strike and stuck to her free-market economic principles, saying to those who doubt her, 'The lady is not for turning.'

But she's undermining things that I think are precious. The post-war consensus about welfare, health and education and our belief in the common good are being destroyed by a form of Middle English bigotry called Thatcherism, a euphemism for greed. I hate what she's doing to Britain, but I'm now one of her weapons of change. How stupid is that?

Thatcher has already made a significant impact on the insoluble problems of Northern Ireland. Her rhetoric and arrogance have inflamed the situation. Republicans see her as part of a long lineage of English bullies. They put her on a par with Henry II, Oliver Cromwell and William of Orange – a select group, indeed.

Despite the ill-fated carnal liaison at my previous school and the subsequent hole in my CV, it proved to be remarkably easy to get an appointment at my new Belfast school. There'd been only two other applicants at my interview before Christmas, and both of them looked like they'd only just left school themselves. The gap in my employment record was easily filled thanks to Gower Street's forgery talents. I didn't ask how they'd managed to get a copy of my old headmaster's signature, but it looked perfect. What he wrote was also very complimentary, perhaps too much so, but it impressed the stony-faced interview panel. It also helped a lot that I'd played semi-pro football in London. One of the governors mentioned that he was Club President of the Hibernian Club football team and asked if I would be available to turn out for them. I said I'd be delighted, if the manager thought me good enough. The governor smiled. He knew I would be – mainland semi-pro is several levels above Belfast's local amateur leagues.

I was asked only one difficult question: why did I want to come and teach in Belfast of all places? My answer was blatantly obsequious: I blathered on about my Irish Catholic roots and how I wanted to help the people of the local community in their troubled times. It also helped that I was able to mention that my girlfriend, Maureen, was teaching in their neighbouring school and we were both committed to helping our Irish brothers and sisters. It was mendacious, of course, but there was a grain of truth in it. Anyway, my blarney brought smiles of admiration from the school's governors seated before me and I was given the job before the taxi arrived to take me to Aldergrove Airport.

Mona's Queen begins to slow and I see the Port of Belfast come into view. I feel a sudden shiver of trepidation.

My first and only previous visit was but a six-hour snapshot, most of which was spent inside dull school premises. Now I'm approaching the troubled city on a permanent basis. It's raining, of course, there's a biting wind from the north-east, and the city looks murky and hostile. I think of what's happened here over the years: the bombs, the firefights, the murders, the tortures. I suddenly think of Robert Nairac from the Grenadier Guards, a fellow Irish Catholic, and, unlike me, a devout one, who went undercover for 14 Intelligence.

A tremor of fear runs down my spine. Nairac was abducted from a republican pub in South Armagh, tortured and shot. They're still looking for his body. One of the men who killed him admitted at his trial that Nairac never revealed his real identity. He was well trained and incredibly brave.

Am I as well honed? Could I do the same? Even now, I know I'm nothing like as well prepared.

And certainly not as courageous.

12. St Anthony's

As I walk through the arrivals hall at Belfast Ferry Terminal, there's a sudden squeal of female delight close by. I look around to check which of my fellow passengers is being greeted so rapturously. Then the shriek gets louder and I'm grabbed around the neck by a pair of demanding arms. My face is covered in kisses and I hear my new name being shouted out loud. Then there's a whisper in my ear.

'It's Maureen; remember, we're supposed to be lovers and you haven't seen me in weeks!'

I feel really stupid; it's not a very good start. I return the kisses as avidly as I can.

'That's better, lover boy.'

'Sorry, Maureen, you took me by surprise.'

She looks me up and down and, despite the superficial smiles, is clearly not impressed.

'Come on, there's a taxi waiting to take us to the flat. Then I'll take you on a tour of everything you need to see. Be careful in the taxi. Most of the drivers are the eyes and ears of the bad boys.'

I spend the taxi ride with my eyes glued to the squalid streets of Belfast. Much of it is an intimidating war zone: a panorama of barricades, barbed wire, military patrols and devastated buildings.

Maureen pays the taxi and we climb the narrow stairs

to our flat above a corner shop on Estoril Park, at the western edge of the Ardoyne. It's hardly a penthouse. One bedroom, a sitting room, a small kitchen and a few modest pieces of furniture will be all our worldly possessions for the next few months, or however long our assignment takes. Gower Street wouldn't be specific. Maureen has prepared for my arrival by buying a fold-up sofa bed for our sitting room. It will be where I will sleep for the duration of our op; unless, of course, Maureen invites me to join her in her bed!

As I look out of our sitting-room window at the long rows of the Ardoyne's terraced houses, I can't help but think of *Coronation Street*. They're the same red brick as in the soap opera, not millstone grit – the lovely Pennine stone of my native North-East Lancs – but they remind me of home all the same.

'It took forever to find a place within the Ardoyne. I had to get my headmistress to put in a word, and Father Nulty, who's on my board of governors as well as yours, spoke to the landlady.'

'Weren't they curious about why you wanted to live in the area?'

'They were amazed; no one wants to live here unless they have to.'

'So what did you say?'

'That I was hoping you would join me next term and that we both believed we should live within the community where we taught.'

'And they bought that?'

'It seems so, though they must have thought us young and naive.'

'Well, they were right about that!'

Maureen shows me our hidden arsenal of weapons, ammunition, comms equipment and other bits of military paraphernalia, all hidden in the false back of a large wardrobe. Recently delivered in a van disguised as that of a local furniture retailer, it's a brilliant piece of carpentry designed by Belfast Det HQ. We also review the emergency telephone numbers we've been given, which we've had to commit to memory, both for Gower Street in London and Det HQ in Belfast. Thanks to the DG's passion for cricket, we agree on 'Is Botham batting?' as the emergency phrase to be used should we stumble across British security personnel, or if we need to gain access to military or police premises. Conversely, if Control needs to contact us, they will use the expression 'Is George Best fit?'.

Maureen grabs me by the arm.

'Come on, let's take a stroll to our respective schools; it'll take in a big part of the Ardoyne, and you can get to know it. Have you studied the maps and intel you were sent?'

'I have. I'm good at maps. I know the Ardoyne like the back of my hand. But it'll be good to see it for real.'

'Excellent, then you can brief me as we walk.'

Clever girl, she's called my bluff, testing me. But I'll be fine; maps are my forte. We hold hands as we walk down Estoril Park. It's remarkably like every working-class terraced housing estate in Britain, except that many more of its houses are empty shells, left derelict by years of devastation. It's obvious that no one ever comes to clean the streets or remove the detritus of decay and dereliction. The whole place is a depressing mess. Several streets have disappeared altogether, leaving large tracts of waste ground covered in the rubble of demolition. The scene resembles the shattered landscapes of Britain's cities in the aftermath of German bombing during the Second World War.

The devastation is a product of the mass torching of whole streets when the minority population of Protestants moved out and set fire to their own homes so that Catholics couldn't use them. Then the loyalist gangs came, ably supported by the RUC, to burn down whole rows of Catholic homes. It was over a decade ago, but the memories are still raw.

What remains of the housing is ostensibly normal: net curtains at the windows, front steps kept immaculately clean. There's pride in the appearance of many of the houses, but not all; some are barely fit for human habitation.

'It's smaller than I imagined, Mo.'

'Yes, I know, only a few dozen streets. It would be just a village if it was in the countryside. And, by the way, don't call me "Mo".'

'Why not? "Maureen" sounds a bit formal, a bit British, doesn't it?'

'I suppose it does, but I'd prefer "Maureen".'

Wow, she's prickly! But I think I'll carry on calling her "Mo". I can't let her have everything her own way. I look around at the tiny, impoverished Catholic enclave and find it hard to believe that so much violence and hatred could occupy such a small space.

'So, with the Protestants having moved out, they're surrounded on all sides by loyalists and hemmed in by the RUC?'

'Right, and by our army. The siege mentality is very powerful. As you'll have read in the notes, the IRA is more than politics here. They're about the survival of the community. They're heroes in these parts. The story of them going from street to street, with just two weapons between them, firing a few rounds on each street corner, to convince the loyalist mob they were well armed, has become a local legend.'

We soon see very recent remnants of mayhem. Burnt-out vehicles litter several streets. There are piles of cobbles, recycled as weapons, and the scorched residue of countless Molotov cocktails smears the tarmac at strategic crossroads. Less tangible, but very real all the same, is the aura of tension and danger. I can smell it, lingering in the air, amidst the odour of smoke and cordite. This is a front line – an invisible one but all too real, nevertheless. When the clashes happen, the battle lines form and the fight is fought. Then the two sides melt away and a bizarre normality returns . . . until the next time. I've seen it on television, read about it and been told about it in briefings. Now, I can feel it all around me, and Maureen and I are clandestine combatants in the struggle.

A disconcerting truth suddenly hits me: we're acting out an odd perversion. While actively working for their sworn enemy, our job is to convince the locals that, although we're civilian neutrals, we're nevertheless sympathetic to their cause. It's a bewildering feeling. I'm not sure how many other operatives are undercover like this, but Gower Street intimated that we're a unique experiment. I feel isolated and anxious. No, not anxious, scared shitless!

In the distance, there's but one breath of fresh air: the moorland hump of Divis Mountain, rising almost 500 metres to the west. It reminds me of my Pennine home and makes me wish I was back there.

There are no buildings of any scale in the Ardoyne, except for the high, grey-stone walls of Ewart's Linen Mill on Flax Street, long since a source of work, and, on the other side of the Crumlin Road, the tall twin towers of Holy Cross Church and Monastery, lording it over Belfast's poverty. I peer at the preposterous mock-Romanesque ostentation of Holy Cross; it's so typical of the arrogance of Rome.

'What about the clergy? How much do they support the IRA?'

'Some do, tacitly. They've no time for the Protestants, of course. But they wouldn't endorse the violence. They're a positive influence, on the whole, but the local hard cases don't trust them an inch.'

Curtains twitch as we pass. There are lingering stares from anyone we meet in the street. The women wear headscarves and their shabby winter coats are buttoned up tightly against the winter chill. Most of their children look clean and well turned out. Occasionally, to remind us how deprived this community is, a sorry little mite appears who looks unwashed and unkempt and is wearing too few clothes for the harsh weather.

Every now and then, Maureen smiles broadly and offers a warm greeting. 'Good evening to you, Mrs Toohey. How's Bridey?'

'Oh, she's well, Miss O'Brien, thank ye.'

A little group of adolescent girls comes up to us, giggling excitedly. One of them shouts out.

'Is this yer man, miss?'

'Yes, it's Mr Dowd. He's starting at the boys' school next week.'

They run off, mouthing what I'm sure are suggestive or obscene comments, but I haven't yet tuned in to the accent well enough to decipher them.

St Anthony's School for Boys was established in the middle part of the twentieth century to provide a good secondary education for the boys of the Catholic community of West Belfast. It's situated off the Antrim Road, just east of the Ardoyne. Its sister school, St Hilda's Secondary School for girls, is a little further north, but within walking distance. They're both like the 1960s comprehensive schools you can see anywhere in the land. But there's a difference. As well as the usual crop of future secretaries, factory workers and recruits to the legions of the unemployed, the schools are breeding grounds for radical republicanism and its derivative, the IRA.

After school, for the boys in particular, off comes the school blazer, to be replaced by hooded jackets and scarves, which are used to hide their faces. Then they serve as 'dickers' – lookouts – and whenever there's a flashpoint of violence, they make ready to hurl missiles at the British Army and RUC.

My first week at St Anthony's proves to be fairly uneventful. I'm timetabled to teach middle-school English and history, one senior group of 'A' stream English literature, and one of history.

In English, I have to begin *The Tempest* with them. As I try to introduce one of the most original and difficult of the Bard's plays, I can't help thinking how hard it must be, even for the brightest of these boys, to see the relevance of the machinations of Prospero, Duke of Milan, to their lives in the Ardoyne. Over several lessons, I try to develop metaphorical links between Prospero's misery on his little island and Ireland's woes, but I give up when it becomes obvious that the boys see Shakespeare much as I did when I was their age: much ado about nothing in a language that is not as they like it. I revert to teaching by the numbers: forget trying to decipher the play; just get them through the exam by rehearsing the answers to examination questions, over and over again, until they can recite them like parrots!

They're better in their language essays; several of the boys write well, but most of what they put on paper is highly political in content and angry in tone, some of it stridently so. Nevertheless, they're writing coherently; I can't ask for more.

In history, they're studying 'World Affairs from the Russian Revolution to the Present', but it's hard to keep them focused on anything beyond the island of Ireland. The dogma of the late sixties republican uprising is too powerful in their ears. They've heard it many times and know it's true: they're living through a colonial war, experiencing first-hand the dying embers of one of the last vestiges of the British Empire.

As I try to wade through the complexities of the Russian Revolution, the boys want to talk about Ireland and teach me its history. I spend a lot of the week listening as they put into historical context the issues that are in the news bulletins every night. One of the boys, Michael

Kearns, a very bright boy with an almost pathological dislike of the British, does most of the talking and becomes my putative tutor in republican history.

'Sir, ye know the men in the Maze who went on hunger strike in October?'

'Yes . . . well, I've read about them.'

'Well, there were seven, to match the number of men who signed the Proclamation of the Republic in 1916. One of the fellas who signed the proclamation was Seán Mac Diarmada. He lived in the Ardoyne for a while. He was shot by the Brits after the Easter Rising.'

A look of fierce pride plays across the boy's face.

'Before he was executed he said, "I feel happiness the like of which I have never experienced. I die that the Irish nation might live!"'

I feel a shiver of emotion run down my spine. The boys in the room stare at me, wondering how I will react to this powerful evocation of the Gaelic cause. I smile at them.

'A brave man. I'm not surprised you're proud of him.'

Young Michael, warming to his cause, continues.

'So the boys in the Maze chose seven in honour of the 1916 signatories. One of 'em, Brendan Hughes, is one of us. A Belfast boy from the Lower Falls, not far from here.'

'What's he in the Maze for?'

'What d'ye think? For killing British soldiers. He's Officer Commanding, Belfast Brigade, IRA, so he is.'

'Do you know him?'

'Course! Everyone around here knows Bren.'

I'm fascinated as the boy, not yet sixteen years old, holds court. I sit on the corner of my desk and look at the faces of the other thirty-three boys in the classroom. They're all under Michael's spell. He's clearly a future leader in his community and it's a certainty that'll mean he'll be a prominent figure in the IRA.

'It was an Ardoyne man who started the hunger strikes last year, Martin Meehan. The man's a legend. When the Prods came to burn us out ten years ago, the RUC were in on it and the British Army nowhere to be seen. It was Martin and a couple of others who held them off. They'd hardly any weapons and almost no ammunition, but they saved this community and everyone here. Now he's banged up in the Maze on false charges. He went on hunger strike before all the others and only stopped when Cardinal Ó Fiaich begged him.'

Although I would've preferred to go on talking all morning, I decide to call a halt.

'Fascinating, Michael, thank you. But we must get back to 1917.'

'But that means nothin' to us, sir.'

'Are you sure? It was the first great revolutionary struggle of this century. Can't you see the link? Besides, Ireland's not on the syllabus. So let's crack on.'

One of the other boys, a surly lad, hard to win over, shouts from the back of the room. There's a hint of menace in his voice. Several others, all the leery ones in the class, egg him on.

'My da says you're a filthy Brit and wants to know what you're doin' in the Ardoyne?'

A sudden wave of discomfort washes over me and I feel my face redden. I try to think of an answer as blunt as the question.

'It's "sir" to you, Brian. And never use that expression in my classroom again, understand? You can tell your father that if he wants an answer to that question, he can come and ask me himself.'

I'm pleased with the answer. But it's broken the ice, and several boys ask the same question at the same time, though more politely: *Why have you come to the Ardoyne, sir?*

I can't not answer.

'If you must know, two reasons. My girlfriend, Miss O'Brien, teaches at St Hilda's and I came here to be with her.'

There are plenty of sniggers and knowing glances. Maureen has clearly made an impression on the male population of the area.

'But also, we're both of Irish Catholic descent and know that, because of the Troubles here, there's a need for good teachers in Northern Ireland. So we thought we'd like to help, and find out what's going on.'

A smiling, happy-go-lucky boy, Danny Barrett, continues the interrogation.

'So you're a republican, then, sir?'

'Yes, I am, in both senses. I believe in a United Ireland. And I'm also a republican in the UK and believe in a head of state, rather than a monarch.'

There are smiles around the room. I've been prepared for that question since I arrived in the city and it rolls off my tongue effortlessly.

'So will youse be helping us fight the Brits and the Peelers?'

'No, Tommy, I'll be helping you little ear-'oles pass a few exams!'

My candour prompts a few smiles and brings the conversation to an end.

That evening, sitting having dinner in our tiny kitchen with Maureen, I tell her about my Irish history lesson. She's concerned.

'Jim, you should be careful, young Kearns is the nephew of Jimmy McKee, the head of one of the most well-known families in the Ardoyne. McKee is quartermaster, Ardoyne Battalion, and high on the army's wanted list. His daughter, Kathleen, teaches with me at St Hilda's; very pretty, but a very strident republican. I don't think she likes me very much.'

'Her little cousin is very committed as well. I got well and truly grilled today.'

'And?'

'OK, I think it was fine. I told them the truth . . . well, something like the truth!'

'What do you mean?'

'I've been thinking . . . d'ya reckon Gower Street's got any idea what they're doing?'

'I think so. We're intelligence officers beginning a surveillance operation.'

'But they've chosen us because of our Irish Catholic credentials – credentials which, if they had the wits to put two and two together, might make six and be likely to give us qualms of conscience.'

'Speak for yourself.'

'I am.'

'Look, get used to it; we're here now and we've a job to do.'

'But, other than sit and wait, we don't even know what the "job" is.'

'Don't worry, that's bound to come in due course.'

'I know, and that's what bothers me, wondering what it'll be.'

'Observation and intel, Jim. That's what we're trained for.'

'Perhaps, but you've heard the rumours, as I have, about what the Det boys are up to.'

'Rumours, Jim, just rumours. Anyway, we have another test to face on Saturday. Kathleen McKee has invited us to the Hibernian Club for a drink. It's just round the corner, a big wooden hut at the end of Brompton Park. It's the heart of the community and the Provos' unofficial HQ. I've been through the initiation, now it's your turn.'

'Into the lion's den, then.'

'Exactly. Kathleen said they'd heard about your reputation as a footballer and their manager wants you to play for them. But the main reason is to vet you. They want to make sure you are who you say you are. I went through it when I arrived in September.'

'How was it?'

'Friendly enough. But they're not daft; you'll have to be careful. Drink a lot, but keep your wits about you.'

'Who'll we meet?'

'Barry Kennedy, for sure; he's the heart and soul of the club. A republican, but I don't think he's got a balaclava in his wardrobe. He was interned for a year when the army lifted anyone who whispered the words "United Ireland"; the locals say he got arrested just because he's an expert on Gaelic culture and Irish history. He's got a sociology degree from Queen's. They call him "the Brain". You'll also meet the football manager, a man called Donal Cleary, who loves football. I don't think he's IRA. We might even meet Kathleen's father, Jimmy; and Sean Murphy, OC-Ardoyne, may be there as well.'

'The man himself! I've read the brief about him, the most wanted man in Belfast.'

'Yes, him. If he's there, he'll be surrounded by a posse of guardian angels, all armed to the teeth. The army has wanted him for years, but can't get close. He's never been arrested. He moves from house to house, never sleeps in the same bed two nights running. We've no idea if or how he gets in and out of the Ardoyne.'

'My intel's very clear, he's a low-life piece of shit who should have been topped a long time ago.'

'That's the boy. His file makes harrowing reading.'

'I know, I've read it. I do my homework, Mo.'

'He's very close to the McKees, first cousin to Jimmy. So watch your step, especially with the Kearns boy. Every word you say in class will go straight back to Ardoyne Battalion HQ.'

'Where do they meet?'

'The McKee house or the Hibernian.'

'You know what, Mo. You're right about how to play it – drink a lot!'

13. Saturday Night in the Hibernian

As the hub of a large community in the middle of a major city, the Hibernian Club could not be more modest. Not much more than a shebeen, and the furniture is a motley collection of cast-off chairs – several of them taken from hijacked buses – discarded sofas and an array of old kitchen tables. The bar is a fake mahogany worktop screwed to some melamine shelves, embellished by an improvised assembly of bits and pieces from burnt-out pubs and bars.

Tracks from the album *The Woman I Loved So Well* by Irish folk group Planxty is being played far too loudly from huge speakers on either side of the bar. Irish tricolours cover the bare walls and the atmosphere is thick with cigarette smoke and heavy with laughter. Above the din, most of the conversation seems to be about a bloke called Sutcliffe who's been arrested in the Yorkshire Ripper case. The view seems to be that he's an evil-looking bastard and definitely the killer.

We get a few stares as we sit near the bar. The Hibernian doesn't see too many outsiders, but getting in was straightforward. The elderly man on the door recognized Maureen and smiled as we passed. I try to relax; they've seen Maureen before, so everyone's eyes are on me. Reassuringly, when I do catch somebody's glance, I get a smile from the women and a nod from the men. It looks like word has got around: Miss O'Brien's fella, a Brit, but he's alright, a left-footer, Irish blood, good footballer.

I'm not fond of Guinness but, as there's no choice, Guinness it is. Maureen has the same. We're into our second pint when our host appears. Kathleen McKee is a sight for sore eyes. Maureen said she was 'pretty', but that's a gross understatement. She's stunning. I can't help thinking, 'Jesus, it's Maureen O'Hara in *The Quiet Man*!' Her hair, lighter than Maureen's, is a lustrous copper colour, and it flows in waves rather than in Maureen's tight curls. Her skin is as pale as parchment and her eyes are a sparkly light grey.

Instantly smitten, I jump to my feet to shake hands, a politeness more appropriate in suburban England than in Belfast's republican clubs. She's almost my height, about as tall as Maureen, at least five foot ten. They could be sisters.

'Hello, Jim, Maureen's told me lots about you. Pleased to meet you in person.'

'Pleased to meet you, Kathleen. What can I get you to drink?'

'No, you're my guests, another Guinness?'

'Come on, let me get them.'

'Will ye sit down, man! This is the Ardoyne; I'm buying. A Guinness for the both of ye.'

Without spilling a drop, she returns from the bar carrying a triangle of pint glasses adroitly cradled between her outstretched hands. We chat away animatedly for thirty minutes before anyone else arrives. Much to Maureen's disapproval, I can't keep my eyes off this Angel of the Ardoyne. She's great company, bright and full of mischievous humour. With the Guinness adding to the mood, I forget the reason for our invitation until several large silhouettes block out the light. They're already clasping their pints of Guinness.

Barry Kennedy, bespectacled, clean shaven and with the air of a man of learning, introduces himself, as does Donal Cleary, a pot-bellied, red-faced man who hasn't kicked a ball in anger for many a year. The other men in the group walk to another table without speaking. Kathleen smiles at them and one of them, a solid, craggy-looking man in his forties, winks back. I assume that's Jimmy, her father.

Barry does most of the talking.

'You've been here before, Maureen, haven't you?'

'I have, Barry.'

'Well, welcome back. And welcome to you – is it Jim, or Jimmy?'

'Either way, I don't mind.'

'We have a lot of Jimmys, so let it be Jim.'

'Fine by me.'

'Father Nulty, a governor at St Anthony's – you met him at your interview – tells me that you played semi-pro over the water?'

'I did.'

'Tell us more. We don't often meet players of that calibre over here.'

He pronounces calibre with a lovely Irish burr – *cal-iber* – that makes me smile.

'I played for the UAU and British Universities, and then Leytonstone and Ilford in the Isthmian League.'

'What position do ye play, Jim?'

'Left back is my strongest suit, but I can play centre back, especially if my partner's a big stopper, or centre midfield if the standard's not too high. I'm a ball winner.'

Donal, who has said very little, smiles broadly.

'Are ye fit?'

'I haven't played this season, but I'm fit. I run a lot.'

'Great. Ye'll walk into our first eleven. Centre midfield it is. We need a ball winner. Our league is full of nasty little fuckers who take man and ball without batting an eyelid. Excuse my French, Miss O'Brien.'

'Don't worry, I've heard it all before, Donal.'

'Not from my Mary, I hope.'

'No, she's a good girl.'

Donal turns to me.

'Training, Mondays and Wednesdays. We play over at Andytown . . . sorry, ye're new to Belfast, Andersonstown. We've got a game against Malachians on Saturday. I'll bring the league forms for ye to sign on Monday.'

There are handshakes all round, and glasses are raised in a toast. Barry then gets up and gestures to us to go with him.

'Come on, there's some fellas over here I'd like youse to meet.'

I feel my heart beat against my chest like a drum. We're two members of British Intelligence, and I'm SAS – the two organizations most despised by the Catholic community – and we're about to be introduced to the leadership of the Provos' 3rd Battalion, Belfast Brigade. We're in their lair and no one knows we're here. We have no comms and no escape route. One mistake, one word out of place and we're goners . . . and in a very nasty way. What if our

77

cover is already blown? What if they've known all along and were just waiting for me to arrive to join Maureen? No one would ever know the truth; we'd just be two more British soldiers who've died on active service.

The famous black-and-white image of a lantern-jawed Robert Nairac, wearing his Grenadier Guards beret while talking to children of the Ardoyne, pops into my head. A few years later, when he was caught operating undercover, he claimed he was Danny McAlevey, a 'sticky' – a member of the Official IRA – from the Ardoyne. The parallels are too uncomfortable to contemplate. I swallow hard. They haven't found Nairac's body. Perhaps they'll never find ours. We could be ground up into dog food, or fed to the pigs. My hands are shaking; I clench my fists to try to stop them trembling.

Nairac got tumbled by a few rural lightweights. Maureen and I are in front of real hard men; clever, battle-hardened veterans. I glance at Maureen. She's met this lot before and seems incredibly at ease. There's ice in that girl's veins! Her resolve makes me feel worse; I feel the Guinness churn in my belly. For fuck's sake, lad, don't puke now – or worse, shit your pants!

Jimmy McKee smiles broadly as we approach.

'Miss O'Brien, how're ye doin'?'

'Very well, but please, it's Maureen.'

'Good enough, Maureen, I think ye've met Sean Murphy before?'

'I have. Good to see you again, Mr Murphy.'

The big man, who looks like he should be a club bouncer – and probably has been, in his time – beams at Maureen.

'Sean, please. How's St Hilda's? Girls behaving themselves?'

'Very well, they're all good girls.'

'Very pleased to hear that. Make sure to tell me if any of 'em step outta line.'

Murphy looks at me. His expression is warm and welcoming.

Words and phrases from his file ring in my head: kneecapping, torture, beatings, a vicious temper, violent towards friend and foe, drug-running, summary executions, extortion. It's hard to marry what I see in front of me with what I've read on paper. He stands up to shake my hand, as do Jimmy McKee and the other men, none of whom offers his name. Murphy beckons to us to sit. I look at his minders to see if I can see if they're armed. Nothing is obvious, but I'm sure they'll have shoulder holsters or weapons in their belts. I checked the door as I came in and couldn't see anyone who was obviously an armed guard, but I feel sure that, very close by, will be an automatic weapon and somebody able to use it.

'So you're Maureen's boyfriend. You're a lucky man.'

'Indeed I am.'

If only he knew that I sleep on the sofa!

'How do youse find St Anthony's?'

'Fine, it's just like any other inner-city school. You have to win over the boys. You have to build their trust.'

'And how do ye do that?'

'By convincing them that you care about them and then reminding them who's the boss.'

Murphy seems to like the answer. He looks at the others around the table and smiles. They all nod approvingly.

'I'm told you've got Irish roots like Maureen.'

I break into a thick Lancashire dialect to reinforce my working-class roots.

'Aye, St Theodore's Catholic Secondary Modern, Burnley. Maternal grandmother, Mary Cooney, Tyneside Irish; family frae Armagh. Father unknown; thought t' be a doctor at St James's Dublin, wheer me mother, Eileen, were a nurse. But for all I know, 'e could've been t'hospital winda cleana!'

More smiles, they're amused by my aping of the unique East Lancs accent. I'm doing well. Then the crunch question comes. Murphy's face retains its smiley glow, but there's a hint of gravity.

'So, Jim, why here? Belfast's not most people's career choice just now.'

I try to make light of it.

'That's easy, Mo's here.'

Murphy's smile widens.

'Well, she'd have any man on a string, that's for sure. Anything else? Perhaps to be with your Irish brothers and sisters in their hour of need?'

Cleverly put. I'll have to be very careful. Several sets of eyes are boring into me.

'That plays a part, of course. I went to university in '68, and in my first year I went to listen to some visiting students from Queen's Belfast who were part of the civil rights campaign. Up to then, I had no idea what was going on. Then Burntollet Bridge happened. I've been a convert ever since.'

'So, have you come here to fight, Jim?'

Here goes, this is the big answer to the big question.

'No. I've come here to teach. I'm English; it's not my fight. But I want to help the Catholic community build for the future.'

There is a pregnant silence. Murphy looks at me like the interrogators during my selection. I feel like I did then: fragile and frightened. At least I've got my clothes on this time! The other faces give nothing away. They're waiting for their godfather to speak. Then he smiles again.

'OK, Jim. I know Maureen thinks the same. Youse two are very welcome here, especially to help educate our heathen children. The Ardoyne's a very small family. We look out for one another. You take care of us and we'll take care of you . . . and make sure you keep the Hibernians in the First Division.'

'I'll try my best, Sean . . . and thanks for the welcome, it's much appreciated.'

There's a round of warm handshakes and, with only the slightest wave of his hand, Sean calls over the barman. Two trays of Guinness arrive quickly, each one accompanied by a Jameson's chaser for a toast. Several choruses of *sláinte* follow. I feel like I've just been reprieved from death row. My heart is pumping even faster, my hand is shaking even more than before, but this time the dynamo is euphoria not dread.

Saturday night in the Hibernian soon descends – or ascends, depending on your point of view – into a drunken evocation of Gaelic pride, complete with rabble-rousing speeches, collections for displaced Catholic families and mass renditions of Irish rebel songs. It's not hard for me and Maureen to become wholeheartedly involved.

The atmosphere is electric.

*

81

When Maureen and I get back to our flat, we flop on to the sofa like we've just finished Long Drag on SAS selection. I break out our bottle of Jameson's and pour two hefty measures.

'You did well, Jim. They like you.'

'No suspicions?'

'If they had, we'd be two lumps of slaughterhouse meat by now.'

I take a big swig and try to gather my thoughts. They're confused.

'How do you feel, Mo?'

'What d'ya mean?'

'How about guilt? You know, being in the Hibernian, welcomed like that, but lying through our teeth.'

'Jim, we're intelligence officers, we're spooks. It's what we do.'

'But is it right?'

Maureen looks at me sternly but, this time, doesn't admonish me. She takes a swig of her own and ponders for a while before answering.

'That's not for us to decide.'

'Fuck me, Mo, we're not robots; we're allowed to think.'

'Jim, come on, we've had a lot to drink, so let's drop it.'

'Bollocks! When I told Murphy we're here to help, I meant it. I couldn't have said it unless I meant it.'

'I mean it too. But if we're going to help this community, people like Murphy, the godfathers – criminals – and the iron fist of the Provos have to go.'

'OK, but the IRA is all they've got. No one else is looking after them.'

'I agree, I think that's part of our job as well, to make sure communities like this are never neglected and oppressed again. But, first, we have to restore order and get rid of the bad boys.'

Maureen's argument confuses me even more. I can see her point. My training and the British view of the problem seem logical, but I wonder how much we really know and how much of the intel we've read has been manipulated by Westminster and its appointed agencies. Somehow, being here in the heart of the Ardoyne makes everything look and feel different.

'Jim, leave it. It'll gnaw away at you.' She puts her hand on my arm. 'I'm off to bed. See you in the morning.'

She goes into the kitchen to put her glass in the sink. When she comes back, she pauses. I think she feels sorry for me.

'No girlfriend at home?'

'No, why? You offering?'

'Jim, out of bounds! It's just that I watched you drooling over Kathleen.'

'Any man would, Mo, she's to die for.'

'That's as may be, but she's got to be off-limits too.'

'Why? I signed up for a military mission, not to a fucking monastery.'

She looks exasperated.

'For all the reasons you've just talked about. It would be a lie . . . and a very dangerous one.'

'Has she got a fella?'

'Don't think so. Belfast isn't exactly crawling with Richard Gere lookalikes. Anyway, that doesn't matter, leave her alone.'

'What if she comes on to me?'

'I don't think so, lover boy. But if she does, let her down lightly; be nice, but say no.'

She's right, of course.

14. The Rites of Spring

The early weeks of 1981 pass quickly. The humdrum of ordinary life takes over. Teaching is tiring, I have my football three times a week, and the fitness regime Maureen and I follow religiously fills the remaining evenings. So time flies. We go to the Hibernian at least once a week and into Belfast city centre at weekends, usually after a day tabbing across some of Northern Ireland's beautiful countryside.

Our favourite spot is the Mourne Mountains and their highest peak, Slieve Donard. It's not unlike Pen-y-Fan in Wales, and about the same height, so we hurtle up and down it as often as we can, doing our own little Fan Dance. Maureen can still slaughter me on the flat, but on the almost vertical I'm still king of the mountains!

Our preferred haunts in the city are the Crown, Madden's Bar and Kelly's Cellars, and we rotate between them. Like on the top of Slieve Donard, they seem far removed from both the humdrum of normal life and Belfast's interminable internecine woes. At least in its oldest pubs, there's still good booze, good music and good craic – thank God. The Crown reminds me of the legendary Philharmonic in Liverpool. We try to bag one of its charming private snugs, complete with etched glass, leather banquettes and bells to ring for service, but it's usually impossible.

Maureen and I are getting along well. We don't agree on much, but have a deal not to talk about politics in general – and Northern Ireland's in particular – unless its machinations have implications for our op. However, as of the beginning of March, we still have no idea what our 'op' entails.

As the weeks pass, my private musings lead me to imagine all sorts of scenarios, most of them too horrendous to contemplate. During selection, and especially from the regulars at Hereford, I heard all sorts of stories of covert operations – what the republicans call 'dirty tricks' – being perpetrated by British forces in their many guises. I guess that Maureen may well be having the same thoughts as I am but, if she does, she doesn't mention them.

My concerns are exacerbated by two particular conspiracies that are repeated, over and over again, in the Ardoyne. One is the long-held view that British forces are colluding with loyalist paramilitaries, particularly through rogue elements within the RUC and Special Branch, and that loyalist assassination squads are being fed intel and encouraged to attack republican targets. The other is a growing belief that, carried out by SAS teams and supported by 14 Intelligence, a covert shoot-to-kill policy is in operation, particularly since Thatcher's government came to power in 1979. Whenever these thoughts come into my head, I suppress them as soon as I can.

I often see the gorgeous Kathleen in the distance, but stick to Maureen's advice and steer clear of her. Once, she waved at me animatedly, but I resisted the almost overpowering temptation and just waved back. She came to a couple of the Hibernian's matches and cheered from the sidelines, despite the worst that Belfast's climate could throw at her. She wore a thick parka coat with a fur-trimmed hood and I fantasized about her as Julie Christie in *Doctor Zhivago*. But again, I was a good boy. I played particularly well that day and ran the game from the middle of the park. I pretended I was playing like Glenn Hoddle – if only!

The Hibernians have improved. We've only lost twice since I started playing, and we're now mid-table. The level isn't bad, but more kick, bollock and bite than silky skills. Even so, I enjoy it; I don't mind a bit of a scrap, and it's over after the game.

Dull normality is suddenly shaken out of its slumber in late March, a miserable rainy day. In the distance, I see a car pull up next to a young man as he walks along Berwick Road at the corner of Cranbrook Gardens. He's dressed in a dark duffel coat, jeans and labourer's boots. I'm about seventy-five yards away. The driver of the car seems to be talking to the pedestrian; I assume he's a friend, or asking for directions. Checking for cars as I cross the road, I turn away. A single shot rings out. By the time I look back up the street, the young man is already a crumpled heap on the ground.

The driver revs his engine. I see the brake lights go out, then go back on again. A tall man wearing dark clothes and a balaclava exits from the rear door of the car and, at point-blank range, aims a pistol at the stricken man's back. A plaintive hand is raised from the man on the floor, pleading for mercy. None is forthcoming. I begin to run towards the scene as another round retorts down the street. The victim's body quivers from the impact; then it's still. It will never move again.

The car speeds away down Berwick Road, then turns right along Estoril Park towards the Crumlin Road. Estoril is my road. Forlornly, I wish that I could alert Maureen, who could arm herself and shoot the bastards as they escape. It's yet another sectarian killing; another pointless death.

When I reach the boy, several people are there before me. There's blood everywhere. There isn't much panic, few hysterics; they've seen it all before. Only one young man is distressed and angry. He shakes the body and shouts, 'Paul, get up, get up! Ye'll be fine, so you will. Get up!'

I kneel down; my knees, clothed in my schoolteacher's grey flannel trousers, drop into the sticky pool of blood that surrounds the body. His eyes are open in a fixed stare, a stare of abject terror. He knows he's dying. I can't check for a pulse at his neck because the first bullet has gone through his throat. I check his wrist, and there's a faint pulse. I look at his neck; blood is still pumping in spurts. His heart is still trying to nourish his body, but then the flow stops. The beat at his wrist disappears. His eyes remain open, but the impassioned stare becomes a gentle repose. I try to console the distressed friend.

'He's gone, mate. I'm so sorry.'

My accent gives away my alien status. The man's distressed face turns venomous.

'Who the fuck are youse?'

'I live round here.'

'Oh, yer, you're a fucking Brit. What are you doin' 'ere?'

It's obvious that he – and everyone around him – is putting two and two together. And making six.

I hear someone mutter, 'He's a fuckin' Tan in civvies! Go and get the boys.'

A surge of blind panic rises in the pit of my stomach. A youth turns and runs in the direction of the Hibernian. He's going to get Sean Murphy and his henchmen. I want to run to the flat and get a weapon, but that would only confirm my guilt. I'm still holding the victim's hand; I don't let go. Surely it tells the onlookers that I care.

But their faces mirror the opposite. They're looking at me like I'm a callous enemy, responsible for the death of their friend. Do I run and face a certain death, or stay and face the same? What about Maureen? Perhaps I could warn her? I try to call on my training. Stay calm; think through your options; then act quickly and decisively. I decide I have to run. The op's over!

Suddenly a female voice shouts.

'It's alright, Kevin, he's one of us. It's Jim Dowd, the schoolteacher.'

I look round. My saviour is Kathleen; she smiles, but only weakly. There are tears in her eyes and her chest is heaving. She kneels down beside me, oblivious to the blood that immediately soaks her tights and skirt.

'It's Paul Blake, a good friend of mine. We were at junior school together. He's the nicest boy in the world.'

She starts to wail uncontrollably and rock backwards and forwards on her knees. After a while she begins to speak.

'We called him "The Big Sleep", because he could nod off anywhere. Now, he's asleep forever.'

I put my arm around her. It only makes her sobs worse. Paul's friends from the Hibernian arrive: Jim Dickson, Martin Kane and Hughie Burns. They're wild with anger. Burns starts to shout.

'It's the fuckin' UFF for sure, bastards! Fuckin' Prod bastards! They'll be from the Shankill, let's go over and find 'em.'

His friends try to calm him down. Kane grabs his arm.

'No one does anything until we speak to Sean. Come on, he'll be in the Hibernian, let's go.'

As Kane pulls Burns away, Burns turns to me, his face still red with rage.

'And youse, ye Brit bastard, ye can fuck off where you came from; ye're not fuckin' welcome 'ere!'

Kane rebukes his friend.

'Shut it, Hughie.'

Hughie doesn't listen.

'And you can take your fuckin' hands off our Kathleen. We don't want some English ponce touching her, you cunt!'

Burns' invective snaps Kathleen out of her grief.

'Get lost, Hughie! Paul's lying here dead. Behave yourself.'

Eventually he's led away and everyone relaxes and turns their attention back to the victim. The man who had turned on me smiles apologetically.

'Sorry, Mr Dowd, I thought you were a Brit agent.'

'It's Jim.'

'Kevin Connor.'

He holds out his hand to shake mine. It's drenched in blood, but I shake it anyway. Kathleen gets to her feet and takes several deep breaths before looking at me, pain etched on her face. She goes over to sit on a garden wall. After a while, with sirens closing in on the scene, she calls over to me.

'Jim, will you walk me home? It's over on Herbert Street.'

'Course I will.'

As we walk, the sirens blare and people rush past us to see what's happened. She's a little unsteady on her feet and I offer her my arm to steady her. She takes it and smiles. She seems composed now, resigned to the horror of it all. After a while, she looks me in the eye.

'There's Flax Cabs on Flax Street. Do you fancy going into the city for a drink? I need to get away from the Ardoyne for a while.'

'That's a good idea.'

'Are you sure Maureen won't mind?'

'Course not, she'll understand. But what about our clothes? Don't you want to get changed?'

'No, everyone's used to blood in Belfast. Besides, it's Paul's blood, I'm proud to have it on me.'

We go to Kelly's Cellars, Belfast's oldest pub. It's very Irish and very old; its low arches, whitewashed walls and open fire could easily be in a medieval tavern. Irish is widely spoken in the pub and Kathleen exchanges pleasantries in Gaelic before sitting down. The atmosphere helps her relax. We talk idly about the pub, Belfast's history and anything else, rather than about what's just happened. But suddenly, she looks down at her bloodstained dress and sighs.

'Will it ever stop, Jim?'

'I don't know. It's only just started for me. I've read about the violence, now I've seen it for real.'

'I'm afraid it's a way of life here.'

'Why did they target your friend? Was he in the IRA?'

'No, Paul loved football – Manchester United – he liked a drink and chasing the girls, he didn't have a political thought in his life. Jesus, Jim, he was just twenty-six. His girlfriend lives just up the road, he must have been going to see her.'

'So why did they shoot him?'

'Probably for no reason except that he lived in the Ardoyne and was a Catholic. A loyalist councillor, Sammy Millar, was shot in the Shankill last week. I reckon they just sent an assassination squad over for revenge: pick out a Taig and shoot the fucker! To those in the Shankill we're all Fenian bastards.'

Kathleen takes a swig of the Jameson's she's cradling.

I put my hand on her arm.

'Thanks for what you said when Paul's friends got angry.'

'That's OK, you are one of us.'

'I'd like to think so.'

'We were all very suspicious when you first came. Not so much Maureen, a woman on her own, but when you appeared a few people asked questions.'

I shudder; hopefully, only on the inside.

'But you were checked out.'

'Really?'

'Of course. An Englishman suddenly arriving out of nowhere? We're not stupid.'

'The IRA?'

'The Provos. Sean Murphy is Officer Commanding in the Ardoyne, which is the 3rd Battalion of the Belfast Brigade. Brigade made some inquiries.'

I try to look innocent about Sean's status and suitably shocked that they had verified my status.

'I assumed Sean was a bigwig in the IRA, but didn't realize he was the main man.'

'Oh yes, Sean's a god in Belfast, part of the Provos' inner sanctum. But don't worry, word came back that you are who you say you are.'

I try to sound appropriately naive.

'Can I ask how you find out things like that?'

'Jim, you've lived and worked in London. Do you know how many Irish Catholics live in London?'

'Point taken.'

I hesitate, then I decide to ask a question I would ask if Jim Dowd was real.

'I hope you don't mind me asking; is your father in the IRA?'

'He's the Battalion Quartermaster.'

I ponder whether it's a good idea to ask my next question, but decide that Jim Dowd would definitely ask it.

'Can I ask if you're a member?'

'Of course you can. I'm a member of Sinn Féin.'

'Is there a difference?'

'Yes, Sinn Féin's a political party. There's a new view among republicans; the armed struggle must go on, but we need a political strategy as well.'

'Does that mean you know you can't win the military battle?'

'Not at all, it's just two parallel strategies.'

'So what do Sean and your father think about that?'

'They support it; only a few hardliners are against it.'

'Isn't Sean a hardliner? He's quite an intimidating man.'

'D'ye think so? He's a hard man, so he is, but his heart's in the right place.'

'Really? I don't think I'd like to get on the wrong side of him.'

'He does look like a heavyweight boxer, but his bark is worse than his bite.'

I decide it's a good time to push my luck and probe a little deeper.

'On the mainland, the press say that the paramilitaries – republican and loyalist – are criminal gangs in disguise and that they run all sorts of dodgy rackets and campaigns of violence and intimidation in their own communities.'

Kathleen raises her eyebrows, but then smiles.

'You should know better than to believe what you read in the British press. There are some rogues, for sure, on both sides. Jim Craig, who's the top man in the UFF in the Shankill, is up to his ears in crime and a very nasty piece of work. But Sean's a good man. And remember, there's no formal law in the Ardoyne. The RUC can't be trusted, and it's a no-go area for them. So we take care of our own justice.'

'According to whose rules?'

'Ours.'

I decide that's enough questions for one night. Kathleen looks at me quizzically.

'What about you, Jim? I heard what you said to Sean. But you've just seen what's happened to Paul. What would it take for you to get involved in the fight?'

'Jesus, Kathleen, that's a hard one. I know all about how the Catholics were discriminated against here for decades and how the Protestants turned on them after '69, and all that. But I'm just a schoolteacher. I know I'm from a part of the North of England with a big Irish heritage, and was brought up a Catholic. But I'm English; it's not my fight. I disagree with the way the British government has handled the situation, but that doesn't make me want to take up arms.'

Kathleen puts her hand on mine.

'I understand; it's just that incidents like today make my blood boil. Like the Prod bastards who've just killed Paul, I want revenge.'

'Then it'll never stop.'

'I know, and I'm sorry; I'll have calmed down by tomorrow.' She glances at her watch. 'Jim, it's really nice of you to bring me here and listen, but we should go. Maureen will be worried about you.'

15. The Hunger Strikes

As the spring of 1981 moves towards Easter, the situation in Belfast and the Ardoyne deteriorates. For Maureen and me, it poses a significant challenge, both in terms of our operation and how we perceive its morality.

Maureen had been surprisingly understanding about my excursion into Belfast with Kathleen. I expected a bollocking, but she took a pragmatic line, saying that my attempts to help after the killing of Paul Blake and my support for Kathleen would significantly enhance our reputation in the community. Nevertheless, her position about getting any closer to her colleague at St Hilda's remained emphatic: don't you dare!

She was much more concerned when I told her that IRA Brigade had had us checked out. My cover is more or less watertight, given that I was a full-time teacher throughout my selection for both 21 and 14 Intelligence. On the other hand, Maureen is a professional soldier, with no genuine civilian credentials as a teacher. But Gower Street has been clever and constructed a pedagogical career for her in an English language school in Japan, a story even the resourceful IRA will find hard to verify or refute.

Spring has brought a sea change in the Troubles. Along with several other IRA men, Bobby Sands, former OC-IRA in the Maze prison, has begun a hunger strike in its

H Blocks. He began refusing food at the beginning of March, quickly followed by three others: Francis Hughes, Raymond McCreesh and Patsy O'Hara. More strikers are scheduled to join the strike. The protest is a replica of the seven-man strike from the year before, but is a significant escalation of a prison dispute that's five years old. Sands is a totally committed Irish patriot; many see him as the leading poet and philosopher of the republican cause. This development has changed everything.

The suffering of the men on hunger strike has roused the anger of republicans everywhere and there are confrontations on the streets of the Ardoyne almost every night. As I walk home on Thursday, 9 April, the tension on the streets is palpable. It's a special evening. Bobby Sands, forty days into his strike, has been nominated as the republican candidate in a by-election to choose the MP for Fermanagh and South Tyrone. His candidature is recorded as 'H Block/Armagh'. The result of the vote is expected at the end of the night.

Maureen and I meet at the corner of Brompton Park and Balholm Drive, on the residents' side of a hastily erected barricade. The crowd of young men manning the obstacle consists almost entirely of teenagers, most of them boys I teach at St Anthony's. They're hurling rocks at a row of armoured personnel carriers about thirty yards away and a line of police and soldiers stood behind the vehicles. The barrier is nothing more than a burnt-out car protected by a row of corrugated iron sheets. It's a pathetic sight. The defenders are no more than children; several of the younger ones can't throw very well and their missiles are either way off target or land yards short of their intended victims.

A group of adults is watching in the shadows. I recognize two of Sean Murphy's men among them.

'Jim, Maureen, move away. It's not safe!'

It's Kathleen; she runs over to us, shouting over the din.

'Move back! They've got new plastic bullets. They'll start firing soon.'

I look at the kids standing on top of the car, the top half of their bodies exposed.

'What about them?'

'They know what they're doing.'

'Isn't that a bit callous?'

'Is it? We're at war, Jim. Haven't you worked that out yet?'

Trying to stop me responding, Maureen pulls me away.

'Come on, Jim, let's make Kathleen a cup of tea at our place.'

Kathleen smiles mischievously.

'I'd prefer a shot of Jameson's.'

Maureen smiles back.

'Not a problem, Jameson's it is.'

As the three of us move off, there's a volley of shots from behind us. Missiles ping off metal, brick and tarmac. It's as if we're trapped in a pinball machine. Maureen's hit in the leg and falls to the ground with a yelp. One of the boys on the barricade is not quick enough to avoid the fusillade and is hit in the chest, catapulting him backwards on to the ground. Several men rush forward and pick him up. He's in floods of tears, but is conscious and seems to be no more than badly bruised.

Kathleen and I help Maureen to her feet. She's in pain and a huge swelling is already forming on her calf. The three of us move away as a group of men replace the boys on the barricade and unleash a broadside of Molotov cocktails at the security forces. In response, another fusillade of plastic bullets is fired. I look around. Flames light up the advancing dusk, making everyone either a ghoulish silhouette or a brightly lit face distorted by rage. The defenders shriek and dance like banshees, goading the line of police and soldiers. In stark contrast, the men in uniform look like automatons, mindless storm troopers from *Star Wars*.

It's horrible, primordial; Kathleen's right, this is a war.

When we reach our flat, while I pour the drinks, Kathleen packs Maureen's leg with a towel and a bag of frozen peas.

'Those plastic bullets are lethal. They used to be rubber and bounce everywhere; these plastic ones don't bounce as much, but they're still deadly, mainly because the Brits and the RUC scum fire directly at people's faces instead of their legs. They've killed children and old people; it's criminal, so it is.'

Maureen winces as Kathleen tightens the towel around her calf, but encourages her to carry on venting her spleen.

'So why's the hunger strike happening again?'

'It's complicated, and not everyone agrees with it. There's a big split over it. Prior to 1976, Provo prisoners had Special Category Status within the Maze, a situation that meant they were treated like prisoners of war. As such, they could live in dormitories, wear civilian clothes and undertake military drills and so on. Special Category Status had been won a few years earlier through a hunger strike led by one of our heroes, Billy McKee, a cousin of ours. He was close to death when Willie Whitelaw, the Secretary of State, relented. But when Roy Mason became Secretary of State in '76, a tough little bugger, he immediately took a hard line. Boys were taken to places like Castlereagh and had the crap beaten out of them until they confessed to every crime under the sun. He gave the SAS and military intelligence free rein, and they immediately went on the rampage. They're everywhere, and they shoot anything that moves. It's like the Wild West!'

I look at Maureen. We both gulp.

'The little bastard – and remember, he's supposed to be a Labour man – ordered the revoking of Special Category Status, branding the IRA as common criminals. The boys refused to wear prison clothes and took to wearing blankets to cover themselves. That was the "Blanket Protest". It escalated into the "Dirty Protest" when the boys, who were being beaten daily by the prison officers, refused to "slop-out" their chamber pots. It started to get really nasty. The boys were angry and the screws were out of control. They came in and started kicking the slops all over the cells and humiliating the boys. So, without approval from the Army Council, they decided to up the ante and started to daub their prison walls with their own shite. No one knows how it started. Can you imagine the filth, the smell? There are maggots everywhere; anyone who goes in there to visit comes out puking up their guts.'

I look at Maureen. I can see her squirm at the thought. Kathleen takes a mouthful of her whiskey.

'When the government refused to give any concessions, the prisoners – led by Bobby – chose to begin another hunger strike. Bobby has so much influence now inside the Maze that he can go against the Army Council. They're not inside, he is; so the other prisoners listen to him. He said, this time, the strike will be on a much bigger scale. And he's vowed that, unless their demands are met, this time it will be to the death.'

Kathleen looks at us sympathetically.

'How are your stomachs?'

'Why?'

'Let me give you an illustration of the barbarity of it all. Maureen, I'm sorry, you'll need another swig before you hear this.'

Maureen steels herself by doing as Kathleen suggests.

'Go on.'

'OK, the boys on the inside are naked and living in shit, right? Bizarrely, a piece of shit has become the only way to communicate with the outside. Notes are written in tiny writing on sheets of cigarette paper. They're rolled up and put in a plastic bag. The carrier – mother, girlfriend – then hides them in her mouth and transfers them to the boys with a kiss. When they eventually shit them out they have their message.' Kathleen continues. 'The screws have got wise to it. So rectal examinations are now a daily procedure. There are two techniques: one is called "the squat", where the screws put on Marigolds and make the boy squat over a mirror. Then they get some gynaecological forceps and ram them up there. The other is called the "bum boys' delight", where the lad is bent over and the screw sticks his hand in and roots around to his heart's content!'

Both Maureen and I take a deep draught of Jameson's simultaneously. Kathleen looks at us sternly.

'That's what we've come to in the Protestant North of Ireland.'

There's a long silence, as we look down at our drinks, ashamed of what we – all of us, Brits and Irish alike – have let happen within our borders. We like to think we live in a civilized country, but there's very little that's 'civilized' about this part of the realm!

Eventually, the conversation turns to other things, particularly the tragedy of seeing the kids we teach engaging in running battles with the police and the army.

Two hours later, with the whiskey bottle almost empty, there's a sudden uproar from outside. It's not the din of violence, but the clamour of celebration. Kathleen jumps to her feet.

'Can we put the telly on?'

Maureen grabs the remote control and puts on *Newsnight*.

The headlines proclaim: 'Bobby Sands has won and is the new MP for Fermanagh and South Tyrone.'

Kathleen shrieks out loud.

'Jesus Christ! We've won an election – this changes everything.'

She kisses both of us in delight and we try to seem as pleased as she is.

'Come on, let's go to the Hibernian, the craic will be great.'

Maureen doesn't move.

'You go with Kathleen, Jim. This leg has swollen up really badly and is giving me gip. I'm off to bed; I've got netball with the girls in the morning.'

'Sure?'

'Course, it's a night for a big celebration. You go and enjoy yourselves.'

Kathleen was right, the craic in the Hibernian is great. From the dancing, singing and laughter, you'd have thought that Maggie Thatcher had just announced that Northern Ireland will become a part of the Republic at midnight tonight!

Kathleen becomes more and more inebriated and I become more and more lustful as I stand at the bar and watch her cavort from group to group, exchanging hugs and kisses. Eventually she reaches Sean Murphy's table and kisses him and her father. She then turns to one of his henchmen, a hard case with a scar from his eye to his chin on the left-hand side of his face. He's obviously the worse for wear and responds to her embrace rather too amorously. He places both his hands on her backside and pulls her hard against his midriff. Kathleen backs away, but he pulls her back and starts to cover her face in kisses.

Kathleen raises her hand to slap him, but he grabs her wrist violently. Her father notices what's happening and jumps to his feet. As he does so, he pulls a revolver from his belt and positions it six inches from Scarface's nose.

'Take your hands off my daughter or I'll blow your fuckin' head off!'

Murphy steps between them and slaps his minder across the face with the back of his hand, sending him sprawling across the Hibernian's alcohol-soaked floor. He turns to his other minders.

'Pick him up and take him home.' He then puts his

hand on Jimmy's shoulder. 'Jimmy, put the pistol away and sit down.'

Jimmy does as he's told and I walk over to check that Kathleen's OK. She's a little shaken, but the alcohol has helped and she's not too upset. Her father notices me and stands up again.

'Jim, would you take Kathleen home? She's had enough and has school in the morning.'

'Course I will.'

'Number 10, Herbert Street. Her mother's not home; she's gone to Dublin for a while.'

'I'll see she gets home safely.'

'Thanks, Jim.'

The fresh air outside the Hibernian is a welcome relief. There's still the hubbub of celebration coming from several houses along the way and, for once, the Ardoyne seems like a happy place. And I feel elated; I'm walking the Angel of the Ardoyne home at her father's behest!

But my euphoria doesn't last long. As we enter the small alleyway that leads from Brompton Park into Butler Place, the goon who grabbed Kathleen steps from the shadows. It's very dark, the only light a faint glow coming from the window of a nearby house.

'So, walking home with the Tan, are we, Kathleen?'

She spits back at him.

'Fuck off, Michael! Go home to your bed.'

He steps towards her and, instinctively, I step in front of him.

'Michael, behave yourself. He's not a Tan, he's Jim Dowd. And my daddy asked him to take me home. Now piss off!'

Michael's a big man with a fearsome aura about him, not

improved by his hideous scar. He's obviously been drinking, but is in control of his faculties. I need to be careful.

Kathleen begins to walk around him, but he steps in her way.

'You weren't so cold when we had that cuddle last Christmas. You came on strong that night. Is it this Brit schoolteacher you fancy now?'

I decide enough is enough. Suddenly, it's Saturday night, Burnley town centre, two lads having a set-to over a lass.

'Michael, Kathleen wants to go home. You're in her way.'

Inevitably, he launches a punch with his right hand. In situations like these, there are three rules: move faster than your opponent, turn his aggression against him, and strike back as venomously as possible. Unfortunately for Michael, my training has added professional CQB skills to the nous of street fighting. As I duck to avoid its arc, his punch sails over my head. In the same instant, I raise my left foot, my stronger leg, and, with all my might, slam it into the outside of the joint of his right knee. He yells loudly as his knee is hyper-extended and he collapses in agony. When he hits the ground, he reaches to his belt and pulls out a pistol.

Certain that he would have already released the safety catch, I move quickly. I stamp on his right knee again and grab his wrist with both hands, turning it violently against the joint. I then collapse both my knees into his back and pull his forearm against his elbow. He has no choice but to allow his elbow to bend and I now have his right arm locked against his body. I hit him hard in the side of the neck, stunning him for a few moments. The pistol drops to the floor and I grab it, allowing me to unclip the magazine, remove it and put it in my pocket. I then throw the pistol over the wall of the alley and let Michael get up.

He staggers to his feet, then falls back against the wall.

'Come on, Kathleen, he'll be alright, but he'll have more than a hangover in the morning and it'll be a while before he can use that knee properly.'

Kathleen stares at Michael's stricken form with incredulity.

'Holy Mary, Mother of God! Where the fuck did you learn how to do that?'

As soon as she's finished asking the question, I realize what I've done. I've responded instinctively, my training's taken over. It's only when you meet an enemy for real, intent on inflicting mortal damage, that you know whether you're a soldier or not.

Either you find the moment exhilarating, or it renders you helpless. Until it happens for the first time, you never know. This is my first time. I'm relieved and elated, but my instincts and training have seduced me into making a big mistake: I've revealed skills held only by a very few. I have seconds to think of an answer and it can't be 'the Boy Scouts'. I rush Kathleen away down the alley before I answer.

'Martial arts, karate. I started at university and joined a dojo when I moved to London.'

'You must be a black belt or something?'

'Yes, fourth dan.'

'What does that mean?'

'It means you can take a weapon off someone who's going to shoot you.'

When we get to Kathleen's house, she's beginning to wilt from the alcohol and the excitement of the evening. She invites me in and immediately heads for her father's drinks cabinet. I decline, sobered by the thought of what will be the consequences of damaging and disarming big Michael.

'I should go, Kathleen, we've both got to teach tomorrow.'

Her eyes begin to swim, but she shakes her head trying to stop the room spinning. As I make for the door, she manages to get to her feet and grab me around the neck.

'Jim, thanks for looking after me tonight.'

She then thrusts a gyrating groin at me and smothers me with slobbering kisses. How can I resist this? I'm not a fucking monk! Months lusting after Maureen, and now this – the Angel of the Ardoyne offering up her delights for the taking!

If only Michael hadn't interfered, but he's taken the edge off the moment. I need to get home to Maureen and work out what to do next. I pull Kathleen's arms from my neck and gently sit her down on the sofa. She flops backwards, all but comatose. I lift up her gorgeous long legs, rest them on the sofa and cover her with her coat. Then I put the loaded magazine from Michael's pistol on the table and make my exit.

As I close the front door behind me, I think back to all the outrageous risks I've taken in my life, especially those involving women, and sigh.

I must be going soft in my old age.

When I get back to the flat, Maureen's still awake. She has her leg up on the kitchen table and is clearly in pain.

'I can't sleep. My calf's come up like a balloon. I think it's still bleeding internally.'

'Do you need it looked at?'

'No, it needs elevation and rest. How was the celebration?'

'Raucous.'

She sees the anxiety on my face.

'And?'

'Not good.'

I proceed to tell her the whole story. The furrows on her brow get deeper with every further detail.

'Are you sure you didn't shag her?'

'Mo, for fuck's sake!'

'Are you sure she won't wake up in the morning thinking that you shagged her.'

'She might wake up wishing that I'd shagged her!'

'Jim, you arrogant bastard. Do you realize that by kicking his arse, you may well have blown the whole op?'

'What the fuck do you think I should have done, let him beat the shit out of me?'

'Yes.'

'Well, fuck you, I'm not a fucking machine! I'd had a few drinks and he came at me with his fists and a 9mm semi-automatic. I should've slotted the ugly fucker! As for Kathleen, I should have shagged her. I reckon only me and St Francis of Assisi could have chosen not to give her one . . . and he ended up preaching to birds!'

She goes very quiet and winces several times as she adjusts the position of her leg. Eventually she speaks.

'Get some rest. We need to speak to HQ in the morning and make sure you're remembered at the best karate dojo in London. Do you know one?'

'That's easy; it's the Budokwai, in Chelsea. They need to speak to Master Yamagishi. He'll vouch for me.'

'Did he teach you?'

'No, I've never been near a karate dojo. But I helped his daughter with A-Level history. He's a one hundred per cent British patriot. He'll do whatever you want him to do.'

'We need him to send us one of those white suits; and get Gower Street to create one of those black belt photographs and a certificate. I'll take the day off and go over to Det HQ to sort it. We're hanging by something a lot thinner than a karate belt.'

'Don't fret, Mo, it'll be fine.'

16. Hanging by a Black Belt

I was wrong; it isn't fine. It's Easter Saturday morning, nine days after the incident with Michael. I'm walking to the newsagents on Flax Street. Jimmy, Kathleen's father, is walking towards me. Since the fracas, Maureen and I have considered carrying our Brownings, but decided that it was a death sentence if we were ever challenged, quite apart from the problems of carrying them during the school day. So I'm unarmed and feel very vulnerable.

Via Belfast Det HQ, Gower Street has delivered everything we need to authenticate my martial arts credentials. But deceit always breeds fear, and we're living with a mountain of deceit already. All has been quiet since what happened after the celebrations of the 9th, but I know the reckoning is certain to happen, sooner or later. It looks like this is the day.

Maureen has taken some of her girls to see a netball tournament in Lisburn, so I'm alone. Surely, they won't top me this morning? We've got a big game away to New Lodge Celtic this afternoon.

'Good morning to ye, Jim. How are ye?'

'I'm well, Jimmy. Fine day, isn't it?'

'It is, Jim. Come on, walk with me to the Hibernian. Sean and I want a word.'

It is indeed a beautiful spring morning; bizarrely, the Ardoyne looks vaguely normal. Divis Mountain is verdant with new colours, and even the birds are singing. I think of St Francis of Assisi again . . . and back to my abstinence with Kathleen. Sadly, if this is to be my last day in this vale of tears, I don't think sainthood is on the cards as a reward for my momentary celibacy.

I'm as nervous as a virgin in a brothel as I stroll with Jimmy to the Hibernian. I try to make polite conversation, all the time thinking that once I cross the club's threshold, I may never again hear the birds sing.

'Jim, thanks for taking care of Kathleen the other night, I appreciate it.'

'I'm just glad I was there, Jimmy.'

He then stops and looks me in the eye.

'Listen, Jim, Michael Donnelly's a nasty piece of work. There aren't many men who could tackle him. Sean wants to know how ye did it.'

'Why?'

'Because Michael swears youse is SAS.'

I swallow hard and try to concoct a good answer.

'I think Michael's trying to restore his damaged pride.'

'That's as may be, but how did ye manage to hurt him so badly? Then you disarmed him and emptied his pistol.'

'Not difficult, Jimmy. He's a big fucker, but he's not quick enough for a street fight.'

'From what I've heard from him and Kathleen, what ye did was a lot more than street fighting.'

'Just martial arts, Jimmy.'

'Really?'

'Yes, over many years. I'm in pretty good shape.'

'That's what Kathleen said. She also said you behaved like a proper gent. I'm very grateful to ye for that.'

'Not at all, Jimmy. She's a great girl. I wouldn't see any harm come to her, or hurt her in any way.'

'Thanks, Jim. Come on, let's go and talk to Sean.'

I hesitate, trying to think like an innocent Brit would.

'Jimmy. I'm a teacher in this community, answerable to my board of governors, not to anyone else.'

Jimmy's face turns from friendly warmth to furrowed harshness.

'Jim, this is the Ardoyne. We're an ostracized community, beyond the normal way of things. This isn't London, it isn't even Belfast; once ye turn right off the Crumlin Road, ye're in Tombstone. Sean Murphy's Wyatt Earp – the only gun in town. Get used to it.'

I know Jimmy's right, but continue to appear indignant.

'I understand, Jimmy. But do I have to account for how I protected your daughter from a thug?'

'Yes, ye do, because of the way ye did it, especially as an Englishman living in a community under siege by the British State.'

I decide I've protested enough.

'OK, let's get on with it.'

'Don't worry. Sean's a hard man, but he's fair and he likes ye. So do I. You'll be OK . . .' He pauses. 'Unless, of course, Michael Donnelly's right!'

He smiles wryly.

I smile back, as calmly as I can.

The Hibernian's deserted. Murphy is sitting at a table at the back of the club. He's reading a newspaper; it looks like the *Guardian*. For a moment, I think his bodyguards are not there, but then I see them skulking in the shadows. Will one of them be my executioner, or will Murphy do it himself? According to military etiquette, Murphy is a brigadier, so I decide to refer to him as such from now on.

The Brigadier folds his newspaper carefully and smiles. It seems to be a warm and genuine gesture.

'Hello, Jim, come and take a seat. I know ye've a game this afternoon. As a proper player, I don't suppose ye'll take a stiffener before the match. Will ye have a soft drink or a cup of tea?'

If only he knew how a 'stiffener' would be perfect right now!

'Tea, please, Sean.'

For a while, we talk football. He's very complimentary about my contribution to the team.

'They tell me ye're a fine player.'

'Fair to middlin', Sean.'

My tea arrives with what looks like Coke for the Brigadier. The big man takes a large mouthful of it.

'Jimmy tells me that ye're also good with yer feet at other things?'

'I can handle myself.'

'Sorry, Jim, I should have started by thanking you for looking after the lovely Kathleen. My apologies.'

'I like to think anybody else would have done the same.'

'Perhaps they would've tried, but I don't know anyone who could've flattened Michael Donnelly like that . . . except ye, of course.'

'As I said to Jimmy, he's big, but he's slow.'

'By the way, ye won't be seeing him again. He's gone to see his relatives in America and won't be coming back.'

Then the Brigadier produces Donnelly's pistol and rests it on the table.

I wasn't expecting this!

'Ye've seen that before, Jim?'

'I assume it's Michael's?'

'Was. Would ye like it as a souvenir?'

'No, thanks. I wouldn't know what to do with it.'

'Really? D'ye know what type of gun it is?'

I have to be careful here. I can't pretend to be too naive; on the other hand, I mustn't appear to have any familiarity with weapons.

'It looks like a Luger.'

'How do ye know?'

'The Germans always have them in the movies.'

'It's not a Luger, it's called a Walther P38. A bit old, but a good weapon. Ever handled a pistol before?'

'Only when I took that one off Michael.'

'How did you know how to take out the magazine?'

'You don't have to be a weapons expert to work out where the clip is.'

'In the dark, Jim? There's no street lamps left in the Ardoyne.'

Fortunately, the clip to release the magazine on a P38 is very prominent and easily found, even by a novice.

'There was a bit of light from the house next door, but I'm sure I could unclip a pistol even in the dark, Sean.'

'D'ye know what Donnelly said before he left?'

'Yes, Jimmy told me. He said that I must be SAS.'

'Are ye?'

'What do you think, Sean?'

He seems surprised that I've thrown the question back

at him. He bristles, and I regret that I've given him the opportunity to condemn me there and then.

'Where did ye learn to disable a man like that? Ye tore Michael's knee ligaments, and that blow to the side of his neck nearly killed him.'

'But not quite. I made sure it wouldn't kill him.'

Both Jimmy and the Brigadier look at me long and hard. My heart's pumping so hard, I daren't pick up my mug of tea for fear of spilling its contents out of my quivering hand.

'So how do ye know how to do that?'

'I was taught by Master Yamagishi at the Budokwai, in Chelsea. It's the oldest martial arts dojo in London, first established in Victorian times.'

'Kathleen said that youse has a black belt in karate?'

'That's right, fourth dan.'

'That sounds good?'

'It is, very good. Very few reach fourth dan. Fifth and sixth take many years. Anything above that is just honorary, to indicate great respect for older masters.'

There's another long silence, only broken when two men I've never seen before come through the door and walk towards us. Is this it? Are these boys the firing squad? More likely they'll torture me first. Perhaps they're the inquisitors?

'Jimmy, take Jim outside for a minute, I need a word with these fellas.'

When we reach the open air, I realize that my face is pink with anxiety. I'm fair-skinned and my cheeks are burning like hotplates. As Jimmy lights a cigarette, I look around and consider my options. It's still a beautiful day;

I can still hear birdsong, but I need more than their harmony for comfort. I'm close to deciding that I should just run for my life when I notice that two of the Brigadier's minders have exited from the rear of the club and are standing between me and my escape route down Brompton Park.

I take a deep breath. I've been trained for moments like this; keep calm, stay disciplined. Jimmy breaks my train of thought.

'You alright, Jim?'

'No, I'm not, Jimmy. This is like the Spanish Inquisition.'

'Sorry, we have to be careful; lives are at stake.'

'I know, that's what's worrying me!'

Jimmy smiles at me. He changes the subject and we talk about the prospects for this afternoon's game.

Within five minutes, the Brigadier's visitors leave and Jimmy leads me back inside.

The Brigadier is smiling.

'Sit down, finish yer tea.'

'Thanks.'

I manage to slurp some tea without shaking it all over the floor. There's an exchange of glances between Jimmy and the Brigadier, followed by another pregnant silence.

'Jim, would ye ever reconsider yer decision not to join us in the fight against the Brits? We need men like ye. We've lost a lot of good boys in the last few years, and the Brits are really turning the screw at the moment.'

'I'm sorry, Sean, I have thought about it, especially since the start of the hunger strike. But I'm a schoolteacher, not a soldier.'

'Except with the skills ye've shown, it wouldn't take you long. Jimmy here could teach you how to use a weapon.'

'I appreciate the offer, but I don't think I'd make a soldier. Besides, although I was conceived in Ireland, I was born and bred in England.'

He looks at me with narrowed eyes, trying to read my mind. He takes another swig of Coke.

'OK, understood. On yer way, then. Make sure ye turn them over this afternoon.'

'Thanks, Sean. I'll try my best.'

As I walk towards the door, the Brigadier calls out to me.

'Jim, sorry about the third degree – we have to be very careful. The Brits have eyes and ears everywhere. And since Nairac, we're suspicious of everyone.'

I don't answer, but nod my head in acknowledgement.

Jimmy walks me all the way to our flat. When we part, he shakes me by the hand.

'I'm glad Sean's happy. I thought he would be. Ye're a good man, Jim, and ye and Maureen are a lovely couple. By the way, me and Kathleen are coming to watch ye play this afternoon. New Lodge are top of the league, should be a good game.'

When I get into the flat, it's immediately obvious why the Brigadier is happy. As expected, the flat's been searched; carefully, with no mess. But there's no doubt that a thorough search has gone on. The key is easily got from our landlady, especially if Sean Murphy is asking for it. It had to be the two men who came to the Hibernian. They must have given us a clean bill of health.

I make sure to check the secret compartment in the wardrobe – undisturbed. But the karate suit and belt I left in the bottom of our chest of drawers have been moved and my photograph and certificate examined. I know this for certain, because I took care to use Fairy Liquid to stick a length of my hair across the gap at the top of the drawer, and I arranged its contents in a particular way.

That afternoon, I play a blinder. I score twice – one from a free kick outside the box, the other a cool side-foot into the bottom corner – and make two more for our forwards. We win 5-2, and move to third in the table. Promotion is suddenly a possibility; we must win our last three games.

As I walk off, I get warm handshakes and embraces from Jimmy and the other Hibernian supporters but, much more satisfyingly, I get a big kiss and warm hug from Kathleen!

Later, I'm the local hero in the Hibernian. I'm bought drinks and get handshakes from all and sundry. The Michael Donnelly incident has become Ardoyne folklore. Nobody liked Donnelly. So good on Jim Dowd, the Ardoyne's Bruce Lee. Don't mess with him, he's a mean fucker. And he's mates with Jimmy McKee and Sean Murphy.

Maureen appears in the Hibernian about nine thirty. She's had a long day. When I tell her what happened during the morning, she takes a gulp of her whiskey.

'Jimmy boy, living with you is like living with a time bomb! Try to stay out of any more trouble.'

Maureen's relief is obvious, and I detect a grudging

admiration. But I'm not really paying attention. Kathleen's on the other side of the club. She's celebrating like she did on the night of Bobby Sands' election. She keeps looking in my direction.

Maureen notices, but I don't care any more.

17. Martyrdom

'Bobby's dead, Bobby's dead!' The words are being repeated, over and over again. The anguished sentence will live long in the memory. It's Tuesday, 5 May 1981. The eyes of the world are focused on the escalating crisis, and Margaret Thatcher's increasing intransigence is hardening opinion on both sides of the sectarian divide. Now, after refusing sustenance for sixty-six days, Bobby Sands has starved himself to death.

I'm trying to shepherd the boys of St Anthony's into morning assembly, but they're angry and volatile. They're already relishing the adrenalin rush of the inevitable confrontations with the security forces later in the day. The atmosphere is febrile and the boys are antagonistic towards anyone in authority. They refuse even the mildest encouragement to go into school.

Within minutes, as a mark of respect for the man who is already a martyr to the republican cause, the headmaster has taken the decision to close for the day. He well may have made the right decision in terms of local public opinion, but I suspect it also has a lot to do with him escaping to the safety of Belfast's leafy suburbs to be with his wife and kids. For those of us trapped in the Ardoyne, like American settlers in their wagon trains encircled by the Indians, it means the rioting will begin by mid-morning, rather than later in the day. St Hilda's is also closed for the day and Maureen is home before ten o'clock.

People of moderate persuasion rush to their homes to bar their doors against the mayhem they know will engulf the city within hours. But there are few 'moderates' today; almost everyone is on the streets, either mourning the loss of a hero or protesting against those they regard as his murderers and their oppressors.

Maureen and I decide to walk the short distance to the Crumlin Road to see what's going on. What we witness can only be described as theatre of the most absurd kind. While small groups of women hold impromptu prayer gatherings, within yards of them gangs of boys and men collect empty bottles and start filling them with petrol from plastic containers. There are pneumatic drills in use, digging up paving slabs to make missiles, and huge barricades are being built. Most worryingly, in broad daylight, men in boiler suits and balaclavas carry automatic rifles and shout orders at anyone prepared to listen. The Crumlin Road itself is full of people driving out of Belfast to avoid the violence that will soon paralyse the city. In their midst are dozens of police and army vehicles, their occupants making their own preparations for the battle to come.

It's going to be a long day and an even longer night.

Like the pipes and drums of ancient warfare, whistles and dustbin lids summon the combatants to the battle lines. The percussive rhythm is primeval and intimidating; the shrill sound of the whistles assaults the ears.

Clashes continue throughout the day in an ever-escalating orgy of violence. By dusk, the city seems to be one huge battlefield. There is the baleful glow of flame in every direction and wave after wave of screaming voices, breaking glass, sudden explosions and intermittent gunfire fill the air. Armour-plated vehicles rush down streets trying to disperse rioters, but they soon retreat, swamped by the flames of Molotov cocktails.

The rioters are emboldened when news circulates about the strength of international reaction to Sands' death. It seems to represent a major victory for the republican cause around the world. Fearing a resurgence of Catholic militancy, loyalists pour on to the streets, to goad their republican neighbours and indulge in riots of their own. The police and army are stretched to breaking point.

Maureen and I look at one another. She's the one who mentions it first.

'This looks like civil war!'

Distraught by what we see all around us, Maureen and I adjourn to the Hibernian. It's packed with exhausted rioters, many of whom are enlivening themselves with Guinness and whiskey for yet more encounters at the barricades. The Brigadier is there with his men. Behind them, Jimmy McKee is checking a table full of weapons: Armalites, AK47s, shotguns and pistols and several boxes of ammunition. It's clearly a fully functioning command centre. Kathleen, who's helping her father, comes over when she sees us.

'This is really bad. It started as a wake for poor Bobby, God rest his soul, but now it's out of control.'

Maureen sees the arsenal of weapons and looks at Kathleen anxiously.

Kathleen notices.

'There's a rumour that the UFF might come over gang-handed. We have to be ready in case they do. We won't get any protection from the army; they'll just look the other way.'

'Can I help with anything?'

'Not unless you know how to strip down and clean a rifle.'

Of course she does – and could do it faster than anyone in the room.

Maureen smiles a sweet smile that is a masterpiece of contrived innocence.

'Fair enough, I'll get some drinks. Jameson's, Kathleen?'

'Please . . . and a Guinness.'

'Jim?'

'Same.'

It's important to be there to offer tacit support to the cause but, other than buying a few drinks and mopping a few brows, we do little to help – how could we?

At about one in the morning, the level of violence begins to subside and we get ready to leave the Hibernian. The UFF attack hasn't materialized, and the arsenal has disappeared. The Brigadier is still here, sitting with Jimmy. He waves us over. He looks tired – and nothing like as formidable as usual. As always, he's polite and friendly, and today he's in reflective mood, addressing his thoughts towards Kathleen.

'A sad day, Kathleen.'

'Very sad, Sean.'

'This changes everything.'

'I know.'

'It will strengthen the young turks: Adams and McGuinness. They're arguing for a velvet glove with an iron fist in it. Bobby's death is a political victory, and now the reaction to it makes Adams' case for him.'

Kathleen responds by directing a question at Sean.

'What do you think will come of it?'

'I'm not sure, but I think it means Sinn Féin will carry on the fight in the future and we'll move into the background. But I'm nervous about undermining the military campaign.'

The Brigadier looks at me and Maureen and suddenly realizes that we shouldn't be privy to this conversation.

'We shouldn't be talking shop with our friends from over the water. Come on, it's –'

The Brigadier doesn't finish his sentence. There's a cry from the doorway.

'Grenade!'

I'm closest to the Brigadier and I see the fear in his eyes. Strangely, my instincts compel me to push this IRA warlord to the floor to protect him. Kathleen screams as Jimmy and Maureen pull her behind the pillar next to our table. There is a blinding flash and an almighty bang which deafens everyone. Shattered glass and splinters of wood fly everywhere. There are screams of anguish and shouts of anger. Then there's an eerie silence and unnerving stillness for several seconds.

Gradually our hearing returns. Muffled voices and the crunch of feet on debris bring us back to life.

There are no wails of pain; we're lucky. The device has stayed in the unoccupied space between the inner and outer doors of the club. While one of them stands guard over him, pistol at the ready, the rest of the Brigadier's men rush to the doorway, weapons in hand.

He gets to his feet and looks at Maureen and Kathleen.

'You alright, girls?'

Maureen helps Kathleen to her feet. They both nod to say that they are.

Ten minutes later, although the explosion has destroyed both the inner and outer doors, all is calm. No one's been hit by shrapnel. Although there are some cuts from flying glass, the human damage is minimal.

I look at the Brigadier. He suddenly seems very vulnerable and he knows that I saw the fear in his eyes. Strangely, it creates the hint of a bond between us.

'Thank ye, Jim. That was close.'

'It was. Who was it?'

'Could have been anybody: UFF, UVF, the Red Hand boys. Who knows? It's not the first time, and it won't be the last.'

The clearing up begins immediately. And life, such as it is in the Ardoyne, goes on.

18. The Big Match

It's Saturday, 23 May, the Hibernians' last match of the season. The warmth of early summer has arrived; it's more cricket conditions than football weather. It's a long time since I've felt the adrenalin of a big match.

It's the day of the cup final for Division 2A of the Northern Amateur Football League. After an excellent run in the second half of the season, the Hibernians have already won the 2A title and, with it, promotion to 1B, just one league below 1A – the top league. We're going for a cup and league double, which would be a first for the Hibernians. Our opponents are Shankill United, as fiercely loyalist as we are republican, and they're our next-door neighbours across the sectarian chasm that is the Crumlin Road. We beat them into second place in the league and they've a score to settle; it will be a full-blooded encounter, and the word is that they're going to try to kick me out of the game.

Astonishingly, despite the viciousness of the Troubles and the hatred on both sides, the Northern Amateur Football League carries on as normal. Games are not cancelled; where teams have to enter the other team's 'territory', the visitors are met on the 'boundary' and safely escorted in and out. Hospitality is laid on and friendships are formed. Sport declares its own truce, even in these most horrendous times. It's one of the many anomalies of

Northern Ireland's Troubles – and one of sport's many gifts.

We're playing at Andersonstown, a neutral venue. One sideline will be as orange as King Billy himself, the other will be as green as a leprechaun. Stewards will keep order; there'll be no trouble, beyond the heated exchanges typical of amateur football anywhere in the land.

Everyone in our dressing room is dealing with the pressure in their own way. Some are pacing up and down, others are sitting quietly, trying to compose themselves. Our manager, Donal, is like a man possessed. There's fire and brimstone in his eyes as he goes from man to man, invoking everything from the Easter Rising to the Almighty Himself to rouse his men. He comes to me last.

'How're ye feelin', Jim?'

'Good, Donal, I just want to get on with it.'

'Will ye say something to the lads to fire them up?'

It's the last thing I want to do, but I know I should keep Donal happy.

'Course I will.'

'Quiet now, boys! Our Jim's got something to say to youse.'

I stand and try to appear calm and collected.

'Listen, lads, the first fifteen minutes will be like the Alamo. They'll come at us with tackles waist-high. Don't get riled up, don't retaliate; let the ref do his job. Just concentrate on your first touch. Get the ball under control – pass and move, our usual game. Their storm will blow itself out, then we'll take control, just like we did last time we played them. If they do score early, don't panic; we're better than them, and we'll get better as the game goes on. Remember, if they provoke us into a brawl, we'll lose. If we play football, we'll win – simple as that.'

The words seem to strike a chord and I get lots of handshakes and pats on the back as we go out. It's the biggest crowd we've played in front of all season, perhaps two hundred souls, more than half from the Ardoyne, including Maureen, Kathleen, Barry Kennedy and Jimmy McKee. I'm told that the Brigadier will be watching from a parked car nearby, but nobody will know which one.

The game starts disastrously for me. My first touch is poor and the ball runs away from me. I try to win it back in a fifty-fifty challenge, but my opponent goes over the top of the ball and slams his studs into my right shin, catapulting me into the air. When I come down, I can't feel much below the impact point and fear that I've broken my leg. Amazingly, the referee hasn't given a foul and play goes on. I look around just in time to see my assailant hit a wonderful drive into the top corner of our net. Three minutes played, one-nil down!

As he runs on with his medical kit, Donal berates the referee and tries to illustrate the official's incompetence by pulling down my sock and removing my shin pad to show him a set of welts that are a perfect match for the pattern of my assailant's studs. He soaks my leg with painkilling spray and repeats his rebuke to the referee.

'He could've broken the boy's leg!'

The referee glances at the injury and smirks.

'He shudda jumped outta the way, Donal. He wouldn'a got hurt then, would he?'

Thanks, ref!

I have to leave the field for at least ten minutes. Slowly, the feeling comes back in my right foot, and I'm able to go back on. But my shin hurts like buggery and I can't make any tackles. I spend the next ten minutes hobbling around, hoping that the pain will subside. We're soon two-nil down and hanging on until half-time.

The mood in the dressing room is grim. Everyone knows that without me winning the ball in midfield, ensuring good distribution, we're in a hopeless position. I have my leg raised on a chair and Donal has packed it with ice from the fishmongers across the road. Inevitably, I stink of fish, as does the entire dressing room. Perhaps the stench will upset the opposition.

'Make yourselves decent, boys, wee girlies coming in!'

The voice belongs to Kathleen. She's with Maureen. They come over to me like they're in a scene from *Emergency – Ward 10*. Maureen gives me a handful of pills.

'Here, get these down your throat. They're painkillers and a couple of other things Kathleen's brought.'

'Where did you get them from?'

'We rushed home when we saw the state you were in.'

I swallow the lot and wash them down with a bottle of Guinness, intended for the victory celebration.

'So what've you given me?'

Kathleen winks at me.

'Don't ask, but you'll have wings in the second half, so ye will!'

She's right; the second half comes and goes in a blur of adrenalin, flying tackles and high drama. I seem to float above the scene, looking down on the action. I know I'm playing but it's more like a dream, and I seem to be oblivious to any pain. There are several punches thrown and the crowd becomes very animated, but the team officials on both sides keep a lid on tempers.

We win 5–3; the league and cup double is ours.

The game ends with wild celebrations on our side, muted admiration from the opposition, and handshakes all round.

I score the all-important third goal from a direct free kick to give us the lead. It's nothing special, I just hit it; their defensive wall bottles it and parts, allowing the ball to fly into the top corner.

It looks better than it is.

Outside the Hibernian, seven minibuses have disgorged their passengers, who have already managed to consume several crates of Guinness. The celebration's in full swing. After a long speech by Barry Kennedy, extolling the virtues of the Ardoyne, the Hibernian and all things Gaelic, in which I get an honourable mention, the drinking begins in earnest.

Feeling on top of the world, I look for Kathleen. Sadly, she's nowhere to be seen.

It's a warm May evening. Maureen's been back to the flat to change and has put on a very fetching skimpy dress that accentuates her amazingly long legs. She looks like a million dollars. She gives me a big kiss and seems in a lively mood – perhaps she's also taken some of Kathleen's half-time wonder drugs!

'Everyone's talking about you, Jimmy boy. You're the local hero; I know nothing about football, but even I could see how good you were. I'm proud of you.'

The evening disappears in a fog of inebriation as I drink more Guinness than seems humanly possible.

I wake up in the morning with a head like the football I kicked all afternoon the day before. The frightening thing is, I'm not on my sofa bed in our Estoril Park flat, but on the sofa in Jimmy and Kathleen's house. I rack my brains to remember what happened the night before, but everything's a blur.

Don't tell me I've done something stupid again?

I'm bollock naked under a blanket, with my shoes on the floor next to the sofa. *Oh fuck!* What have I done now? Then I hear the crackle of a frying pan doing its work.

'Jim, ye awake?'

It's Kathleen's honeyed voice.

'I am, but I feel like shit.'

'That's not surprising. You were in a right state last night. I'm doing you a real big Irish fry-up. It'll sort you out.'

I almost puke at the thought.

An hour later, although I find it hard to stand on my injured leg, I'm dressed and feeling vaguely human. Kathleen has had to wash and dry my clothes. I don't ask why; I'm too ashamed to inquire. We're sitting at the kitchen table, at which I've managed to eat a mountain of food. And Kathleen was right, it has made me feel a little better. Her father's not here; he left early to drive to Dublin. Kathleen says he's gone to see her mother. I get the impression that her parents are separated – but, for all I know, he could be collecting a new IRA arms shipment.

We talk about the game. Apparently, I'm now a legend, having turned the game around on one leg. I look at my right shin; the impact injury is so severe, the bruising is coming out at the back of the calf.

'What the hell did you give me at half-time?'

'Just a little pick-me-up that some of the lads in the Hibernian sell.'

'Pick-me-up! I felt like I was floating on air.'

'You played like it too – brilliant! We're all so proud of ye.'

I'm struggling with how to phrase the next question.

'Kath, I'm sorry if this sounds like a silly question . . . but why am I here?'

She looks embarrassed and repeatedly stirs her tea before answering.

'Wishful thinking on my part.'

'How do you mean?'

'You're not getting on with Maureen, are ye?'

My mind is working overtime.

'Why do you ask?'

'Don't you remember anything?'

'Not much . . . we didn't . . . ?'

'No . . . I hope you don't mind me saying this, but I've fancied you since the first time I met you.' She looks down sheepishly. 'When I was drunk and made that play for you after you sorted Michael out, I really appreciated the way you dealt with it, out of respect for Maureen and for me. But it didn't alter my feelings for you. So when I heard that things weren't right between you two, I went for it. I'm an Ardoyne girl, Jim; we call a spade a feckin' shovel round here.'

She crosses herself mockingly. 'So here's the God's honest truth, so help me. Daddy and I got you home and got your kit off. We put you to sleep on the sofa and went to bed ourselves. But as soon as Daddy was snoring, I crept back down to see if I could wake you up, but it was like trying to raise the dead.'

She's already asked me if everything's alright with Maureen; something else bad has happened.

'How do you know things are not right with Maureen?'

'Well, that's obvious; you don't act like an item. There doesn't seem to be much warmth between you. Anyway, last night, you had the mother and father of a row, so ye did.'

'Oh fuck. Was it embarrassing?'

'Not for me, but I don't think Maureen was very pleased.'

'So what happened?'

'It was late, she wanted to leave, but ye didn't. She pulled you up from your chair to get you to leave and ye started to get amorous. When she didn't respond, you started shouting at her about being fed up with sleeping on the sofa.'

I'm desperately trying to work out whether I've blown our cover, or just revealed a total breakdown in our so-called relationship.

'Ah . . . not good.'

'No, not great.'

'So then what happened?'

'You made a grab for her and started smothering her in kisses. Maureen slapped you good and hard and pushed you away. You were legless and went arse over tit, right across Sean's table, glasses and Guinness everywhere. That's why I've washed your clothes.'

'I'm really sorry, Kath.'

'No problem, you were really kind to me once, remember?'

'Was Sean annoyed?'

'No, he laughed his socks off!'

'And what happened to Maureen?'

'She stormed off; she's not happy with ye, Jim.'

I try to think through my dilemma as quickly as possible. I know I need to get home to Maureen and take my punishment, but I don't want to. I put my head in my hands, desperate for inspiration. Then, to make matters even worse, Kathleen leans over and puts her hand on mine.

'Do you want to stay here? Da won't be back for a few days.'

I so want to stay with Kathleen. I even think of telling Gower Street to fuck off – and staying in the Ardoyne with her. I don't know how to answer her at first but, eventually, I make a decision, based entirely on instinct rather than logic, and start to dig a very big hole for myself, the consequences of which I can't even imagine.

'Kath, I've fancied you from the first time I saw you. You're right, Maureen and I are not getting on at all. It's been like it for a while. She's looking for a flat of her own.'

'Poor you.' She smiles at me provocatively. 'Well. I've got a big bed upstairs, plenty of room for two.'

'Jesus, don't tempt me!'

'No brewer's droop today, then?'

'Kath, don't! Look, I'd love to stay here, but I have to go and square things with Maureen.'

'Jim, we're big boys and girls. What will happen will happen.'

'I know, and that's what I want more than anything. But I have to talk to Maureen.'

'You mean try to patch it up with her?'

'No, but I need to tell her what you and I feel for one another. I owe her that.'

Kathleen's eyes fill with tears.

'You know what? You're a fine man, Jim Dowd . . . God, I want you so much, but you're right to be kind to Maureen.'

Kathleen's generous comment cuts through me like a butcher's knife. If only she knew what a complete bastard I am!

She grabs me around the neck and sticks her tongue deep into my mouth. She goes for the belt on my trousers with her hands.

'Make love to me, Jim . . . please.'

I think my hangover and bad leg save me from diving straight into the hole I've just dug. I'm desperate to have it both ways: to get out of here, but to keep alive my opportunity with Kathleen.

'Tomorrow, Kath. We'll go into town and have dinner. I want our first time to be special. I'll feel a lot better tomorrow.'

'Promise?'

'Promise.'

19. Hell Hath No Fury

I walk into our flat feeling timid. My hangover's still making my head throb like a piston engine and my stomach churn like a washtub. I try to think of the positives. First of all, my relationship with Maureen is fabricated, so why do I care? Secondly, Kathleen and I have declared our feelings for one another, so that's great news. Finally, my hangover will be gone in the morning and I, the local hero who can walk tall in the Ardoyne, will be taking Kathleen out to dinner. And there's magic awaiting me at the end of it.

But I know I'm deluding myself. I am what I am; Maureen knows it, and I know it. No matter how enticing the prospect of a relationship with Kathleen may be, unless I jump ship entirely and abandon my mission, it's certain to end very badly.

What if I do jump ship? Do I really know these republican zealots?

If the intel's kosher, the Brigadier's a ruthless monster, Jimmy's a gunrunner and probably a bomb maker; they're surrounded by a posse of brutal hatchet men who, with no more than a nod from the big man, would happily turn me into dog meat.

And what of Kathleen? How callous is she prepared to be for her cause?

Not only that, if I do jump, I become a treasonous

enemy of the British state. Not an enviable position to be in!

As I close the door behind me, I decide to stop trying to analyse my predicament and just accept the bollocking that's coming my way.

Carpe diem.

Maureen's in her dressing gown, she has her feet up on the table and is reading the *Sunday Times*. The news is not good. Northern Ireland continues to dominate the headlines all over the world. Three more hunger strikers have died, the riots have intensified, and a large mob has tried to storm the British embassy in Dublin. Two young girls, both Catholics – one aged fourteen and one only twelve – have been killed by plastic bullets in south-west Belfast. Northern Ireland has never been in a more perilous situation.

Maureen's sympathy – and mine, for that matter – for the republican cause has been moderated by the IRA's slaughter of five British Army lads in an APC near Camlough, South Armagh. It happened only a few days ago, when they were blown up by a huge landmine – what a cowardly way to conduct a war. Four of them were 1st Battalion Royal Green Jackets, a unit Maureen has been fond of since she met one of their future officers at Cambridge.

Nevertheless, for the moment, my own personal dilemma overshadows the dire political situation. I decide to play it nonchalantly.

'Lazy day, Mo?'

'Not at all, I got up early. I've been up Divis and back.'

'No hangover?'

'A bit, that's why I went for a tab, got it out of me.'

Her face hardens; here it comes.

'I presume you went home with Kathleen. Did she tell you what happened, or were you too preoccupied?'

'She told me most of it, I think. Made a prat of myself . . . sorry, Mo.'

The eruption begins.

'Sorry? A prat of yourself? You made a complete prat out of me, announcing to the whole of the Ardoyne that our relationship is on the rocks!'

'I know, I'm really sorry.'

Now she's volcanic!

'I suppose you fucked her?'

'No, I didn't. Slept on the sofa – or, I should say, I was unconscious on the sofa.'

'I don't believe you; you were gagging for it last night. Anyway, apart from the personal embarrassment, you fuckin' well put our op under threat and almost blew our cover, you arsehole!'

'I know, but whatever you gave me at half-time was dynamite. I don't remember much after that.'

'That's the excuse of a weak-kneed civilian. You're supposed to be an elite professional soldier. You're supposed to be able to hold your drink and keep your dick in your trousers!'

Now my mood is beginning to boil.

'I told you, I didn't fuck her!' I decide to throw caution to the wind. 'But I'm going to! I'm taking her out tomorrow night.'

Maureen gets to her feet, throws the newspaper on to

the floor and stomps into the kitchen, berating me as she goes.

'Jim, I have to tell you that your behaviour is beneath that expected of a serving soldier.'

'Listen, Mo, there are no ranks on this op, so don't talk to me like my CO. This whole thing's bollocks. Our job is to become part of this community. That's what I'm doing. I'm teaching their kids, playing for their team, and now I'm going to get involved with one of their girls. That's my brief; Gower Street can't have it both ways.'

She walks back from the kitchen and stands in the doorway, her arms folded defiantly.

'I don't accept that. You can't get involved with Kathleen, given who she is.'

'I'll tell you who she is: she's the most desirable creature in Belfast. Why shouldn't I?'

'Because it's fucking dangerous for the op ... and for us.'

'You should have thought about that over the weeks when you turned me down. I'm not a monk! Would it have been that dreadful for us to have had a bit of fun?'

'You what? I'm not a plaything to "have a bit of fun" with!'

'That's not what I meant. We would've been much stronger if we'd let our bond grow.'

'That's not fair, Jim. I agree, it would've been far easier if we'd become an item, but it can't happen, it would complicate things too much.'

A wistfulness suddenly settles on her face.

'It's not easy for me either, you know.'

'But you've got ice in your veins.'

'No, I haven't.' She sighs loudly and looks desolate. 'I suppose I'm jealous that you've found someone and will be having some "fun", as you put it.'

'I'm sorry, Mo. I realize it's hard for you as well, but I'm not as strong as you; you're the real warrior here.'

She comes over and sits next to me.

'Jim, are you really serious about Kathleen?'

'Yes.'

'OK, I'm not trying to be your CO, just your partner, but I think I have to tell HQ.'

'Here or Gower Street?'

'Gower Street.'

'Why?'

'Because it may persuade them that the op is no longer viable. We have to give them the option to pull us out.'

She's right; I just nod my head in approval. I put my hand on her arm.

'So where do we go from here?'

'Well, you're going out tomorrow night to fuck Kathleen and I'm staying in to do some marking.'

I suddenly feel sorry for Maureen. Even her resolve must be wearing thin. She also sleeps alone every night and is under the same pressures as I am.

'I'm sorry about embarrassing you last night, and I promise I won't let the situation with Kathleen undermine our op.'

'OK, you'd better get some rest. You look like death warmed up.'

Monday becomes one of the most memorable days of my life.

We manage to forget that we're in troubled Belfast, and I black out the fact that the foundations of my budding relationship with Kathleen are built on quicksand. We have dinner at Kelly's Cellars.

What follows would fill several searing chapters in an erotic novel but, suffice to say, it's a blissful odyssey. Time stops; nothing matters. I have died and gone to heaven!

We compound our delicious tryst with the mischief of taking Tuesday off work. We spend the whole day making love. Kathleen is a perfectly formed creature. If God really did create Eve for the comfort of Adam, Kathleen is His pièce de résistance.

Suddenly, it's pitch dark again and Kathleen and I start to cook dinner. We make a full Irish: sausage, bacon, fried eggs, soda bread, potato bread, black and white pudding, beans, mushrooms and tomato. I grill the sausage and bacon; Kathleen does the rest. It's the ideal earthy feast to match the coarseness of our passion.

We're halfway through our food when there's a knock at the door. Kathleen looks anxious and glances at the clock. It's turned 9 p.m. Calls at this time in Belfast could be lethal. I'm wearing only underpants, so I rush upstairs to get my trousers. Kathleen's in her bra and knickers, so she puts on her dressing gown and shouts, 'Wait!' at the impatient visitor, who continues to rap on her door.

By the time I get back downstairs, Kathleen has positioned herself just to one side of her front door. She's crouched on one knee and a black-barrelled pistol, gripped firmly in both hands, is trained just above the door's letter box.

There's another loud knock.

'Open the door, Kathleen.'

'Who is it?'

'It's Eamon, Eamon McCabe. Sean's here, he needs to talk to ye.'

Kathleen gets up and hands the pistol to me. She whispers in my ear.

'It's one of Sean's boys, but take this in case it's an ambush and Eamon's got a gun to his head. If I scream, shoot whoever comes through the door!'

She opens the door. There are three men huddled together.

'What do you want at this time?'

'Sean needs to talk to ye.'

They push past her and walk into the living room. As they pass, they stare at me with barely disguised contempt. Sean walks in behind them, followed by two more of his men. He smiles at me, but only thinly.

'Good evening, Jim. Scored again, I see!'

My mind races. Have I broken some code of behaviour? Is it me they want to see? Am I being brought to heel for seducing the Angel of the Ardoyne?

Sean looks at his men.

'Wait outside, boys.'

As they leave, Kathleen offers Sean a drink or a cup of tea. He declines both. He looks at me and looks back at Kathleen, who stares back anxiously.

'What is it, Sean?'

'It's not good news, Kath.'

Sean looks at me again.

'I want Jim to stay.'

'OK, fine ...' He hesitates and looks at his hands

before continuing. 'Listen, Kath, your da's been lifted by the Garda in Dublin. He's being held in Phoenix Park.'

Kathleen looks down and begins to tremble; she doesn't speak for a while. Sean breaks the silence.

'Is Jim here yer man now?'

She looks up, her eyes full of tears, and grasps my hand. 'Yes, he is.'

Sean turns to me.

'There'll be a car dropped off here for ye at eight in the morning. Take Kathleen down to Dublin and take care of her. There'll be an envelope in the glove compartment with an address for ye to stay at and a wee bit of cash for spending money. I'll talk to the heads of your schools, they'll be fine about it.'

I look at the Brigadier, in awe of his power. He really is the master of all he surveys. He looks down at my hand and I realize that I'm still holding the pistol that Kathleen gave me.

'I see you've got your hands on another pistol, Jim. You're like a magnet for weapons!'

'Kath gave it to me when your boys knocked. I think she thought I would know what to do with it.'

He holds out his hand and I pass it to him.

'Do ye know what it is?'

'Haven't a clue.'

'It's an American classic, Jim, a Smith & Wesson 39, a lovely little gun.' He hands it to Kathleen. 'Put it away, don't take it to Dublin with ye . . . and put the safety back on.'

Kathleen has composed herself.

'What have they arrested my daddy for?'

'Illegal possession of guns and explosives, arms smuggling, bomb making. They've thrown the book at him; it's not good, Kathleen. We're trying to get him out on bail, but it's not going to happen. Take a few days. It might be a while before he gets out.'

'How did they get him?'

'It must be an informant; the Brits have been using more and more of them. I've just issued a new order in the Ardoyne: immediate execution for anyone colluding with the British state, no matter what the circumstances.'

I swallow hard. But my mind is already racing ahead.

I know I don't need a passport to travel to the Republic, but I don't have my driving licence on me either; it's a false one, so I don't carry it around much. I have a good excuse to say to Kathleen that I need to go via the flat in the morning to collect it.

That'll give me a chance to tell Maureen what's happening.

20. Dublin's Fair City

The news about Jimmy McKee's arrest puts a dampener on any more passion with Kathleen. She just wants to be held and talk about how lonely she's been since her mother left home, six months ago.

'She begged me to go with her and get away from everything that's happening here. She's a fully committed republican, but can't bear what's happening to ordinary people caught up in the war.'

'It can't have been an easy decision.'

'It wasn't. But, for all its sins, this is home, and I will always fight for the people who live here. It's bizarre; Daddy's been arrested by the Irish Republic. Can you believe it! All governments are the same when it comes down to it. That's why the Ardoyne and Belfast mean so much to me. And – you know what? – that would include Protestants in the fight against oppression, if they could find common cause with us.'

'That's a big "if", isn't it?'

'I suppose it is. But a lot of republicans don't believe in a united Ireland being a Catholic state. I have no fondness for Rome and all its trappings. I want an Irish Free State for all the people of this island, no matter what they believe in or what their background is. That's why there's orange in the flag of the Republic; we've always wanted that.'

'Was it the violence that persuaded your mother to leave, like Sean's new order tonight?'

'Yes, she doesn't like Sean and the leadership.'

'And you?'

'He's a necessity; not a necessary evil, but a necessity. He's what you have to have when you're engaged in a war and you're living in a war zone.'

'And you? How far are you prepared to go to win the war?'

'That's a good question, Jim. I haven't been tested yet. I'm a girl – not asked to bear arms, except to defend myself – and just a schoolteacher. So I'm a civilian. But, in principle, let me quote one of your countrymen, your man Churchill, who said something like: "We are at war against a tyranny never surpassed in human history. We must have victory, victory at all costs, however long the road may be; for without victory, there is no survival."'

'I'm impressed. That sounds pretty much word for word to me. I thought Churchill was fairly low down in Irish popularity polls?'

'He is, but I'm not averse to using a good quote when I find one.'

'But wasn't Churchill talking about Hitler and the Nazis?'

'Yes, but an enemy is an enemy . . . and Thatcher's a fascist. She looks like a well-to-do housewife. But if she's not stopped, she's a dictator in the making. You Brits will have to deal with her in your own way, but we're not going to let her destroy our communities over here.'

'Is that how you still see me, Kath? As just a Brit?'

'Sorry, Jim, no, you're not "just a Brit". You're my hero;

the Ardoyne's hero.' She smiles at me and kisses me on the cheek. 'Thanks for taking me to Dublin tomorrow. I'll feel better when I've seen Daddy. Then we can see the sights and have some fun. I also want you to meet Mammy. Do you mind?'

'No, I'd love to meet her.'

My excursion to the flat in the morning is fortuitous as, to my surprise, Maureen is delighted to hear about the trip to Dublin, concluding that it could be a very positive development for our op.

She wishes me luck.

Our journey south is uneventful, except for a long delay at the border as every vehicle is stopped and searched and all passports or driving licences checked. Sean has left us a thick wad of cash and booked us into O'Neill's, just opposite Trinity College. I had visions of a fleapit but, far from it, it's wonderfully atmospheric – all mahogany and stained glass – and has apposite 'form', having been used as a safe house by Michael Collins during the War of Independence. We check in and drive over to Phoenix Park so that Kathleen can see her father.

I wait in the car as she meets a Dublin solicitor who will accompany her on the visit.

Phoenix Park is a sight to behold. There's blossom everywhere and the resident deer graze without a care in the world. It's obvious that Kathleen will be some time, so I walk down to see the giant obelisk erected in tribute to Arthur Wellesley, the Duke of Wellington, one of Ireland's most famous sons. Although born into the Anglo-Irish Protestant Ascendancy that ruled Ireland for over three hundred years, he remains one of those Irish enigmas: as Irish as a four-leaf clover by lineage and adored by the British, but reviled by most of his kinsmen in his own land.

I then walk down to the River Liffey and cross over it on a pretty little bridge on the South Circular Road. Again, I think how familiar it all looks. So much of this island bears the imprint of its neighbours to the east, especially the English. Since Norman times, various versions of 'the English' have dominated Ireland, usually exploiting it for their own ends. In doing so, they've changed it completely. I wonder, given what's currently happening in the North, if the Irish and the other tribes of the British Isles will ever acknowledge their similarities and shared history, rather than their diversity?

The English may well have invented 'Britain' and 'the British' to persuade reluctant Celts that we are all part of a big happy family; even so, the people of the British Isles retain a potent shared identity and enjoy a unifying language and many cultural similarities as well as differences.

When Kathleen finally emerges from the Garda headquarters, it's early evening and I've long since fallen asleep on the back seat of the car. As I clamber back into the driver's seat, she shakes hands with the solicitor and smiles warmly at me.

'Come on, Jim, I think I owe you a big dinner. I'm sorry it took so long, but the Garda gave me a real grilling. They obviously think I know where Daddy has his arsenal hidden away.'

We go to the Trocadero on St Andrew's Street, a restaurant loved by Dublin's theatrical luvvies, a place festooned with signed photographs of the greats of screen and stage. It could easily be off Shaftesbury Avenue in London's theatreland. The food is out of this world and inordinately expensive but, as the Brigadier's paying, we eat well and drink from the top end of the wine list. It's only a short walk from O'Neill's, so we can drink to our hearts' content without having to worry about finding our way home. Kathleen has one of the Troc's classics, Kilmore Quay black sole, and I have a sirloin that I can cut with a fork.

It's a great evening, not only because of the food and the setting, but also because Kathleen's much more relaxed after seeing her father and hearing his news.

'The solicitor says Daddy won't get bail and it might take a few months before there's a trial, but he doesn't think there's enough evidence to convict him, not without finding one of his arms dumps south of the border.'

'And there's no chance of that?'

'Not a chance; only Daddy knows where they are. They're in communities that have been nationalist for generations – and so well hidden, on remote farms, no one would ever find them.'

'So how's your father feeling?'

'OK, it's not the first time he's been locked up. But he's annoyed that, this time, it's the Irish who've arrested him. He sends his regards, by the way, and says he's delighted that we're now an item.'

'That's very nice of him; I'm relieved he approves of us.'

'He also told us to be careful about where we go and who we speak to, as we're sure to be watched at all times.'

*

We spend the rest of the week in Dublin visiting all the tourist sites and behaving like young lovers on a romantic getaway.

We call on Kathleen's mother, who's living in the suburbs with her sister, and several other members of Kathleen's extended family, a tribe that seems to be the size of a medium-sized town!

Our best night is probably at the legendary Mulligan's pub on Poolbeg Street, closely followed by a magical night of storytelling and live music at the Brazen Head, down by the Liffey.

I'm falling in love with Dublin, all things Irish and – especially – Kathleen.

21. The 12th

A calm has settled over my relationship with Kathleen and it's now an accepted fact in the Ardoyne. Her father is still in custody in Dublin and I spend most of my time at her home. Maureen seems relaxed about the situation and has no problem being seen with us, including having a drink together in the Hibernian. There have been some innuendoes about a ménage à trois, but we ignore them.

In early July, after sixty-one days of refusing sustenance, Joe McDonnell becomes the fifth IRA man to die on hunger strike. His death will pour yet more fuel on to the fires of hatred that are raging in the city. There's tension in the air, just like in the days after the death of Bobby Sands; the schools are closed for the summer holidays and large numbers of people are on the streets.

The next day, the sheer brutal horror of life in Belfast comes very close again. Kathleen and I, still in our running gear, are on our way to the Hibernian for a drink. As usual, there are outbreaks of disorder all around the Ardoyne. We hear plastic rounds being fired and the distinctive crash of exploding Molotov cocktails. For several weeks, much to the fury of the locals, a British Army observation post has been located on the rooftop of Ewart's Mill on Flax Street. It offers a commanding position over the entire area of the Ardoyne and makes the locals feel that, not only are they surrounded in their tiny enclave, like inmates in a prison camp, they're also watched over by armed guards in a watchtower.

We're walking down Havana Way, having just said hello to a smiling Danny Barrett, one of the nicest lads in my senior history and English classes at St Anthony's. After he passes us, he turns into Havana Court and we lose sight of him. Moments later, the impact of a high-velocity bullet catapults Danny over a garden wall, mortally wounding him. Even though several people are trying to stem the bleeding, by the time Kathleen and I reach him, a deep pool of blood is seeping into the earth beneath his stricken body.

The next day, we hear that before it reached the Crumlin Road, the ambulance that took Danny away was twice stopped by army patrols, each insisting that they search the vehicle. It was stopped again by an RUC patrol when it reached the Crumlin. By the time Danny reached the nearby Mater Hospital, he had already been declared dead in the back of the vehicle.

I feel ashamed to be a Brit.

To make matters worse, 12 July falls on a Sunday this year, so the annual Orange Day parades, the Protestant marches – or 'walks', as they prefer to call them – are being held today. A bright and warm Saturday morning heralds the most contentious day in Northern Ireland's calendar. Kathleen, Maureen and I are watching the parades on the Ardoyne side of the Crumlin Road.

Always volatile and the source of sectarian violence for decades, this year's parades are particularly explosive.

Red, white and blue bunting and Union flags festoon the city. The Orangemen, in their bizarre uniforms of black suit, bowler hat, rolled umbrella and strident orange collarette, march down their traditional routes to reaffirm their Protestant Ascendancy. The martial music of their pipe and drum bands echoes around the terraced rows and housing estates of the city, generating either joy or loathing among all who hear it.

We're joined by Hibernian stalwart Barry Kennedy, the Ardoyne's philosopher. He sees a marcher who was at Queen's with him and bellows an insult at the large Orangeman just yards away.

'Harold, you prat, look at ye, all dressed up like an English ponce!'

'Fuck off, Barry, you little leprechaun!'

Barry shakes his head.

'If only they realized how daft they look with their bowlers and brollies.'

He then holds court about the significance of the 12th for both sides of the community. He begins with a surprising expression of sympathy for his loyalist fellow citizens.

'Poor Protestant buggers, cooped up on an island dominated by us Catholics; that's why the 12th is so important to them.'

Startled by what she's heard, Maureen turns to stare at Barry.

'Compassion for the loyalists, Barry?'

'Pity more like! They're cursed by their past. We all are. Ireland's history is its curse; peace would be so much easier if we could bury our past. But, without our history, we can't define ourselves and so create a new future. It's a conundrum no one can solve.'

'But you'll have to, sooner or later.'

'You're right, Maureen, but I doubt it will be in my lifetime.'

I look down the Crumlin Road. It's a scene full of images of arrogance and prejudice, fear and hatred. I can't help thinking Barry's right. As far as the eye can see, there's a long stream of marching Orangemen strutting their stuff. There are roars of approval from the Shankill side of the road and howls of abuse from the Ardoyne side. Missiles are thrown, insults hurled, rude gestures exchanged; it's primeval and deeply disturbing.

Kathleen disappears to go back to the Hibernian for a pee. Barry, probably in need of the same relief, keeps her company. Shortly afterwards, a middle-aged man approaches Maureen and me. He smiles oddly, almost as if he's not quite a full shilling, or has had too much to drink. We've never seen him before but, from his heavy accent, he's clearly a local. He prattles on about several things and seems to know about my prowess on the football field.

Then he hits us with a bombshell. He uses an expression we knew we would hear one day, but had almost forgotten.

'So, Jim, they tell me youse was magic against Shankill, a bit like the wee great man himself. By the way, how's he doing? Is George Best fit?'

Maureen and I look at one another, incredulous at

hearing the coded expression after all these months. Then the stranger leans close to us and, in a much more earnest voice, gives us a short, sharp message.

'Madden's Bar, nineteen-hundred hours tomorrow. Two men, both in collar and tie.'

Then, with all the nonchalance of a man without a care in the world, he walks away, talking twenty to the dozen as he goes.

'Well, good to meet ye, Jim Dowd. And ye, Maureen . . . Jim Dowd, Ardoyne's hero! Good on ye, Jim, good to meet ye . . .'

Maureen looks as shocked as I feel. She begins to walk back to the flat, beckoning to me to do the same.

'Can you tear yourself away from the wondrous Kathleen tomorrow night?'

'Steady, Mo.'

'Sorry . . . but seriously, nothing planned?'

'No.'

'Good. Why don't you tell her that I'm going to look at a flat of my own and that I want you to come with me?'

'That's a good idea. I'm sure that'll be fine.'

Maureen smiles warmly.

'Go down to the Hibernian and find Kathleen and Barry and have a few drinks. I'll go back to the flat for the evening.'

I smile back.

'So, do you reckon we've finally been given something to do?'

'Looks like it. I'll see you at the flat at eighteen thirty hours tomorrow evening. We'll get a Flax Taxi, right?'

'Right, see you then.'

An evening of mixed emotions follows for me. I'm relieved that an ostensibly meaningless assignment might, after all, have a purpose. But I'm also anxious. Once again, the future becomes open-ended.

And I'm reminded of the shallow foundations of my bond with Kathleen – a relationship that, in every other respect, is wonderful and going from strength to strength.

The next day is a long one. I just want to get it over with, and to find out what our op is going to involve.

I've been helping Kathleen get fit and we go on a long walk in the Mourne Mountains. Not surprisingly, we almost bump into Maureen as, in the middle distance, we see her lithe form tabbing up Slieve Donard.

As Kathleen and I drive back to the Ardoyne in her father's car, she drops another colossal complication into the already toxic mix of my bizarre life in Belfast's most notorious ghetto. She smiles coquettishly in her irresistible way.

'So, Jim, if Maureen's moving out of Estoril Park, why don't ye move in with me?'

I try to think through the implications as quickly as possible, knowing full well that Kathleen would think it very odd if I were to say no.

'Are you sure?'

'Of course. Wouldn't it be great?'

'It would. But what about when your father comes home?'

'He'll be fine with it. We're not short of room. Of

course, I could move in with you in Estoril when Maureen leaves.'

That's an option I hadn't anticipated.

'But I'd prefer to be at home with Daddy; he hasn't a clue on his own.'

That's a relief!

'So, do you want to shack up with me and play mummies and daddies?'

'Course I do, Kath, but I'm not sure about the "mummies and daddies" bit just at the moment.'

Her face suddenly becomes serious.

'Jim, I've got a bit of a surprise for you. I hope you think it's great news . . . I do.'

Shit! I've got a very bad feeling about this. I try to concentrate on the road and stay calm.

Her face beams, full of excitement; she almost shrieks the news.

'I'm pregnant. You're going to be a daddy, Jim!'

I know I can't be anything less than enthusiastic. But – fucking hell! – how has this happened?

'That is great news! Are you sure?'

'Course I am. I'm twice overdue . . .' She pauses, looking guilty in an impish sort of way. 'I know, I'm supposed to be on the pill. But they're hard to come by around here, and I must've missed taking them for a while when Daddy got lifted. You know, the stress and all . . . and meeting you, that sent me skew-whiff for a while. I didn't know Tuesday from Thursday week. I hope you don't mind?'

'Course not, it's wonderful. But it changes a few things.'

'I know – isn't it exciting?'

Poor, sweet Kathleen, what am I doing to you?

I drop Kathleen at her home on Herbert Street and leave the car. Then I walk back to Estoril Park to collect Maureen. All the while, as I pass house after house in this strangely alien but beguiling community, I think to myself, what am I doing to these ordinary yet extraordinary people?

Behind their commonplace front doors, there's poverty and no little depravity; there's plenty of prejudice and ignorance. But there's also courage and the nobility of the human spirit. I'm sure the same is true in the Shankill, not much further away than a boundary throw in cricket, but my lords and masters haven't asked me to infiltrate that particular world, so I can only care about the one I'm in.

By the time Maureen and I sit down in Madden's, my mind has stopped reeling a little, but only a little. I can't yet tell Maureen the appalling news of the day; I'm dreading that prospect. Life is suddenly even more terrifyingly Byzantine.

Our scheduled visitors at Madden's are about as nondescript as spooks tend to be. We assume they're RUC Special Branch as they both have Northern Irish accents, which is a surprise, because we'd assumed they'd be Anglos – Det boys. They insist that, although they know our names, we may not know theirs. After a round of drinks and some banter about life in Belfast, when it comes to the operational brief, to Maureen's all-too-obvious anger, they speak to me rather than her.

'What do you know about Sean Murphy?'

'Only what we read in the briefing notes before we came –'

Maureen interrupts.

'But we see him at least twice a week in the Hibernian Club.'

'You come and go to the Hibernian?'

'Of course we do, we live and work in the Ardoyne. Anyway, you have a message for us, so why don't you just get on with it?'

'OK, Townsend, listen carefully. Sean Murphy's a ruthless killer. He's committed all the usual sins: murder, torture and a long history of shooting and bombing soldiers. But many more things have since come to light through informants. So much so that we're led to believe that no one, even within the republican hierarchy, would mind if Sean was soon to meet his Maker.'

Maureen looks surprised.

'What sort of things?'

'Prostitution in the city, hard-core drugs, illicit alcohol, two cases of rape – both teenage girls – several sexual assaults and a lot of intimidation to keep the families quiet.'

We're both astonished at the revelation and ask for elaboration, which is immediately forthcoming.

'One example: in front of his henchmen, he was responsible for the sexual humiliation of the mother of one of the girls who went to confront him.'

An unpleasant leer plays across their faces.

'Do you get the picture, Townsend, or would you like a few more graphic details?'

Maureen, angry and distraught, doesn't answer. But they tell us anyway.

'One of the girls was just fourteen at the time. She was held over a weekend and repeatedly raped by Murphy and several of his men. They threatened to shoot both her parents if anything was said.'

Another pause.

'She's one of your pupils . . . Anne Brady.'

Maureen's face contorts in horror.

'Little Annie; dear God, no!'

'Dear God, yes, Townsend.'

'Her father was shot by loyalists last year.'

'No, he wasn't. Her father, Fergus, confronted Murphy, who beat him to a pulp. Fergus then went to the RUC, so Murphy had him executed. He was shot through the back of the head and dumped on waste ground off Oldpark Road.'

'What did the RUC do about it?'

'They don't have enough evidence. Murphy's impregnable. That's where you two come in.'

'Is this intel accurate and verifiable?'

'One hundred per cent –'

I interrupt. I look at Maureen, who seems as disconcerted as I am.

'And what do you want us to do?'

'You hit him.'

We're both in shock. Maureen is stunned into silence, but I've heard that ops like this have been happening, so I'm a little less surprised. Nevertheless, I shiver at the suggestion and question it.

'Are you kidding? That's James Bond and MI6 – and only in the dark corners of the world.'

'Oh, and this isn't one of the world's dark corners?'

Maureen has got over her initial shock.

'Who's sanctioned this?'

'HQ here, Gower Street in London, and the politicians.'

'Which "politicians"?'

'All the relevant ones.'

'Is that gospel?'

'It is.'

'So we have an official order to assassinate Sean Murphy?'

'If you mean you want it in writing, I can tell you now, you won't be getting a piece of paper. If you mean are you protected? Yes, you're protected. But let me reiterate, this is a covert operation. And as far as the public and press are concerned, it won't be happening. You will make it look like either an internal IRA hit, or a loyalist revenge attack. Clear?'

Maureen bristles at their attitude.

'Yes, I suppose that's clear. No more instructions?'

'No.'

Maureen gets up to leave. I get up to follow her, but have two more questions.

'Is there a timescale?'

'As soon as possible.'

'And afterwards?'

'Don't know; Control didn't say.'

Maureen and I leave Madden's at a gallop and rush down College Avenue to the Crown in Great Victoria Street.

When we get there, Maureen is adamant about her choice of beverage.

'No more Guinness. I need a proper drink, a large cognac.'

'I'll join you.'

For once, we're able to bag one of the private little booths and settle down to come to terms with what we've just heard. An hour later, after several large cognacs, we're still going over it, still not sure what to do.

'Look, Jim, by the book. We should do as ordered.'

'Which "book"? There isn't a book for this. It's certainly way beyond any civilized rules of engagement, in breach of the Geneva Conventions, and against the law of the land. Other than that, it's fine.'

'I know, but governments sometimes have to use extreme measures in extreme circumstances.'

'But the Brigadier, is he "extreme" enough? Do you buy all that stuff – the rapes, the sexual assaults?'

'Why should I doubt it, Jim? If it's true, he's certainly a monster. I can't bear thinking about what he did to Annie; she's the sweetest little thing you could possibly meet. No wonder she's so quiet and shy.'

'I don't like the sound of it. It's all too convenient. If it's kosher, why don't we hear it on the ground?'

'What does Kathleen think about him? Have you ever asked her?'

'She calls him a "necessity", the kind of man you need "in a war zone".'

'That doesn't tell us much. Can you find out a bit more?'

'I'm not sure. Let me think about it.'

My mind's in a whirl. Do I tell her Kathleen's news now? No, not yet.

By the end of the evening, we're both a little the worse for wear. Is now the right time? Probably as good a time as any. She's got to be told, sooner or later.

22. Despair

'The little cow. Is that what she told you: "I must have forgotten to take them for a couple of days"?'

'That's what she said.'

'It's the oldest trick in the book, Jimmy. She's stitched you like a kipper.'

Maureen looks down at her cognac, checks how much is left in the bottom and, in one gulp, drains the residue.

'What the fuck are we going to do now?'

'I don't know, Mo. It's a right mess.'

'You can say that again.'

She pauses, scrutinizing me like a headmistress interrogating a disobedient schoolboy.

'Are you sure it's yours?'

I hadn't even thought about that.

'I think so. There's been no one else around, as far as I know.'

'Bloody hell, it was quick, she must have conceived straight away. So much for accidentally forgetting to take the pill. What a conniving cow!'

'Don't be too harsh, Mo. I'm very fond of her, you know.'

'You don't say! That's really good news; now you can live happily ever after ... except for the small matter of you actually not existing, Jim. You're a fucking myth, an SAS soldier disguised as a schoolteacher!'

Maureen begins to boil with anger.

'What are you going to do now? Take her back to Hereford and move into married quarters? Perhaps the Regiment will invite Sean and her dad to the wedding and put them up in the officers' mess at Stirling Lines! Jim, you're a nightmare, a fucking nightmare!'

There's nothing I can say. She's right, of course. I've fucked up big time. And I've no idea what to do about it.

'You'd better go home to your sweetheart. I need time to think.'

Like a dog with its tail between its legs, all I can do is look pathetic. I'm lost for words, except the predictably banal.

'What can I say, Mo?'

'Don't say anything. I don't want to hear it.'

There's a long pause as she takes stock. Then she looks me in the eye.

'By the way, are you in love with her?'

I don't want to answer, but I suppose I owe Maureen an honest response.

'Yes, I think I am.'

'And does she love you?'

'I think so.'

I don't see Maureen for several days because Kathleen and I go down to Dublin to see her father. During the journey, she begs me to allow her to tell her parents about our news, but I persuade her not to – at least, not until we've decided on our future together. Inevitably, that tactic only focuses her mind on the one subject I want to avoid: our future.

To delay matters, and knowing that it will give her a dilemma to wrestle with, I play a cunning but grossly unfair gambit. I suggest we move back to England, because – with all its ills and traumas – Belfast is not a good place to bring up a family, etcetera. Although it creates a bit of tension and some argument, she agrees to think about it and postpones any firm plans for a future in Belfast.

However, it deepens my despair. I'm hurting someone I love and I'm letting down Maureen, a comrade who's been totally loyal and supportive.

I'm digging a bigger and bigger hole for myself.

A few days later, Kathleen trumps my ace about our future. Brimming with excitement, she wakes me early in the morning by tickling my ribs and whispering in my ear.

'How easy would it be for us to get jobs in London?'

I immediately sense the ominous implications of the question, but can't avoid answering truthfully.

'Fairly easy; there's a shortage of good teachers, especially in the inner city.'

'But isn't Inner London just like Belfast?'

'In terms of the schools and kids, yes, but not in any other way. We don't have riots every night, and paramilitaries aren't running the housing estates.'

She props herself up in bed and looks at me with a disconcerting intensity.

'If you really want to go back to England, then I'll come with you. But you must promise that our baby will be just as much Irish as English. We must come back here all the time. I want this place to mean something as our baby grows up.'

This conversation's like a runaway train. I try to answer as she would want me to.

'Of course. My half makes the child three-quarters Irish; it's a good start.'

'Is that a deal, then?'

Jesus! I've just hit the buffers and careened across the platform.

'It's a deal.'

She squeals like an eager schoolgirl.

'Let's go into the city in the morning and get the *Times Educational Supplement* and start looking for jobs.'

My despair deepens.

The next few days become an ever-worsening crisis. My anxieties begin to affect my libido. Every time I make love to Kathleen, it reinforces the deceit, until it begins to turn our trysts from heavenly experiences to hellish ones. At that point, of course, I can no longer perform.

She gets upset and can't understand what's wrong. I run out of excuses to explain what the problem is. I think I might ask Maureen to put me out of my misery and shoot me instead of the Brigadier!

Inevitably, after a few days, Kathleen and I end up having our first row. Then, over the next twenty-four hours, the rows escalate. Her Celtic temperament soon comes to the fore; the conversations become more and more heated. Then the lid comes off.

'I don't understand, Jim.'

'I'm sorry, Kath, it's no big deal, just give me a few days.'

'Is it the baby, or going to London?'

'No . . . I don't know what it is. But I'll get over it, don't worry.'

'I'm not worrying; I'm upset because you don't fancy me any more.'

She looks at me piercingly. I know full well that she can sense that something serious is playing on my mind.

'You've got cold feet, haven't you? I can tell; why don't you tell me the truth?'

'It's nothing serious, Kath, believe me.'

'Don't lie to me, Jim. I can tell when someone's lying.'

Her temper begins to boil over. She gets up and opens the front door.

'You're no fucking use to me at the moment. I'm going to Dublin to see my mammy and daddy. You can fuck off back to the ice maiden. Perhaps she can put some lead back in your pencil! When I come back, Jim, I want the truth. Think about it.'

'Please, Kathleen, aren't you overreacting?'

'No, I'm not! I can cope with whatever your problem is, but I can't cope when you won't tell me what's wrong.'

She's right. I can't tell her what the problem is.

Kathleen's decision to go to Dublin is a blessing in disguise. Within half an hour of her leaving, with my tail firmly between my legs, I'm back at Estoril Park. Kathleen's trip gives me the chance to talk to Maureen about our multiple, intertwined dilemmas and how we're going to extricate ourselves from them.

Later that day, we decide to go into the city, to Kelly's Cellars, to eat and drink and see if we can find a miraculous solution.

Maureen is far from sympathetic.

'So you've been thrown out on your ear?'

'It's a disaster. She's bewildered. We've stopped making love. I just can't make our situation any worse by carrying on deceiving her. I've thought about it, over and over, and looked at it from every conceivable position and, no matter what I do, it's totally buggered.'

'Do you still love her?'

'I must do. If I didn't, I think I would be able to carry on with the charade. But I can't hurt her any more.'

Maureen smiles at me with a gentleness I haven't seen before.

'Jim, you're about the most disaster-prone person I've ever met. But this is a nightmare to end all nightmares. You've got yourself into a right mess, haven't you?'

'Yes, and I've dumped you in it as well.'

'Never mind about me for the time being. Let's see what we can sort out for you.'

'I don't deserve that, Mo.'

'Perhaps not, but you're my partner, right?'

I look down at the floor. I feel completely helpless. Slowly, I shake my head, trying to rid my consciousness of the pain that invades it.

Maureen rests her hand on mine.

'Come on, let's get rat-arsed. It'll make us both feel better, at least for a few hours.'

Like all cowards, I take up Maureen's offer with relish.

We order a large sirloin each and a bottle of Rioja and try to forget everything. We get through another Rioja and a couple of stickies and, at least for a few precious hours, the world seems a better place.

As usual, I sleep on the sofa. It's not a comfortable night.

*

Too much alcohol wakes me early and the mental anguish soon starts to swirl around in my head with a vengeance.

As we prepare breakfast, Maureen puts her hand on my shoulder.

'How do you feel, Jim?'

'Didn't sleep much after about four in the morning.'

'Neither did I. It gave me a chance to think, though.'

'I hope you've had a brainwave?'

'No, but I've got a least-worst position.'

'Go on, then.'

'OK, my status first. I'm not happy with what we're doing here. I signed up for military intelligence work, not for schoolteaching and then a dubious order to assassinate someone for Queen and country. But I'm a servant of Queen and country, and will obey orders. So, for me, I think I should get it over with, complete the mission we've been given, present a good case to go back to Blighty and resume a "normal" career in the army. As for you, Jimmy, it's more complicated, but the end point's the same.'

'Elaborate.'

'You need to get out of here, preferably with Kathleen on your arm, right?'

'Correct.'

'Then you need to complete the mission as well, get posted back home and take her with you.'

'Two problems with that. How do I conceal my army identity from her? But, more pointedly, I don't think I'm prepared to shoot the Brigadier in cold blood.'

Maureen looks at me like I'm an immature adolescent – which is not an unfair assessment, given my recent behaviour.

'Look, you're going to have to tell her about the army eventually. Gower Street has already made you ex-army. So get yourself a teaching job, and make the army distant history. In due course, you can tell her the truth. Not about here, of course, but the pre-Belfast bit. As for the Brigadier part, are you sure about that?'

'I think so.'

'Then that gives us a big problem. We've been given an order.'

'No, we haven't – at least, not a legitimate one. We've been issued an illegal command that we'd be mad to agree to.'

'Jim, somewhere between the carnal delights of Kathleen and the laddishness of Hibernian football, you've gone native.'

'Bollocks, Mo! What do you mean by "native"? Do you really think the Brigadier's guilty of that charge card we were given?'

'Why shouldn't I? Are you suggesting that the intel isn't accurate?'

'Yes, I am.'

'For what reason?'

'When I was at Hereford, I heard strong rumours that RUC Special Branch was directing British units and their missions, and that the RUC was working hand-in-glove with the loyalist paramilitaries.'

'To do what?'

'Get rid of the IRA's leadership and anyone who supports them, and generally discredit the republican cause. I thought most of the rumours were exaggerated. But then, when we were given the order to slot the Brigadier, everything dropped into place.'

'Jim, he's a one-off; exceptional circumstances demand exceptional solutions.'

'I don't agree. He's not a one-off. He's a target of a conspiracy that goes right to the top.'

'What about his charge sheet? Are you saying it's a pack of lies?'

'It is, isn't it? It doesn't ring true to me. You've met him, what do you think?'

'I don't know, but we have to accept what our colleagues tell us, otherwise the whole stack of cards comes tumbling down.'

'That's my point. The whole thing's a carefully constructed pack of cards. The truth is, the web is so intricately woven, you can't tell the good guys from the bad guys any more.'

'I can, Jim. What you're suggesting is state terrorism. I don't believe that's happening in our country. This is not a tin-pot Third World dictatorship! Sean Murphy is a brutal murderer, rapist and torturer; it's a legitimate military assassination.'

'That's a contradiction in terms and you know it. You're not thinking, Mo. Listen to what you've just said. We're involved in classic counter-insurgency; it's a terrifying feature of the world we live in. Over the years of the Troubles, the Brits have had to decide which side they're on – the loyalists or the republicans. Instinctively, people on the ground here, and back on the mainland, have aligned themselves with those loyal to the Crown. It's human nature.'

'No, Jim, you listen to yourself. You're talking about "the Brits" as if you're not one of them.'

'I know I'm one of them, but I don't agree with what's happening.'

Maureen relents. She knows we're never going to agree.

'We both have a decision to make. We either make it together, or we go our separate ways and live with the consequences.'

Maureen has an uncanny habit of pointing out the stark facts of life. I don't know how to respond.

'I need to think, Mo. My brain's in meltdown.'

23. Danny's Death

It's August, but the warmth of high summer hasn't tempered the fear and anger on the streets of the Ardoyne. In fact, the mood has become even more febrile.

Four more hunger strikers have died, and each death has been followed by ever-escalating riots. After one overnight skirmish, just off the Falls Road, Nora McCabe, a 33-year-old Catholic woman who seemed to be guilty of nothing more than walking home from the corner shop, was killed by a plastic bullet that hit her in the back of the head from close range.

The shooting took place at 7.45 in the morning when, although strewn with debris from the riots, the area was relatively quiet. Local witnesses claimed that an RUC armoured vehicle came to a halt close to her, from which a single shot was fired, mortally wounding her.

Sadly, such incidents are now so frequent, they no longer make the headlines. They have become the norm, rather than the exception.

The situation in Northern Ireland escalates significantly on 5 August, when the IRA explodes a series of car bombs and incendiaries throughout the province. No one is killed in the attacks, but the damage to property is substantial and the propaganda impact significant – especially in the United States, where sympathy for the republican cause is growing by the day.

Mainland UK is also in turmoil. Margaret Thatcher's stringent economic policies have led to an unemployment rate of over two and a half million, a number not seen since the Depression of the 1930s. Serious rioting first began in Brixton in April, and in July erupted in almost every inner city in the country. Even the fairy-tale wedding of Prince Charles and Lady Diana Spencer at the end of the month has failed to lighten the menacing mood that pervades the land. With powerful figures like politician Enoch Powell talking about impending civil war, the country seems to be heading towards Armageddon.

My own Armageddon is approaching fast and my position about our operational orders has hardened even more today, a beautiful Monday morning in the second week of August. In the early hours, a young Catholic lad, Liam Canning from Glengormley, north of Belfast, was walking his girlfriend to her home in the Ardoyne. When they got to the corner of Etna Drive and Alliance Avenue, two pistol shots rang out. It was 3.15 a.m., all was quiet, and the crack of the bullets echoed around the Ardoyne like a double clap of thunder.

Liam was hit in the head and the spine, and died immediately.

Angered by the news, I immediately go round to Estoril Park and confront Maureen.

'So, at the moment, I think I should be accepting the Brigadier's offer to join his battalion, not putting a hole in him.'

'So when do you get your balaclava and Armalite, Jimmy?'

'Don't be bloody stupid, Mo. These people are being

murdered. Those boys on Ewart's Mill, our army colleagues, shot Danny in cold blood. He was sitting on his garden wall, minding his own fucking business. And now this lad's been shot walking his girlfriend home. The rumour is that his killer's in the UDR – a regiment of the British Army, for Christ's sake!'

'OK, but how do you know that while Danny was sitting there his mates were not filling bottles with petrol to throw at the army?'

'That's bollocks, Mo. Danny wouldn't have known a Molotov cocktail from the hole in his arse!'

'But, Jimmy, that's the problem; no one knows who the good guys are any more. You've no idea what Danny got up to when you weren't looking. Just like we don't know what the Brigadier's up to.'

'And that's a good reason to slot him?'

'He's OC 3rd Battalion, Belfast Brigade, IRA, and the intel on him couldn't be more damning; that's good enough for me.'

'Well, it isn't for me.'

We continue to argue for some time, until Maureen gives up on me.

'OK, Jim, here's the solution for both of us. I'll fulfil the mission and carry out the order to eliminate the Brigadier. That will get him off the streets and make the Ardoyne a safer place – one less thug.'

'That assumes his replacement's an improvement.'

'True, but not our problem. We complete our mission. I go home to continue my real army career; you take Kathleen to London. And we all live happily ever after.'

'As simple as that?'

'Yes, as simple as that.'

'Tell me something; if you go ahead with this, what makes you any different from the Brigadier and his thugs?'

'Well, I'm following an order handed down from the legitimate government of our country; he's a cold-blooded terrorist, a brutal thug and a serial rapist.'

'Allegedly!'

'Come on, Jim, you're being stupid. Do you accept the solution or not?'

'It's not right if I do it, and it's not right if you do it. Who pulls the trigger is irrelevant.'

'I think it is right, and I'll make the hit.'

I realize that Maureen will not be dissuaded.

'Is that it?'

'No, you don't get off so lightly. You have to cover my back. I'm not going after Murphy on my own. You'll be my backup if anything goes wrong. Will you do that for me?'

I think hard. Is an accomplice to a murder any less guilty than the one pulling the trigger? Of course not, but Maureen knows that if I refuse her, I put her at enormous risk.

'Are you sure you can trust me, given everything that's been said?'

She gives me one of her rare smiles.

'Of course. You're still a professional soldier and a member of the finest military unit in the world. What's more, besides being a walking disaster area, strange as it seems, I trust you.'

'Flattery usually works.'

'Well, you're not getting any more!'

I decide that 'backup', although not a legit part of my

role, is within the bounds of what's morally right, if it means keeping my partner safe.

'OK, agreed. How are you – or should I say we – going to do it?'

'I think I've already worked that out.'

'OK?'

'What's the Brigadier's Achilles heel?'

'Women.'

'Exactly. I'll brief you when I've worked it through.'

24. Eyes in the Hibernian

Maureen's strategic plan has relieved a lot of my anxiety. Her single-mindedness has lifted a weight off my shoulders. It has also helped my libido return. Kathleen came back from Dublin full of remorse for not being more understanding and explained how much she missed me. We made up and normal service has resumed. We've both applied for supply teaching jobs in London and been accepted. Specific roles in named schools are expected any day. The news has added extra zest to Kathleen's demeanour and even more spice to our relationship.

As I spend most of my time at Herbert Street with Kathleen, Maureen has no need to move out of our flat in Estoril Park, so that means it's easy for us to talk. Kathleen's fitness regime has intensified since she became pregnant, and so, bizarrely, the three of us sometimes go running together.

Kathleen's father is expected to be released in September, by which time Kathleen thinks we'll be living our new life in London.

I've managed to find out more about the Brigadier from Kathleen and relayed the intel to Maureen. Kathleen admits that he's a notorious womanizer and has several 'girlfriends' in the Ardoyne with whom he stays on a rotating basis. The names of these women are closely guarded secrets, as are their addresses. Kathleen did admit that, one Christmas, he tried to kiss and fondle her when she came back home from college, but he was drunk and apologized the next day. She didn't regard it as a big deal.

Maureen takes the view that Kathleen's account verifies the intel from RUC Special Branch. I still disagree, arguing that there's a huge moral chasm between being a womanizer and a rapist of teenagers.

Through a process I find hard to fathom, Maureen thinks she's identified at least two of the Brigadier's mistresses. She's confident she knows a third, but two suffice for her strategy.

'How d'ya know?'

'Instinct, Jimmy; body language in the Hibernian; a look here, a look there. Eyes tell you a lot.'

'So where does that take us?'

'At least I know where he is most nights of the week.'

'And his goons?'

'Well, I'm pretty sure that when he's shacked up with his concubines, one of his boys sleeps downstairs and another in a parked car outside.'

'Just two?'

'Correct.'

'So have you got a plan?'

'No.'

It's obvious that Maureen is thinking of using her femininity to find a chink in the Brigadier's armour.

'Mo, be careful. Don't get too close to the Brigadier, or his goons.'

'Worry not, Jimmy. I'm the ice maiden, remember?'

Two days have passed since my conversation with Maureen. The Hibernian is packed, as usual. Kathleen's in high spirits; we've just heard that we've both been offered teaching jobs in the same school in London.

Maureen is either drunk, or pretending to be drunk. She's giving the Brigadier the look; the one that women use when they offer men the world. My hackles are rising. I'm fucked off with her, and see the Brigadier like a lusty young gorilla sees an ageing silverback. Jesus, this is not good; manageable if Maureen's sober, but a nightmare if she's drunk.

She's entitled to be drunk, of course. She's seen me the worse for drink, time enough. So why not?

Kathleen's noticed.

'What's going on with Maureen? She's cosying up to Sean.'

I try not to seem too concerned.

'She's a big girl, Kath.'

'Do you think she's trying to wind you up?'

'Don't think so, we're beyond that.'

There's a very pointed expression on Kathleen's face.

'Sure?'

'Sure.'

Kathleen continues to stare at Maureen as she flirts with the Godfather of the Ardoyne. I realize that she's worried.

'You seem concerned, Kath.'

'Oh, it's nothing, Jimmy, but there are several women in here whose noses might be put out of joint at what Maureen's up to.'

Maureen continues to entice the Brigadier, a routine that makes my jealousy turn to anger; then I find it repulsive. I want to go over and drag her out of the place.

Suddenly, I begin to see the Brigadier as the intel has painted him. Kathleen notices my discomfort.

'I thought you weren't jealous, Jim?'

I find it hard to be nonchalant.

'I'm not. But, as you said, there are lots of eyes on the two of them.'

'I know, it's not good . . .' She hesitates. 'Jim, if I tell you something, it mustn't go any further.'

'Course it won't.'

'OK, Sean's got a few girlfriends in the Ardoyne; he likes the ladies. Everyone knows, but not many know who they are.'

'Do you know them?'

'Only a couple, and they're both in here now.'

'Ah, not good.'

'Right, not good.' She looks around the room, then turns back to me. 'Do you want me to try to get her out of here?'

'Could you?'

'I could try.'

'That might be for the best.'

'We may need to go back to the flat with her. If she goes home on her own and Sean's been tempted, he's likely to go round there.'

Kathleen gets up and walks over to Sean's table. Half the eyes in the room follow her progress. Maureen only has eyes for the Brigadier and doesn't see her coming. The two women speak briefly before Kathleen turns on her heels and walks back.

'Nothing doing, Jim.'

'What did she say?'

'She told me she was fine. I probed a bit and suggested that Sean was a fairly big fish to be frying – or words to that effect.'

'And what did she say?'

'She told me to mind my own business – or words to that effect.'

I know what Maureen's up to and I don't like it. Apart from the fact that it's a risky gambit, I'm very concerned for Maureen's safety and very jealous that the big Irishman is slobbering all over her.

'Come on, Jim, let's go home.'

'Do you mind if we stay a bit longer?'

'Come *on*, Jim. As you said, she's a big girl. I'm sure she can take care of herself.'

I'm in a dilemma.

Maureen and I are supposed to have ended the relationship we never had. So, as far as Kathleen knows, she's now just an unattached schoolteacher, not a member of British Intelligence's elite unit in Northern Ireland. I decide that no matter how distasteful it seems, having abnegated my own responsibility for our op and handed control to Maureen, I should let her get on with it.

After all, she is indeed a big girl.

25. Safe House

I don't see Maureen until lunchtime the next day. With every hour that passes, I go over and over my decision to leave her in the Hibernian. Did I do the right thing? Is she OK? Has the big bugger done something horrible to her?

After Kathleen and I have eaten breakfast, on the pretext of going for a run, I manage to get away. When I arrive at Estoril Park, Maureen, still in her dressing gown, is sitting at the kitchen table. She's looking a little the worse for wear.

'You OK?'

'Yes, thanks. A bit hung-over, but I'm OK.'

'That was a pretty risky tactic last night.'

'It had to be done, Jim. I couldn't think of any other way.'

'Were you really drunk?'

'Course. D'ya think I could've done that sober?'

'Suppose not.'

'Well, the gamble worked.'

'Really?'

'Yes.'

I'm feeling like a jealous lover trying to find out if his girlfriend has slept with somebody else.

'So what happened?'

'Well, I didn't pay the ultimate price for Queen and country, if that's what you mean.'

She looks out of the window. A grimace plays across her face.

'But I came close enough for it to be pretty unpleasant. I suppose you want to hear the details?'

I do, of course, but try not to appear prurient.

'Only as far as it affects the op.'

'Well, it's best you know. Besides, I want to get it off my chest.'

I don't say anything, but hope and pray I'm not about to hear anything too repugnant.

'Don't look so horrified, Jim; it's all in a day's work.'

'If you say so.'

'Anyway, I decided the only way I could find a chink in the Brigadier's armour was to exploit his weakness . . . and we both know what that is.'

'I warned you to be careful.'

'I know; it was sweet of you to be concerned about me, but I chose the only route that made sense. Your relationship with Kathleen made it so blatantly obvious. Then, when you lost it in the Hibernian after the cup final and told everyone in the Ardoyne that we were no longer an item, you gave me the perfect entrée. And him . . .'

I try to defuse the seriousness of the situation and Maureen's discomfort.

'I did, didn't I? See, now you realize that the whole thing with Kathleen was just a clever ploy to help us accomplish our objective.'

'Of course, Jim! I hadn't realized: the most subtle double bluff in the history of military intelligence.' Maureen's demeanour becomes serious again. 'The Brigadier made his intentions clear a few days ago. He kept probing me about us, and my feelings towards you and Kathleen. He wasn't very subtle, casting himself as a strong shoulder to cry on, but subtlety is not one of his strong suits.

'So last night, I had a couple of stiffeners at home and went for broke. It wasn't difficult. Strange as it may seem, he likes you, so he didn't want you to see too much. He didn't want to antagonize any of his women either. So, with the strict understanding that there'd be no hanky-panky, and definitely without his minders coming in, I agreed he could follow me home to the flat so that we could hatch a plan to see one another.'

'Don't tell me he came round here!'

'He did. Two of his goons waited outside.'

'So they know where he was!'

'Yes, I was aware of the danger of that; I'm not daft, Jim. I suggested he tell them that we were meeting a mother from school whose daughter had a problem with one of her male teachers.'

'And he agreed to that?'

'Of course.'

'So how did it go?'

'We struck a deal.' Maureen swallows hard, as if recalling a bad dream. 'At some point soon he'll send word about an appropriate safe house in the Ardoyne. I insisted that, although there can be one of his men outside, no one must be in the house at the time. And none of his men must know who he is meeting – I have my reputation to keep up, you understand! Otherwise the deal is off. He agreed, but it cost me a close-quarters clinch and a bit of groping before he gave in.'

'Fuck me, Mo. The poor fucker doesn't realize he's in thrall to Mata Hari herself.'

'Thanks, Jim. I'll take that as a compliment.'

'It was meant. But tell me, how do you delude a man like that – hardly someone with the looks of a Hollywood star – into believing that you find him attractive?'

'That's easy. Ask his girlfriends: power, Jimmy. Power is irresistible. Henry Kissinger, who resembles a cheap garden gnome, said women started to throw themselves at him when he became US Secretary of State. He said that power is the ultimate aphrodisiac.'

'So, do you find the Brigadier attractive?'

'Kind of; he certainly has an aura about him.'

'But I thought you said he's a horrible monster?'

'He is, but that's different. But now's not the time for a discourse on female psychology.'

'OK, so then what happened?'

'It was difficult to get him out of the door, but I managed it with the promise of much greater delights to come.'

She looks at me like she's in front of her headmistress, who has just found out she's seduced the school grounds-man. I try to ease her sense of shame.

'Mo, I'm embarrassed. Here's me whining about the morality of what we're up to, and you're sucking up to the Godfather of the Ardoyne for the greater good.'

'Don't drown me in kindness, Jim. I'm just trying to get us both out of here in one piece.'

I put my hand on her shoulder and squeeze.

'Well done, partner. What now?'

'We wait for word from the Brigadier.' She looks me in the eye with an intensity that's unnerving. 'We have to be ready. Everything must be watertight: you, me, weapons, logistics, timing. It must run like a ticking clock, to the split second. Understood?'

'Completely.'

'And Kathleen. Thanks to you, we have to include her in it. She's our greatest liability and our greatest asset. She's central to our exit strategy.'

'Go on.'

'She has to be our cover. If we can make the Brigadier's exact time of death hard to determine, you and I must appear to have been with Kathleen, preferably in the Hibernian.'

We spend a couple of hours thinking of various scenarios which would allow us to carry out our orders, but without any questions being asked within the community. The key is to devise a plan that gives us an exit strategy out of the Ardoyne without anyone raising an eyebrow.

Maureen looks down at her coffee cup. It is still half full, but must be stone cold. She's lost in thought; her usual aura of supreme self-confidence has evaporated. In her dressing gown – pale-faced, hair dishevelled – she looks like a depressed suburban housewife.

'You alright, Mo?'

She snaps back to the here and now.

'Yeah, fine . . . just about. How about you?'

'I'm OK . . . just about . . .' I pause and look her in the eye. 'Are you sure you can pull the trigger when it comes to it? It's a big ask.'

'It is. The honest answer is, I don't know. But two things will make it happen: my training, and the thought of what he did to little Annie.'

'OK, good enough. But don't go in there unless you're certain you can do it.'

'Agreed. But listen, Jim, I don't want to go over old ground about the rights and wrongs of all this. Just tell me that you won't let me down. I can't do this without you.'

'Don't worry, Mo. You're the one putting yourself in harm's way. Of course I'll protect your back.'

26. Walking a Tightrope

It's the third week in August. The weather has been kind and the warm temperatures have taken a little of the edge off the confrontations in the city. But even good weather can't lift the spirits of the local community. The hunger strikers are still dying, three so far this month. Even some diehards are suggesting that Thatcher's cruel obduracy may be impossible to overcome and that the boys might be dying for nothing. There's a deepening despondency spreading through the little streets of the Ardoyne.

The wait for the Brigadier to send Maureen a message about the time and place of their intended tryst has taken far longer than we anticipated.

We are beginning to be concerned that our prey has got cold feet, but a letter arrives at the flat one morning and we get our explanation in a most surprising way. Handwritten in a neat and precise script, and presumably posted by the man himself, he apologizes for the delay, explaining that he's been waiting for someone to go on holiday. That's now happened and Maureen has been invited to an end-of-terrace house in Highbury Gardens. The rendezvous is 10 p.m., Friday night. The letter is short, but with a very sweet, childlike ending. It's signed 'S', with several kisses embellished by a very finely sketched four-leaf clover.

The next few days are an agony of anticipation, anxiety and fear.

The first spanner in the works is the news of Jimmy McKee's sudden release from prison in Dublin. At first, Kathleen wants to drive down to meet her father but, thankfully, he's already arranged transport and is home on Wednesday evening. Kathleen is thrilled that her daddy's back, of course, but the worry for Maureen and me is that the Ardoyne's other IRA big cheese is back in the community; not only that, but I happen to be living under the same roof as him.

A huge celebration is held in the Hibernian to welcome Jimmy home. Good news has been rare in the Ardoyne for several weeks and the mood is upbeat. However, the main topic of conversation, as it has been for several days, is the health of hunger striker Michael Devine, who is approaching the sixtieth day of his fast and is very close to death. If he dies, he will be the tenth protestor to do so.

Barry Kennedy's already had too much to drink and is arguing with the Brigadier. Their differences typify the split in the republican community.

'Sean, they're brave boys, so they are, and remind us of all the martyrs to the cause who've gone before them. Don't they make you proud of your kith and kin?'

'They do, Barry, but that's not the point. They're playing into Thatcher's hands. She's such a hard-nosed bitch, she doesn't care how many die; she'll stand her ground. It's a tactical disaster. The resolve of most of the families of the boys still alive is crumbling. They'll crack before she does, mark my words. Thatcher will then be an even bigger hero over the water than she is now. So where will we be then?'

'The strikers have won the sympathy of the world.'

'You don't win wars with sympathy, Barry. You have to defeat your enemy, and we're making ours stronger.'

Kathleen intervenes. For once, she challenges Barry, the man she admires so much.

'Sean's right. The families have had enough, and if they agree to the boys being fed, it'll be over. And the dead ones, God save their souls, will have died for nothing.'

'Not for nothing, Kathleen; for Ireland.'

Sean's temper rises.

'That's just nostalgia, Barry, no use to anyone!'

The three agree to differ and get back to the celebration of Jimmy's return. At least there's consensus on one thing; the British Prime Minister is reviled by everyone as the most wicked British oppressor of them all, even when compared to hated figures such as Cromwell and King Billy.

Even when the revelry becomes raucous in the Hibernian, Maureen wisely keeps her distance from the Brigadier. I watch the big man closely. Despite my reluctance, he's now my prey and I need to know the beast I'm about to hunt. He looks at Maureen many times, not with a leer but with a self-satisfied smile, like the big fat tomcat who's got the cream. I'm trying to dislike him enough to be party to his demise. I also watch Maureen closely. She's not exactly squirming with discomfort, but I can tell that she's ill at ease. Her eyes meet the Brigadier's only once, when she gives him the faintest of smiles – but alluring, nonetheless.

Kathleen notices the exchange as well.

'Did you see that, Jim?'

'What?'

'That glance between Maureen and Sean. There's something going on there.'

'You reckon?'

'Definitely.'

'You heard any gossip?'

'Yeah, there's lots of talk among the women that Sean's taken a fancy to Maureen and that she's game on.'

'You said that wouldn't go down too well.'

'It hasn't. You should tell her to be careful.'

'Surely Sean can protect her?'

'From the men, yes, but not necessarily from the women; "hell hath no fury" and all that.'

I wasn't there when Kathleen's father arrived at Herbert Street. So when he sees me, Jimmy comes over to say hello, Guinness in hand and clearly well inebriated.

'So how are you two lovebirds doing, then?'

'We're doing great, Jimmy, thanks. It's good to see you. You look well, they must have looked after you OK.'

'They did, Jim. Remember, I was in an Irish prison, not a British dungeon. Although the screws are not fond of the IRA, they're all republicans and have no time for the Brits.'

'So, you out for good?'

'I think so; the Garda couldn't make the charges stick.' He sits down beside us. 'Now then, Jim, I've got a couple of bones to pick with ye . . .' He adopts a severe demeanour. 'First, you get my daughter pregnant, then ye persuade her to run away to England with ye.'

I hesitate, not sure how serious he's being. Then he grins widely.

'Don't worry, Jim; I'm only kidding. I'm delighted for the both of youse. You make a fine couple, so you do.'

'Thanks, Jimmy; we're both very happy.'

Kathleen leans over and gives me a big kiss on the cheek. As she does so, several women nearby shriek their approval and some of the men raise their glasses. I take a deep breath. Jesus, Mo and I are walking such a tightrope here! The image of that French bloke who walked between New York's Twin Towers comes into my head. I look at Maureen and think that, like him, we're both crazy. I remember the guy doing a little jig in the middle of his walk.

That's what we're doing – dancing with death.

I suppose Kathleen's trying to be helpful, but she then proceeds to make matters much worse.

'Daddy, there's something ye should know. It may not be true, but I'm pretty sure Sean and Maureen are having a fling, or at least are about to start one.'

In an instant, Jimmy's demeanour changes from sunny to thunderous.

'Are ye kiddin' me?'

'No.'

'Jesus Christ, has he lost all reason? We all know Sean likes the ladies – but not Maureen, the local schoolteacher. She's a Brit, for fuck's sake.' He looks at me. 'Sorry, Jim, I know you're a Brit, but this is different.

194

Kath's not a senior member of the Provos!' He takes a big swig of his Guinness. 'Kathleen, are you absolutely sure?'

'Not absolutely, but I'd bet my last pound on it.'

Jimmy peers at me with a fearsome intensity I've not seen before.

'So do ye know anything about what your ex is up to?'

'No more than Kathleen, Jimmy. It's not my business any more.'

'Well, you'd better make it your business. Whatever's going on needs to stop – for both their sakes. There'd be a lot of jealousy and anger in the Ardoyne, and word would get back to the Army Council in the blink of an eye. And not even Sean's immune from the wrath of the Army Council.'

'There's already a lot of gossip, Daddy.'

'Then I'll talk to Sean in the morning. Jim, are ye able to talk to Maureen?'

'I think so.'

'Then do it tomorrow morning. If she wants still to be here after the summer holidays, then get her to understand that Sean Murphy's off limits . . .' He pauses and looks at Maureen. 'She's gorgeous; how does he do it? He's a big ugly fucker, but the ladies can't resist him.'

Maureen's stood at the bar, talking to a couple of mothers of her girls, and then glancing across at Sean, who, surrounded by his minders, is in his usual place close to the bar. Jimmy walks over to Sean's table as if he has the weight of the world on his shoulders.

Kathleen turns to me and puts her hand on my arm.

'Go and see her after breakfast in the morning and tell her the facts of life.'

'I'll try, Kath, but Maureen doesn't take kindly to being told what to do.'

'I understand that, but she could get herself into very hot water . . . and us.'

Thursday is even more tense than the day before.

It's only 9 a.m. but news has already swept through the Ardoyne that Michael Devine has just died. Another day of violence will follow. Today is also the day of the by-election in Fermanagh and South Tyrone. In an attempt to replace Bobby Sands, whose death in May caused the by-election, Sinn Féin activist Owen Carron is standing as the 'Anti-H-Block/Proxy Political Prisoner' candidate.

Following Sands' election, Thatcher has rushed through a new act of parliament, the Representation of the People Act, which specifically prevents serving prisoners from standing for election. However, the move may have back-fired in that it opens the door for Sinn Féin to become the vanguard for the republican political cause. If Carron wins tonight, a day of bitterness and violence will be followed by a night of joy and celebration. It's going to be a toxic twenty-four hours.

Maureen is very tense as I talk her through Jimmy McKee's reaction to the rumours about her and Sean.

'Why did Kathleen have to open her big mouth?'

'She's concerned, Mo, for everybody. It's under-standable.'

'Bugger! We only need another thirty-six hours.'

'I know, but let's turn it into a positive.'

'How? The risk is going up by the minute. Besides, what if Jimmy persuades the Brigadier to call tomorrow off?'

'I guess that's possible, but I doubt he's often dissuaded from doing what he wants. And you're a hell of a temptation, Mo.'

'I suppose that's meant to make me feel better.'

'Does it?'

She smiles for the first time.

'No.'

'OK, assuming the meet's still on, here's how we turn it to our advantage. I go back to Kathleen now and tell her that you've agreed to think about it. You need time to think, but you've agreed to have a drink with me in the city tomorrow night. I'll then tell her that we'll come to the Hibernian afterwards, by which time I'll have talked you round.'

'And how will you do that?'

'By telling you that having a fling with Sean would be a disaster; and not having one would be an equal disaster.'

'Why?'

'Because, besides making a fool of yourself, you fear Sean will be very upset that, having led him on, you then spurn him. So you don't want to be living in the Ardoyne having annoyed its Godfather.'

'And?'

'So you've decided to go back to England before next term. It fits perfectly.'

Maureen thinks for a while before answering.

'Not bad, Jimmy boy. Now what?'

'Let's rehearse our hit and exit strategy one more time. It's our last opportunity.'

'OK, and then I think I should catch the Brigadier's eye a couple of times in the Hibernian tonight – just to make sure he's still nibbling at the bait.'

'I suppose you must. I'll have to look the other way.'

27. Bad Friday

'So how're you doing?'

'OK, I suppose, other than the fact that we're surrounded by Red Indians and I'm about to shoot Sitting Bull right under the noses of his braves. Oh, and one more thing; I've never shot anyone before!'

'Let your training take over, Mo. Go into autopilot – and, remember, I'll have your back.'

Maureen is as tense as I've ever seen her. The noise and hubbub from a packed and very boisterous crowd in Kelly's Cellars isn't helping her mood. Owen Carron has been elected to succeed Bobby Sands and there are celebrations in every republican watering hole in the city.

But there's no alcohol for us tonight; not until the deed is done.

We rehearse and rehearse every detail of our plan and repeat it to one another.

'OK, so, no comms. We're doing it the old-fashioned way: stealth, silence, speed, severity. I'll have my silenced Browning in my handbag; you'll have yours in your belt holster. We'll both be wearing new clothes that no one will have seen before. You'll have a baseball cap, jeans and hooded jacket. I'll be in jeans and a bomber jacket, heavily made-up like a cheap tart and wearing a bottle-blonde wig. Thankfully, by ten p.m., it'll be dark, so it will be almost impossible to recognize us, even at close quarters.'

I repeat the next part.

'The distance between the house in Highbury Gardens and our flat in Estoril Park is a round trip of only nine hundred yards. It's then only another five hundred yards to the Hibernian. So, we've plenty of time to return our weapons to our armoury, lose our disguises and change our clothes. Then we relax in the club, establish our alibi with Kathleen and Jimmy, and get rat-arsed.'

'Not too rat-arsed.'

'If we pull this off, try stopping me!'

'OK, I think we're ready, Jimmy.'

'If you are, I am.'

'I'm as ready as I'll ever be.' She looks at the clock above the bar. 'Come on, let's go; time to rock 'n' roll.'

As we get ready in our flat, there's no conversation. The only noises are the rustles, snaps and clicks of our meticulous preparations.

As it should, our training's taking over. Like automatons in a science fiction movie, we're robotic in our movements. It takes us almost thirty minutes to prepare, and by 10 p.m. we're walking up Estoril Park towards our target.

Maureen has decided to be ten minutes late: a) because it's what she'd do if the tryst was for real, and b) because it will ensure the Brigadier is already inside the love nest.

'What if he doesn't show, Jim?'

'He'll show, trust me.'

'Why so sure?'

'You're the most desirable creature he's ever met, that's why.'

'But Jimmy will have told him the facts of life – about word getting back to the Provos' Army Council, and all that.'

'Relax, Mo; he'll be there.'

'OK . . . OK . . . I'm just shitting myself, that's all.'

'Training, Mo, training; switch to auto.'

'I will, I will. No more talking. Let's get this done so we can go home to England.'

When we reach the bottom end of Highbury Gardens, we can see a dark blue Vauxhall Astra parked outside the last house on the left. There's a shape in the driver's seat and the outline is far too slim for it to be the Brigadier. The elbow of the occupant is protruding out of the open window and cigarette smoke is wafting into the air.

After squeezing Maureen's arm and giving her a reassuring nod, I cross over to the opposite side of the road, to the corner of the junction, and take out a packet of cigarettes. I hate fags, but I have to have a reason to stop there.

In case the Brigadier has positioned a backup to the man in the Vauxhall, I peer in every direction and check all the windows and doors I can see. Except for a single tabby tomcat on the prowl and a dog barking in the distance, there's no sign of life; just a few lights on in some of the houses and the flicker of tellies in their living rooms. There are the usual muffled sounds of confrontations in the distance, probably on the Crumlin Road, but nothing particularly untoward. Most people are either in the Hibernian or in the city.

As Maureen turns into the narrow walled drive in front of number 78, the goon in the Astra turns his head to watch her.

The front door is slightly ajar. Maureen pushes it open and walks in. I check my watch: it's 10.11 and 20 seconds.

By the numbers, Mo: stealth, silence, speed, severity.

Leaning on a garden wall, I pull on my cigarette, which nearly makes me retch, and watch the seconds ticking round.

It's 10.12, plus 10 seconds.

We're fifty seconds in; Maureen will be out soon.

Two double taps: two in the chest, two in the head, just to be sure. It doesn't take long. Then take a deep breath, check for a pulse and walk out calmly: sixty seconds, max.

It's now 10.13; something's wrong!

I walk towards the Astra. As I do, Maureen appears at the front door. There must be an issue with the kitchen door. She's walking out just like she walked in – nonchalantly, like a true professional.

The goon in the Astra is suddenly galvanized. He grabs the door release handle. My adrenalin has been pumping for most of the day; now it's surging like a mill race. He's going to get out of his car. This is not good. I need to slot him before he moves. We'd planned that Maureen leave via the kitchen door to avoid the minder, but if he became a problem he'd be tapped at the wheel so that I could push him into the footwell, out of sight. With no street lighting left in the Ardoyne, he probably wouldn't be seen until the morning.

I move quickly to get level with his window. Then time slows down and I feel as if I'm hovering above myself. Everything's happening in slow motion. In a long fluid arc, I see myself pull out my weapon, bringing it to rest against the temple of my victim.

To my horror, although I don't know his name, I recognize him immediately; I've seen him in the Hibernian many times. He's not one of the Brigadier's more menacing, older lieutenants. This one's the pasty-faced, acne-pitted kid who's always fidgeting and ill at ease. I've always assumed he's the son of a senior Provo commander who's only in the Brigadier's entourage because his daddy's fixed it for him.

He begins to turn his head towards me. The look of terror on his youthful face chills me to the bone. He's some mother's son, some nice girl's boyfriend, probably harmless, and I bet he's never used in anger the handgun hidden under his seat.

Despite my revulsion, I don't hesitate. An elite military training teaches you to do two contradictory but powerful things: react instinctively, but with precision and control. I pull the trigger, slowly and firmly. Muffled by the silencer, the bullet farts as it bores a small hole in the side of the young man's head. It's a neat hole; there's no blood. It's almost surgical in its precision. On the other hand, the opposite side of his head explodes. Blood and brain matter are sprayed everywhere, making a shocking splash as they cascade across the inside of the windscreen.

His short life is over in an instant. All his memories, thoughts and feelings are extinguished forever. His brain and body are transformed from whatever it is that makes us sentient human beings into a carcass of dead meat. Spewing more gore as it lands, his head flops on to the passenger seat.

I still don't feel; I only see. As I'm conditioned to do, I put two more taps into the back of his head, just where the neck enters the cranium, destroying his cerebellum and severing his spinal cord. His head is now just pulp; his brain is like crimson scrambled eggs.

I open the car door and, taking care to avoid any bloody bits, use my foot to push his limp body into the footwell. I have to kick at him a bit as the gearstick gets in the way, but I soon make him disappear into the void at the bottom of the car. I close the door carefully and check the windscreen. In the gloom of night, it's hard to see the bloody smears on the inside.

Job done.

I'm still not feeling anything; I'm still watching a movie. I take two long, deep breaths. Once again, I look at all the doors and windows that I checked along Highbury Gardens and Etna Drive.

All is as it was; there's not a murmur, not a movement anywhere.

I see Maureen coming round the back of the car. She seems calm; she's breathing deeply. There's no hint of panic or anxiety as she leans towards me and, almost inaudibly, whispers in my ear.

'All done?'

'All done. You?'

'All done. Sorry you had to deal with the minder; the kitchen door was locked, no key. Let's take a stroll.'

Within minutes, we've stored our weapons, changed our clothes and cleaned ourselves up. Once again, we end the mission as we started it – in a silent ritual. It's only when we're walking to the Hibernian that we cease to act like robots and begin to speak. Suddenly, Maureen's body loses its rigid tension. She looks like she's had the weight of the world lifted from her shoulders.

'It nearly went tits up, Jim.'

'How?'

'When I walked in, the Brigadier was nowhere to be seen. I hesitated, thinking about a million frightening possibilities. Eventually, I called out. When he answered, I realized he was in the bath. He shouted to me to go up. He had lit candles and dimmed the lights in the bedroom. He was playing Barbra Streisand, "Woman In Love", on the stereo.'

'What a romantic!'

'Yeah, right! The bathroom door was half open, so I walked in, weapon in hand. It was a hell of a shock for both of us. He was covered in soapsuds, stark bollock naked, and also had his weapon in his hand. Thankfully, it wasn't a 9mm Browning!'

All sorts of extraordinary images jump into my head.

'Anyway, my weapon was a lot more potent than his.'

'And?'

'Let's just say, seeing him in that obscene pose made it easy. Two in the chest, two in the head. He's now face down on the bathroom floor, a fitting end for someone who's done what he's done.'

'Jesus, Mo, I hope to God I don't come up in front of you on Judgement Day!'

'Quite right! Be warned, Jimmy boy.'

She's on a high, of course. There are two kinds of reaction to what she and I have just done: morbid reflection born of guilt, or unashamed euphoria driven by adrenalin. Maureen's got the latter. I think I'm going to experience the former.

Even as I walk, I can see the petrified face of the boy in the Astra and the images of the revolting slaughter I inflicted on him. Maureen interrupts my brooding. She's still euphoric.

'Just the last chapter, Jim. Let's go over it again. You laid into me in the pub and convinced me what a fool I've been with Sean. I'm acutely embarrassed. Tomorrow morning I'll write a letter resigning from St Hilda's. I'll get the ferry home, probably on Sunday afternoon. I should probably say sorry to Sean, but will say I'm too ashamed, so I'll write to him via you and Kathleen. Your turn . . .'

Lost in thought again, I don't answer. I'm beginning to feel very fragile. My hands are shaking. I have to go home with Kathleen tonight, and I'm sure that she'll be feeling horny; she always is. That thought makes me feel even worse. I want to go home with Maureen. I'm not sure why, but I'm feeling weak and cowardly. I've just done something I'll regret for the rest of my life; I'd give anything to curl up beside her and draw on her strength.

What a prat I've been. Having decided that it was wrong to kill the Brigadier because I didn't believe he was the monster the intel said he was, I've murdered a lad who was probably as innocent as anyone can be in the mire of Northern Ireland.

'Jim, you OK?'

'Just a bit shaken. I assumed his minder would be one of the ones you wouldn't want to meet on a dark night, but it was that quiet one who looked like he wouldn't say boo to a goose.'

'Sorry, Jim. Sorry I couldn't get out at the back. Not very pleasant?'

'No, it wasn't.'

'As you told me, let your training take over.'

'I did, that's why there's a lump of cold meat in the bottom of a Vauxhall Astra. But there's no training that helps with the way I feel now.'

'I understand, but you've got to stay strong; the op's not over yet. Come on, take me through your part of our exit strategy.'

Very reluctantly, I recite my lines like a catechism.

'I'll stay with Kathleen until it's time to leave for our jobs in London. You'll square everything with Gower Street and tell them what our exit strategy needs to be. I'll go to Belfast Det HQ in ten days' time to hear the feedback from London. Then we'll take it from there.'

28. Facing the Music

This is the worst bit. After the most traumatic moments in our lives, we have to walk into the Brigadier's lair and act as if nothing's happened. I'm absolutely terrified. Right now, it's as if my uniquely demanding training is no more exacting than the tests to become a Boy Scout. I hope I don't look as frightened as I feel. On the other hand, Maureen, although she looks a little pale, appears remarkably calm.

When we arrive at the Hibernian, despite his anger when he first heard about Maureen and the Brigadier, Jimmy is very gentle with her. He finds her a chair and gets one of the bar staff to bring over some drinks.

'So, yousuns have had a heart to heart, have ye?'

I draw in a deep breath and Maureen takes a deep draught of Guinness.

'We have, Jimmy. Jim has read me the riot act and I think I've come to my senses.'

Kathleen smiles at me; the relief on her face is all too plain to see. Jimmy looks delighted.

'That's good news, Maureen. It can all be forgotten now.'

'I wish it was that easy, Jimmy. Too many people know, or have their suspicions.'

'Perhaps, but it'll all be forgotten in a few weeks.'

'No, it won't, and you know it . . .'

She pauses and looks at Kathleen and Jimmy. There's a silence that screams that there's a bombshell coming.

'I've decided to go home. I'm too embarrassed to stay.'

Kathleen looks astonished.

'That's a bit sudden. What about St Hilda's? The girls are very fond of you.'

'I know, and I'm very fond of them. But now I realize what an idiot I've been, I couldn't look them in the eye – quite apart from their mothers.'

Kathleen and her father look at one another.

Are they buying this?

Kathleen furrows her brow.

'So when are you leaving?'

'As soon as possible. I'm going to try to get a ferry tomorrow.'

'Really, that quickly?'

'The sooner the better, Kath.'

Jimmy looks concerned.'

'So, Sean knows?'

'Not yet.'

'But I thought ye were seeing him tonight?'

Jimmy's words are like a dagger into the heart. The game's up; we're toast!

Maureen looks like I feel, but she manages to blurt out a brilliant answer.

'How do you know? That was supposed to be between Sean and me.'

'He told me when I tried to get him to see sense. He wouldn't tell me where, because he probably knew I'd come and spoil the party.'

'So did you persuade him to change his mind?'

'No, he told me to fuck off and mind my own business.'

He gives Maureen a look that I've never seen him give before. It would shatter stone.

'So why didn't ye meet him?'

Their exchange has given me time to think.

'I told her not to go.'

Jimmy snaps at me with a ferocity that I've not witnessed before.

'Why?'

'Because I assumed Sean would be angry when she told him and thought it best if she wasn't alone with him.'

'What do ye mean by that? Sean's a soldier, a man of honour. He'd never hurt anyone unless they were a military enemy.'

Then, anxiety leads me to say something that's probably unwise.

'But what about his reputation?'

'What do you mean, "reputation" . . .?' He pauses and scrutinizes me like he's interrogating a known criminal. 'Have youse been listening to British propaganda?'

Jimmy looks at me even more intensely. Is he beginning to put two and two together? I'm feeling sick to my stomach. I'm a quick runner, so is Maureen. I just want to run, but I know I have to answer.

'Well, I've heard a couple of rumours.'

'From who?'

'A couple of teachers I met in the city at an in-service seminar. We went for a drink afterwards.'

'Who were they?'

'I can't remember now, just two colleagues from another school.'

'They'll have been loyalists for sure. For fuck's sake, Jim, that's RUC propaganda. They've been spreading that filth for months. He's a womanizer, not a psychopath. None of it's true. I bet they said he assaulted a child. One of Kathleen's girls. That he did horrible things; fuck me, it's all a pack of lies.'

He looks at Kathleen, who swallows hard and looks at the floor.

'Tell them, Kathleen.'

'It's an awful story; impossible to imagine that it could happen, but it did.'

Kathleen tries to compose herself with a hefty swig of Guinness.

'Just over a year ago, a wee girl, no more than fourteen, was repeatedly raped by her own father over a weekend. Some of his friends from down south, including two women, were there and watched the whole thing. The mother, a pathetic creature herself, was away.'

Her voice is breaking and she has to take another drink.

'The RUC wouldn't do anything; the mother was too frightened to say anything, and the girl too traumatized. So the man was walking free right here in the Ardoyne; everyone was worried for their children. There was a lot of soul-searching in the community. Eventually, Sean had him executed. No brutality, mind; it was done like an official execution. He was blindfolded and they put a single bullet in the back of his head. His friends ran for their lives before we could get them and never came back. There wasn't a single person in the community who didn't think Sean had done the right thing.' Tears form in Kathleen's eyes. 'What else could we do?'

Maureen's face turns from pale to deathly white and she begins to shake.

'Did you know the girl?'

'Yes, I'm the one she told. I pleaded with the RUC to do something, but they refused.'

'What reason did they give?'

Kathleen almost spits out her answer.

'They said that if we wanted to run our own community in the Ardoyne, then we'd have to clean up our own shite.'

Maureen's emotions begin to boil. The trembling fear on her face has been replaced by an ever-deepening expression of horror.

Kathleen continues.

'Anyway, not long after, the story starts to circulate that Sean was the rapist and that when the father challenged him, Sean murdered him. Can you believe that?'

Maureen gulps hard.

'What happened to the girl?'

'She's OK. She lives with one of Sean's women, who takes good care of her. But she'll never get over it. I won't tell you her name, but she's in one of your classes.'

Maureen knows exactly who the girl is, of course, because those SB bastards we met in Madden's told us. Now we're hearing a completely different version of events. I can't imagine what Maureen must be feeling. We've both been duped into inflicting a terrible injustice on a community that has taken us to their hearts.

I glance at Maureen. She's beginning to lose it. Her head's on her chest and she's beginning to heave. Jimmy has no inkling about the real cause of her trauma. He just thinks she's a silly girl who's made a lot of trouble for everyone. Kathleen puts her hand on Maureen's arm.

'Maureen, Sean's a hard man, but he's a good man. We all look up to him. He's been silly with you, but you're an attractive woman. There've been a few feathers ruffled, but they'll calm down. Talk to him; you owe him that.' Kathleen then turns to me. 'As for you, Jim Dowd, you should be ashamed of yourself. Is that why you kept asking me about Sean, because of what you heard in a fucking pub?'

'Yes, I suppose it is. They didn't mention rape, but I was worried. We're living in his domain, after all.'

'Well, you should thank your lucky stars it's his domain. If it wasn't for Sean and his men, the Ardoyne would be a waste ground and all of us would be on the streets.'

Maureen begins to cry.

'I've had enough of this. I need to go home.' She looks at Kathleen imploringly. 'Do you mind if Jim takes me home?'

'Course not. I'll come with you. We'll have a drink and get you to bed.'

A great ploy, Mo, but it hasn't quite worked!

Jimmy nods his approval and we get up to leave. Then Jimmy calls over the Brigadier's praetorian guard. You don't have to be a mind-reader to know that he'll be despatching them to find their leader. Let's hope he was telling the truth when he said he didn't know where the rendezvous with Maureen was going to happen. He must assume it's the home of one of his women. The Ardoyne's a tiny place. It won't take them long to scour the entire enclave. We've got fifteen minutes at most to make our escape, perhaps less. Not only that, Jimmy knows exactly where we're going.

There's one grain of comfort. He hasn't yet added two and two together and made four. Otherwise, he wouldn't have let Kathleen come with us. But what the fuck do we do with her! She doesn't deserve any of this. What kind of ignominy am I about to pile on top of ignominy?

As we walk along Estoril Park, my mind is trying to calculate like a chess master. If we make this move, then this happens; but if we make an alternative play, then there'll be that consequence, then this, then that, then . . . My brain begins to ache. My pounding heart is making it impossible for me to think clearly. I can only pray that Maureen's superior intellect is thinking multiple moves ahead. Please God, she'll know exactly what to do when we get to the flat.

Despite her distress, Maureen's still acting like a clear-thinking pro. She walks along briskly, but not with any hint of panic. I'm like a greyhound in its trap; all I want to do is run like buggery! Eventually, we reach the momentary sanctuary of the tiny home that Maureen and I once shared. Kathleen knows where the Jameson's is and pours three glasses. Maureen thanks her and moves towards the bedroom.

'Thanks, Kath. I'm just going to get changed.'

Kathleen sits down with her back to the bedroom door, gulps a big mouthful of her whiskey and releases a deep sigh.

'Bloody hell, Jim. I can't believe this is happening.'

'Neither can I.'

Kathleen continues to talk, mainly about the Brigadier

and how she feels sorry for him. I can tell that she thinks Maureen's been a stupid bitch.

As she speaks, Maureen appears behind Kathleen with a roll of grey duct tape in her hand. She hasn't changed; she's still fully dressed. Instantly, I know what's expected of me. As Maureen pulls a long piece of tape from the roll, I get up and put my hands on Kathleen's shoulders. She hears the unfamiliar sound of stretching tape and the alien focus in my eyes. A look of bewilderment forms on her face, then a scream begins in her throat, but my hand is at her mouth before any sound can pass her lips.

As Maureen wraps the tape across her mouth, Kathleen's face becomes a contortion of confusion, fear and hatred. Despite the gag, I know what she's trying to say: 'Jim, why?'

Her head shakes; her eyes flood with pools of tears. They cascade down her face and trickle over the tape that is preventing her from damning me to hell and back. She struggles and fights like a trapped animal, but we're too strong for her and she's soon taped to her chair like an Egyptian mummy.

I look at my watch. It's been eight minutes since we left the Hibernian. We're on the edge. This is no-man's-land. They may have found the Brigadier, they may not; but the odds are stacking up against us with every second. Maureen seems to have gone into shock; her hands are quivering and she's not breathing easily.

I assume command.

'Mo, get the comms out, call in: emergency evac. Crumlin Road, now. Five minutes, max. Break out the Brownings, leave everything else.'

215

As Maureen goes to make the comms call, I pull Kathleen and the chair to the kitchen sink and wrap yards of tape from the chair to the taps.

'Mo, ready?'

She can barely speak, so just nods that she's ready.

I kneel in front of Kathleen.

'I know you'll never forgive me. Falling for you was a huge mistake, but I couldn't help myself. I'm so sorry.'

I can see Kathleen pursing her lips. She thrusts her head forward; she's trying to spit in my face. I look at my watch. Nearly eleven minutes have elapsed; we have to go. I take one last look at the Angel of the Ardoyne. She's writhing and squirming, trying to loosen her bonds. She shakes her head violently in a vain attempt to bellow screams at me.

Maureen tugs at my arm.

'Jim, let's go!'

At the top of the stairs, I take one last look. The hatred in Kathleen's eyes is a picture from hell I will remember for the rest of my life. I know now it will be a daily haunting that, no matter what else happens in my life, will be the last thing I see as I take my final breath.

We bolt down the stairs, but stop at the bottom to check the road. It seems clear. There's no point in a pretence of normality now, so we fly out of the door and start to run towards the Crumlin Road. Our rendezvous should be the pedestrian triangle where the Ardoyne Road meets the Crumlin.

It's only a little over a hundred yards – fifteen seconds to safety!

Everything's quiet as we sprint down the road, our

rhythmic breaths pumping bursts of mist into the night air like a steam engine. The frenzied thumps of our long strides strike the tarmac like beats of a drum. But we've only travelled thirty yards when we hear the roar of two cars hurtling up Estoril Park. We look behind us. Two pairs of main-beam headlights blind our eyes. Our pursuers will reach us before we reach our sanctuary.

I turn and take up a firing stance.

'Mo, keep going!'

I check the street. The moon's approaching its third quarter and is quite bright. I can see a handful of people walking on both sides of the road. So I can't aim at the tyres; the ricochets could go anywhere and harm the civilians. I have to aim at the windscreen. Maureen appears beside me. She adopts the standard firing stance and we each release four rapid rounds at the lead car. At least one shot shatters the screen. The car swerves wildly before mounting the pavement, demolishing a garden wall. We concentrate on the second car and pump four rounds into it. One smashes into the radiator grill and the other three hit the windscreen. The car screeches to a halt in the middle of the road. Four men dive from it and make for cover. Another four have clambered from the lead car and crouched behind the rubble of the wall. The scene is illuminated by the cars' headlights and, from his baseball cap and burly outline, I can see that one of the men is Jimmy McKee.

We have a choice to make: take cover, get involved in a firefight and pray that someone will come to our aid; or make a run for it. The problem with the second option is that there's almost no cover between us and the Ardoyne

Road. I can see weapons being raised. They're only sixty yards away; we're sitting ducks!

'Mo, let's move!'

Thank God, we can both run. There are two parked cars on the left-hand side of Estoril Park that offer some cover. Also, just before it meets the Ardoyne Road, the street dog-legs a little to the left. We have about forty yards of perilous exposure to navigate before we reach the safety of the bend. Let's hope they can't hit a barn door at ten paces.

Using the cars as a shield, we weave our way up the road like Olympic sprinters. Bullets ping everywhere: tarmac, cars, brick walls. They whistle past us more than once; but none strikes us. Maureen reaches the safety of the bend first and scans the area like a radar beacon.

For once, thanks to Owen Carron's election victory, there's no rioting. The area is clear of pedestrians. The firing has made everyone run for cover, but the Crumlin Road traffic seems to be running normally for a Friday night. Maureen turns to me with a look of terror on her face.

'Where's the fucking wheels, Jim!'

'They'll be here, don't worry.'

Knowing that at least half a dozen Provos will be sprinting towards us, we run across the triangle so that we can look up and down the Crumlin Road. There's no sign of a rescue vehicle, either Army or RUC!

I take a quick decision; we're going to hijack the next decent-looking set of wheels. So, with Maureen in my wake, I run north into the oncoming traffic.

'Mo, raise your weapon, I'm stopping that black cab.'

As I raise my hands high in the air, directly in front of the taxi, the driver swerves and accelerates to go round me, but Maureen fires a single shot into the air. The round makes the driver slam on his brakes and the taxi screeches to a halt.

I raise my weapon and bellow at the driver.

'Leave it running and get out!'

In fear for his life, the driver, his beer belly wobbling like a jelly, makes a pathetic attempt at a sprint as he runs towards the petrol station on the opposite side of the road. He doesn't get far; a bullet bounces off the tarmac and smashes into his leg, spewing blood everywhere. Hollering expletives, he collapses on to the road and rolls like a barrel.

'Mo, you drive!'

I turn and fire most of the rounds remaining in my magazine at the knot of men who have appeared behind us. I take care to aim just above their heads; even though they're intent on our elimination, I don't want any more blood on my hands. My shots make our pursuers scatter for cover.

Maureen does a three-point turn in the blink of an eye and the taxi skids to a halt right next to me. As I move to dive into the passenger compartment, two olive-green British Army Pigs approach at high speed. They're level with us in moments. As Maureen and I run round to the rear door of the nearest one and dive in, several squaddies open fire from the second one.

Within seconds, we're heading towards the city at speed, bullets bouncing off the heavy armour of our olive-green cocoon. Our rescuers are men from 2 Para, good lads in a crisis.

I get my breath and smile at the young officer in command.

'Good of you to turn up!'

'You're lucky we got here at all. It's kicking off big time in Short Strand.'

'What took you so long?'

'These boys were about to go off-duty when you called; they've been at it since first thing this morning, so thank your lucky stars. What are you two up to, anyway?'

Maureen answers in that way of hers.

'Don't ask; just take us to Palace Barracks, in double quick time!'

'Alright, keep your wool on, missus.'

'It's "ma'am" to you, Lieutenant . . . What's your name, by the way?'

'Sorry, ma'am; it's Winfield.'

'Very well, Palace Barracks, Lieutenant Winfield, pronto. My colleague's also your superior officer, so mind your Ps and Qs.'

It's not true, of course, but it makes me smile as we cross the city in silence. Maureen and I glance at one another from time to time as we slowly come to terms with what's just happened.

Then she breaks the silence.

'I think we need to pay a visit to RUC HQ in the morning.'

'Agreed.'

29. Knock Road

When we get to Palace Barracks, we say nothing about ourselves or our operation, except to quote our security code greeting, *Is Botham Batting?* After making several telephone calls that get him nowhere, an infuriated duty officer agrees to our demand to get the adjutant out of the officers' mess. A Scots Guards officer, Captain Collingwood – a man who embodies all the pomposity the name of that august regiment implies – is not happy when he arrives.

'So who the bloody hell are you two comedians?'

I leave it to Maureen to respond; she speaks his language.

'Det, Captain, and this is not a comedy routine – far from it.'

'And?'

'That's it, Captain.'

'What do you mean, "that's it"?'

'That's all we can tell you.'

'Name and rank and the nature of your op, or I'll have you put back on the Crumlin Road.'

'No, you won't. The DG, MI5 would not be very amused.'

The adjutant pauses, his ace trumped.

'You cloak-and-dagger types drive me crazy. Who the fuck do you think you are!'

'Serving soldiers, just like you. And by the way, I'm going to stop calling you "Captain" until you behave like a gentleman officer. Have you forgotten what you were taught at Sandhurst?'

'What do you know about Sandhurst?'

'Not much, except they taught us girlies exactly the same at Bagshot. The difference is, I haven't forgotten my training . . . or my manners.'

'Listen to me, whoever you are. As you're refusing to give me your names, I'm going to have you detained until you do.'

I've had enough of this! I walk up to the archetypally tall guardsman, stick my nose close to his chin and give him what's called the Para's Stare.

'No, you listen to me, you leery twat. I'm only an NCO but, in my regiment, that's out of order. So, if you don't behave yourself, I'll knock your fucking block off!'

The adjutant, his second ace trumped, looks at both of us. Realizing that Det operatives are usually SAS, he decides that discretion is the better part of valour and backs down.

'So why haven't you gone back to your unit?'

Maureen answers.

'Because we don't have one. We're not operating out of Det Belfast. We came straight from MI5 London at the beginning of the year. Except for one emergency visit to Det HQ in April, we've had almost no contact with anyone here since then.'

'That's a new one on me; what will they think of next!' He relaxes and goes towards the telephone. 'Who do you need to speak to here?'

'No one, we just need wheels to RUC HQ in the morning.'

'So why did you come here?'

'Safety – we're in a hell of a bind.'

He calls in his duty officer.

'Transport for these two tomorrow morning, as soon as it can be arranged.' He then turns to us. 'Anything else?'

'Two drinks each on your tab in the mess. We'll send you a cheque!'

He looks horrified, but barks another order.

'See to it, Maclean. Escort them to the mess, then get them a bed for the night.'

Maureen corrects the order.

'Two beds!'

After hatching our plan until 1 a.m. in Palace Barracks' Officers' Mess, at six the following morning, we're rudely awakened by several members of the Parachute Regiment, who storm into our rooms like gangs of thugs. They use considerable force, ignore our protestations, confiscate our weapons and march us to a couple of cells used for prisoner interrogation.

The doors are locked and we're incarcerated for the rest of the day. A tray of food arrives at midday, but for the rest of the time we're ignored. By the time we're released, early in the evening, steam is coming out of our ears, but, fortunately for him, Captain Collingwood is nowhere to be seen.

Instead, we're shown to the office of the CO, a Colonel Grierson, a very polite infantry officer who apologizes profusely for having us locked up for the day. He explains that the 'MoD in London' had insisted that we be detained until our credentials were checked and our story verified by Gower Street.

He offers us dinner in the mess, guarantees a fine repast and assures us that the regimental cellar is second to none. The old boy obviously assumes that we're both officers and I decide not to mention my lowly NCO status. We accept readily; at least the day's solitary confinement has allowed us to calm down a little. We put our revenge mission on hold for a few hours and spend the evening enjoying Grierson's hospitality. Our operation is not discussed, and no questions are asked at the table, but, as we leave, the Colonel pulls us to one side and asks us to join him for a digestif in the bar.

'My adjutant told me that you were pulled off the Crumlin Road in something of a predicament, that you were in civvies, but not operating out of a base in Belfast?'

Maureen and I look at one another. We have to be careful. This is more Maureen's realm than mine; I let her answer.

'That's correct, sir.'

'So you're 14 Intelligence, but not based here?'

'That's also correct, sir.'

He then looks me in the eye, but with a benign, almost paternal expression.

'And you're 22, seconded to Det.'

'Yes, sir, but I'm actually 21.'

'Isn't this all a bit odd?'

To my relief, Maureen answers.

'How do you mean, sir?'

'Well, two Det operatives with no operational base here – and one of them from a reserve regiment.'

'All we can tell you, sir, is that we both fitted very particular criteria for the op – the details of which must, I'm afraid, remain with us.'

'I see. Well, it's a new one on me. I suppose I should mind my own business, then . . .' He pauses and smiles. 'Get yourselves another tipple on my tab, and get some rest. I hear you're off to Knock Road tomorrow. I won't ask why.'

At breakfast the next morning, Grierson appears again and comes over to us. He waves away our attempts to get up and salute, and sits down next to us.

'Mind your backs at Knock Road today and make sure you know who your friends are when you get back to London. There are things blowing in the wind at the moment that are not to my liking, and you two seem to be caught up in them.'

I'm pleasantly surprised by his comment.

'They're not to our liking either, sir.'

He looks at us like a worried father.

'Let me quote George Washington, a man I much admire, a great soldier and an equally great politician: "Government is not reason. Government is not eloquence. It is force. And, like fire, it is a dangerous servant and a fearful master."'

After breakfast, we meet with a sympathetic intelligence officer who Colonel Grierson sends to see us. He tells us which department of RUC Special Branch we need to ask for.

At 11 a.m. we're pulling into RUC HQ on Knock Road, a relatively leafy part of Protestant East Belfast. We request 'E3A, Intelligence Division, Republican Groups' and are waved through security.

Sadly, given that our mood puts murder high on our agenda, we have to relinquish our weapons. It takes more than thirty minutes of walking along labyrinthine corridors and negotiating an interminable series of byzantine security procedures before we think we have finally arrived at the office of the man we seek.

After keeping us waiting for almost twenty minutes, when he walks in our quarry has a crown and a pip on the epaulette of his dark green uniform. That makes him a Chief Superintendent, not quite the rank we were hoping for – we wanted an Assistant Chief Constable, as a minimum – but he'll have to do.

Folder under his arm, he goes behind his desk. We remain seated. Our presence doesn't make his hackles rise as we'd hoped, which would have made it easier to begin a confrontation. Instead, he nods at his juniors to leave the room. Then he speaks to us in a very guttural Belfast drawl.

'I've been reading the reports. You got out by the skin of your teeth, but mission accomplished. The Ardoyne has gone berserk, but we can live with that. Well done, you two!'

I begin the interrogation calmly.

'There was nothing in the papers today, we checked. How will it be reported?'

'It'll be all over the news tonight. A loyalist assassination. One of our informers on the inside has just called in. There's a meeting in the Hibernian tonight, which will be chaired by Jimmy McKee. It's expected he'll take over as OC 3rd Brigade . . .' He pauses and attempts a paternalistic smile. 'By the way, I'm sorry it got a bit tricky with the McKee girl.'

I look at Maureen. This is a cool customer, that's for

sure. Riled by his mock sympathy, I fire our opening volley at him.

'Who were the two goons you sent to meet us in Madden's?'

'What's that got to do with anything?'

Maureen fires the broadside.

'Because they're a pair of low-life, lying bastards, that's why!'

'Steady, Townsend, remember where you are and who you're talking to.'

Maureen gets to her feet, places her hands on his desk and leans towards him menacingly.

'I know exactly who I'm talking to. You're also a lying bastard, but you're a real piece of work: you're an evil, murdering, lying bastard!'

Suddenly realizing that we mean business, the Chief Super begins to push himself out of his chair. But I'm at his back in a blur of movement and put him in a headlock. He's a big bugger, but he's sitting down and it doesn't look like he's done any exercise for years. He tries to push me upwards and backwards, but I have his throat locked against my forearm and my other hand at the back of his head, forcing it against my tightening grip. I push his legs further under his desk, making it even more difficult for him to wriggle. He tries to shout out, but I jam my hand over his mouth. He starts to go puce.

Maureen takes the belt off her jeans and uses it to secure his upper arms to the back of his chair. Now we have him where we want him.

Sitting on the edge of his desk, she smiles at him in a way that says, 'Now I'm about to hurt you.' She then picks up a pencil from his desk and rams its sharpened point up his nose.

He struggles like a mackerel in the bottom of a boat, but I just tighten my grip.

Maureen begins the inquisition.

'Tell us about Sean Murphy, the intel brief. How much of it was concocted by your department?'

I release my grip a little so that he can splutter an answer.

'None of it; it's all genuine.'

I intervene in the interrogation.

'You're fucking lying. Whose tune are you dancing to – Westminster's? Or are they dancing to yours?'

Instead of answering, he makes an almighty effort to free his mouth from my grip and shout for help. Maureen pushes the pencil even further up his nostril until he yelps in pain.

Seconds later, two junior officers burst into the room. They stop dead in their tracks when they see their boss's predicament.

There's little reason to continue our inquisition; we're unarmed and surrounded by an entire building of policemen, all of them armed. We've made our point. I relax my grip and Maureen unties his arms.

Our prey is embarrassed and angry and takes a while to compose himself.

'London told me that you're a thug, Waddington, but I expected more of you, Townsend.'

Maureen hisses back at him.

'And we expected to be deployed on a legitimate op, not a political assassination!'

'You two have a lot to learn. This is a war zone, and our

enemy is a bunch of murdering bastards. It's our job to defeat them with all the means at our disposal, including operatives like you two.'

I begin to seethe again.

'But you're no better than they are!'

'That's a matter of opinion. But what really matters is who wins the war, and getting rid of Sean Murphy is a big victory.'

'And what about the young lad I shot?'

'Caught in the crossfire, Waddington.' He shakes his head dismissively. 'I always knew it was a mistake to put two fucking left-footers into the Ardoyne. Never trust a Mick, even an English Mick! You've obviously gone native. All that "British oppression" bollocks, you've fallen for it, haven't you?'

I hate this callous bastard. If I had a weapon, instead of a pencil, I'd definitely put a bullet up his nose.

'You've no idea what I think, you bastard. But what's certain is that men like you are the problem, not the solution. I hope you can sleep at night.'

Maureen, who has finished putting her belt back on, moves towards the door.

'Come on, Jim, let's go.'

The two junior officers block her way. I suddenly realize how easy it would be for these buggers to terminate us and dump us in an alleyway.

Maureen turns and looks at the man who has been pulling our strings for months.

'There's transport waiting for us outside. It's arranged by Colonel Grierson, CO, Palace Barracks. We have to be on a Hercules out of Aldergrove in two hours' time. We're expected at Gower Street for a debrief at eighteen hundred hours.'

The RUC man ponders for a moment before nodding at his men to step aside.

As we leave, he tries to have the last word.

'Make sure you hide yourselves where no one can find you. There are some very angry people in the Ardoyne, and they're sure to come looking for you.'

We don't bother to answer. He's not worth the breath.

Later that day, our Hercules, full of squaddies going back to Brize Norton, banks as it crosses the city. We can see the linear streets of Belfast in the distance. We know we'll never see the Ardoyne again.

Inevitably, my thoughts turn to Kathleen. Not only have Maureen and I done a terrible thing in killing the Brigadier and his minder, I've also destroyed the life of a beautiful young woman and her unborn child – a child that's my flesh and blood.

There is no more adrenalin to keep me going. No amount of training can anaesthetize me against what my conscience is accusing me of. I feel myself unravel, physically and mentally.

My heart starts to race and my breathing becomes laboured. I clasp my hands between my thighs to try to stop them shaking. It doesn't do any good; my whole body is quivering with anguish. I begin to sob in contorted spasms.

Maureen puts her arms around my shoulders.

I hear her saying, 'Jim, it's OK. We're on our way home, it's OK.'

I'm fairly sure I reply, saying that I don't want to go

home. I see Maureen's face; she's frowning at me, a portrait of anxiety.

I look down the two rows of passengers on either side of the Hercules' fuselage. They're all staring at me. Some are concerned, some are embarrassed; a few are hostile.

Their faces begin to blur.

Then the lights go out.

30. Stony Silence

Gower Street is very quiet.

It's very late when I finish my story. I'm exhausted; it's been a marathon of detail and an unexpurgated baring of my heart and soul. My audience must be even more fatigued than I am. Maureen is smiling at me warmly. But of the senior MI5 figures only 'S' shows any empathy. The other three look sombre, giving nothing away.

Wank breaks the silence.

'Remind me how long were you hospitalized for after the flight from Aldergrove?'

'About six weeks in a psychiatric unit at the Duchess of Kent, in Catterick. I don't remember much of the first few weeks, I was in cloud cuckoo land on drugs. Then they transferred me to the Cambridge in Aldershot.'

'From which you discharged yourself in April of this year.'

'Correct.'

'Why?'

'Because I wanted to go to the Falklands.'

'Do you think you were in a fit state to do that?'

'Course. Probably would've got myself killed, but that would have solved all sorts of problems, wouldn't it?'

'When did the heavy drinking start?'

'After I got the envelope.'

Everyone in the room stares at me like voyeurs leering

at a peep show. This is taking me back to some very dark places.

'I was in a pub in Clapham when a lad walked in and came right up to me. He was in civvies, but was obviously a soldier. He said to me, "The CO thought you should have this." Then he just turned around and left. It was addressed: *Jim Dowd, aka British Intelligence Undercover Piece of Shit, c/o The Commanding Officer, SAS, Hereford.* The letter was posted in London and found its way to Stirling Lines. It didn't take Hereford long to find out who "Jim Dowd" was.'

Wank springs to his own defence.

'They didn't come to us.'

'I'm sure they went straight to Det Belfast.'

'What was in the letter?'

The question cuts into me like a scalpel. I'm feeling that unbearable pain again, the agony of intolerable loss. I'm going to regret this.

'Just a Polaroid.'

Maureen grabs me around the shoulders and hugs me tightly as I answer.

'A foetus ... covered in blood ... the most terrible thing I've ever . . .'

I don't finish the sentence; I can't. I find it hard to breathe. I'm reliving my breakdown on the flight from Belfast.

Maureen whispers in my ear.

'Hold on, Jim. Look at me. Stay focused.' She pulls me to my feet before turning to the DG. 'I'm taking him home, sir. He needs more time.'

The DG nods sympathetically.

'We'll get you a car.'

'No, sir, we'll make our own way.' She turns to Wank. 'Don't have us followed. We'll come back when Jim's ready.'

Wank nods his agreement as Maureen guides me to the door. As she does, 'S' – the only other woman in the room – whispers in Maureen's ear. I'm not supposed to hear, but I get the gist of it.

'You know that a termination is illegal in Northern Ireland and the Republic?'

'I know, ma'am.'

'The odds are that Kathleen came to England for the abortion. As the letter was posted in London, there's a good chance we can find her.'

Maureen manages to get me back to Kent.

I know not how. I have no recollection of the journey.

It takes me a week to recover from the ordeal at Gower Street. Maureen listens and listens as I slowly describe the burden of guilt I'm carrying.

'I'm not sure why I told them about the photograph. I was exhausted and had already revealed the dark recesses of my soul. So why not show them the darkest corner of them all? I suppose I also felt that they shared some of the guilt, and therefore needed to know what they've done to me.'

'I don't blame you. They ought to know the consequences of their scheming.'

'If you've never seen a dead foetus, I wouldn't recommend taking a look; you'll never forget the horror of a human being in embryo, a tiny creature denied its first breath of life.'

'Why didn't you tell me?'

'I didn't want anyone to know.'

'What did you do with the Polaroid?'

'Threw it in the fire in the pub.'

'Good. You've got to burn it out of your memory as well.'

'That's easier said than done.'

'Jim, you're torturing yourself with it.'

'I know, but I have to learn to live with it. It happened; it's real.'

31. Thud in the Woods

I don't hear the bullet in flight. There's no whistle, no swish. I hear only the tearing of flesh, a choked scream, then a dull thud as the bullet buries itself into a huge beech tree behind me. The second bullet passes over my head. My instincts, honed by my training, impel me to dive for cover. The second thud comes from another beech, just beyond the first one.

I look behind. Maureen has curled herself into a ball. I can see only the curve of her spine and the fingers of one hand gripping her right shoulder. Seeping through her taut fingers is her thick, ruby-red blood. I know we shouldn't move, or speak. So does Maureen. I see her chest heaving; she's breathing. Then I see her thumb rise, signalling that she's OK.

I can hear footsteps coming towards us; at least two pairs of feet, possibly three. They're running, thrashing the ferns and snapping the broken branches of the undergrowth.

They're closing fast.

I'm about to yell at Maureen to run before our attackers reach us, when a dog barks, followed by a human voice telling it to be quiet. The dog, like most of its species, ignores its owner's command and continues to bark even more aggressively. More dogs bark, followed by more human voices, male and female. It's a party of walkers, arguing over an Ordnance Survey map.

The onrushing footsteps stop. There's a pause, then our attackers move away, but much more stealthily, avoiding the walkers who have regrouped and are moving off, calling their dogs to heel.

As I must, I wait and wait for what seems to be an eternity, all the while observing the flow of blood from Maureen's shoulder. It's covering the top half of her singlet, matting her hair and dripping into a small hollow in the ground beneath her. Fortunately, the dogs don't get our scent and they and their owners move away.

I call to Maureen in a whisper, asking how she is and, once more, she sticks her thumb in the air. But I can see that there's a distinct tremor to her body; the ground is very wet. She's in pain and getting cold.

It's time to move, regardless of the threat.

I jump to my feet and look around. The adrenalin's pumping through my body, making my movements elastic and smooth. We're alone. I take three strides, reach Maureen and help her to her feet. She's very pale and unsteady.

'How is it?'

Her breath caught by the pain, Maureen answers shakily.

'I think I'm the luckiest bugger alive. It's gone right through, but above the collarbone. It bloody hurts, though.'

I gently prise away her fingers.

'I'm not surprised. You've got a hole there I could put my knob in.'

'Tiny, then!'

We both start to laugh, but Maureen stops quickly as the movement sends a jolt of agony through her body. We look at one another, both knowing that our already precarious situation has become even more perilous.

Everything has changed.

Maureen begins to sag, and I struggle to keep her upright.

'You're icy cold, you might be going into shock. We need a plan.'

Maureen tries to clear her head.

'We can't go back to the Pilgrim's, so we've only got what we're standing up in, which is bugger all.'

'What about our cash?'

'Always prepared, Jimmy. It's in a money belt around my waist.'

I say a silent prayer to the God I don't believe in and kiss Maureen – the goddess I do believe in.

I help her walk towards the A26.

'We need a car; I'll have to hot-wire one. There must be a car park at the edge of the forest.'

'Then we must go to Hastings. My parents have a flat there, on the promenade. I stashed lots of kit there, ages ago – enough to go to ground for a while.'

'What kind of kit?'

'Weapons, ammo, comms, money, the lot.'

'Of course you did. I don't suppose you've got a battlefield medical kit as well?'

Maureen smiles through the pain. I realize it's a stupid question; of course she has.

I use Maureen's singlet to strap her wound against the bleeding and leave her sitting on a thick branch, clear of the wet ground, with her back propped up against a tree. Slumped in her bra and running shorts, covered in blood, she looks like a casualty from a war zone.

I know time's against me and begin to sprint along the

A26. I soon find a car park for visitors to the forest by using a simple subterfuge: I flag down a motorist and tell him that I've been running in the forest and can't find where I left my car. The elderly driver is kind enough to drive me to a roadside parking area he knows. Noticing how cold I am, he even offers me an old pullover he keeps in the car in case of emergencies. I accept readily, knowing it will be a godsend for Maureen.

Fortunately, the car park is occupied by almost a dozen vehicles; they must belong to the party of walkers who saved our lives. I give the old boy a thumbs up and walk purposefully to the furthest car. Thankfully, he drives off quickly before it's obvious that I don't have keys to any of the vehicles.

I soon choose one that's ideal. It's an old Ford, ancient enough to allow me to force down the driver's window and start the engine by crossing the terminals of its ignition switch. I check that there's enough petrol and drive to collect Maureen.

She's been alone for over thirty minutes and is losing consciousness. I put my hand on her forehead and her response is minimal. She's very cold to the touch and pale as a ghost. It's only a hundred yards to the road and, although it's a struggle for her, the effort gets her adrenalin going.

When I get her to the car, I put her in the old boy's pullover and check the bleeding, which is still under control. I turn up the car's heating and wrap her in a blanket that, mercifully, I find in the boot. Her pain is still intense, but she's bearing it. I keep her talking, desperate that she doesn't fall asleep, which would soon turn into unconsciousness.

After stocking up with fuel, food, drink and painkillers

at a roadside garage, we're soon cruising towards Hastings. I drive like a weekend driver. Although my training included high-speed escape and evasion driving, the last thing we need is to be stopped by a police traffic patrol. I'd love to get Maureen to Hastings more quickly, but being pulled over would be a disaster.

I look back at her, who is curled up on the back seat.

'How're you doing?'

'OK. I suppose I should be counting my blessings.'

'You should. Shame your shoulders are so muscly, though; that hole will have ripped them to shreds.'

'Then you'll have to stitch them, won't you, Doc?'

'I'll try, but my battlefield casualty training didn't include surgery.'

'Don't worry, closing a wound is just like repairing torn jeans.'

'I've never done that either.'

'I have, many times. I'll guide you through it.'

'I hope your kit includes some local anaesthetic.'

'So do I! Don't worry, I think I have bupivacaine. It works a treat.'

'For your sake, I hope so!'

Maureen winces as she changes position.

'Mo, I'm baffled. How far away do you think they were?'

'Difficult to say; fifty to eighty yards. Why?'

'How come they missed? They only winged you, and missed me altogether.'

'We were moving pretty quickly.'

'But pros don't miss at those distances.'

'Some of the Provos are hardly sharpshooters; they're just lads off the estates.'

'Ordinary lads assigned to an ASU on the mainland? I doubt it. I've had another thought: are we a liability at Gower Street to the point that we're expendable?'

'Christ, Jim, if it was those boys, we'd both be brown bread now.'

'Not necessarily. Like you, I trained with them; some couldn't hit their own arse with a banjo!'

'Do you know what you're saying?'

'Course I do. We may have two lots of bad boys looking for us.'

'I can't believe that the spooks would be that callous.'

'Can't you? You're the one who told me that they were paid to take ruthless, pragmatic decisions. Think about it. We got into deep shite, and much of it was our own doing – well, most of it mine. We haven't handled the fallout very well, at least I haven't. My behaviour when we went to Gower Street wasn't exactly positive. I'm a liability. Downing Street's position on the IRA is hardening by the day. The decision that I'm too big a risk could've been taken in the last few days. And I make you expendable too.'

'No, Jim, I don't buy it.'

'Well, humour me for a minute. Are you sure nobody could know about the Pilgrim's Rest?'

'Sure.'

I listen as Maureen goes over every detail, every step we've taken since we left my flat in Clapham. She's trained in surveillance – how to do it, and how to spot it. But she concedes it's hard to tell if you're being followed on busy public transport. She then repeats the steps from the Gower Street meeting. The look on her face betrays the doubts that have come into her head.

'We could have been followed from the meeting. Wank agreed he wouldn't have us followed, but I wouldn't trust him as far as I can spit.'

'And I was in a right state. An elephant could have stepped on my toe and I wouldn't have noticed.'

I carry on driving. We're both deep in thought.

'Here's another theory, Mo. What if the spooks used one of their channels to get word to the Provos about our whereabouts? They could let them do their dirty work for them. That would explain the poor marksmanship.'

'A conspiracy too far, Jim.'

My mind is racing. Every time I think through a scenario an even more bizarre possibility comes into my head. I decide that I've done enough speculating for the time being.

I look at the car's clock.

'The poor bugger whose car I've nicked will have reported it by now. If the local woodentops have been asked to report anything unusual to Gower Street, they could have this number plate.'

Maureen's suddenly much more alert.

'A stolen car in Kent's not unusual.'

'Agreed, but if they know about the Pilgrim's, then it will appear on their radar.'

'Good point. And they're sure to know about my parents' flat.'

With Maureen stricken, the responsibility is all mine. It does me good. I'm suddenly feeling much better. I'm up for anything. I smile at her cockily.

'Right. So, I need to be in and out of the gaff like a cat burglar. Tell me what it's like and where to park.'

Maureen goes through the layout of the flat and the building in detail.

'There's a torch in the kitchen drawer, left of the sink. My stuff's in the spare room. It's obvious.'

'Will I get it all out in one go?'

'There's a bergen in the cupboard. It'll all go in there. The M16's bagged up in pieces, and the MP5 should fit in whole. It'll be a heavy load.'

'How many pistols?'

'Two Brownings.'

'How the fuck did you get hold of that lot?'

'Through that bastard boyfriend of mine. They'd been decommissioned, but I nabbed them and made them good as new.'

'I won't ask how. But are you sure they're operational and have enough ammo?'

Maureen doesn't answer; she just smiles and makes a face that says, 'Are you kidding?'

'You know what? Fuck the cat burglar bit! I'm just going to drive up to the front door, walk in, walk out and drive off.' I glance at Maureen in the rear-view mirror. 'What do you think?'

'It sounds like a recipe for getting us both slotted, but you're in charge . . . for the moment.'

32. Two Rabbits Down a Hole

It's difficult to tell if her parents' place is under surveillance. It's as quiet as the grave. I check every car, every vantage point, but with Maureen in urgent need of medical care, I do what I said I'd do and walk in through the front door. My audacious plan goes smoothly.

With Maureen's key, I'm into the flat and out again in less than ten minutes. I put her heavy bergen on my back and hold a large shopping bag in each hand. I empty the fridge and larder and pick up any household items I think might be useful. Although I'm prepared to drive like a rally driver to lose anyone trailing us, there doesn't seem to be any need. I'm confident no one is following us.

Desperate to treat Maureen's wound, I drive to a small, seedy hotel just behind the Grand Parade in nearby Eastbourne. I deposit Maureen and all our kit in a top-floor room and give her three doses of painkillers and an anti-tetanus jab, before disposing of the car several hundred yards away. I then sprint back to the hotel.

I remove the borrowed pullover and inject Maureen's shoulder with a local anaesthetic. I have to be careful removing the singlet that has been staunching the bleeding. The blood has dried, fusing the material to her skin. Antiseptic helps loosen the singlet from the wound and, thankfully, the flow doesn't resume as I pull away the blood-soaked top.

Worryingly, the wound weeps and looks deep. I surround it with towels and pour antiseptic into it. Maureen winces a little, but is concentrating on using the dressing-table mirror so that she can help me with the procedure. I inject the anaesthetic and prepare the needle and surgical sutures.

We wait for fifteen minutes for the anaesthetic to take effect, during which time I read Maureen the stories from the newspaper I bought at the petrol station. Northern Ireland is still making the headlines and still haunting us. Earlier in the month, a bomb planted at a disco at the Droppin Well in Ballykelly, County Londonderry killed seventeen people: eleven British soldiers and six civilians. The INLA has claimed responsibility, saying that the civilian deaths were justified because they were 'consorts' of the British soldiers.

Maureen looks very pale and weak. It's a testament to her physical strength and mental toughness that she's still conscious and hasn't collapsed emotionally in the face of the trauma she's suffered.

'How's it feel?'

'Numb, I think. Stick that needle in somewhere and we'll soon find out.'

I plunge the needle into her shoulder several times, each time more deeply.

'Nothing, Jim. Let's get on with it.'

I've never darned a sock before – never mind sown up a wound – but, carefully and calmly, Maureen tells me what to do. There are a few hitches.

'Can't you keep the stitches in a straight line?'

'I'm trying, Mo, sorry. I can make a dovetail joint or put

245

a thread on a bar of steel, but needlework wasn't on my school curriculum.'

'Bloody hell! All boys should do home economics and learn how to sew. But, if you're so good with your hands, concentrate on what you're doing.'

'I am concentrating!'

Under her guidance, I'm able to repair some muscle tissue and then slowly close the wound. It doesn't look too neat, but it'll serve the purpose. Eventually, the wound is dressed and the shoulder heavily strapped.

I have to remove Maureen's bra to do the strapping and move her right breast towards the middle of her chest to do the binding. I caught many glimpses of most of her anatomy when we shared a life together in Belfast, but this is the first time I've seen her at close quarters and put my hands on an intimate part of her body. It's an electrifying experience.

'Don't start to get any ideas.'

Her comment makes reality kick in.

'OK, sorry. It's late. We have to sleep. I'll get another car in the morning, but I want us out of here before dawn.'

Maureen smiles appreciatively.

'I'm glad "Mr Gold Star" is back.'

'How do you know that name?'

'You told me once, in the flat. You'd had a skinful and were trying to get in my knickers. You said that was what the DS called you on selection. Don't tell me it wasn't true.'

'Well, it was, but only in the classroom – map-reading, I love maps and bearings. I was pretty average at everything else.'

'I'm sure you weren't.'

'Believe me, I was. I got through by keeping my head down and working out the path of least resistance.'

'Sounds like being a good soldier to me.'

'Not really; survival instinct, more like.'

'You know what, Jim? You talk yourself down too much. They showed me your service record when you were picked to go with me to Belfast. You were in the top three on your course and excelled in Continuation, so don't be so bloody modest.'

'Being modest keeps me out of trouble, Mo.'

'So that's why you've lived such a trouble-free life, and why we're now holed up in a fleapit in Eastbourne?'

'OK, point taken.'

'Have you got a plan for tomorrow?'

'No, I've no idea. Let's think of one in the morning.'

'Jimmy, I don't know how you do it. You excel at pretending to be clueless, but I know you're not. Thanks for getting me out of that forest.'

'Don't mention it. All in a day's work in the service of Her Majesty's armed forces, or whichever bunch of bastards we're running away from.'

I kiss Maureen on the cheek and tell her to sleep. I find it difficult to do the same. The adrenalin of the day is pumping and my heart racing. Maureen drifts off quickly, the drugs soothing her pain and bringing the luxury of sleep. I look at her and smile with admiration. What a warrior she would make, if the top brass would only allow her on the front line. I'd have her in my platoon any day of the week! Then I remember that she's a captain and I'm a mere NCO. I hope she would have me in her unit. Not only is she a top pro and an outstanding soldier, she's also beautiful.

I crawl into bed next to her and gently hold her around the waist. The intimacy should make my desire for her spiral, but it doesn't. I feel so protective, like a brother. I squeeze her a little and she responds by nestling her backside closer into my midriff. It feels wonderful, and I fall asleep feeling more content than I can remember for many months.

It's difficult to rouse Maureen the next morning.

I've already stolen a car and packed it with our meagre belongings and far from meagre cache of weapons. It's just before 5 a.m. and I want to be on the South Downs before daylight. We're both still in our running kit, but Maureen also has her pullover and is wrapped in the car blanket from the day before. I have to carry her down the stairs and into the waiting car. Fortunately, I've nicked a Ford Cortina Estate and folded the seats down so that she can spread out.

I have two priorities: clothing and a new place to hide. As Maureen sleeps, I speed westwards towards Brighton, my mind working overtime to devise a way out of our dilemma.

By the time we reach the A27, I have a plan. Daylight has arrived and, with it, glowering skies, strong winds off the English Channel and squalls of heavy rain – all of which is a bad omen for my plan.

Maureen stirs in the back.

'Where are we?'

'Just coming into Lewes.'

'Do we have a plan yet?'

'Yeah, you'll love it.'

'The way you said that tells me that I'll hate it.'

'No, you won't. Stage one: Brighton. Army surplus – clothes, more kit for a bivvy. Head north by car, staying off the motorways and bypassing the big towns. They'll be watching those.'

'To where?'

'Stage two: the Pennines. Up the A6 beyond Preston and then over to Kirkby Lonsdale and on to Barbon, a tiny village. I've got an old schoolmate there, Jed; he's got a hill farm. He'll hide the car in his barn. No one will find it there.

'Stage three: we'll tab it high into the Pennines. I know some places up there where we can lose ourselves for months.'

'On the Pennines, in a bivvy? Bloody hell, it's the middle of winter!'

'You said you wanted to do selection for Hereford. This is your chance.'

'Then what do we do?'

'Stage four: we wait until they know they can't find us, and we're sure they've given up searching, then Jed drives us to Liverpool. We get the ferry to Dublin and an international flight to wherever we want to go.'

'Do we really want to be going to Dublin; isn't it like going from the frying pan into the fire?'

'Exactly, it's the last place they'd think we'll go.'

'So then where?'

'Stage five: Timbuktu, Tbilisi, Tehran, Tierra del Fuego; somewhere where we can disappear and start again.'

'Great, but not the kind of places I had in mind when I dreamed my dreams as a kid!'

'Don't be so pessimistic – new life, new adventures.'

'Hmm, not convinced. Anyway, we don't have enough cash for flights.'

'Ah, that might be a problem, then. Jed might lend me some cash. We can pay him back when we can.'

'Or my dad can square him up.'

'See, I told you, it's a good plan.'

Maureen's not persuaded.

'Oh, Jim. It's a lot to think about. What the hell are we going to do in some godforsaken place in the middle of nowhere?'

'Teach, build a school, open a dive centre. We could learn how to farm: pigs, sheep, grow mushrooms. We could start a vineyard.'

'I suppose then we get married and start a family?'

'Exactly!'

33. Swardle

In Brighton, I buy everything we need for our winter hibernation, then begin the long drive north.

We change into casual clothes and mountain boots and look like a young couple on their way north to do some hillwalking. Maureen sleeps most of the day as we take the old roads to the North. It's a slow and tedious journey but avoids the motorways, which I fear our pursuers will be monitoring.

Every time we pass a depiction of normality – milkmen and postmen doing their deliveries, children going home from school, mothers with prams, old ladies going shopping – I think, if only you knew what it's like in Belfast or Londonderry. If only you knew what your government is doing in your name. Most pointedly of all, I think, if only you knew what the two people in the car driving along your streets have done in your name.

When we cross the East Lancs Road, west of Manchester, I begin to feel like I'm home: dark satanic mills, Gracie Fields, flat caps and whippets. More clichés than a cheap novel, but it's home and I wish I'd never left it.

When Maureen wakes, just north of Preston, she's feeling much better and takes in the view of the high Pennines in the distance.

'Happy to be back?'

'Certainly am. God's own country where we're going. How's the shoulder?'

'Don't ask; aching like buggery.'

'Take some more drugs.'

'I've had enough for now. More importantly, where exactly are we going after your mate Jed's place?'

'As we say up here, "a reet long tab over t'moors". I want to be a long way from his farm, just in case they trace him as a friend and come looking. So, right over towards Swaledale, near Muker and Keld. It's a long way.'

'I can't tab carrying a bergen with this shoulder.'

'You won't have to. I'll do two tabs.'

'You sure?'

'No problem, do me good.'

Maureen smiles contentedly and curls herself into an even tighter ball in the back of the Cortina.

'Muker and Keld – strange names.'

'Strange place. It's Old Norse up there. The locals speak Swardle; it's a kind of Old English, with bits of Norse. "Keld" means spring, "muker" is a small field, "laithe" means barn, "thwaite" means meadow and "beck" means stream. You won't understand a word of it.'

'Fascinating.'

I look back at Maureen. She's laughing at me.

'Are you taking the piss?'

'No, wouldn't dream of it.'

'Above the Swale is Great Shunner Fell. No one ever goes there. It's like the moon on the top.'

'You wouldn't make an estate agent, Jimmy.'

'Listen, it'll be fine. We'll find a sheltered spot hidden in the trees, with a fresh stream, probably the top of Cotterdale, a small side dale. I'll build a proper bivvy with a stone base, mat it out, we'll have a sod roof, all the mod cons.'

'Loo and shower?'

'Definitely. Twenty yards downstream, one of those new open-air types, they're all the rage.'

'What about food?'

'No open fire, I'm afraid. The farmers will see the smoke. We'll have to cook with hexamine.'

'And where do we get provisions?'

'Well, we won't need a freezer up there. We can stock up with stuff once a fortnight. I'll get Jed to drive over from Kirkby with supplies and we can meet him at the top of the track through Cotterdale.

'How do you know the area so well?'

'You won't believe this.'

'Try me.'

'Duke of Edinburgh's Award.'

Maureen starts to laugh, but soon stops as the movement makes her wince with pain.

'And what will we do all day?'

'Books? Jed's got loads. He can bring more every time he comes over. We can do lots of tabs, the terrain is like the Brecons; I can be your DS on SAS selection and beast you.'

'Oh, great, can't wait!' Maureen's mood changes, and she looks puzzled. 'Listen, if Jed can drive over with scoff for us, why can't he drive us up there in the first place?'

'Cos the tabbing will be good for us. Are you sure that bullet didn't go through your brain before it minced your shoulder?'

'OK, agreed. Good thinking, Mr Gold Star.'

*

We turn off the A6 north of Lancaster and head for Kirkby Lonsdale, a haven of Pennine life unchanged for generations. Jed's farm is higher on the fells, beyond the tiny village of Barbon, a one-pub village that sits in its picturesque setting like it's been there since God was a boy. There's a dim light on in the Barbon Inn, which projects like a beacon of temptation. I'd love it if Maureen and I could sit and enjoy a pint of Theakston's Old Peculier in front of an open fire in an archetypal Pennine pub. However, expediency tells me it's impossible.

As we drive into our host's farmyard, the clammy fingers of a dank moorland mist wrap themselves around us. The air is wet, the wind chilling; I immediately feel at home.

Jed is bewildered by our sudden arrival through the murk, but proves to be an excellent host. A roast dinner and half a dozen bottles of beer appear; we eat with our plates on our laps in front of a roaring fire. After what we've been through, it's like being in heaven.

Jed's ex-Coldstream; got shot in the back in Londonderry, lost a lung, got invalided out on a piss-poor pension. His recovery took a long time and he became depressed. His wife left him and took the kids. But he's getting better and has a new girlfriend, Bonny, a local from Kirkby. She cooks dinner and fusses around us like a mother hen. She's very sweet – a real North Country lass – full of freckles, with a shock of strawberry-blonde curls that fall way below her shoulder blades.

Jed's full of questions. I answer some of them.

'So a reet to-do, then?'

'Aye, mate, a reet to-do.'

I look at Bonny, concerned about what I can tell Jed in her hearing.

'Tha can talk in front o' Bonny. She'll say nowt.'

'Can't, Jed, no more details, not even to you.'

'Bad as that?'

'Aye.'

'So, tell us abaht yon Maureen. Tha knows she's too good fo' thee, lad.'

Jed talks about Maureen as if she's not there, which makes her hackles rise.

'You're right, Jed, yon Maureen is definitely too good for him. Thanks to you and Bonny for an excellent meal and for putting up with all this cloak-and-dagger stuff.'

'No problem, lass. If thee an' Gary's in a spot o' bother, nowt more needs be said. I'll cover yon motor outside wi' a tarpaulin and stick it in t'back o' t'old shippon. You two can be on yer way in t'mornin'.'

Jed turns to me and smiles the smile of an old comrade-in-arms. He busies himself, helping Bonny with the residue of dinner.

'I'll start puttin' some cash aside for thi flights, an' I'll come o'er to Cotterdale, top o' track, every other Saturday mornin'.'

Maureen gets up and kisses Jed on the cheek.

'We'll get the money back to you. If we can't manage it, my father will. You'll like him.'

'Bit of a toff, is 'e?'

'No, he's an Irish navvy.'

Confused, Jed looks at me. I grin at him and nod. Jed looks at Maureen and raises his eyebrows.

'Well, t'bugger must o' done a lot o' overtime!'

*

255

Jed's sheep farm is high above Barbon village. When dawn breaks the next morning, I clutch my Ordnance Survey map of the High Pennines and put a trusty Silva compass in the top pocket of my jacket. The hills are covered in low cloud and the air is even wetter than it was last night.

Jed grabs the map from me.

'Can you remember t'way?'

'It's been a while, but I think so.'

'Just north of east along t'track at our gate.'

'Yeah, I remember.'

'Is Maureen ready?'

'I think so; she's just gone for a pee.'

'So you two aren't an item?'

'Sad to say, no. But we're real buddies. She's a top girl.'

'I can si that.'

Jed looks at me. I can tell he's ill at ease.

'Look, lad, I know tha can't tell me any o' t'details, but if it's reet serious, a've one question.'

'I know, Jed. Am I putting you and Bonny in danger?'

'Well, that did cross me mind. Am gettin' me'sen sorted up 'ere. Bonny's great.'

I put my hands on Jed's broad shoulders.

'What can I say, mate? I don't think there's any threat to you. But, to be honest, we're stretched out to breaking point. Mo's already taken a tap in the shoulder and they missed me by a whisker. I wouldn't have come here if it wasn't our only option.'

'Who's they?'

'Can't, Jed. It's best for you not to know anything. I'm sure they won't be able to trace any link between us.'

'Gary, don't fuck wi' me. This seems bad. Who's "they" – IRA? It sounds like deep shit for thee, and tha's just dropped a big pile on my doorstep.'

Jed looks at me with a streak of resentment in his eyes. I decide to adopt an operational tone.

'Get rid of the car today. Bury it. Destroy any trace of our presence here and don't come over to Cotterdale for a fortnight. You know these moors; you'll know if anyone's up here who shouldn't be. Keep your eyes open.'

The ire doesn't subside in his eyes.

'You givin' me orders, Gary, lad?'

'Yes, I have to do this by the numbers to keep us all safe.'

'But I'm not in t'fuckin' army any more.'

'I realize that, but it's the only way I know. If any damage has been done, it's done. We're here now, so let's deal with it.'

I try to look at Jed like a hard-nosed NCO, his sergeant major, telling him the facts of life. He stares at me, pondering what I've said. The sternness of his glare melts and he smiles at me.

'OK, you shithead, but if tha gets us all killed, I'll fuckin' murder yer!'

I laugh at him.

'Come on, let's get you an' yon lass out o' 'ere.'

Maureen appears and we all say our goodbyes. Bonny gives Maureen a big hug, then slips a foil package into her pocket.

'A few sandwiches fer yer suppa t'neet: a bit o' last neet's lamb on me mam's oven-bottom cakes.' Bonny grabs me, kisses me on the cheek and whispers in my ear. 'Our Jed

thinks t'world o' thee. I don't know wot tha's done, an' a
don't care, if Jed sez tha's a good lad, that's reet enough
fer me. Tek care o' Maureen, she's luvly . . . an' very keen
on thee.'

My ears prick up.

'How do you know?'

'A'm a lass, aren't a?'

I call to Jed as we stride up the track.

'I'll be back early tomorrow morning for the other bergen. Leave it outside the kitchen door, but put some
breakfast in it.'

My bergen's heavy, and no amount of tabbing on the Kent
Weald can replicate the precipitous slopes of the Pennine's
moors. My chest is straining and my thighs burning.

Maureen's not doing too well either. She winces with
every step as the stitches of her wound pull against her
skin.

We make several stops and drink gallons of water. I
check Maureen's wound. It's looking angry and swollen.
She uses a small stainless-steel mirror to examine it.

'I think it's infected.'

She's right.

'Do we have some antibiotics?' I ask her.

'Yes, I put the medical kit at the top of the bergen.'

'Take a double dose now and a couple of painkillers.'

'Yes, boss.'

Our going gets harder and harder.

To avoid being seen, I decide to take the most remote
route. A weak sun breaks through the grey moorland
gloom and we stop to eat something. Bonny's oven-bottom

cakes went mid-morning, so I delve into my bergen to find my favourite army field rations: a tiny tin of steak and kidney pudding, followed by an equally small tin of cling peaches. As always, I've taken care to put the peaches in a pouch on the outside of my bergen, so that they're as cold as the Pennine air.

I open the tins and Maureen lights our little hexamine stove.

'How's the shoulder?'

'Not bad. The painkillers have kicked in, but the buggers have given me a headache.'

'We'll be there soon, and you can get your head down.'

'What will we do for shelter? There's no time to build a lean-to tonight.'

'Jed let me have his two-man tent. We can use that until I can build a proper bivvy.'

Reinvigorated, we're soon on the move again, striding high on the side of the narrowing valley of Cotterdale. The narrow road up the dale is dotted with quaint dales' cottages until they finally give out and the thin strip of tarmac disappears.

As the rough track rises on to the sides of the huge mound of Great Shunner Fell, there are several stands of pine plantation. The evergreens are incongruous amidst the wild open spaces of the once heavily wooded fells. Long since deforested, the bleakness of the high moorland is assaulted by these recent plantations, but they offer ideal cover for an inconspicuous abode. From previous visits, I know that the last plantation on the highest part of the eastern side of the dale has a clearing at its heart, which can only be reached after a difficult hack through the almost impenetrable darkness of the dense pines. There's also a small stream running through the trees, ideal for washing clothes and people.

Typically, dusk brings a gentle drizzle that rolls down from the moors. It takes us a while to reach the spot where I hope we can make camp. After some searching we eventually find the place I remember from more than a dozen years earlier.

I manage to get the tent up and the sleeping bags unfurled just before total darkness descends. Maureen clambers into her bag as I light our small gas lamp in the bell end of the tent and prepare our modest dinner of dried minced meat and mashed potatoes. It's not haute cuisine, but made bearable by an item Jed gave me as we left Barbon. I show it to Maureen, who smiles appreciatively as I pour her a hefty measure of cognac.

'This will do you more good than any painkiller.'

'Possibly. Two shots a night, no more.'

'Don't worry, Jed will bring us more.'

'That's not what I meant.'

34. Misery on the Moors

It doesn't take us long to make a more permanent hide in our moorland retreat. Everything we need – branches, foliage, stones, sods of earth – is readily to hand, and we soon have a tolerably dry and warm yet discreet haven.

However, as time passes in our wild hermitage and the days turn into weeks, our morale plummets. It's much worse than a surveillance operation. At least an op has a defined objective, but, because we've agreed we need to see out the winter before making our bolt for Dublin, our self-imposed hibernation is purgatory. Although we're trained to endure conditions like these, and despite the quality of our bivvy's construction, the constant chilling damp and perpetual cloying mist of the high Pennines sap our resolve. Worst of all, when the wind blows, it drives the rain into every nook and cranny of our shelter. Everything is wet, even the insides of our sleeping bags.

Mercifully, the antibiotics help heal Maureen's shoulder. But even so, she's beginning to be worn down by the tedium and discomfort.

To try to ease the tedium and keep in shape, we've taken our daily tab to the top of Great Shunner and are both tired, hungry and miserable. It's a particularly cold day and there is sleet in the air as we work our way through the trees to our refuge.

'Jimmy, tell me there's a sirloin in the fridge and that you've decanted a bottle of claret.'

'Yes, of course. But the wine's a Rhône, a rather good Châteauneuf.'

'That'll do nicely. Where's the corkscrew?'

'Don't worry; I'll get the butler to do it.'

'Good, and ask him to bring a hot-water bottle. I'm a little chilly.'

Maureen sits down next to me as I light our little hexamine burner. I can smell her stale sweat and unwashed body. She notices my nose wrinkle.

'Yes, we're both going in the beck tomorrow morning – no matter how cold it is.'

'So, what's the really good news? Dinner tonight is . . .'

'A lovely bag of dehydrated minced beef and powdered mash . . . and to finish, dried apricots.'

'Mmm, can't wait.'

'We're running low on rations, but Jed's due tomorrow morning. He'll have lots of fresh scoff for us.'

After yet another uncomfortable night, Maureen and I rise early the next morning and make our way to our concealed lookout point above Cotterdale's farm track, where we wait for the first glimpse of Jed's dark green Land Rover.

When it hasn't appeared by noon, we both know he isn't coming. Maureen looks worried.

'What should we do?'

I try to remain calm.

'Wait another week.'

Maureen grimaces at the suggestion.

'He's been as regular as clockwork, every fortnight. Something's not right. We should check it out.'

I also have a strong feeling that something's amiss, but I don't want to get unduly alarmed by one no-show.

'He could have problems on the farm, or may just have broken down.'

'Perhaps, but let's tab it down there – just to be sure.'

I can see that Maureen is determined to go and make sure all is well.

'Weapons?'

'Definitely. Let's leave the hide intact. But we should take everything else, in case we aren't able to come back.'

'Isn't that a bit over the top, Mo?'

'I don't think so. We have to be ready for anything.'

'Can you manage a bergen with that shoulder?'

'Needs must, Jimmy. You can strap it tightly, and I'll just have to put up with it!'

'OK, boss, let's get our arses in gear.'

The gloom of a rapidly advancing dusk is descending as we approach Jed's farm. There are no lights on anywhere and the place looks deserted.

I decide on a direct, frontal approach.

'I'll go in with a Browning. You cover me with the M16.'

'Not a good idea, Jim. The kick on that beast will do my shoulder no good at all. I'll go in with the pistol. You cover me!'

She's right, of course.

'OK, but be careful.'

My eyes scan every inch of Jed's farm buildings and the surrounding fells as Maureen makes her stealthy approach across the farmyard towards the kitchen door. If anyone is lurking, they're well concealed. Of course it's possible that Maureen could be walking into an ambush. If she is, my reactions are going to have to be lightning fast.

She keeps her pistol rigidly in front of her as she pushes the kitchen door inwards. It's not locked, not even on the latch. She hesitates, waiting for any signs or sounds of movement. There are none and she steps inside, out of sight.

I clamber down and follow her in. As I reach the middle of the yard, Maureen reappears. She's no longer alert, but her face is drained of all colour.

'Come on, get inside and lock the door behind you.'

As I move inside, she stops me.

'Not a pretty sight, Jimmy.'

A blind panic grips me as I realize that something terrible has happened to Jed. I rush inside and see him hunched over on a chair. His hands are tied behind his back. I know he's dead. There's blood on the floor beneath him and an entry wound at the base of his skull.

He's been assassinated. I pray that he hasn't been tortured, but the bruises to his face say otherwise, as do two bullet holes, one in each knee. I begin to shake with anger and revulsion. This is my mate from schooldays. We played football together and escaped on to the moors in the summer, where – in exchange for a two-bob bit and as much milk as we could drink – we helped the hill farmers with odd jobs. We went to Morecambe together and stayed in a caravan to which we would lure gullible girls in vain attempts to get their knickers off.

Now, thanks to me, he's dead. And he met his end in excruciating pain and unbearable fear.

Fighting my trembling fingers, I begin to untie his icy cold body. It's difficult, rigor mortis has set in. The blood on the floor is dark and dried out. Jed has been dead for a while. I know we don't have time to bury him but, at the very least, I want to move him to a more dignified position and cover his body.

Then I hear an anguished call from Maureen.

'Jim, up here . . .'

There's an agonizing pause.

' . . . it's Bonny.'

I meet Maureen at the top of the stairs. The look on her face tells me that even more horror is behind the bedroom door. Maureen grabs my arm.

'This is not the IRA and not Gower Street. This is a psycho. She's been bound and tortured, and it looks like they raped her. I'll get something to cover her.'

I feel like I've been kicked in the guts. It's hard to breathe. I cry out, 'No!' with an intensity that could be heard in the bowels of the earth. I've brought the worst nightmare to this innocent couple.

As I cut loose Bonny's wrists and ankles, Maureen pulls a curtain from the window to throw over her body. My guilt forces me to look at the agony they put her through. The baler twine they used to tie her has cut deeply into her flesh as she fought against her restraints. Her fingers and toes are blue from lack of circulation. Her young body is bruised and blotchy; her groin is obscenely exposed. Her pubic hair is matted with semen. I close my eyes to try to eradicate the awful images and hold back the tears. What kind of monster would do this? Maureen leans over me. She closes Bonny's legs and crosses her arms over her stomach. She then gently covers her still form with the curtain.

'Not full rigor mortis, Mo. She can't have been dead for more than four to six hours.'

'They must have killed Jed last night and Bonny this morning. It's too horrible to think about.'

'Fuck! *Fuck!* What have I done?'

'Turn away, Jim . . .' Gently, she lifts me up by my arm. 'But never forget.'

We find refuge in the sitting room where, all those weeks ago, we had supper in front of the fire.

Maureen is soon in operational mode.

'We need to move quickly. They can't be far away.'

'Jed can't have told them anything; otherwise, we'd be dead by now.'

'We can't be sure. They could be in Cotterdale now. They wouldn't have seen us, high on the fells. Let's take Jed's wheels.'

'OK, but only as far as Kirkby, or perhaps Lancaster. We need a new car; his is too recognizable.'

'Where then?'

'Further south, and then back up the moors.'

She looks horrified at the thought.

'What about a cheap B&B somewhere? At least we can stay warm and dry.'

'Yeah, Mo, but the locals talk; and then the bobbies get to know.'

'What about a fleapit in Blackpool?'

'Perhaps. Let's talk in the car. Whatever we do, everything's changed. We have to deal with whoever did this. We're the hunters now.'

266

Maureen's face hardens.

'Agreed. It's personal.'

As comrades-in-arms, we embrace in a symbol of our unity of purpose.

Less than a mile from Jed's farm, there's a rarely used track. It snakes up above Leck Fell Farm, an impossibly remote place, the stone walls of which sit heavily in the steep moorland peat but still don't look like they belong. Beyond the farm, there's a vantage point where we can see the whole valley and Jed's farm.

We decide to wait there until nightfall to see if our quarry returns. They don't.

The air on the fells has cleared and a full moon appears to bathe the high Pennines in mercury-silver light. So, instead of going back down the valley, I decide to drive further up the meandering trail, as far as Jed's Land Rover will take us.

Maureen looks at me.

'Where are we going?'

'I'm going to tab up to Gragareth. It's a special place, the highest point in Lancashire. You can see forever from up there. I need to breathe clean air.'

'So do I. I'll come with you.'

An impossible journey without a full moon, it takes us almost two hours to make the ascent. Gragareth is over 2,000 feet high, but we're rewarded by an awesome vista when we reach the top. We can see the lights of Kendal, Lancaster and the whole of Morecambe Bay shimmering in the distance and, behind us, the menacing saddleback of mighty Whernside.

We say nothing to one another for a long time.

Maureen breaks the silence.

'I've been thinking, Jim. We can't just leave them there.'

'What else can we do?'

'Call Gower Street. They'll send a team to clean up.'

'Jesus, Gower Street might be responsible, Mo.'

'No way, Jim. This is a nutter; in fact, more than one.'

'But if it's not the spooks, it's got to be the IRA: the kneecapping, the bullet to the head.'

'No, Jim, they're evil fuckers, but they don't tie up women and rape them.'

'Well, they do now.'

'I think it was meant to look like the IRA. Something's not right, Jim. The tube attack, the one in Kent; they weren't right. This isn't right. Let me call in. We'll do it from a phone box. I'll ask to speak to Control directly.'

'They'll trace us.'

'I know, but we'll do it from the motorway. We could go anywhere from there. Besides, somebody knows where we are, anyway.'

Maureen's right. Somebody has been able to track us down three times, so there's little to be lost in calling in. At least Bonny and Jed's families will be spared the true horror of their demise. The clean-up team will arrange an 'accident' of some sort. It sounds so callous, but it's better than the truth.

'OK, let's do it before somebody stumbles across them. It's Saturday night. No one will go up to the farm until Monday at the earliest.'

By the time we get back to the Land Rover, it's five in the morning.

As we drive away from the horror of what's happened on the bleak fells above Barbon, Kirkby flashes by unnoticed. We're soon speeding down the M6, which is eerily deserted.

Finding a new set of wheels in Lancaster isn't difficult. A battered, navy-blue Ford Capri Mk II, which will go unnoticed everywhere, presents itself on a side street next to the canal.

Maureen makes the call from Forton Services, just south of the city, and tells the Gower Street duty officer about the carnage at Barbon. She then tells him that she'll call Wank, our Control, at precisely 10 a.m.

I take up Maureen's suggestion of a seaside fleapit and suggest we drive to Fleetwood; it has a few.

We have a big fry-up at a greasy spoon on Dock Street before Maureen goes off to a phone box to make the call. She's gone less than five minutes. When she returns, she's as pale as a ghost.

'Where next, Jim?'

'Waterloo Road, Liverpool Docks. No one notices anyone there. It's been full of strangers for centuries.'

'Let's go. I've got bad news.'

35. Waterloo Road

The drive south to Liverpool becomes a journey fraught with anxiety. Maureen's report from Gower Street could not have been more precise, nor could it have been more ominous.

Control was very clear. There's a rogue unit at large: right wing, disaffected. They're on our tails and feeding intel back to the RUC which, in turn, may be leaking it to the IRA and its ASU in England. Control is still unable to identify the culprits, but they're close to pinning them down. In the meantime, we're to disappear as completely as possible, and not to make contact for at least a fortnight.

After mulling over everything Maureen has said, I try to come to terms with what it all means.

'Was it Wank?'

'Yes.'

'How did he sound?'

'Matter-of-fact.'

'No hint of concern for our welfare, I suppose?'

'Course not.'

'Do we trust him?'

'We don't trust anyone.'

'Agreed.'

I look across at Maureen. The expression on her face is one of distinct unease.

'Mo, I can't figure it out. Why would right-wing rogue

elements be so concerned about us that they would want us dead?'

'Doesn't make sense, does it? All I can think is that someone in Gower Street has written a report about our reaction to our op in Belfast and that's been interpreted as an accusation that we've gone "native" and are now a major security threat.'

'That seems a bit far-fetched.'

'Correct, but have you got a better interpretation?'

We pass the grim red-brick warehouses and shabby pubs of Liverpool's Waterloo Road. The street lighting's very dim, adding to the gloomy atmosphere of an area that has seen much better days. It's an early Sunday evening and the pubs don't open until seven, except for the one that's perfect for us – the Marine, an old dockers' spit-and-sawdust dive with a couple of bedrooms on the top floor. We take both.

Maureen's not impressed.

'I think I prefer Cotterdale.'

'How about going into the city tonight for a decent bite to eat?'

'That's a wonderful idea, but we honk; we must both jump into that immaculately clean shower first.'

'Together?'

'No room, Jimmy, but nice try!'

After we've cleaned ourselves and spruced up our hikers' clothing, we head for one of the greatest public houses in the world, the Philharmonic, in Hope Street, a glorious homage to Liverpool's Victorian heritage.

'You've got to have fish and chips, Mo, fresh from Fleetwood this morning.'

'Just like us! Sounds good to me. But aren't we making ourselves a bit obvious in Liverpool city centre?'

'Not in the Phil. It'll be so packed, we'll be lost in the crowds.'

Squeezed into a tight corner of the Philharmonic, we muse about our predicament over fish and chips and two pints of Higsons local bitter.

I'm still not totally convinced about the rogue unit.

'If the bad boys are wound up by an internal report about us, shouldn't we be more worried by whoever's writing it?'

Maureen raises her eyebrows and picks up the thread, her mind working overtime.

'The author would have to be quite senior and privy to the op.'

'Right, so that makes for a very small group.'

We look at one another and the same names come to us in the same moment. Maureen takes a large mouthful of her Higsons.

'Wank and Dank?'

'Correct. More like Wank for me. He's a creepy little fucker and treated me like shite.'

Maureen warms to the conspiracy and takes another swig.

'Could be both.'

'Then Spank is our only hope.'

'And it's impossible to get to him without going through the other two.'

It's my turn to take a big gulp of Liverpool's finest.

'So we may have a legit team on our tail trying to track us down and persuade us to come in, plus a unit of rogue cowboys and an ASU of balaclava boys?'

'You've got it, Jim. And we won't know which is which.'

'Correct.'

'We need a plan.'

'We do. I'll get another round in.'

By the time I get the beers back to Maureen, I have the outline of a strategy.

'Let's ambush the ambushers.'

'Great. Is that it?'

'Don't you like it?'

'Not much, I'd prefer a few more details. Besides, it's easier said than done.'

'I know, but we have to nail whoever killed Jed and Bonny. Let's lure them into a trap and blow them away.'

Maureen's eyes widen.

'I'm up for that. Any idea how?'

'None whatsoever. But I will tomorrow. Now it's time to get legless. It'll help us sleep in the Marine.'

'OK, I'm on for that as well. But back to basics in the morning.'

'Deal.'

We eventually get to the Marine long after midnight.

The landlord of the salubrious premises has locked up and gone to bed and is none too pleased by our loud banging to let us in. His accent is so Scouse, it's difficult to understand him. But the gist of it is that we're a pair of fucking arseholes and he won't be doing breakfast, because we're a pair of . . . We'll have to go to Joe the Greek, who runs the greasy spoon around the corner; he'll be open from six.

*

What a relief to sleep in a bed again, even if only for five hours – and even if it ends with a thumping hangover. The trouble with giving up drinking is that when you go back to bad habits, you get wicked hangovers!

I look at Maureen, who looks as bad as I feel. Joe the Greek's fry-up helps us both feel better, even if it is a disgusting mess of fatty bacon, gristly sausages, greasy fried bread and runny eggs. Maureen takes a gulp of dark brown builder's brew from a tea-stained chipped mug that looks like it's not been washed for a month.

She stares at my grey face.

'Do you feel as bad as you look?'

'Worse.'

'Any brilliant ideas overnight?'

'I did think of knocking on your door and asking for a cuddle, but then I thought better of it.'

'Good decision. Any bright ideas this morning?'

'OK, how about this? I've got the perfect cure for a hangover. And when we get to the top, I'll have thought of a plan.'

'Oh, great. That sounds ominously like another tab up a mountain.'

'But it's an enchanted mountain. It has magical properties that will help us with our plan.'

'Pray tell.'

'We're going to King Cotton, a mecca for pleasure seekers from all over the world.'

'I'm not going to Barnsley, for Christ's sake!'

'Not Barnsley, that's in bloody Yorkshire. Burnley – it makes St Tropez look like Clacton. You'll love it.'

'No, I won't, Jim. We haven't got time for trips down memory lane.'

'Fear not, there's method in my madness.'

The journey from Liverpool into North-East Lancs doesn't take long. By the time we reach Whalley, we've lost what I call 'Lowland Lancs' – red-brick and dull – and are into the foothills of the Pennines, or 'Proper Lancashire' – mills, moors and magnificent.

Maureen has been snoozing most of the way, but my cooing about familiar landmarks wakes her up.

'Where are we?'

'The Gates of Heaven. I've had a word with St Peter. He says you can come in, as long as you speak with flat vowels.'

'You mean gr-*ass* instead of gr-*arse*?'

'You're in!'

'So tell me what the "method" is in this "madness"?'

'An ambush.'

'I know, you've said that already. Elaborate, please.'

'My origins are on file. And if they check on Jed, they'll see that we were at school together. So they may think I might go and see Jed's family, after what happened in Barbon.'

'Go on.'

'I'm not sure where his parents live, and I definitely don't want to go and see them, but I could ask around a bit and make it obvious that we're in the town.'

'OK, so we become the bait. Then how do we set the trap?'

'Don't know, haven't thought about that bit yet.'

Maureen smiles at me.

'You will give it some thought *before* we become bait, Jimmy boy?'

'All in good time, Mo.'

'Do you want me to drive for a while?'

'OK, but when we get to Burnley, I'll take over and give you the guided tour.'

'Wow, what a treat.'

'I know, another tick on your "ten things to do before I die" list.'

I do the tour quickly: my old school, where I lived, where I had my first snog with Janet Shufflebottom, the pubs I used to go to, the Mecca Ballroom, scene of many nights of boppin' and feightin'.

I buy us fish and chips from the Wynotham Street's wonderful old chippy, the street where my mother was born. She got chips from there when she was a girl during the Great War, as I did during the 1950s, when chips were a tanner and cod a bob. Sadly, they're not as delicious as I remember. New owners; probably don't use beef dripping any more!

We stay in the Rosehill House Hotel, one of the town's better hostelries, and spend the next few days making ourselves visible in the area. We're conspicuous in pubs and ask lots of questions of my old friends and people who knew Jed.

We only stop when the news of Jed's death arrives.

The story makes the front page of the local paper, the *Burnley Express*: 'Burnley Hero Killed in Tragic Accident'. The report says that Jed and his girlfriend were found in her burnt-out car in a deep gully near their farm in Cumbria. It's thought their car must have come off the road in bad weather.

The report brings back the horror of Barbon all too vividly for us, so we decide to drive out of Burnley for a change of scene. I take Maureen around the base of Pendle Hill, the area's most famous landmark, and into the picturesque village of Downham, one of the most charming villages in Lancashire. Pendle towers above it; ducks inhabit the village green, through which Heys Brook babbles away towards the Ribble Valley; and the beautiful medieval houses look like they've been there forever.

Maureen and I stand by the brook and watch dusk turn the huge, dark green hump of Pendle into a brooding silhouette.

'There you are, Mo, the magical mountain. The Pendle witches cavorted up there. It's always been mysterious. I told you it's a special place.'

'And we're going up there tomorrow, right?'

'Right. Come on, let's walk up to the Assheton Arms. You'll like it; it's a proper pub.'

The Assheton has a warming fire and hand-pumped real ale, but the landlord, a bucolic cove with long sideburns and hairy nostrils, doesn't believe in the latest 'gimmick': pub grub – chicken in a basket, scampi and chips. But we can have a packet of crisps or a bag of nuts, if we want.

Maureen sips her beer. She looks disconsolate.

'So the clean-up team did their dirty work with Jed and Bonny.'

'It's for the best, Mo.'

'I know, but I can't stop thinking about it.'

'How do you think I feel? It's all my fault. Coming back here has made it even worse. Jed and I used to come here all the time. We'd climb up the Burnley side of Pendle, come down this side and catch the bus home.'

Maureen puts her hand on mine.

'Sorry, Jim. But you must stay strong; we have a job to do, for their sake.'

I pause, pushing my sadness and my guilt into my subconscious.

'I know, so here's the plan. I know Pendle and the villages around here like the back of my hand.'

'Here we go, yomping again!'

'Course we do. We've outstayed our welcome at the Rosehill. If our plan is working, the bad boys will be moving into the area about now. So we sleep there tonight, pack everything into the car in the morning and drive over here.'

'The car's the bait?'

'Yes, we park it at the bottom of the main track up Pendle and set the trap.'

'So far so good.'

'I was crap on the range, but I bet you were pretty shit-hot.'

'Not bad.'

'Good, you've got the job. I'll be spotter, you're the shooter. Use the scope and the silencer on the M16.'

'Sounds reasonable, Jimmy, not bad for an NCO. But from what I saw, it's very exposed on those slopes.'

'You're right; I've thought of that. We've got comms. There are a few trees lower down, so you can be hidden quite close, and I'll help camouflage you. I can be high up with a wide field of vision. There's a good camera shop in Preston; we can go there first thing and buy a fuck-off pair of binos so that I can see a gnat's arse from miles away.'

'I like it. But don't you want to slot the fuckers yourself?'

'I want them brown bread, and that's more likely if you pull the trigger.'

'Jimmy boy, for a dreamer about people and politics, you're a hell of a realist when it comes to soldiering.'

'Thanks, Mo, that's a big compliment, coming from you.'

36. Broomsticks in the Mist

We find exactly what we need in Preston – a pair of Carl Zeiss Jena binoculars I've always wanted. With them, I'll be able to see whether or not anyone who comes calling had acne as a kid.

By the time we get back to Pendle and unload all our paraphernalia for the ambush, it's lunchtime.

'Hungry, Mo?'

'Are you kidding? We had breakfast ages ago.'

'There're a few places where we can eat in Clitheroe – known to us as "Clit-hero", of course – a nice little market town.'

'Aren't we pushing our luck? They could be ready to pounce by now.'

'Possibly. Let's tool up with the Brownings. Quick lunch and back in position by three.'

'Agreed.'

As we scoff our lunch of cottage pie and chips in the White Lion in Clitheroe's ancient Market Place, we discuss our rules of engagement.

Maureen poses the obvious question.

'Do we slot them straight off, or give them the benefit of the doubt.'

'Slot them without hesitating.'

It seems bizarre to be proposing a cold-blooded killing in a pleasant pub in the middle of a quaint English market town, but it's the measure of the predicament we're in. Even so, Maureen seems surprised by my ruthless response.

'Hang on, let's look at the options.'

'Bollocks to that! If a hit team appears, odds on they'll be the ones who did for Jed and Bonny.'

'But they might not be.'

'OK, if it's the Provos, they're not going to show us any mercy either.'

'Agreed. But what if it's the legit team from the spooks?'

'OK, but what if they're under orders to do for us as well.'

'I don't think so, not yet. They'll be tasked with bringing us in – either to get us out of harm's way, or for one last chance to redeem ourselves.'

'They may think they've already given us our last chance. You give them too much credit, Mo. Let's just take them down, whoever they are.'

'I don't like it. Besides, there's likely to be three or four of them. We'll be lucky to take them all down.'

'If you hit two, with the advantage of cover and elevation, I can get them in a crossfire with the MP5, then double it down the hill to finish them off.'

'Still a big ask.'

'Not easy, I agree. But it depends how good they are, and how good we are. Not getting windy, are you?'

'Not windy about the op, just about whether it's the right thing to do.'

'Come on, let's think about it along the way. We need to get our skates on.'

*

By the time we park the car, make its contents look like we've gone tabbing up Pendle, and get our kit sorted, the light is beginning to fade.

I go through a last check with Maureen.

'Weapons, silencer, scope?'

'Check.'

'Comms?'

'Check.'

'Scran?'

'Check.'

'Poncho/sleeping bag?'

'Check.'

'Happy?'

'No, we haven't decided on the outcome of the op.'

'Blow the fuckers away.'

'I don't like it, Jimmy. We've got comms. So can we decide when we see them; use our instincts?'

'Not good, Mo. We need to know what we're about, before we put two hundred yards between ourselves. You can't decide on the hoof, based on "instincts".'

'You're right, but that's the only deal I'm happy to agree to.'

I have a real dilemma. I know Maureen's not being 'weak' or succumbing to 'female sentiments'; she's too good a soldier for that. Although it goes against everything I've been taught, my gut feeling tells me to trust her 'instincts'.

'Are you sure, Mo? It goes against the grain, all our training.'

'I know. I just don't want us to make another mistake. Belfast, Barbon; two's enough.'

I smile at her as warmly as I can.

'OK, deal; your call. Let's get into position. This could be a long haul: twelve hours, or twelve days.'

I can sense Maureen's apprehension. She knows this is my territory – not the glamour of front-line battle or embassy sieges, but the mind-numbing grind and physical hardship of undercover surveillance.

I try to reassure her.

'You passed Phase 1 Selection in Cotterdale. If you pass this one, you get your beret and badge.'

'No pressure, then.'

We scan the hillside to identify positions that grant us clear sight, then leave the car at the bottom of the track to Pendle's summit and tab up its precipitous slope. We move a hundred yards away from the much-trodden path, where I help Maureen sort out her hide behind one of the few small trees that survive on the barren hillside and prepare its camouflage. We help one another with cam cream, and I repeat the standard procedures for eating, peeing, crapping and sleeping, and wish her luck.

We part with an embrace, and I make my way higher up to a position in a small gully where I have a commanding view of everything below. I camouflage my position with foliage, branches and twigs, put my poncho down, clamber into my sleeping bag and roll over, making myself into a cocoon against the elements. For a while I'm warm and dry, but I know these are comforts that won't endure.

It's all but dark. Pendle's huge presence makes me feel insignificant and vulnerable. It's easy to understand why it's been such a source of mystery and intrigue over the centuries. I steel myself for what's to come by remembering my training and thinking of the countless others who've gone before me in miserable hides in even worse conditions. Like the G Squadron lads who hid in tiny scrapes in the freezing earth of the Falklands to call in air strikes against Argie fuel dumps; or the poor buggers from D Squadron who, wet and cold in muddy hedgerows in Armagh, waited for Provo quartermasters to return to their arms dumps.

After a while, I make my first comms call to Maureen.

'How are you?'

'This place gives me the willies, Jim. It's not like Cotterdale.'

'Don't worry, it's all in the mind. But if you see any witches, give me a blast.'

'Don't worry, if I see any old hags up here, I'll be in your bag before you can say, "Hubble, bubble, toil and trouble . . ."'

'Sounds promising. I'll see what I can get the Devil to conjure up.'

'Yeah, right.'

I check everything and go over all the things that Maureen has to think about – to make sure I haven't forgotten anything. I polish the lenses of my binos, then strip, clean and reassemble my Browning and MP5 – not easy in the dark – and check my watch, a gift from Mo for good behaviour.

I give her another blast.

'Seventeen hundred hours, Mo. Two hours on, two hours off. I'm on first, OK?'

'Understood. Call me at nineteen hundred hours.'

'Feeling better?'

'Are you joking? It's black, wet and cold. And I can see witches on broomsticks everywhere.'

'Really? How intriguing. You know what they use their broomsticks for?'

'Fuck off!'

37. Witch's Ambush

A long, miserable night on the side of Pendle follows. We keep one another alert and crack jokes at the end of each watch, but it's scant comfort. The damp air and cold ground invade the body and weaken even the firmest of temperaments.

Nothing much stirs beneath us. On my watch, I count four cars overnight; Maureen clocks three. A milk lorry passes by at 06.15 and a white van at 07.25. A steady increase in traffic heading for the metropolis of Burnley follows. At 08.15 it's still dark, and a vehicle passes every two or three minutes.

'Another glorious day in nirvana, Mo!'

Her response is just a grunt of discontent.

As daylight replaces the black gloom of a Pennine night with the grey misery of a Pennine day, we both wonder which bright spark thought of two-hour watches! We decide that tomorrow night, if we survive that far, we'll do four-hour stints.

Everything is wringing wet. We decide to clean our weapons to ease the tedium.

'Magic up here, isn't it, Mo? Some people pay money to experience the charms of the "Backbone of England".'

'Fuck me, Jim, all this bollocks about God's own country is very dull.'

'Got out of the wrong side of the bed, did we, darling?'

'Fuck off!'

*

Two days pass.

Nothing happens, except that life goes on as it always has in this quiet corner of England. We begin to wonder whether anyone will ever come looking for us and reach the obvious conclusion that we could be lying in our self-imposed torture chamber until doomsday.

The morning of day three dawns just like all the days before: bloody grey and bloody miserable. Although she hasn't moaned once, I'm certain Mo feels as I do. Fuck this for a game of soldiers! Our rations are running low and, without more food, our wait is unsustainable. We decide that we'll give it until midday, then decamp to Clitheroe for a good scoff, a bottle of plonk and a rethink.

When lunchtime arrives, it brings the brief respite of clear air and warm sunshine. We decide to stick it out for another few hours. I check my watch: 15.15. The clouds come back; there's more rain coming.

I'm suddenly guilty of nodding off. I can't help it. One minute I'm peering into the distance, the next minute I'm gone. Then, after what is either thirty seconds or three hours, Maureen is whispering in my earpiece.

'This looks promising . . . *Jim*, this looks promising!'

The light switch is suddenly thrown.

'Sorry, Mo, you broke up then.'

'Bollocks, you nodded off! I think I get the beret and badge.'

'OK, they're yours. What's going on?'

'Dark green Range Rover, coming up the road at two o'clock. You won't be able to see it yet . . . moving slowly. Not many Range Rovers in these parts.'

'It must be military.'

'For sure. The Provos wouldn't be in anything as conspicuous as that. It's either the good spooks or the bad spooks.'

'OK, Mo, remember what I said. Let's assume it's the bad boys.'

She doesn't respond for a while, then speaks with an urgency.

'I think they've seen our wheels. They're stopping.'

The Range Rover suddenly comes into my view and I see its red brake lights cut through the Pennine gloom.

Maureen calls again.

'They're pros. They're parking hard against the wall next to where we've parked.'

She's right. The high dry-stone wall by the road covers all but the top part of their car, giving maximum cover from above. There's no movement from the vehicle for several minutes. The windows are open slightly and I can see the thin mist of cigarette smoke escaping into Pendle's moorland air. My heart begins to beat faster as I realize that dusk is not far away, when we'll lose sight of our quarry.

'Jim, they must be deciding what to do.'

'Correct. Their dilemma is not knowing where we are. We could be yomping around Pendle and, as it's the end of the day, be due back about now, or we may have abandoned the vehicle. They may even think it's an ambush. Hopefully, they'll come up to hunt us down, at least three of them, preferably all four.'

'Jim, if they're half-decent pros, they won't buy it.'

'You may be right, but let's keep our fingers crossed.'

'Hang on, Jimmy, the door's opening.'

'If they're as good as they seem, only one will get out

288

for a recce of our wheels. Stay absolutely still. If he comes up the track towards you, put a hole in him.'

'Don't worry, I will.'

The man doing the recce might just as well be in combat uniform, his dress is so Hereford: jeans, monkey jacket, baseball cap and heavy horseshoe moustache. As he walks around our vehicle, pistol in hand, I train my binos on the Range Rover. Both the passenger and rear on-side windows are slightly open, and poking out of them are the silencers of a pair of high-calibre rifles.

Mr Regiment finishes his tour of our car and begins a hesitant walk towards the track.

'Only one shot, Mo. He's got cover from their car. Don't give away your positon.'

'I see them. If he reaches that big puddle thirty yards up, he's a dead man.'

'OK, I'll pin down the shooters from here. They're certain to go for the cover of the wall next to the vehicle. I'll keep their heads down until it's dark, then you leg it out of there.'

'OK.'

Our visitor only walks ten yards up the track, where he scans Pendle's precipitous flanks intently. Realizing that it makes for an ideal hide, he stares at the little clump of vegetation where Maureen is hidden. He's weighing up whether to take a closer look. I flex my trigger finger, but he looks at the boggy ground, then at his pristine adidas trainers, and decides it's a recce too far.

When the wanderer returns to his vehicle, there are more long minutes of inactivity.

'They don't know what to do, Mo. There's not much

daylight left and on the basis that we might still be here, they'd like to flush us out before dark.'

'OK, boss. So what do we do?'

'So, I'm "boss" now?'

'Your territory, Jimmy.'

'We wait. We have all the cards.'

It begins to rain and the wind starts to swirl it around. It's like being in a cold shower. I didn't think there was any bit of me that wasn't already sodden by days of rain and damp, but this latest squall manages to blow rivulets down the back of my neck. They merge into a stream that tracks between my shoulder blades and into the small of my back. I mutter expletives to myself.

'Quiet, Jimmy. I'm trying to concentrate.'

'Sorry, Mo. But the rain is running down my back.'

'As you lot say up here, stop "moitherin".'

More interminable minutes pass. Dusk is blending into darkness.

Maureen strangles a cry of alarm.

'Fuck! A police convoy's coming up the road. No sirens, but lots of blue neon! There must be half a dozen of them.'

It takes me a few moments to work out what's going on.

'Very clever. They've called in the woodentops. Probably told them we're a Provo ASU. They knew darkness would allow us to get away, so they've brought in the bobbies to flush us out before it gets dark.'

'So what do we do?'

'Give me a minute.'

I look to the sky and the advancing darkness. The rain is still coming down in typical Pennine torrents.

'Let's hold our ground. I think our visitors have under-estimated nightfall and overestimated the professional-ism of Lancashire's constabulary. By the time the boys in blue have got themselves organized it'll be pitch black and the plods will want to be off home for plate pie and chips.'

'Are you sure?'

I check the skies again and survey the flurry of activity below. It's illuminated by strobes of blue light and seems chaotic, like a scene from the Keystone Cops.

'We'll be OK . . . just. But the fuckers have brought dogs!'

'How long before I can move?'

'Another ten minutes, then leg it up to me, double quick. Leave everything except weapons and ammo.'

It seems like the longest ten minutes in history but, as the seconds tick down, below us the animated policemen are still telling one another what to do and their dogs are still barking rabidly. I can no longer see them, so I'm sure they can't see us.

'Mo, move! As fast as those long legs will carry you. Keep your head down, weapon at port arms, and your arse in the air like the best fell runners.' Maureen's athleti-cism gets her to me in no time at all. She's hardly drawing breath. We check our precious weapons and make for Pendle's summit.

'OK, Mo, this is your Fan Dance, up and over Pen-y-Fan; your final selection test.'

'You lead, Jimmy.'

We're able to use our red-filter night torch once the gradient of Pendle's huge cleavage takes us out of sight

of those below. Its soft glow makes it much easier to nego-
tiate the hill's treacherous ground. My guess about Lancashire's bobbies turns out to be accurate. No one seems
to be following us up the bulge of Pendle's south-east
flank.

'So, we go over the top and down the other side to Pendleton, another place almost as pretty as Downham.'

'Great! I suppose it'll be pissing it down there as
well?'

'Course, this is Lancashire.'

'Will you be fucking quiet about Lancashire? You're
like a broken record!'

'Sorry, Mo, just keeping you amused.'

It's hard going, especially with only a compass to guide
us. But by the dead of night, we're at the bottom of Pendle's north-west slopes, trudging into the pretty village of
Pendleton.

'Mo, we need to hide our weapons and get rid of our
camouflage.'

'OK, but I don't want us to be defenceless.'

'Let's keep the Brownings in our belts. I'll hide the
heavy artillery in the churchyard over there. You find a
quiet spot near the pub down the road. It's about two
hundred yards.'

'Name?'

'The Swan with Two Necks.'

'Very appropriate – we're also a protected species with
our necks on the line.'

'Take it as a good omen.'

I hide the weapons in an overgrown hedgerow behind

All Saints Parish Church and walk down to find Maureen. She's opposite the Swan, hidden behind a low wall, and makes her presence known by lightly tapping her pistol on the top.

'So far so good, Mo. We need some wheels. What about that Range Rover outside the boozer?'

'That's what I thought, until I went over for a close look under the street light. I stopped halfway.'

'And?'

'Dark green, blackened windows!'

'You're kidding?'

'No, I'm not. It's them.'

I peer across into the darkness and the familiarity is suddenly obvious. I try to make light of it.

'Well, I suppose they have to sleep somewhere.'

'So what do we do now, Jimmy boy?'

'Wait until they leave in the morning. It'll still be dark; we can get close. Let's turn them into human colanders.'

'Not your smartest idea, Jim. Four bodies in the middle of a small Lancashire village might raise an eyebrow or two!'

'Who cares?'

'We do! I don't want us all over the papers and every copper in Britain looking for us. If we're going to eliminate these boys, let's at least do it discreetly, so the mess can be cleaned up.'

'Suggestions?'

'There must be a few flashy cottages in this village – holiday/weekend homes?'

'Lots.'

'Let's find one. I'll borrow a few glad rags and some

make-up and we can set a new trap. Which way will they leave?'

'That way, towards the A59.'

'Is there a quiet spot?'

'Yes. Good thinking, Mo. The damsel in distress routine?'

'Correct.'

38. Damsel in Distress

It's easy to find a well-appointed holiday cottage in Pendleton. At one, nestling some way from Pendleton Brook on quaintly named Tary Barn Lane, the neatly manicured lawn, immaculate paved driveway and expensive bronze-finish exterior lights reek of big-city brass, not Pennine muck.

One of the many gifts of 14 Intelligence training is the ability to pick locks. However, without one of their neat little tool kits, we resort to a cruder methodology. The cottage has no alarm so, with the help of a large stone from the garden, we make an easy entry through the downstairs cloakroom window.

As I keep my eyes peeled, Maureen disappears inside to make herself look glamorous.

After what seems like an eternity, when she reappears the transformation is extraordinary. She's found a short denim jacket, sky-blue blouse, fetchingly tight black skirt and a pair of racy nylons. The shoes are perfect: black shiny stilettoes with a heel that makes Maureen even more Amazonian in stature. She has washed and blow-dried her hair, which makes her look just like Sigourney Weaver in *Alien*, and put on enough make-up to suggest she's off to spend the day with a clandestine lover in a country hotel.

'Fuck a duck, Mo, I must remember this address. It looks like the lady of the house may be worth a visit one day.'

'I shouldn't bother, Jim. The man of the house must be a giant. You could get both of your size nines into one of his shoes!'

'Shame . . . but you look fabulous, just the part. I'd definitely stop to help you start your engine.'

'Yer, right! These bloody shoes don't fit; I'm in agony. Let's get on with it.'

'I'll go and see if I can purloin some wheels that match your outfit. Something ostentatious that goes like fuck!'

'Steady, boy!'

She gives me an uncharacteristic swivel of her slim hips and pushes me towards the front of the house.

'Go on, I'll wait here. Bring the heavy artillery.'

I find the perfect vehicle on the way up to the church. It's a relatively new navy-blue Ford Escort Cabriolet – ideal for Maureen's honey trap – and it's easy to get into and start.

Ten minutes later, we're in position to strike. The lane to the A59 is not very long, and quite narrow. But there's a place to pull over about a hundred and fifty yards from the village, where there are gates into the fields on both sides of the road.

Maureen tucks her Browning down the front of her skirt and opens the bonnet of the Escort. She sticks her head into the engine compartment, leaving her backside poking provocatively into the air. I find a spot obscured by the hedgerow and check that the MP5 is ready to create mayhem.

Then we wait. I check my watch: 08.15.

Those idle fuckers will be having a big fry-up. It could be a long wait. They'll go back to the other side of Pendle to check our car and see that it's still there. They'll think we've abandoned it and so make for Lancashire Police HQ in Preston for a rethink and a call to Gower Street.

It is a long wait.

A few commuters to Clitheroe and Blackburn trundle by; Maureen waves away any who offer to stop. One of them, whose tongue almost slides along the tarmac as he drools over her stunning outline, has, with reassurances that an anxious husband is just around the corner, to be all but manhandled back into his white van by Maureen. He blows her a kiss as he drives off, then toots his horn repeatedly. His day's been made.

Just after nine, our quarry appears.

They're moving slowly. There's every chance they'll sniff a trap, but we have to take risks. And my hunch is that, after checking the car, they'll think we're long gone from this part of the world. Maureen turns and leans deep into the Escort's innards. Her skirt all but disappears over her backside. I flick off the safety of my weapon.

The Range Rover slows and Maureen immediately straightens herself and turns towards the approaching vehicle. She looks stunning. A rare shaft of sunlight catches her auburn locks and makes her garish burgundy lipstick glisten. Drawn as if by a powerful magnet, a baseball-capped head peers from the driver's door window.

It must be the long months listening to my flat Lancastrian vowels but, with almost perfect tone and inflection, she calls out coquettishly.

'Oh, bloody 'ell, lad, you're a sight fer sore eyes. This bloody thing's died a death on me.'

The driver buys the deception and rolls his Range Rover

behind the Escort. He gets out and walks towards Maureen. His masculine homing device is locked on. He doesn't even look sideways. When he gets close to Maureen, she flashes him the sort of smile that promises every conceivable carnal delight. But in the same moment, her Browning appears within six inches of the end of his nose.

I take my cue and before the Rover's windows or doors can move, I step forward and point the Heckler & Koch MP5 at the blackened windows.

Maureen issues very short, sharp orders.

'Tell your mates to leave their weapons behind, get out of the vehicle and walk through the gate. You drop your weapon on the ground and go with them. When you're there, get on your knees, hands on heads . . . and be good boys.'

'Fuck you, Townsend! You and that drunk twat Waddington are in so much trouble, you'll soon be dead meat. We're here to help.'

Within half a second of our captive's scathing comment, Maureen has pulled her trigger. The round, its discharge echoing around Pendle's slopes like a rumble of thunder, passes close enough to our prisoner's ear to make him wince.

'Fucking hell, Townsend, are you mad!'

'Yes, I am, mad enough to put the next one through what passes for your fucking brain. Didn't they brief you about me being a man-hating, lesbian psychopath?'

So convincing is Maureen's threat, its menace produces an instant reaction. Within seconds, four men are in the field and on their knees in front of us.

I grasp the tone Maureen has set.

'Listen, you fuckers. After what happened to Jed and Bonny, as far as we're concerned, this is now very personal.'

Maureen takes over.

'If you're who you say you are, you can tell Control that we're now the hunters and that we'll treat anyone who gets in our way as fair game. D'ya get that, limp dick?'

Our prey has got himself together and begins to fight back.

'Look, I've been threatened by some real hard cases, so dykes like you don't even register.'

Such is the fury on Maureen's face, for a second I think she's going to slot him on the spot. I decide to intervene.

'Whatever story you've been fed by Gower Street, we're just a couple of operatives trying to survive this bag of shit. We got stuffed in Belfast; we're not going to be fucked over again.'

My candour seems to strike a chord.

'OK, you're obviously declining our offer to come in, so here's the way it is. Control wants you to know that a Provo ASU is active on the mainland and has already made contact with a sleeper unit, we think in London. They have a single agenda – vengeance. It's personal for them too.'

'I think we'd worked that out for ourselves.'

'Fair enough, but that's not the worst of it.'

'Go on.'

'There's a rogue element on the loose.'

'We know that as well.'

'Yes, but we have more intel.'

Before he can continue, a passing car stops in the gateway. Its driver stares straight at the scene – kneeling men, guns – it must look like a Sam Peckinpah movie. He slams his car into reverse and screeches his way back towards the A59.

I realize that we've got not much more than ten–fifteen minutes before a posse of police vehicles arrives at speed. I step towards our quarry and point my weapon at his face.

'We're now in a hurry, so get on with it.'

'Ex-Selous Scouts, mercenaries. We think as many as a dozen, organized into three units. They're led by a sicko who's so crazy they threw him out of South Africa's Bureau of State Security. He ended up in Rhodesia.'

The shock of hearing the notorious Scouts' name hits me like a thunderbolt. I look at Maureen; she recognizes the name as well.

'We think they're financed by disaffected businessmen, very rich, some onshore, some offshore.'

Maureen speaks. Her tone is less aggressive, more anxious.

'What's their problem?'

'All sorts. Selling out Smith's regime in Rhodesia to Mugabe and his rebels. Not dealing with the left here, and letting the unions run the country. Northern Ireland is the final straw.'

I look at Maureen. The same cogs begin to whirr in her brain as they do in mine.

Our man continues his ominous outline.

'When word about your exploits in Belfast reached this disaffected group, you two became public enemy number one.'

Maureen snaps at him.

'We went "native", became IRA sympathizers?'

'Something like that. We're guessing a bit, probably got blown into a thing about how the left has infiltrated MI5. You in particular, Waddington; your left-wing tendencies at university, and all that.'

My hackles begin to rise.

'Are you Regiment, or ex-Regiment?'

'Ex.'

'So what're you doing at Gower Street?'

'What does it look like?'

'How the fuck is all this intel getting in and out of Gower Street?'

'We think there's a mole, but we can't pin him down.'

I look at Maureen. Suddenly a lot of what's been happening begins to make sense.

She fires another question.

'How close are you to our Control?'

'I'm under his direct orders. I report to him, and him only.'

'OK, so tell him that we're on the offensive; tell him to keep out of our way.'

'Not wise, Townsend. Let me tell you about these Rhodesian boys. The units that attacked you in Clapham and the Weald are not the ones you should be worried about. They're hard cases, but not in the same league as the boys who did Barbon. They're the really bad boys. Smyth, Tyler, van Zyl and Hendriks, a crack unit. Assassins, dirty tricks; they've done the lot. Hendriks is a psycho, a right nutter. Stay well clear, if you value your well-being.'

I take my turn to assail our captive.

'What's your fucking name?'

'What's that got to do with anything?'

'You know our names. We want to know yours. What's your fucking name?'

'Peters.'

'Well, Peters, I don't value my well-being. I don't give a fuck. You know they tied Bonny up and raped her?'

'We know. Hendriks has done it before.'

'Hendriks?'

'Correct.'

He looks at Maureen.

'I know you don't need any advice from me, but don't try the short skirt routine with him. He's a killer and a sadist –'

I interrupt him.

'Hendrik, or whatever the cunt's name is, doesn't scare me, or Maureen. Thanks for giving us his name. You can tell Control that Mr Selous Scouts is a dead man.' I look at my watch. 'Mo, let's go.'

'Yeah.' She looks at Peters with an intensity that could melt granite. 'These "disaffected businessmen" with "friends" in Gower Street. What more can you tell us?'

'Nothing. That's all we know.'

'Don't fuck me about, Peters. You don't get from "businessmen" to Gower Street without intermediaries.'

He stares at Maureen, weighing up whether he should divulge any more intel.

'OK . . . there are obvious links to politics, high up, and the senior military. We think their hub is one of the old boys' clubs in St James's, but we can't be sure. The connections with Gower Street are strong in all of them, so it's hard to find out.'

Maureen curls her lip.

'The old boys' fucking network!'

I smile at her.

'Careful, Mo, Peters will be reporting back that you've gone pinko as well.'

'I don't give a fuck!' She then turns back to Peters, with a renewed hostility, and asks an obvious question. 'If you know who these Rhodesian Boy Scouts are, why hasn't Gower Street brought them to heel?'

Peters stares back at Maureen with a plaintive, even remorseful, look on his face.

'That's a good question. Several of us have made the same point, including Control . . .' He pauses and lowers his head.

Maureen doesn't relent.

'Go on!'

'The word is that they're protected.'

'What do you mean, "protected"?'

'Who knows? It's forbidden territory. If you value your job, don't ask, don't get involved; one of those "keep your mouth shut" jobs.'

'That's fucking bollocks!'

He now looks distinctly sheepish.

'I know.'

'What about Control and the DG?'

'Who knows? That's beyond my pay scale. You'll have to ask them yourself.'

I step forward.

'Don't worry, we will.'

We grab all their weapons and ammunition and, taking care to put holes in all four of the Range Rover's tyres, prepare to make a rapid departure in the Escort.

Just as we pull away, Peters calls out to us.

'Be careful, you're running out of options.'

Although he seems to be genuinely concerned for our welfare, we ignore him and, with the wail of sirens emerging in the distance, we leave long strips of tyre burn on the local tarmac and head back towards Pendleton like shit off a shovel.

'Where to now, Jim?'

'Over the tops above Burnley, a little moorland road that avoids civilization until we're miles away from here.'

'Don't tell me, another idyllic part of God's own country?'

'Not quite. It's a wonderful place but, sadly, it's in Yorkshire. Even so, other than the Tykes, it's great; you'll love it.'

'Will I? Not if it's all "ee, by gum", whippets and flat caps!'

'What did you read at Cambridge?'

'English, why?'

'Do you like *Jane Eyre*, *Wuthering Heights* and all that stuff?'

'Course.'

'Well, we're going to Haworth. It's all fish and chips and Yorkshire pud for the tourists, but it's still a proper literary shrine. We can go to the Parsonage, where you can tell me why *Jane Eyre*'s so good. I hated it at school.'

'That's because you're pig ignorant, Jimmy.'

39. Darling Daddy

We drive to Haworth over Widdop Moor. On the way, I take Maureen to see the ruined Wycoller Hall in a tiny Pennine village, all but frozen in time from the days when it thrived on wool in the eighteenth century. When I tell her the hall was the inspiration for Ferndean Manor, in *Jane Eyre*, she's impressed and relents a little on her 'pig ignorant' view of me.

When we ascend Widdop, its desolation and rugged beauty captivate Maureen.

'No wonder Emily wrote *Wuthering Heights* with such vivid imagery. Just look at it, it's magnificent.'

'Careful, Mo, we're still in Lancashire. Don't let me think you're beginning to like it.'

When we reach Haworth, we book into the White Lion and go for dinner at the Black Bull, where Branwell Brontë drank himself into oblivion.

Although it's raining and Haworth's Main Street is dominated by commercial premises devoted to emptying the wallets and purses of pilgrims to the memory of literary greatness, its aura has an effect on Maureen. But it doesn't quite lift her pensive mood.

'Jim, are we planning on being obvious, attracting attention again?'

'Yes, we'll leave a few clues for the bobbies. I'll park the Escort where it'll be spotted. Eventually, some eagle-eyed woodentop'll drop in and word will get back to Gower Street. But we have a few days.'

'OK, listen, we have another problem.'

'Don't tell me – you've found Jesus and you're joining a nunnery?'

'Be serious . . . we're running out of money. We're nearly at rock bottom.'

'Ah, that's not good. And our job prospects are not great at the moment.'

'Exactly.'

'We could always do a Bonnie and Clyde.'

'They didn't live happily ever after, Jim.'

'But they did go out in a blaze of glory.'

'Yes, full of holes. No thanks.'

'Butch Cassidy and the Sundance Kid – Bolivia?'

'Same ending, even more holes.'

'But we could become legends, like them.'

'I'd prefer a long life, grandchildren and a tranquil death in my nineties.'

'You need a marriage in there somewhere. Other than me, I'd like to meet the bloke who could persuade you to settle down and have kids.'

She ignores the comment; she's being practical.

'I'll write to Daddy. He'll send more money to keep us going. God, he's a saint, that man. But we'll have to be very careful.'

We spend the next twenty minutes working out how a wad of cash can be sent to us. Eventually, we devise what we think is a watertight delivery method. Maureen begins to write the letter on the White Lion's notepaper.

Darling Daddy,

. . . I'm sending this to you at the golf club for obvious reasons . . .

Cut out a hole in the pages of a hardback book for the cash . . . package it up securely and address it to me here at the White Lion. Use the name 'Nelson' – that's what we're using at the moment . . .

Drive off to the golf club as usual. Leave the package with Mummy. Tell her, after you've been gone for an hour or so, to go next door with the package . . . the back way, where no one will see, not the front door . . .

Mummy should tell Mr Lloyd-Elliott that she's not feeling well and that you've gone off and forgotten an important package . . .

Would he mind taking it to the post office? You know how the old boy fancies Mummy, he'll be off like a shot . . .

Sorry not to be able to tell you more and to impose on your generosity yet again. You'll get the full story when I'm home – and I promise that will be soon . . .

Try to help Mummy. I know she'll be worried sick. Trust me, I'll come through this. I'm with a top man. Together we're a formidable team. I'd like you to meet him one day.

I love you, Daddy.

D

xxx

My eyes light up at the last paragraph.

'Do you mean that "top man" stuff? You're not just trying to reassure your father?'

'What do you think?'

With the letter written, Maureen's mood deepens from pensive to sombre.

'What did you mean earlier when you said you'd like to meet the man who could persuade me to settle down?'

'Jesus, Mo, you're a formidable woman, a daunting prospect for ordinary mortals.'

'Am I . . .?' She pauses and looks distinctly fragile. 'You know what, Jim? I'm fed up with being formidable. I think I just want to be ordinary. I don't want to intimidate men and be a hard case. I've heard them all: "Amazon", "dyke", "should've been a man".'

She tries to compose herself. 'Look at me. I've blown my career and let my parents down. I've been shot at, I've brought death to innocent people and I'm on the run, with only a slim chance of surviving . . . and I've just turned thirty-three. I'll soon be a middle-aged spinster. What a fucking mess!'

'Yes, but we'll sort it – as you said, we're formidable. And you've still got me, Mo. With your help, I'll get you through this. Don't crack; don't go under, like I did. From bitter experience, I can tell you it's not a good place to be.'

She doesn't say anything for a while. I need to change the subject. So, seeking inspiration, I look out at the dank mist that has wrapped itself around Haworth. I think of the Brontës and the harsh, secluded life they led in this moorland backwater. Where did they find the inspiration when, as far as we know, they led such sheltered lives? Maureen must know, so I ask her.

'Who knows? We'll never know for sure. I suspect it came from the power of the human imagination, which knows no bounds, even for lonely girls up on the moors.' She smiles at me with a wistfulness that's endearing. 'Do you know Tennyson?' She still looks glum.

I don't think my ploy's worked, so I try humour.

'There's a pub in Scarborough called the Tennyson Arms.'

'Jesus, Jim, did you just make that up?'

'No, there is. I've been there. Scarborough Festival – university football.'

She looks at me. My silly comment nearly lifts her mood, and a little smile plays across her face, but it's soon gone and the solemn vein returns.

'In *In Memoriam*, Tennyson wrote: "So runs my dream; but what am I? / An infant crying in the night; / An infant crying for the light, / And with no language but a cry."'

'Jesus! Don't be so morbid, Mo.'

Her passing smile now long gone, there's a profound sadness contorting her face.

'The truth is, I really feel like I'm crying in the night – a dark night, like up on Widdop Moor. I am crying for the light, but there isn't any.'

'But there is. There is light, a light that comes from within us. We're special, both of us, and together we're very special.'

Maureen looks up at me. Her eyes glisten with tears. She takes a long and deliberate, deep breath.

'Jim, will you do me a big favour?'

'Anything.'

'Sleep with me tonight.'

'You know that question doesn't need an answer.'

'Not for sex, Jim. I don't want that. I need you, not as a lover but as my guardian angel. Will you do that for me?'

Part of me is devastated. But I also know I'm being paid a huge compliment. It's enough.

'Mo, it will be a privilege.'

'My Tristan?'

'Whoever you like. But weren't Tristan and Isolde lovers?'

'Yes, but not tonight.' She smiles. 'Hang on, you're pig ignorant. How come you know about Tristan and Isolde?'

'I just guessed!'

Maureen looks me in the eye and puts her hand on mine. 'Thanks, Jim.'

'Come on, girl, let's get some sleep. Fish and chips tomorrow. Iron rations until Daddy's money arrives.'

My night with Maureen curled up in my arms is heavenly.

She keeps her bra and knickers on. I get a hard-on, of course, but she just accepts my tumescence as normal and snuggles into me. She seems comforted and content, and I feel empowered.

It's enough; my arousal subsides, and I fall into a peaceful sleep.

When I wake the next morning, Maureen has already had a shower and is almost dressed.

'Come on, Jim. Breakfast, then we're going up to Top Withens. I have to see it.'

'You know it probably isn't Wuthering Heights?'

'Doesn't matter. I have to see it.'

She throws some of my clothes at me, then leans over and kisses me on the forehead.

'Jimmy, you are Mr Gold Star. Thanks for last night. I needed that warmth and reassurance. You've made a girl very happy. I'll never forget.'

I kiss her back and slap her on the arse.

*

By the time the money arrives from Maureen's father, our diet of cheap Haworth fish and chips has become a little monotonous, even for me. Astutely, recognizing the address, her father has sent the money in a copy of Anne Brontë's *The Tenant of Wildfell Hall*.

'That's clever. I thought you said your father was a thinly disguised thick-necked Mick?'

'He probably just picked up the first Brontë novel in the bookshop. Her name does begin with "A", after all.'

'I think you do him a disservice. I wonder if he knows it's thought to be one of the first great feminist novels?'

'Jim, are you sure you didn't read English lit at uni?'

'Certain, just modern history.'

'I'm going to have to stop calling you an ignorant northern pig.'

'Don't drag the North into this.'

That evening, we decide to offer one last homage to Britain's greatest gift to international cuisine and settle down at a table at the Brontë Fish Bar, a neat, triangular street-corner chip shop with an inside eating area and tables outside for Haworth's summer pilgrims.

It's a blast from the past. Red gingham tablecloths cover pale pine tables, which are laid with the usual ensemble of glass bottles. There are salt and pepper pots with white Bakelite screw tops, brown sauce and ketchup bottles and pear-shaped, red-topped bottles of Sarson's malt vinegar. The gleaming stainless-steel frying pans are heated by a central coal fire and above them, illustrated by seagulls and an old-fashioned trawler in full sail, sits a painted-glass decorative panel in pale green and yellow. There's a signature on the glass: Henry Nuttall, Rochdale,

Rangemaster. What a perfect name for a manufacturer of deep-fat fryers.

The air is a fug of chip fat, burning coal and spicy vinegar; it's blissful! I smile to myself, content that at least one such Edwardian splendour has survived into the 1980s.

The proprietor, rotund and flushed, wears an immaculate white apron as he stirs his boiling beef dripping. His assistant, bleach-blonde and a little plump, looks like his daughter. She's probably still at school. Her apron's a little crumpled and has black streaks down its front from the newsprint off the discarded newspapers she uses to wrap her wares.

He smiles and is effusive with his greetings and chit-chat; she looks sullen and bored and clearly would prefer to be anywhere else.

The weather outside is a perfect complement to the scene. The only illumination of the murky night comes from the buttery glow of a single sodium street light and its reflections on the wet street below. The rain hits the cobbles like drum taps. The subsequent rivulets become a torrent, which begins to overwhelm the iron grilles of Haworth's Changegate drainage gullies.

I look at Maureen to check if there are any signs of her recent morose mood returning. She's staring at the cascading downpour outside but, thankfully, with no hint of melancholy.

Instead, there's a sudden look of horror in her eyes. I watch as, in a fluid movement, she dives from her chair and reaches for her Browning. My move follows instantly. I turn before I hit the tiles of the greasy floor. Two shots ring out, fired almost in parallel, from unseen attackers. One of the bullets shatters the glass of the counter and produces a blood-curdling scream from the young girl. The other ricochets off the tiles next to me, sending fragments of clay stinging into my face. More bullets explode the glass of the warming pans above the counter; one hits the proprietor square in the forehead. It exits at the top of his skull and deposits a melange of bone, blood and brain on the glass behind him. The cod trawler's sails are suddenly ruby red.

The impact throws the stricken man backwards. He then recoils forwards, towards the scorching fryers. His lifeless form slumps over the hot pans and his left arm falls into the fat. A huge plume of steam rises to the ceiling as his body falls to the floor, splashing fat everywhere. Flames soon follow as the fat reaches the hot coals inside the open fire door.

Maureen has already emptied her magazine through the black holes which were once the shop's windows. I've fired only five rounds so, as Maureen inserts a new magazine, I put an arc of fire into the darkness.

As soon as she's ready, we rush out on to the street. There are two bodies slumped at the bottom of the wall of the house opposite, which has lost all its ground-floor windows. In the distance, we see two silhouettes running into the gloom. We both drop to our knees, take aim and fire simultaneously. One figure judders as it's hit and falls to the ground; a weapon rattles along the pavement. The other figure disappears around a corner.

Maureen shouts at me.

'Do we go after them?'

'No, too far. You check the chippy. I'll check these two and the house.'

The shop is engulfed in flames. Even if, by some miracle, the proprietor or his daughter survived the bullets, they're lost in the inferno. Mercifully, the house opposite is empty of inhabitants. The two assassins are dead. Our aim has been lethally accurate; at least two rounds in each body. They carry no obvious identification.

As our car is in the opposite direction, we decide not to check the body of the third shooter. We run as fast as our legs will carry us to our wheels. The rain beats down on us. Thank God, the deluge means there'll be few, if any, witnesses.

I race through the crucial details in my head: weapons and ammunition in the boot. Good! I shout at Maureen.

'Money?'

'In my belt pouch.'

'Well done!'

'Where to now?'

'London. We've got business there.'

'Too right.'

40. An Audacious Move

It's a rare treat to drive through London with almost no traffic. As we coast across Ludgate Circus, with London's fine buildings towering above us in a pre-dawn half-light, I concede to Maureen that the South does have a few corners of heaven to call its own.

We head for the Hope, a Smithfield pub, where we're sure to find an early-morning breakfast.

After consuming a monstrous feast, a pint of Guinness to wash it down, then a powerful black coffee laced with rum to finish, we're finally relaxed. It's the second week of February. London's air is clear and mild. Many of the Hope's customers are reading the day's first editions. The headlines are all focused on the kidnap in Ireland of the Derby winner Shergar.

'Bet that's the Provos, Jim.'

'Probably.'

'I suppose news of last night will break in the *Evening Standard* tonight.'

'I'm sure it will; should be on the streets early afternoon.'

'How the hell is Gower Street going to deal with last night's slaughter?'

'I can't imagine, but we'll soon find out.' I put my hand on Maureen's arm. 'You did brilliantly last night. Your eagle eyes and quick reactions saved us both. I reckon you slotted all three of them.'

'No, I think you got the one running away, I was high and right. Those poor buggers in the chippy; the girl can't have been more than sixteen. That's two more innocent lives we're responsible for.'

The image of the inferno we left behind comes into my head.

'I suppose there was a mum upstairs. She'd have been lucky to get out alive.'

'OK, so three innocent people. That's five in all, seven if you count Belfast. We seem to be getting deeper and deeper into the mire, and the body count is just going up and up.'

Maureen looks at me earnestly, then stares at the Hope's Smithfield workers, their aprons covered in the blood of the animals they've just butchered.

'Are we just professional butchers like these boys, Jim?'

'No! Come on, it's time to go.'

She doesn't move; she just stares at the very large slaughtermen as they pour Guinness down their throats.

'Mo, you need to snap out of these moods. Come on, you're a pro. Act like it!'

She turns to me. My comment has annoyed her. Then she relents.

'You're right. Sorry, where to next?'

'We'll abandon the wheels and get the tube to Knightsbridge.'

'Why?'

'We'll stay at the SFC.'

'You a member?'

'I am.'

'Isn't that like putting our heads in the lion's jaws?'

'Perhaps. But we need to get some sleep and speak to someone there. He's ex-Regiment and knows everyone. He's an excellent bloke, very bright, a good soldier. His career went downhill when he crossed the CO at Hereford.'

'Over what?'

'The Regiment becoming a plaything of politicians, rather than a crack military unit. He's a man of principle, so he had to leave. He's now head of security at Harrods. It's just round the corner, and he goes to the SFC for a drink every night.'

'What are we going to ask him?'

'What he knows about the Rhodesian nutters, and how we get to Spank.'

'Perhaps we got Hendriks and his team last night?'

'Perhaps, but I'd like to be sure.'

'How can he help us get to the DG?'

'He's a contemporary. They were at Cambridge together.'

'How do you know him?'

I helped his son when he was trying to get a trial at Spurs. He owes me one.'

'Bloody hell, Jim, you do get around . . .' She pauses and looks at her watch. 'Listen, if we're getting the tube, what do we do with the artillery?'

'There's a Blacks on Holborn. We'll drive down, dump the Escort, buy two bergens and some new clobber and join the commuters going to work. When we get to Victoria, we'll stash the kit in left luggage.'

*

The Special Forces Club has a strict dress code. So we spend a small fortune and get togged up at Harrods. Maureen doesn't seem to mind spending vast amounts of her father's money. I suppose that's what privilege means. Anyway, we certainly look the part in the bar that evening.

We sip our pre-prandial gin and tonics, pondering the miraculous story that someone at Gower Street, the Home Office, or somewhere, has managed to concoct about Haworth. The *Evening Standard* headline blares: 'Gangland Gun Battle at Literary Shrine.'

It's a deviously brilliant pack of lies. According to a West Yorkshire Police statement:

Three men from rival underground gangs operating drugs and prostitution rackets in Manchester and Leeds have been gunned down on Changegate, a quiet street in the middle of Haworth, the heart of Brontë Country. Three members of the same family were killed in the crossfire and subsequent blaze as their chip shop became the focus of an exchange of intense gunfire. At least three gang members are thought to have fled the scene, one of whom is thought to be a woman. The police are appealing for witnesses and any information that may help their inquiries. They emphasize that the gang members at large are armed and dangerous and must not be approached under any circumstances. At the moment, the police do not have any descriptions available. The three dead men are yet to be identified.

'Ingenious, Jim.'

'It's like Al Capone and the Mafia! I wonder who thought of that? The good news is that we're still out of the public eye.'

We go to the club's TV room, where several members are glued to the BBC's *Six O'Clock News*. There's a lot of head shaking and tut-tutting as reporter Donald Mac-Cormick presents a live report from the scene. He speaks in that earnest tone unique to reporters and vicars while, behind him in the distance, smoke from the burnt-out shell of the Brontë chippy rises into the air. I look around the room; all are from the military or intelligence communities. I'm curious to know if anyone's suspicious about the veracity of the story. There don't seem to be any furrowed brows, only a few mutterings about sending the lads in to sort out the gangs, once and for all!

Maureen and I go back up to the bar where, on cue, David Carmichael, the man we need to speak to, is propping up the bar.

'Good God, Gary, long time no see. Look at you, suited up like a proper chap!'

'Bollocks!'

'Only kidding. You look well.'

'Thanks. How're the kids?'

'Great. Simon got into Teddy Hall and Tim's playing semi-pro for Sutton. Last time I heard, you'd gone doolally, pissed all the time.'

'Yer, right. Let me introduce Debs Townsend. She got me off the sauce.'

'Colleague, lover or friend?'

'A friend and colleague, 14 Intelligence.'

David grabs her by the hand and shakes it vigorously.

'Very well done. Not many women in 14 Int. Excellent effort! And thanks for getting Gary on the straight and narrow. He's an arsehole, but one of the best soldiers I've ever met. So are you two on an op?'

'Not really, we're sort of on leave.'

'Sort of . . . sounds intriguing.'

I come straight to the point.

'David, we need your help. We're up shit creek. We need to speak to the DG at Gower Street.'

'You mean JJ? Fuck, it must be serious!'

'It is; we can't trust anyone else.'

'Look, Gary. I haven't spoken to him in a while. You'll have to give me something to hang this on.'

'We can't. Our names mustn't be mentioned or anything about us, or our op. We don't trust anyone around him, and can't risk him mentioning our approach to his team – or anyone else, for that matter.'

'OK, but you have to give me something. I'm sorry, Gary, I'm not calling JJ and getting myself involved unless I know why it's so important.'

I look at Maureen. Her expression is non-committal, but she turns and looks David in the eye.

'Gary says you're a good bloke, so we'll have to trust you. But understand this: several people are already dead, most of them innocent civilians. It's a miracle we're still alive. We're being hunted; a Provo ASU's after our blood, plus a rogue element of headbangers – ex-Selous Scouts, led by a nutter called Hendriks. He's ex-South African police, and so crazy they threw him out.'

'Oh, is that all? What about the CIA and Spetsnaz?'

'Not yet! We think the Rhodesians are operating with

tacit and even some overt support at very senior levels in the military, and probably in Gower Street. There's money behind them – and some senior politicians.'

'Sounds pretty unhealthy.'

'It is. And we're targets . . . and very expendable.'

David looks across at the *Evening Standard* lying on the bar.

'I don't suppose . . .?'

We don't answer, and try not to give anything away with our facial expressions, perhaps not too successfully.

'Fuck! I had a feeling something wasn't right about that story when I heard it on the radio. Gangs in Brontë country, for Christ's sake!'

He pauses, staring at the headline. The picture beneath it shows flames lighting up the black night in Haworth.

'Look, an obvious question occurs to me.'

'Go on.'

'How do you know you can trust JJ?'

'We don't. What do you think? You've known him a long time.'

'I've known him since Cambridge; we joined the Royal Artillery together. Good bloke. But you can never be a hundred per cent sure of anything in life, Gary. Husbands cheat on wives and vice versa; people let their best friends down. So when it comes to governments and their spooks, it's anybody's guess. But he's not a right-wing loony, of that I'm pretty sure. I doubt he'd have any truck with the kind of people you're talking about.'

I look at Maureen. She grills David further.

'When I was in training for the Det, there was a lot of idle chat about MI5 conspiracies against Harold Wilson in the sixties and seventies. The DG would have been quite senior then. He must have known about them.'

'Look, Debs, I've no doubt that plans for a coup against Wilson were real and that senior people in MI5 were involved. Indeed, the illustrious founder of our Regiment, David Stirling, was part of the plot – GB75 and all that. I think Stirling's got a bit muddle-headed; he was a great soldier, but he's a very average politician, and I don't think he's the sharpest knife in the cutlery drawer. He's not a fascist, but there're a lot of nutters trading on his name.'

Maureen is warming to David.

'So what's the situation now that Maggie's in power?'

'I'm sure if Michael Foot had got into Downing Street, instead of Maggie, we'd be living under military rule by now. Northern Ireland's keeping the pot boiling, though, which is why she's under so much pressure to sort it.'

'Which brings it full circle, back to us.'

David looks at the pair of us. He takes on the mien of a hard-nosed platoon commander assessing two new recruits. Then he smiles.

'How do you want me to play it?'

Maureen answers.

'Is he a member here?'

'Yes.'

'Can you get him to come for a casual drink tomorrow night?'

'Fuck me, Debs! Anything else? Would you like me to invite the Home Secretary and the PM as well?'

Maureen answers, as quick as a flash, and with a straight face.

'No, just him. We definitely don't trust the other two!'

I laugh out loud.

David turns on me.

'I'm glad you think it amusing. I don't suppose you can tell me what happened in Northern Ireland to start all this?'

'No – one day, but not yet.'

'You two staying here?'

'Yes.'

'I'll call you if I can't swing it. Otherwise, be here, eighteen hundred hours, tomorrow.'

'Thanks, David.'

'I won't say "no big deal", because it's a fucking big deal! At the same time, I don't like what's going on over the water. It's not soldiering; it's fucking politics. And dirty politics at that . . .' David pauses, as if to steel himself. 'Have you heard about Colin Wallace?'

Maureen nods in a way that suggests Wallace is not on her Christmas card list.

'Intel officer, Northern Ireland. Lost the plot, doing time for topping his lover's husband.'

'That's the one. I know Colin – the most loyal and dedicated soldier I've ever met. He had a change of heart about the dirty tricks going on over there, so they got rid of him. He was framed. He's serving time for nothing. A lot of people know the truth, which makes it even worse. That's how far they're prepared to go to protect themselves. That's what you're up against.' He looks at Maureen and then smiles at me. 'So you two aren't an item?'

Maureen answers quickly.

'No, we're soldiers trying to finish a job we should never have started . . . and get out alive.'

'Shame, you deserve one another. You'd make a great couple.'

41. A Spank in the Bar

The Special Forces Club is like a cross between a gentlemen's club and an officers' mess. Its walls are covered from floor to ceiling with paintings and photographs of military intelligence officers and special forces soldiers from the Second World War onwards. Many of them are heroes, some are rogues of various hues, and a few are a bit of both.

As one might expect, the DG of MI5 arrives at the club on the dot of 6 p.m. Leaving his burly protection officer to wait in the hallway, he walks up to the intimate bar on the first floor. Spank sees David at the bar and goes over to him. They greet one another amiably.

Maureen and I have been skulking in the corner, but as soon as the greeting's over we join them. As we do, we catch Spank saying, 'Sorry, David, I've only got forty minutes. How can I help?'

We're already at Spank's shoulder, so I answer for David. 'Sir, I'm afraid we're the ones who need your help. David's done us a huge favour. He's an old friend and about the only man in the world we can trust at the moment.'

Spank doesn't seem ruffled in the slightest by our sudden appearance. I suppose that's what comes from a lifetime as a spook.

'I thought you two were fighting gangs in Yorkshire.' Maureen's hackles rise.

'That's not very funny, sir. Three civilians were killed, and we only got out by the skin of our teeth.'

'I'm suitably admonished, Captain Townsend.'

'Sorry, sir, we're a bit raw at the moment.'

'I understand. So let's get on with it. How can I help?'

'To put it simply, things have escalated to the point where Jim and I – we're still using our op names – have decided that we have to put our trust in you if we're going to survive this mess.'

I take over the conversation.

'I know you haven't got long, sir. We stumbled across Peters up north, who, after a bit of persuasion, gave us a good briefing about what we're up against. It doesn't look great.'

'Peters told me about your ambush. He's a bit embarrassed. Look, let me buy us all a drink and I can update you as of today.'

The barman busies himself with drinks, while the DG takes us over to a quiet corner. We sit directly under a large portrait of the Queen Mother, the club's patron, reminding me that we're in one of the establishment's innermost sanctums.

Then, drink in hand, the DG gives us his sitrep.

'First of all, you two have had us even more worried than before – particularly you, Waddington.'

Embarrassed, I look down at my brand-new black brogues.

'After all, the last time I saw you, you were wobbling like a jelly and Townsend had to all but carry you to the lift. Anyway, the fact that you've made it this far speaks volumes. And, I have to say, your presence here in London gives me a chance to put this thing to bed.' He turns to David Carmichael. 'Listen, David, do you want to hear this? If you do, you must treat it as highly sensitive.'

David looks at me.

'I'd rather you stayed, David. We might need your help again.'

'Fine, happy to be of assistance.' David then addresses the DG. 'JJ, forgive me chipping in, but I'm beginning to grasp what these two have been through in recent weeks. On top of that, Gary – or "Jim", as he now seems to be called – has been to hell and back since Belfast. Anyway, I said this to Debs earlier, in case you're in any doubt: Jim was the best recruit I ever came across, bar none.'

I'm embarrassed.

'That's good of you, David, but, as Maureen and the DG will testify, I've made a right tit of myself more than once over the past two years.'

'That's as may be. But, I should also add, he's all the better for having strong principles. End of eulogy.'

The DG seems irritated by David's words of support.

'I understand. I'm aware of his qualities; but his "principles" are now part of the problem, are they not?'

We choose not to answer, so the DG – obviously keen to get home to his leafy suburb – moves on.

'So we think we've identified some rogue elements in Gower Street and discovered how you got compromised.' He takes a deep draught of his malt. 'Your order to eliminate Murphy should never have come from RUC Special Branch. They weren't even supposed to know you were there. Your Control, Major Martindale – known to you as

Roger – has rooted out those who disclosed your operation to Belfast SB. We're pretty sure Gower Street is now secure.'

I have my doubts about that and raise them immediately.

'What about Martindale?'

'What about him?'

'Can you trust him?'

'That's impertinent; he's your superior.'

'I don't care. Too many people have died to be concerned about military etiquette. I don't trust Thatcher as far as I could spit, and she's the Prime Minister!'

'You don't like Major Martindale, do you?'

'No, I don't.'

'He doesn't like you either. Look, I've known him for donkey's years. He's one hundred per cent. I have no concerns at all.'

'Well, I do.' I look to Maureen for support. 'Mo?'

'Like Jim, I have my doubts, sir.'

'Very well. But that gives me a problem because, only last week, I asked him to bring you two in and persuade you to be our bait in a trap to get this Provo ASU and this Hendriks character: two birds with one stone.'

He's just thrown a hand grenade into the conversation. I feel my blood boiling.

'Really! Who are the birds – them or us?'

'That's also bloody impertinent! What the hell do you mean?'

'Just the fucking coincidence that we got hit in Yorkshire a few days later!'

Maureen intervenes to calm things down by switching to another subject.

'Sir, who's protecting Hendriks?'

'Listen, I didn't come here to be interrogated by my own operatives!'

I begin to lose it.

'Well, you are here and we're asking the questions, so deal with it.'

The DG, now turning puce, starts to get up. David grabs his arm.

'JJ, hear them out. They deserve that.'

'I've heard them out more than once. This is becoming very tedious.'

'But you have a duty to protect your people.'

'Are you telling me how to run my team?'

'Yes.'

'That's got you in hot water before.'

'I know – but a leopard doesn't change its spots.'

Eyeing the three of us like we're an annoying nuisance that won't go away, the DG thinks for a moment before answering.

'OK, five more minutes. What do you want to know about Hendriks?'

Maureen resumes her questioning.

'Everyone seems to know who he is and that he's highly dangerous. Yet he's able to roam the country at will. Not only that, he seems to know exactly where we are.'

'As I told you, we've dealt with that.'

'You mean the same leak at Gower Street was feeding Hendriks?'

'No, we think that's Belfast.'

'And what are you doing about it?'

'Sorting it.'

'What if the leak is elsewhere?'

'Like where?'

'MI6?'

'Not possible.'

'Why not? They think Ireland should be their patch. It's well known that they don't like what's going on there and think that we're buggering it up.'

'Do you imagine I haven't thought about that? We've looked at their possible involvement, we're sure they're not a player.'

I make up my mind to tell our leader the facts of life.

'OK, sir . . . no, I think I'll call you JJ. So here's how it is. We're not being your bait in any trap; we've been caught in several traps already, and we don't like it. If Martindale's involved, we're not playing. And we remain unconvinced that Gower Street is secure.'

I glance at Maureen, who nods her agreement about the facts of life.

'So, like we have up to now, we're going to run our own agenda. If any traps are to be set, we'll be setting them.'

The DG doesn't answer, but turns to Maureen.

'Is that also your position, Captain Townsend?'

'It is, sir.'

'You realize what you're putting at risk?'

'I do, sir – my life.'

The DG hesitates and takes a sip of his Scotch.

'And if you come through it, what then?'

'You mean, what about my army career?'

'Yes.'

'That's history. I didn't join the army to be duped into

shooting a man for no reason other than to serve some-one's devious political agenda.'

He takes another drink, this time a mouthful.

'Well, I have to admire your resolve ... or is it bloody-mindedness? I wish you well. What will you do if you come out the other end?'

'Jim and I are going to start an ostrich farm in Bot-swana, aren't we?'

'I'd prefer a dive school in the Philippines.'

'Sounds very appealing. If that's your position, come what may – survival or otherwise – we will now purge all your files from our records.' He stands up and drains his glass. 'What you do with Waddington and Townsend is up to you. Dowd and O'Brien never existed. You're on your own.'

After the DG leaves, David buys us another drink. He shakes his head.

'That's very harsh. You seem to be back where you started, only worse!'

Maureen looks shell-shocked.

'A fat lot of good that's done us. Purged from the re-cords. That means everyone wants us dead.'

David is still shaking his head.

'JJ's rattled by something. That performance was very unlike him.'

'David, I'm sorry I lost it with him. He was just too glib. And the coincidence of his order to Martindale and the hit in Haworth is a clincher for me. He's either not very astute – which is hard to believe, given who he is – or he's not being straight with us.'

'No need to be sorry, Gary. That's not the JJ I remember.'

Maureen intervenes.

'I think there are forces around him that are way too powerful for him, and he's taking the line of least resistance. He's probably a good guy, but he's got a wife and family. How much longer has he got? Perhaps another two years, then retirement with a knighthood and a fat pension. I'm afraid we're just expendable foot soldiers in the grand scheme of things.'

David looks at us with an intensity that is unnerving.

'I know JJ's an old friend, and I certainly don't want to make this any worse, but it's worth considering. JJ's not stupid, he got a first from Cambridge . . .' He pauses, like he's still coming to terms with what he's saying. 'What if he's the rotten apple in Gower Street?'

'I thought you said he was a good bloke?'

'He is, or at least he was, but these are worrying times and there are some ominous things going on. Remember the Cambridge Five? They were all good guys and were recruited at Cambridge.'

'But they spied for the Soviet Union.'

'Yes, but there are just as many right-wing sympathizers at Cambridge as there are left-wing activists.'

'But you said he wasn't a right-wing loony.'

'People change – or they never tell you the truth in the first place.'

Maureen looks at me.

I say it before she does.

'We need to get out of here.'

42. The Beginning of the End

Maureen goes to the bar and asks the barman to bring over more drinks. When she comes back, she poses an interesting question.

'Do we really need to leg it? This is the SFC. Why don't we make this our Rorke's Drift; there can't be a better place. The Met's Diplomatic Protection Group is just round the corner.'

I sneer at the thought.

'Woodentops with pea-shooters – no thanks!'

David chips in.

'I'm only round the corner as well. I can help.'

'No, you can't. You've got a good job, a family – and you've already done enough.'

'Once Regiment, always Regiment, Gary. I could line up a few lads who are at a loose end. Some of them don't like what's going on. There're a few 21 boys around as well; always on for a scrap.'

'Yeah, I know. It might come to that, but let's keep your powder dry for now.'

Maureen leans over and gives David a kiss on the cheek.

'Go on home to your family. Jim and I need an early night. And thanks for being such a legend.'

David does as he's told. After an old friend's embrace, and with a resounding thump of the heavy door of the club, he leaves us to whatever fate awaits us.

Save for the receptionist and the lone barman upstairs, the SFC is suddenly empty and quiet. Without the military memorabilia and portraits, it could be a posh town-house hotel and, at least for a while, we feel relaxed and safe. We go into the small sitting room next to Reception and finish our drinks, like any middle-class couple at home in the evening. We watch TV, read the papers and chat until Maureen issues an order.

'Bed, Jim! We need to rest. We've got an Isandhlwana coming.'

'I thought it was a Rorke's Drift?'

'Hmm, I think it might be more like an Isandhlwana.'

'No problem, we can deal with four thousand Zulus!'

'Sure about that?'

'Certain.'

She looks at me with a sad expression. She begins to speak, then stops herself. A thin smile breaks across her face and she takes a deep breath. Still she hesitates.

I put my hand on her arm.

'Come on, spit it out.'

'I've just ditched my army career, the only thing I've ever wanted to do.'

'Don't get gloomy, Mo. What about that ostrich farm?'

'Wishful thinking, Jimmy. The odds on us surviving this mess are lengthening by the day.'

'So, let's change them.'

A hint of a smile returns.

'I'm up for that.'

Minutes later, I'm once again lying next to Maureen in her bed. There are no nightmares this night, just dreams of Maureen, imploring me to protect her from those who would do her harm.

Then my dream is interrupted. Surreal feelings merge into real ones. Maureen's lips are on mine; they're soft and warm.

'Jim, make love to me.'

It's like being hit with a sledgehammer. Overwhelmed by excitement, I can barely control myself.

The next hour or so passes in a blur of pleasure, the intensity of which I've never experienced before. It's profound and lasting; two people affirming their deep love and respect for one another. It is a consummation all the sweeter because it's taken so long to blossom.

The next morning, we're like teenagers: grinning at one another like adolescents who've just lost their virginity together. We hold hands at every opportunity, and kiss and cuddle like newly-weds.

Maureen's more relaxed than I've ever seen her. Then she says the words I always hoped she would say.

'I didn't believe that would ever happen. I'm so happy, even in the middle of this nightmare.'

'So am I, Mo. I wanted this from the first time I saw you. I can't believe it's happened.'

'Believe it, Jim; it's real.'

'All we need to do now is survive!'

'Can we really do that?'

'Course we can! We're more than a match for whatever we're up against.'

A moment of doubt casts its shadow across Maureen's face. She hesitates and takes a deep breath.

'What about Kathleen, Jim? You were in love with her; you might still be in love with her.'

'Listen, how can I explain this? She's gorgeous, for sure. I think I fell in love with the Ardoyne and Belfast. She epitomized all that. But I fell into her arms because you wouldn't let me fall into yours. You must believe that.'

'I'm trying, Jim; believe me, I'm trying . . .'

She pauses, looking into my eyes. Her own eyes are teary with emotion.

'Jim, I've been falling in love with you for a while. Now it's complete. I love you so much.'

'I love you too.'

Breakfast at the SFC is always good, and today it sustains us for what lies ahead.

Our first task is to retrieve our arsenal from left luggage and return it to our intended final redoubt. We walk to the tube at Knightsbridge. London offers few comforts. Cold air is blowing from the north, where blizzards are raging, and even in the centre of the metropolis there are snow flurries in the air.

After we store our kit in our rooms, we order coffee in the club sitting room and read the papers.

They don't offer any comforts either. Other than pictures of a huge snowstorm in the eastern United States, there's nothing much to read except the usual sad accounts of a depressed and angry Britain.

It's hard to concentrate on the news so, after a few minutes of idle page-turning, we decide to review our position. I tell Maureen the thoughts that crystallized in my head first thing this morning as I watched her sleep.

'If Spank's the bad guy, he'll have already set the wheels in motion. If he isn't, there are two possibilities. One, he's told Wank that we're here and, if he's the bad boy, he'll have set his wheels in motion. Or two, if Spank has listened to what we said and is checking out Wank again, that buys us a bit of time.'

Maureen's thinking hard.

'So, three scenarios. My instinct is that the DG isn't a villain, just scared. He might not even care whether Martindale is bent or not and will tell him where we are.'

'And allow a bad apple to continue to operate in his department?'

'Why not? The bad apple's obviously got a lot of friends in high places. Besides, there may be lots of bad apples; too many to deal with.'

'Your logic makes good sense, Mo.'

'There's another possibility. If the DG does care about Martindale, then he might go back to the idea of using us as bait again – to flush him out.'

'Either way, the odds are high that the game's in play and it'll suit all concerned if we disappear off the radar. So we need a plan. It's the weekend tomorrow; I think this place will be deserted.'

I go and check with Ramona, the Spanish girl on Reception, then report back to Maureen.

'No other guests tonight and tomorrow, and just two on Sunday night. We'll have the run of the place when the bar closes tonight.'

'When would you try a hit, if you were them?'

'Tomorrow, when no one is around.'

'What about Reception?'

'Carla, the girl who does the night shift, has a flat at the back. She finishes at eleven.'

'Go on.'

'Saturday night in Knightsbridge; Beauchamp Place will be heaving until two in the morning. So, that means three a.m. onwards. It's ideal. It's the dark of the moon, with thick cloud, and it's a Sunday morning, I'd strike between three thirty and four a.m. – not much later, as some silly buggers will begin to stir around then.'

'What about police patrols?'

'They drive past every thirty minutes or so, but randomly.'

'So a hit would happen soon after they'd left.'

'Correct.'

'They'll do a recce tonight?'

'Yes.'

'We are talking about Hendriks, aren't we?'

'Yes, I have a feeling we didn't slot him in Haworth.'

'What if the Provos just happen to pitch up at the same time? The same channel could be feeding the ASU as well as Hendriks, thus doubling their strength?'

'Possibly, but it would be a right bugger if they did. Mind you, you said it was Isandhlwana rather than Rorke's Drift.'

'So what do we do?'

'Check and clean every weapon we've got. Go over every detail of the street, the building, everything.'

'Good so far, Mr Gold Star. I'll do the weapons, you check the building. Anything else?'

'Take a bottle of club claret to our room tonight and see if we spot their recce.'

'Sounds even better. I don't mind drinking on duty as my military career's just gone down the khazi. What about tomorrow?'

'We go sightseeing during the day, followed by an early-evening movie, then a big dinner at San Lorenzo; let them think we believe we're safe at the SFC, and so we're off our guard.'

That night, keeping watch into the early hours, we're not sure if any of the many vehicles that cruise along this quiet Knightsbridge street is a recce vehicle. A couple slow unusually, but neither looks out of the ordinary.

Then exhaustion, the wine and our newly found love get the better of us and, after a tender sexual interlude, we fall into a deep sleep.

The next day is bitterly cold and few tourists brave London's wet and windy streets. Hand in hand, we wander around the city's landmarks like a honeymoon couple.

We go to Leicester Square and weep as we watch Meryl Streep in *Sophie's Choice*, then cheer ourselves up with an inordinately expensive dinner in San Lorenzo.

Honeymoon over, anxiety returns as we let ourselves into the SFC. It's in darkness, save for a small desk lamp behind Reception. It's late and Carla – the overnight girl and cook for breakfast – has gone to bed. Maureen's already striding up the first few steps at the bottom of the stairs.

I make one last survey of the area.

Something's wrong.

Carla is meticulously ordered; her desk at Reception is always a picture of neatness. The guest book is open on her desk. That's not right; Carla would never leave it like that. My mood switches from anxiety to dread. The adrenalin kicks in. I click my fingers to catch Maureen's attention.

She comes back down the stairs and leans close to me so that I can whisper in her ear.

'Something's wrong. Stay here; keep your eyes peeled on the stairs and the door to the basement. I'm going to check on Carla's flat at the back.'

We each draw our weapon and click off the safety.

The door to Carla's flat is not locked. My instincts tell me not to knock. If I'm wrong, I'll just apologize and say I was looking for the loo. I open the door carefully, then I notice that it's been forced, shattering its frame. Her small sitting room is as it should be; there's nothing untoward, but the door to what must be her bedroom is ajar. The light's on. I raise my Browning and point it into the void. There's no noise. Everything tells me that Carla has become another victim of this madness, a sweet girl who's never harmed anyone in her life.

After only three paces, I can see the gruesome evidence. Blood is splashed across the wall behind the bed. It's still fresh. The hit happened only minutes ago. Carla is sprawled across the crumpled bedclothes, naked as the day she was born; a beautiful innocent, no more than a child, with a long life ahead of her. Now her brief life has been ended as it began. Her family, from a town or village in the middle of somewhere or nowhere, will soon have their normal lives destroyed. Her lovely body has been riddled with bullets: three to the chest, one to the forehead. The last one is the 'tap' of a pro, the coup de grâce that makes death a certainty. She must have heard something and was on the way to the door when she was shot. Now her lifeless form is so pale, so much of her blood seeping away beneath her.

Maureen! I turn and move quickly, but silently.

When I reach the narrow corridor that leads back to the club, the lights go out. They're about to strike! I reach for the small Maglite I carry on my key ring. It's not there. But I always carry a light, a blade and a flame. *Fuck!* Because I had my club key with me, and I was certain the hit would come in the early hours, I decided to leave my keys in our bedroom – a stupid mistake. I have no torch.

My euphoria about Maureen has addled my thinking. She said it would, if we became an item. Fuck it, I don't care; what a way to go!

I feel my way along the corridor. I'm a sitting duck. I should stay still and wait, allowing my eyes to adjust. There's rarely no light; there's always a glimmer of something.

But Maureen is in mortal danger, I can't wait. I know there's a step coming, and I try to feel for it with my foot.

Then, with an intense, searing pain to the nape of my neck, all my lights go out and I'm plunged into an unconscious void.

43. Traitors

Consciousness returns, but I'm in agony. It's as if my neck is gripped in a vice, and my forehead throbs like a hundred hangovers. I can see light, but no real shapes. I'm feeling nauseous and assume I'm seriously concussed. I can detect no movement and hear almost no sounds. But it's cold, icy cold.

I'm sitting down. My wrists and ankles are bound so tightly they're stinging with rope burn. And I know why I'm cold: I'm stark bollock naked.

It's like selection, but this is real.

'Ah, Waddington, you're awake. For a moment, I thought Bakkies here had killed you.'

The heavy Boer accent tells me immediately that I'm in the clutches of Hendriks and his henchmen. I try to focus to see if Maureen's here. I pray that she is, rather than lying in a pool of blood like Carla. But I can still see only vague shapes.

'Mo! Are you here?'

There's no response, but I think I hear a muffled cry.

'Mo?'

The same sound. She's here; she's been gagged.

'She's here, Waddington, just where we want her.'

'Leave her alone, you bastard.'

'That's funny, Waddington; you're the bastard in this room. I've read your file.'

342

'I'm the one you want. Leave her out of it.'

'Can't do that, I'm afraid, my paymasters are insistent: you're both history. But we're going to have a bit of fun first. We're waiting until you're feeling better; you're going to watch.'

There's a chilling leer in Hendriks' voice. Images of Barbon and what he did to Jed and Bonny assault my consciousness. I screw up my eyes, blink rapidly and shake my head to try to get my focus back. I'm desperate to see Maureen.

My pain's not receding, but my eyes are beginning to focus. Gradually, a horrifying image forms. There's a spreadeagled shape no more than three yards in front of me. Although I can't see clearly, I know it's Maureen.

At last, my vision starts to sharpen. I can see much better now, well enough to see that Maureen's mouth is gagged, her wrists are bound with para cord and tied to a roof beam above her. Her ankles are also bound, pulled wide apart and tied to the wall. Like me, she's naked, placing her in the most humiliating position imaginable. She's been hit several times. I can see welts on her body, her eyes are swollen and bloodshot, and blood trickles from her nose. This amazing woman, with whom I've just enjoyed the most intimate of moments, is now strung up before these monsters like a carcass in an abattoir. My body shudders at the horror of it all. But she looks defiant. She nods at me, trying to reassure me.

We're in a garage. I'm pretty sure it's the one beneath Carla's flat in the mews at the back of the club.

'We saw you holding hands in the restaurant, Waddington. You've been a naughty boy, you've been fucking your partner. And she's an officer. Very naughty boy! I bet you were thinking about fucking her tonight, weren't you?' A hideous smile distorts his face. 'I'm very sorry, but you're not going to; it's our turn.'

He laughs cruelly and leans over me.

'And Stoffi here's got one about twice the size of that little tiddler you've got. He'll make her squirm when it's his turn.'

'You're a fucking psychopath, Hendriks!'

'So I've been told. It's never dull; I can recommend it.'

He blows cigarette smoke into my face and begins to pace around the garage. He's tall and lean with a weather-beaten face, made creased and leathery by years in the sun. He's an ugly man with a big broken nose and prominent cheekbones.

'So you know my name?'

'I know all about you, you son of a bitch, and I know what you did to Jed and Bonny.'

'Ah yes, now she was a pretty little thing.' He walks back and puts his face right next to mine. 'Screamed like a stuck pig, she did.'

'You'd better kill me, Hendriks. If you don't, you'll die, for sure – and very painfully.'

'That's strange, that's exactly what I had in mind for you. You see, I don't like traitors.'

'We're not traitors, we carried out our mission!'

'But then you went berserk and attacked a senior officer.'

'That's because he'd used us to settle an old score and kill a man in cold blood.'

'The IRA's the enemy. They should all die.'

'Enemies die in battle, not in cold blood.'

344

'You know what, Waddington? You're a fucking use-less soldier – and a fucking commie to go with it. I hate men like you.'

'Not as much as I hate men like you.'

'You're also a fucking coward. You got Townsend to do your dirty work for you. You sent a woman to do a man's job, you snivelling moffie!'

'Listen, Hendriks, she's twice the man – more than the two of us put together.'

'Really, then that will make the next part very interesting.'

I'm desperate to keep him talking so that I can think of some way out of our dire predicament. Although, as I look at the position we're both in, the prospects look ter-rifyingly gloomy. Para cord is very strong; there's no way we could break free. I try to steel myself by thinking about Robert Nairac's bravery, but it doesn't help much.

Unfortunately, I'm not going to be tortured for infor-mation. That would be easy: I'd just tell them whatever they wanted to know. But they're just going to hurt me and then kill me. I look at Maureen. The greatest agony of all will be witnessing her ordeal, being made to watch while they abuse and humiliate her. Jesus fucking Christ, what a mess! All that running, plotting and scheming, all that ducking and diving, all for this.

Anyway, Hendriks likes the sound of his own voice; it's worth delaying things for as long as possible.

'Who sent you?'

'Some friends, patriots.'

'Like who?'

'Don't be stupid, Waddington, I'm not going to tell you that.'

'Why not? If you're going to kill us anyway, I'd like to know who our judge and jury are.'

'They're just people who don't want this country fucked over like Rhodesia. They've let that Kaffir Mugabe take over; the place is fucked.'

'So we're being executed for telling a Belfast policeman a few home truths and sticking a pencil up his nose?'

'You did more than that.'

'We roughed him up a bit, but it was no big deal.'

'Oh, you would've got away with that. But it was when you threatened to go to the press. That's when you signed your death warrant.'

I look at Maureen. I can see the incredulity in her eyes. So that's why we've become enemies of the state. That RUC bastard has leaked more false intel. Everything suddenly makes sense.

'So now you two have to pay your account.'

'What's in it for you? You're not even a Brit.'

'Don't be stupid, man, I'm in it for the money, a lot of money.' He then ogles Maureen and licks his lips. 'And for a few delights along the way.'

'For what it's worth, I never threatened to go to the press.'

'I've seen the letter.'

'What letter?'

'The one you wrote from that pub you were holed up in, in Kent.'

'There was no letter – not then, not ever.'

I look at Maureen again. I can see the astonishment in her eyes. So the damning intel is a fucking forged letter!

'I've read it. That's what started all this off.'

'How did they get hold of a letter?'

'I don't fucking know, man; they must have intercepted it. Anyway, I don't care. I've read the letter. It would have blown the lid off everything we're trying to do to sort out those IRA bastards.'

'It's a forgery, Hendriks; it's a lie, probably concocted by RUC Special Branch.'

'What, those fucking idiots in Belfast? They haven't got the brains! But who knows? As I said, I don't give a shit. I've been given my orders . . . and a down payment. I'm very much looking forward to collecting the other fifty per cent. You went native, Waddington, the worst sin a soldier can commit, and now you're going to go to Hell. You're a fucking Catholic, you know that's the price you pay.'

'What about Townsend? She did her job. You can't condemn her for that.'

'She's helping you, so guilty by association. And she killed a good friend of mine in Yorkshire. She's going to pay for that.'

'I did the shooting in Haworth.'

'No, Morne was there. It was Townsend's bullet that killed Smitty. You shot the other two. I didn't like them much. They were weak, not real warriors. They were the useless fuckers who missed you in the forest in Kent.'

'You really are a fucking nutter, Hendriks. You'd better get on with what you're going to do. I'm sick and tired of hearing your bonehead South African voice.'

Maureen nods her agreement. I see her square her shoulders, ready for whatever is to come.

Hendriks takes his cue. He walks behind Maureen and takes off the black leather gloves he's wearing. He's a fair bit taller than her, so is able to rest his chin on her shoulder. He smiles at me as he does so. It's the fabricated smile of a deranged man. His hands then grab her breasts roughly and he pinches her nipples. Maureen winces in pain. He then unfastens his trousers and lets them drop to the floor. His underpants follow. He then steps out of both of them. He positions himself for his assault. His face reddens, twisted with insane lust.

'Take pity, Hendriks, she's an elite soldier; she doesn't deserve that.'

It's futile, of course. He doesn't hesitate, but just carries on with his hideous torture. The three others in the room are staring at the scene like pack animals. Hendriks moves his hand down between her legs to ease his entry.

Then, perhaps out of dire necessity – we've had a lot to drink – but I suspect it's more an act of defiance, Maureen lets go a torrent of urine. It splashes on the ground like a waterfall, soaking Hendriks, his clothes and his shoes.

'You fucking filthy cow!'

Maureen's eyes smile at me and I smile back. It's at least one little moment of victory before our demise.

But the moment doesn't last long.

Hendriks kicks away his sodden clothes and walks around to face his victim. He then unleashes a sickening punch to her face, followed by a powerful kick to the groin, then aims two more. Maureen throws her head back; she's trying to scream but her gag mutes it. She squirms, wriggles and heaves against her bindings. Blood appears on the inside of her thighs. More urine drips to the floor but this time it's pink with streaks of blood. He'll kick her to death if he carries on. Mercifully, he stops and takes a few deep breaths.

'Give me Waddington's pants, Morne.'

He dresses quickly and picks up a pistol from a bag in the corner. The look on his face is venomous. He's flipped into killer mode. A huge egg has appeared on Maureen's cheekbone, her body is shivering. Even her steely resolve can't stop tears forming in her eyes. Hendriks strides over to her. He rips the tape and gag from her mouth so that he can slaver kisses on her.

'I'm not fucking your messy cunt now, you dirty bitch. So I'm just going to stick this weapon up there instead. Would you like that, Townsend? Bet you would!' He places the muzzle between her legs. 'Trouble is, I'm then going to pull the trigger and blow your insides all over the fucking floor.'

Maureen's tears have stopped. She stares at me with a look that is saying goodbye. Then she closes her eyes to black out what's about to happen. Hendriks is savouring the horror of his cruelty by delaying pulling the trigger.

With an awful tremor in her voice, Maureen hisses at her torturer.

'Get it over with, Hendriks. There couldn't be a better day for me to die. I'm the happiest woman in the world.' She then looks at me and smiles. 'Jimmy, I love you.'

'I love you, Mo.'

Her defiant words have made the Boer beast boil with anger again. This is it.

The next twenty seconds become a blur of intense noise and rapid movement.

It starts with the back door of the garage bursting

open. I'm facing the main door, so I can't see what's happening behind me, but I hear multiple gunshots. Hendriks turns and points his pistol behind me and to my right. But before he can shoot, he's hit at least twice in the chest. He's flung backwards by the impact and falls against Maureen, who's covered with the blood that explodes from the exit wounds in his back. He collapses to his knees in front of me.

He raises his head slightly and looks me in the eye. He tries to say something but another bullet hits him in the forehead, exploding the back of his head. All three of his henchmen are also hit. So engrossed have they been in Maureen's humiliation, they've been slow to react. They've paid with their lives. Only one managed to raise his weapon, and he only got off a single round before he was hit.

I look at Maureen. Her face is contorted in pain. I scan her bloodied body, looking for wounds. It's hard to tell if the blood is from Hendriks or from her. Her knees give way. She's only held upright by the para cord around her wrists. Then I see the wound. Blood is seeping from an entry wound in her chest just below her sternum. That's not good. Even if the bullet's missed the heart, the liver is behind that, and beyond the liver is the spinal column. Her chin is resting on her chest; she isn't moving.

The incessant shouting behind me gets louder. They're Irish voices. I can pick out the words within the din. It's the Provo ASU. We've gone from the fucking frying pan into the fire!

I recognize one of the voices. *Fuck!* It's Jimmy McKee! He's screaming.

'No! Dear God, no! Kathleen?' He repeats her name over and over again.

No, please, no!

Jimmy is weeping like a child. At the same time he's shouting orders.

'Get the garage door open. We've got to get Kathleen some help. Cut that bitch down, but leave that bastard tied to his chair. Gag them and throw them in the back of the van.'

I'm lifted up in my chair. Now I can see our saviours, who've become our captors. I can see Kathleen being helped up by her father. She's holding her midriff; blood is seeping through her fingers and down her legs. She looks at me. It's the look I remember so vividly from when I left her in Estoril Park, a searing glower of hurt and hatred. I assume she's here to be our executioner. I can't help but think that that's only right and proper. I'd rather she did it than anybody else. Now it looks like she's got a terrible wound in the stomach, yet another victim of this disgusting catalogue of deceit and death.

I recognize the young men who pick me up. They're two of the Brigadier's minders from the Hibernian. They step over the bodies on the floor, a concrete floor that is now crimson rather than grey. There's so much blood they almost slip.

I look at Hendriks. He died quickly; he deserved much worse.

The look of loathing on the faces of the ASU boys makes me shudder. One of them hisses into my ear as we near the van.

'Now youse is going to get what you deserve, Dowd, you bastard.'

After they both spit in my face, they throw me into the back of their white van as if I'm a sack of spuds. Maureen follows. Covered in a slick syrup of fresh blood, she lands on top of me like a haunch of meat. Her body is still. She's either dead or dying. Her plight – and the way she's been so horrendously mistreated – makes me want to die as well. I've got nothing to live for.

The wound in her chest is just above my head. Blood is still oozing from the neat round hole made by the bullet. It drips on to my face; it's warm and flowing rhythmically. That means her heart's still beating.

With the ASU's two goons watching over us, the van speeds south down Pavilion Road. We take a left and a right and continue down Sloane Street towards Sloane Square. As my training has taught me, I try to use my modest knowledge of London's geography to keep track of our route but, almost inevitably, I lose track south of Battersea. Even so, my guess is that we speed through Clapham, Balham and on to Tooting. It looks like we're either going to a safe house or to a secluded spot; either way, it will be where we'll be executed.

It's still not late for a Saturday night in London and there are a lot of cars and people about. At various traffic lights, I can hear the hubbub of late-night revelry. It reminds me of big nights in the Hibernian, nights I shared with the two men sitting with us. I look at them; the icy stare of pure hate is still there.

I decide to accept that what will be will be and concentrate on Maureen. She's still not moving and is looking very pale. We reach a piece of straight road and the van runs along smoothly. It gives me a chance to look closely at Maureen's condition. The relative silence allows me to listen for a hint that she's still breathing. To my amazement, although it's very shallow, I'm sure she is.

There's hope.

All I need to do is free myself, kill our captors and get Maureen to a hospital. No problem!

44. Unsafe House

The van suddenly screeches to a halt. The stop is so sudden, everyone in the back is thrown forward with a huge jolt. With Maureen sprawled on top of me, I finish up hard against the van wall. The impact creates one glimmer of hope. The joints between the seat of my chair and its back legs have snapped.

We're dragged out of the van and on to the drive of a semi-detached suburban house. It could be anywhere, but from the direction we took and the time we've been on the road, I guess we're in Croydon or thereabouts. It must be well past midnight. The street is quiet and there's nothing in view that identifies our location.

This must be their safe house, but not for us.

We're dragged across the gravel, bundled down the hallway of the house and thrown down the stairs into the cellar. I go first, tumbling over and over on my increasingly broken chair. I crack my head several times, adding to the pain and injuries already suffered, and land on my knees, which are torn open by the rough concrete floor. Maureen follows me. Still unconscious, she falls like a rag doll, doing yet more damage to her battered body. Fortunately, she lands on top of me, which at least spares her the impact of the hard floor.

The cellar light is switched off, putting us in complete darkness, and the door is locked. The cellar smells musty and the floor is very damp. It's mid-February, of course, and the cold is beginning to get to me. It must be much worse for Maureen, whose injuries make her susceptible to hypothermia.

After a few minutes, I hear a gurgling in Maureen's throat. Then there's a spluttered cough.

'Mo?'

'Jimmy?'

'It's me, Mo. How are you feeling?'

'Not good. I can't see anything.'

Her voice is very weak. I mustn't tell her how bad things are. She has to have something to live for.

'We're in the dark, in a cellar.'

'What's happening to us?'

'We're doing OK. Hendriks and the others are dead. They can't hurt you any more.'

She starts to whimper.

'Oh, Jimmy, he kicked me so hard.'

'I know, darling, but he's gone now.'

'So why are we in a cellar?' Before I can answer, she speaks again, even more weakly than before. 'I'm so cold, Jimmy.'

I try to think of something positive to say, but then I hear a sigh.

'Mo! Mo! You must stay awake. Don't go to sleep, Mo!'

There's no response. She's lying across my chest and shoulders, so at least I'm giving her a little of whatever warmth I've got left. I prod her body with my head, but it doesn't make any difference. She's icy cold to the touch.

At least three hours pass, possibly more. There's constant movement above us. More than one person leaves the house and drives away in the van. It returns some time later. I spend most of my time trying to loosen my bindings to the chair. I have some success. I manage to detach the back from the seat, but my wrists and ankles are still tied firmly to its legs.

When the light comes back on, it hurts my eyes. I immediately check on Maureen, who's still sprawled on top of me. She looks even paler than before; she's now alabaster white, and stone cold. If she is breathing, it's very shallow. I brace myself for the terrible truth that she's dead, but I'm not able to dwell too long on the horror of that thought.

Our captors come streaming down the stairs. We're dragged away from the bottom of the stairs and propped up against the wall.

Maureen's head immediately flops on to her shoulder at a hideous angle. It seems certain that my darling Maureen, the strongest, most wonderful woman in the world, may have escaped the pain and anguish of her brief life.

Jimmy McKee sits down on a box in the middle of the floor. As he does, Kathleen appears. Supported by an older man I've not seen before, she walks gingerly down the stairs and sits on the bottom step. She's holding her stomach, which is swathed in rolls of heavy white strapping, the front of which is stained with blood. In her right hand is the Smith & Wesson 39 that she gave me in her house when the Brigadier came to call, but this time it's got a silencer on its muzzle. It's pointing straight at me. The other two are also holding S&Ws with suppressors.

The gag is pulled from my mouth.

'Hello, Jim, I don't expect you ever thought you'd see me again?'

I gulp, trying not to seem too weak in the face of my executioner.

'How's the wound?'

'Unfortunately for you, it's fine. My belt buckle saved me. The bullet hit it and ricocheted into my belly. It only went in a wee bit, but it bled like buggery. The doc here's one of us. He took it out and stitched me up.'

She then looks at her father, who turns his head, signalling to the doc to go over to Maureen. He tries her wrist for a pulse. Then he opens her right eye and shines a light into it. Finally, he gets out a stethoscope and places it on her chest.

'She's alive, Jimmy, but only just . . . and not for long.'

He puts his finger in the wound in her chest. Then he pulls her forwards and looks at her back.

'No exit wound. The bullet that went in at the front didn't come out at the back. By the looks of it, it's likely to be lodged in her spine. It's about the only thing that would've stopped it at close range.'

Jimmy looks disappointed.

'Can you bring her round?'

'Not without a room full of specialists and the best of medical care.'

Jimmy turns to me.

'So it's just you, then, Jim. Get him up boys, and put the gag back in.'

The two lads, one of whom I remember as Eamon, cut me loose. They try to pull me up, but my limbs are almost frozen with stress and pain. So they start to kick me. It doesn't help my mobility. Then Eamon grabs my hair and slams my face against the wall. Blood gushes from what feels like a broken nose. A much worse pain follows.

Two rounds are loosed in quick succession, one into the back of each of my knees. They say the pain of a knee-capping is one of the worst you can endure. They're right; a nerve-exploding agony shoots up my legs and back and into my head, the intensity of which is impossible to put into words. Behind my gag, I scream like I've never screamed before.

But I don't endure the agony for long. I collapse on to the floor and everything goes black.

I wake in a twilight zone of semi-consciousness. The pain is unbearable, especially when I'm dragged into an upright position next to Maureen. When I look down, blood is pumping out of my right knee. I can feel its warmth on my shin. The bullet has gone right through, leaving a residue of bone and soft tissue all over the floor. The other knee has only the crimson hole of an entry wound, there's no exit hole. But it's much more painful. I guess the bullet has crashed into bone and lodged itself in there. Strangely enough, I feel the greatest pain in my hips. I try to work out why. It's odd what you think about in the most extreme of circumstances.

Eamon removes my gag again, then goes upstairs to get a chair. Kathleen is helped to sit on it, just a yard in front of me. Her face is twisted with loathing. Her eyes are hollow; there are grey bags under them, and she's lost a lot of weight. She casts a glance at Maureen.

'Shame that bitch is dying. I was going to make her pay for what she did to Sean.'

I find it hard to speak, the pain is so intense.

'I think she's suffered more than enough, Kath.'

'Don't you call me Kath, you British bastard!'

'I know this is no comfort and no excuse, but we were set up.'

'I know you were. We told you about the lies being spread by the RUC. But that doesn't excuse anything. You lied, cheated, murdered and damaged a community of good people. Now you're going to pay for it –'

Jimmy interrupts.

'Who were those men who were holding you?'

'Assassins hired by right-wing elements in Britain. They said we'd gone native, and ordered our execution.'

'That's bad luck: two gangs of killers on your tail. How ironic! They thought you'd gone native, but we know that couldn't be further from the truth. Unfortunately for you, we're more professional than they are. Time's up, Jim.'

Kathleen resumes her invective. She points her weapon only inches from my forehead.

'What's your real name?'

'Gary.'

'Did you get the photo I sent?'

'I did.'

'It was a little boy, Gary.'

Tears begin to form in my eyes. A strange smile plays across her face; it's mocking and vindictive.

'Don't cry, Gary. There's no need . . . you see, Gary, it wasn't your baby.'

Her smile becomes a laugh, a celebration of victory.

'It wasn't mine either. It was another poor sod's child, I just used the photo.'

'I don't understand.'

'Did you never wonder how I got pregnant so quickly? You were a very convenient disguise, Gary.'

I don't answer. I'm so thunderstruck it's hard to take it in.

'Sean was the father of my boy.'

My mind is working overtime to process what I'm hearing.

'He's called Liam, a lovely wee lad. He's with my mother in Dublin and growing fast. Don't you remember? I told you that Sean propositioned me when I came back from college for the holidays. Well, it was much more than that. And we carried on being lovers even when I was seeing you. You were just a beard, Gary.' She then leans forward and spits in my face. 'He was twice the man you are, you piece of English shite!'

She then turns to Maureen's limp form. 'Then this bitch wiggled her arse at him and he fell for it.' She aims a vicious kick at Maureen's face, which brings a spurt of blood from her nose. 'Then the whore fucking killed him!'

'Please don't; she's dying, Kath.'

'I told you not to call me Kath!'

The pain of my broken body is now amplified by the mental trauma of Kathleen's onslaught. Is she just making all this up to hurt me? When I think back to what happened between us, I find it impossible to believe what she's just told me.

I'm about to face death, so I'll never know.

Jimmy nods to the two boys, who move forward and pull me to my feet. The pain from my knees is unbearable. Now I just want it to end. I look at Maureen, who is close to death herself. I say goodbye to her with my body, heart and soul.

Kathleen is helped to her feet by her father and the doc. She raises her weapon and points it at my forehead.

Do it, Kath! Bring this horrible mess to an end.

There's an explosion. But it's not my head being blown to pieces. It's much louder than that. It's the deafening bang and blinding light of a stun grenade. The disorientation is so severe, it's like being knocked out. Then I hear the *pop*, *pop*, *pop* of rapid gunfire. The two boys on either side of me shudder and twist as round after round bounces them off the wall. They fall to the ground in a heap. Without their support, I follow them in a heap of my own. Kathleen doesn't move, but the doc pulls her weapon away from my forehead and she drops it to the floor. Jimmy does the same.

I see dark shadows moving behind Kathleen. They're clad in black, their faces hidden behind S6 Respirators. They're carrying MP5s: it's a Regiment anti-terrorism CRW team.

They start to shout orders and force the three people in front of me to the floor before putting their pistols to the backs of their heads.

'No!'

As loudly as my condition will permit, I bellow at the team to prevent an execution.

'No! Don't shoot.'

The team leader shouts back.

'We have our orders. They're only alive because they were standing in front of you!'

'I said, don't shoot!'

'They were about to execute you!'

'For fuck's sake, stand down!'

They hesitate and, although they keep their pistols firmly against the heads of their captives, they don't fire. There's a strange stillness for what seems like an age, before an unexpected face appears at the bottom of the stairs.

It's Peters, the MI5 officer from the Pendleton ambush.

He smiles at me. He's soon followed by several civilian faces, including an even bigger surprise.

It's Martindale.

He turns to the leader of the assault team, who's taken off his respirator. I recognize him straight away. It's Major Collins, the Regiment's best assault specialist. Martindale shakes his hand.

'Excellent job, Major, very well done. Take these three away.'

He walks over to Maureen and me, two crumpled bodies, covered in blood.

'Peters, get the medical team down here!'

I try to speak calmly.

'Martindale, let those three go. They've got rid of Hendriks. And as for what they did to me; well, I had it coming.'

'No can do, Waddington. They're an IRA ASU operating on the mainland. They're going to prison for a very long time.'

'But they came to right a wrong we did to them. Let them go. We're even, quid pro quo.'

'Not my call, you'll have to talk to the DG.'

Major Collins kneels down in front of me and looks at my knees.

'It looks like a few weeks with your feet up for you.'

'Yeah, right! Thanks for the 5th Cavalry bit.'

'All in a day's work, mate.'

The medics are already crawling all over Maureen, assessing her condition. Collins turns to look at her.

'She's in a bad way.'

'I know.'

He looks at the leader of the medics, who responds with a shake of the head.

'Has she gone?'

'Not yet.'

Tears start to run down my face.

Maureen and I share the same ambulance. It's almost dawn as blue lights flash and sirens wail to hasten our way back towards London. There are three medics looking after Maureen. She's on oxygen, a drip and has had several injections. I've been sedated, but the pain is still excruciating.

Martindale looks at me.

'Thought you might thank us for saving your skin.'

'You are fucking joking, aren't you?'

'I wasn't, actually.'

'How did you find us?'

'We finally tumbled to the source in the RUC, the officer you gave a hard time to.'

'And?'

'Well, after a bit of pressure, he gave us enough to track Hendriks.'

'And?'

'He's taking early retirement.'

'Are you serious?'

'Yes, it's bandit country over there; you know that. If we punish him, or expose him, it will only get worse.'

'Great, so the fucker who's responsible for all this walks away with a fat pension!'

'Something like that.'

'Fucking great! Look at the state we're in; couldn't you have got to us sooner?'

'We got to the SFC just as they were driving you away.'

'Fucking hell, man, why didn't you intercept us?'

'We didn't have the right manpower in the right numbers. We had to wait for a unit to come down from Hereford.'

'You mean all the resources of 5 couldn't muster a team to get us out? That's fucking bollocks!'

He hesitates and looks at Maureen's stricken form.

'OK, it was orders, Waddington. It had already been passed to the MoD. Because of the intelligence mishaps and rumours of moles in Gower Street, Downing Street insisted. It landed in the CO's lap. And, as you know, if he says it's Tuesday, it's Tuesday.'

'It's still bollocks! It's cost me my fucking legs – and Maureen's not going to make it!'

'Look, they sent their top team and they got you out.'

'Great, thanks for absolutely fuck all! Where to now?'

'The Mayday, Thornton Heath.'

'Then?'

'Let's get you better first, then we'll talk.'

I lie back. Martindale's right, there's only one priority right now: getting better. Or at least as well as our injuries permit. It looks like I'll make it, even if it's to a future as a cripple.

Maureen's chances are minimal to zero.

Even if she lives, the odds are she'll be in a wheelchair for the rest of her life.

*

When we get to the Mayday, amid a flurry of anxious staff and a tangle of tubes, wires and medical kit, Maureen's wheeled in first and straight into the operating theatre. I follow and I'm soon oblivious to everything as I'm also sedated and prepared for my turn in theatre.

It's dark when I wake, so I assume I've been unconscious for the whole day. The pain from my shattered knees kicks in straight away. It's not as bad as when the bullets went in, but it's intense all the same.

I hear a female voice nearby.

'He's awake. Get Mr Patel.'

I nod off again, but come round later to see the outline of a man in a white coat. I assume he's Mr Patel and guess that he's my surgeon. On either side of him are two more white coats, and behind him are two nurses in blue.

'Well, Mr Waddington, I've done what I can with your knees. They're in a bad way, I'm afraid.'

'Thanks, Doc. What does "a bad way" mean?'

'I hear you're a soldier?'

'I was until recently.'

'So I suppose you'd prefer a straight answer?'

'I would.'

'You face a long period of rehab. It will be painful and may involve more operations.'

'Will I walk again?'

'Yes, but not for a long time. And it will hurt, possibly for years. Then you'll get arthritis.'

'Did my colleague make it?'

'Captain Townsend's remarkably strong, and very lucky to be alive. God only knows how she survived.'

'I think the bullet she took went through somebody else first.'

'That explains a lot. The reduced impact will have made a big difference. She was operated on by Mr Mohamed and in theatre for a long time. For the moment, she's stable. But she's lost an enormous amount of blood and is very weak.'

'What are her chances?'

'Given that she should be dead already, they're minimal. We'll feel more optimistic if she gets through the night.'

'And the bullet she took?'

'We got it out. It missed her heart by an inch and nicked her liver, but only did minimal damage. However, it shattered her T5 vertebra.'

'And?'

'Her spinal cord isn't severed, so there's a chance she won't be paralysed. But there is some nerve damage around the cord.'

'What does that mean?'

'T5 is quite high and connects the mid-chest area. If she pulls through and stabilizes, Mr Mohamed will go in and have another look. Then he'll have to work on repairing the vertebra, and then either fuse it to T4 or put in an artificial disc.'

'It sounds complicated.'

'It is. Like you, she faces many months of recovery. But don't get your hopes up; her chances are not great.'

'When can I see her?'

'Tomorrow.'

Later that evening, Martindale and the DG arrive.

It's embarrassing for all concerned. They don't want to

be here, and I don't want to see them . . . ever again. They engage in pleasantries and platitudes for a while. The DG even bangs on about cricket!

I listen for a bit before switching off.

Eventually, with cursory handshakes, they wander off. I look at them as they go: amoral androids whose only purpose is to do the politicians' bidding and clean up the shit they make.

When they get to the door, I shout to the DG.

'Remember what you said at the SFC: Dowd and O'Brien never existed. Let's keep it that way.'

He smiles sanctimoniously.

'Never heard of them.'

I think of Maureen and everything that's happened. We're like so many others – civilians and military, guilty and innocent. We're all pawns in a game. So many have died; there's been so much pain, so much hurt.

For what?

For nothing.

Nothing other than a macabre game, a game of betrayal.

Acknowledgements

To my loving family, wonderful friends and dedicated professionals who have made this modest book significantly better, both in its conception and in its execution.

Glossary

Adams, Gerry

Gerry Adams was born in Belfast in 1948 into a family with a strong republican background. He has been a leading figure in the campaign against British rule in Ireland since the late 1960s. He was interned in 1972 and again a year later. Adams became the figurehead of Sinn Féin and led its emergence into mainstream politics. Adams has been accused of many things during the Troubles, all of which he denies.

APC

Armoured Personnel Carrier. Most of the APCs used in Northern Ireland in the 1980s were Alvis Saracens, which could transport up to nine occupants. Although armoured, they were vulnerable to high-explosive landmines.

Ardoyne

The Ardoyne is a small Catholic enclave – no more than a couple of dozen streets – in West Belfast, lying just to the north-east of the Crumlin Road. The name means 'Eoin's height'. During the Troubles it was one of the most dangerous parts of the city and a stronghold of republicanism and support for the IRA, which was regarded as the saviour of the community when it was under severe attack from Protestant mobs in 1969 and 1970.

Armalite

A rifle produced in the United States and used by the IRA during the Troubles. The IRA received small quantities of the Armalite AR18 on the black market.

ASU

Active Service Unit (IRA or loyalist). Usually a team of four.

Bagshot

Bagshot in Surrey was the location of the officer training college of the Women's Royal Army Corps (WRAC) until it was closed in 1981. From then on, female officers were trained at Sandhurst (Royal Military College Sandhurst) along with the men. The Women's Royal Army Corps was disbanded in 1992 and female soldiers were integrated into regiments of the then 'men's' army, making it into a unisex force.

Beast/beasting

British Army colloquialism for demanding exercises or endurance punishments given during training.

Bergen

In British Army terminology, a 'bergen' is a large backpack, based on a design introduced during the Second World War.

Best, George

Legendary Northern Ireland footballer, born in Belfast and star of Manchester United in the 1960s and 1970s, who was perhaps British football's first superstar. His life became a sad saga of profligacy, beautiful women and the excesses of alcohol. The latter addiction ultimately claimed his life.

Bivvy

A bivouac (improvised outdoor shelter).

Bloody Sunday

Refers to a notorious incident on 30 January 1972. Twenty-six unarmed civilians were shot during a demonstration against internment, which was taking place in the Bogside, a Catholic enclave in Londonderry (Derry). Fourteen people were killed by British soldiers from 1st Battalion, Parachute Regiment. The initial inquiry into the events (conducted by Lord Widgery, and published in April 1972) laid the blame on the march organizers and said that although the soldiers had fired 'recklessly', they had been fired on and were defending themselves in a dangerous situation. A much more extensive inquiry (presided over by Lord Saville, and published in 2010) concluded that the deaths were 'unjustified' and 'unjustifiable'. It added that all those who were shot had been unarmed, that no one had posed a threat to the British soldiers, and that many soldiers had given 'false accounts' to justify their actions. As a result of Saville, British Prime Minister David Cameron made a formal apology for the incident on behalf of the people of the United Kingdom.

Bonnie and Clyde

A 1967 movie starring Warren Beatty as Clyde Barrow and Faye Dunaway as Bonnie Parker. It is based on the exploits of Barrow and Parker and their gang, notorious bank robbers in the central United States during the Great Depression. The pair became anti-heroes, even within their own lifetimes. They were ambushed and killed by police in Louisiana in 1934.

Botham, Ian

English cricket all-rounder. He played for England between 1972 and 1992, scoring 14 centuries and taking 383 wickets. His most famous match was against Australia at Headingley, Leeds, in 1981 when he scored 149 not out to rescue England from a hopeless position. Fast bowler Bob Willis then took 8 wickets for 43 to win the match. Botham also performed heroically at Edgbaston and Old Trafford. He scored 399 runs and took 34 wickets as England won the Ashes. The 1981 series is now referred to as 'Botham's Ashes'.

Brady, Liam

Liam Brady was the greatest Irish football player of his generation. Dublin born, he was the star of the Arsenal team in the late 1970s and won an FA Cup winner's medal with them in 1979 before his transfer to Italian team Juventus, in the summer of 1980. He won 72 caps for the Republic from 1974 to 1990.

Brize Norton

RAF Brize Norton in Oxfordshire is the RAF's largest and most important base.

Brontës

The Brontë family made a remarkable contribution to English literature. From modest origins and very limited horizons, they were the children of Patrick Brontë, an Irish-born clergyman from

Haworth, Yorkshire, and his wife, Maria Branwell, a Cornish woman. The three sisters, Charlotte (*Jane Eyre*, 1847), Emily (*Wuthering Heights*, 1847) and Anne (*The Tenant of Wildfell Hall*, 1848), each wrote what is regarded as a literary masterpiece. Branwell Brontë, Patrick's only son, was an accomplished artist and poet, but succumbed to alcoholism and drug abuse and died at the age of thirty-one. Patrick Brontë outlived his wife and all his children by many years. Charlotte was the only one to marry, but she died less than a year later, at the age of thirty-eight. Emily died at the age of thirty, unaware of the success of her only novel. Anne died at the age of thirty-nine. Their home, Howarth Parsonage, is now an extremely popular visitor attraction, as is Top Withens, a ruined hall above the village of Haworth, which may have been the inspiration for the Earnshaw family home in Emily's *Wuthering Heights*.

Browning

A 9mm semi-automatic handgun.

Bupivacaine

A local anaesthetic.

Burntollet Bridge

The Burntollet Bridge incident is widely regarded as the spark that transformed a peaceful civil rights campaign into sectarian violence. The Civil Rights Association had been campaigning for improved civil rights for Northern Ireland's Catholic population since its formation in 1967. Although the Civil Rights Association advised against it, a more radical offshoot of the CRA, People's Democracy, organized a march from Belfast to Londonderry (Derry), which passed through Burntollet, on 4 January 1969. When the marchers reached Burntollet, they were attacked by a crowd of loyalists armed with rocks, iron bars and clubs. The loyalists were reinforced by over 100 members of the Ulster Special Constabulary ('B' Specials), an almost exclusively Protestant quasi-military reserve police force. The incident galvanized the Catholic community throughout the North and focused the attention of the world on Northern Ireland's problems.

Butch Cassidy and the Sundance Kid

A 1969 movie starring Paul Newman as Cassidy (Robert Leroy Parker) and Robert Redford as Sundance (Henry Alonzo Longabaugh), with Katherine Ross as Sundance's girlfriend, Etta Place. It is loosely based on the real Butch Cassidy and his gang's exploits as train-robbers in the American West in the 1890s. The pair are thought to have been killed in a shoot-out in Bolivia in 1908, but their deaths remain the subject of conjecture.

Cam cream

Camouflage cream, used to obscure the faces and hands of soldiers in combat. Usually a combination of green, brown, beige or black, depending on conditions.

Cambridge, the

Opened in 1879, the Cambridge Military Hospital, Aldershot, was named after Prince George, Duke of Cambridge. It was the first base hospital to take wounded men from the Western Front and pioneered the use of plastic surgery from 1915 onwards.

Cambridge Five

The Cambridge Five refers to a group of spies who passed information to the Soviet Union during the Second World War and into the early 1950s. Four members of the ring, then known as the Cambridge Four, were originally identified: Kim Philby, Donald Maclean, Guy Burgess and Anthony Blunt. They later became the Cambridge Five when John Cairncross was also named. They were recruited by a Soviet agent while at Cambridge University in the 1930s. After Cambridge they became senior intelligence officers and diplomats.

Capone, Al

Alphonso Gabriel Capone was a Chicago gangster who became notorious during America's Prohibition era. He was the boss of the Chicago Outfit, a notorious Mafia gang, and organized the 1929 St Valentine's Day Massacre, when seven rival gang members were gunned down by machine-gun fire. Capone went to prison for eight years for tax evasion. He died in 1947 at the age of forty-eight.

Carlton, the

The Carlton Club is one of London's most prestigious gentlemen's clubs. The club has had a close affinity to the Conservative Party since its foundation in 1832.

Castlereagh

Castlereagh Police Station in East Belfast (also known as Castlereagh Holding Centre) became notorious after repeated accusations that both republican and loyalist prisoners were tortured there in order to produce confessions. It has since been demolished.

Century House

The Westminster Bridge home of MI6 from 1964 to 1994.

CIA

The United States Central Intelligence Agency is responsible for foreign intelligence gathering and operations for the US government.

Collins, Michael

Michael Collins was a revolutionary leader of the republican cause during the Irish struggle for independence. He was killed in 1922 in controversial and disputed circumstances in the civil war that followed independence.

Continuation

The post-selection probationary training phase of SAS recruitment, when specialist techniques are acquired.

CQB

Close Quarter Battle (Training). This is a generic term to describe both military and civilian training techniques employed over short distances by small groups or single combatants. It can include lethal and non-lethal weapons and various forms of self-defence and hand-to-hand combat techniques, with or without weapons.

Cromwell, Oliver

Lord Protector of England, Scotland and Ireland from 1652 to 1658. He is reviled in Ireland, and by many objective critics, for the brutality of his campaigns against Catholic Irish rebels in 1649–50, especially during the sieges of Wexford and Drogheda.

CRW

The CRW (Counter Revolutionary Warfare) wing is a specialized unit created during the 1970s to prepare the SAS for its counter terrorism (CT) role. The CRW developed advanced pistol-shooting techniques, explosive entry methods and room-clearing drills for use by the anti-terrorist teams. The CRW is responsible for training whichever squadron is on CT standby duties.

Det

The insiders' name for 14 Intelligence.

Dickers

A British Army term that emerged in Northern Ireland during the Troubles. A dicker is a lookout used to observe army patrols, or to warn of the approach of a patrol. Young men and boys were usually deployed as dickers.

Diplomatic Protection Group (DPG)

Formed in 1974, the DPG is the armed unit of the Metropolitan Police tasked with providing protection for Her Majesty's Government and diplomatic premises, including embassies, high commissions and consular sections. The group also provides protection to members of the foreign diplomatic community in London.

Doctor Zhivago

A 1965 film, directed by David Lean, of Boris Pasternak's novel. Julie Christie starred as Lara and Omar Sharif as Dr Zhivago.

Dojo

Dojo means 'the place of the way' in Japanese. As the term is understood in the West, it refers to a training centre for martial arts.

Doolally

A term in military slang, which emerged in India at the beginning of the twentieth century. It is based on the town of Deolali, near Mumbai, which was the location of a military sanatorium and transit camp. Soldiers suffering from various disorders – such as heat exhaustion, fever or stress-related problems – were sent to Deolali for rehabilitation or for preparation for a return to Britain. The suffix 'tap' was often added. *Tap* means 'fever' in Urdu.

DS

Directing Staff on the 14 Intelligence selection course.

Duchess of Kent Military Hospital

This was a large military hospital at Catterick Camp, North Yorkshire. Opened in 1976, it closed in 2001 when all British military hospital services were integrated into NHS facilities.

Earp, Wyatt

See *Tombstone*.

Easter Rising

An Irish nationalist armed rebellion against British rule in Ireland. Organized by seven members of the Military Council of the Irish Republican Brotherhood, the Rising began on Easter Monday, 24 April 1916. Members of the Irish Volunteers, led by schoolmaster and Irish language activist Patrick Pearse, joined by the Irish Citizen Army of James Connolly and members of Cumann na mBan (a women's republican paramilitary organization), seized key locations in Dublin, including the General Post Office, which became their headquarters, from where they proclaimed an Irish Republic. The rebellion lasted only six days before the rebels surrendered to British forces. The leaders were court-martialled and shot (fifteen in total). However, republican sentiment grew significantly in the following years until Irish independence was granted in December 1922, at the end of the Irish War of Independence. The Protestant-dominated north refused to join the Irish Free State and remained part of Britain as Northern Ireland, composed of the greater part of the traditional province of Ulster.

Emergency – Ward 10

A medical soap opera that ran on ITV between 1957 and 1967. It aired twice weekly and was very popular. It is regarded as one of television's ground-breaking soap operas.

Exocet

A French-built anti-ship missile that can be launched from a variety of aircraft.

Falklands War

The Falklands War was a short but decisive conflict between the armed forces of Argentina and the United Kingdom. It began in

April and ended in June 1982. On 2 April Argentinian forces invaded the Falkland Islands (and the neighbouring territories of South Georgia and South Sandwich) in the South Atlantic. The invasion was intended to force Argentina's claim to have sovereignty over the islands, a claim based on geography, as opposed to Britain's position that the vast majority of the islanders are of British descent and wish to remain under British rule. A British task force sailed for the islands and, after a series of air and sea encounters, made an amphibious landing at San Carlos Water on 21 May. After some fierce fighting the Argentina commander, Brigadier General Mario Menendez, surrendered on 14 June. The conflict had lasted 74 days. 649 Argentinian and 255 British military personnel were killed in the fighting, as were three Falkland Islanders. The outcome became a significant victory for British prime minister Margaret Thatcher, bolstering her flagging popularity. Conversely, for General Leopold Galtieri, leader of Argentina's military dictatorship, it was a humiliating defeat. He was later prosecuted for mishandling the war and various other crimes. He was stripped of his rank and imprisoned.

Fan Dance

An endurance test up and down Pen-y-Fan, in the Brecon Beacons, the highest peak in South Wales; part of SAS selection.

Fenian

Originally a word used to describe members of the Fenian Brotherhood and the Irish Republican Brotherhood in the nineteenth and twentieth centuries, it became a name for all supporters of Irish independence. Latterly, it has been adopted as a derogatory term, especially in Northern Ireland, for Catholics. John O'Mahony founded the Fenian Brotherhood, an Irish republican organization, in the United States in 1858. O'Mahony, who was a Celtic scholar, named his organization after the *fianna*, the legendary band of Irish warriors led by Fionn mac Cumhaill (Finn MacCool), a mythical warrior from Irish mythology.

Fields, Gracie

An English singer, actress and comedian who became a star of both music hall and cinema. She was born Grace Stansfield in Rochdale in 1898 and was made Dame Gracie Fields just before her death in 1979.

14 Intelligence

Part of the British Army's Intelligence Corps, 14 Field Security and Intelligence Company operated in Northern Ireland from the 1970s onwards.

4-tonner

The British Army's standard medium transport lorry, usually open-backed with a canvas cover over benched seating.

Garda

The Garda Síochána na hÉireann (Guardians of the Peace of Ireland) is the police force of the Republic of Ireland. It was formed in 1922 at the beginning of the Irish Free State. Its headquarters is in Phoenix Park, Dublin.

GB75

Accurate information about GB75 is hindered by much disinformation from both left-wing and right-wing vested interests. It was certainly created by David Stirling, the founder of the SAS, in 1975 amidst fears that Britain was under threat from left-wing extremism. Rumours circulated (mainly concocted by elements in the intelligence services) that Prime Minister Harold Wilson was a communist and/or in the pay of Soviet intelligence. Stirling recruited to the cause several ex-SAS men, rich businessmen and equally rich fellow gamblers. The plan was to take over the control of the country to protect its democratic heritage when the (inevitable) collapse came. More sympathetic views of Stirling's motives suggest that he abandoned the idea when he realized that it was attracting many people whose views were undemocratic.

Gere, Richard

American actor Richard Gere's career took off in 1980 when he starred as a male escort, Julian Kaye, in the film *American Gigolo*.

H Blocks

The 'H'-shaped buildings used to hold inmates in the Maze prison (also known as Long Kesh).

Henry II

Henry invaded Ireland with a large army in 1171. He built a series of fortifications and demanded that the local Irish kings show him fealty. He was one of the major architects of the eventual English domination of Ireland.

Hercules

The Lockheed C-130 Hercules is a military transport aircraft that has been in production for over sixty years. Highly adaptable, it is in use throughout the world in over seventy countries.

Hexamine

A smokeless, solid-fuel tablet, not unlike a firelighter. It was used in British Army field rations for cooking and came in a retractable metal container that could be opened and used as a small stove.

Higsons

Higsons was a traditional Liverpool brewery that produced beer from 1780 until it was taken over and brewing was ended in 1990. There have been two attempts to revive the brand, in 2005 and 2011, and a new plan was mooted in 2016.

Hoddle, Glenn

England footballer Glenn Hoddle played for his country between 1979 and 1988. He was a midfield player with exceptional balance, control and grace. He went on to manage England between 1996 and 1999.

Horseshoe moustache

A heavy moustache with vertical extensions grown from the corner of the mouth to the jawline; also called a 'biker moustache'.

Hughes, Brendan

Also known as 'The Dark', Hughes was a leading member of the Provisional IRA and was Officer Commanding, Belfast Brigade in the 1970s and early 1980s. He was the leader of the hunger strikers in the Maze in 1980. He was released from prison in 1986 and became an active figure in Sinn Féin, the political party of the Northern Ireland republican movement. Hughes died in 2008 in Belfast.

Internment

A policy of internment – arrest and detention without trial – was introduced in Northern Ireland in August 1971. Initially, as part of 'Operation Demetrius', 342 people suspected of being IRA members or supporters were rounded up in a dawn raid. Internment lasted until December 1975, by which time over 1,980 arrests had been made, only 107 of whom were loyalists. During their time in prison, internees were subjected to interrogation techniques that divided opinion. Sleep deprivation, stress positioning, hooding and white noise methods were used. Many critics described these methods as torture. There were also many accusations that prisoners were beaten and humiliated.

IRA

The Irish Republican Army is a broad term that describes several armed movements in Ireland across both the twentieth and twenty-first centuries. Most are, or were, prepared to use armed struggle to achieve their aims: a united Ireland free of British rule and ruled by a republican government. The original Irish Republican Army was formed in 1917 from those Irish Volunteers who refused to enlist in the British Army during the Great War. The first split in IRA ranks came after the Anglo-Irish Treaty in 1921, with supporters of the treaty forming the nucleus of the National Army of the newly created Irish Free State, while the anti-treaty forces continued to use the name Irish Republican Army. After the end of the Irish Civil War, the IRA was around in one form or another for forty years, until it split into the Official IRA and the Provisional IRA in 1969. The latter then had its own breakaway groups, particularly the Real IRA and the Continuity IRA. The various iterations of the IRA are listed below.

- The Irish Republican Army (1917–1922): Later known as the 'Old' IRA, it was recognized by the First Dáil (Irish parliament) as the legitimate army of the Irish Republic in April 1921.
- The Irish Republican Army (1922–1969): The anti-treaty IRA, it fought and lost the Civil War and refused to recognize either the Irish Free State or Northern Ireland, saying both were creations of British imperialism.
- The Provisional IRA (Provos): In a dispute about philosophy and tactics, it separated from the Officials (see below). Although opposed to the Marxism of the Officials, it became more left wing over time as it engaged overtly in the political process rather than terrorism. The Provisionals declared a final ceasefire in 1997 and decommissioned its weapons in 2005.
- The Official IRA: Incorporated the Marxist elements of the IRA, following the split with the Provisionals in 1969. It is now inactive militarily, while its political wing, Official Sinn Féin, became the Workers' Party of Ireland.
- Continuity IRA: Broke from the Provisionals in 1986, because the latter changed its policy and recognized the authority of the Republic of Ireland.
- The Real IRA: A 1997 breakaway from the Provisionals. Its members oppose the Northern Ireland peace process.
- The Irish National Liberation Army: Formed in 1974 by members of the Officials who were opposed to its decision to announce a ceasefire. The INLA has since rejected violence and decommissioned its weapons.

Isandhlwana

See *Rorke's Drift*.

Keystone Cops

A group of silent-film, fictional policemen created by slapstick actor and director Mack Sennet. The Cops were notoriously incompetent and specialized in chaotic chase sequences. The films were made between 1912 and 1917, but there were several later revivals, imitations and homages. Their name has become a byword for comic incompetence.

Kick, bollock and bite

A colloquial expression, probably of London origin, for the cruder types of local football, where skill is often outweighed by endeavour and aggression.

King Billy

The affectionate name used by Northern Ireland loyalists for King William III, who reigned from 1689 until 1702. A staunch Protestant, he was supported by all those who feared a return to Catholic rule. He gained the English, Scottish and Irish thrones during the 'Glorious Revolution'. His final victory at the Battle of the Boyne on 11 July 1690 is commemorated every year by the loyalist community with parades and marches.

Kissinger, Henry

Kissinger, a former Harvard academic, was US Secretary of State during the administrations of Richard Nixon and Gerald Ford (1973–1977). Controversially, he was awarded the Nobel Peace Prize in 1973 for his efforts in the Paris Peace Accords, which brought about an end to the Vietnam War.

Klebb, Rosa

The fearsome, fictional head of SMERSH (Main Directorate of Counter-Intelligence), the Soviet spy network, who is featured in Ian Fleming's James Bond thriller *From Russia with Love* and the movie (1963) of the same name.

Lee, Bruce

An iconic martial arts actor who starred in several memorable films – including *Fist of Fury* and *The Way of the Dragon* – in the early 1970s. He died in 1973 at the age of thirty-two.

Left-footer

A mildly derogatory term for Catholics in common usage in Ireland (north and south), Scotland and the north-west of England. Its origins are subject to debate. Some believe the term is based on the view in the Protestant north of Ireland that labourers in the south drive a spade with their left foot. Others think it may relate to the feeling that the left foot is like the left hand (unclean or sinister), thus Catholics are not to be trusted.

Long Drag

The final endurance challenge of SAS selection in the Brecon Beacons; 40 miles in less than 20 hours, usually including the notorious mountain Pen-y-Fan, with a bergen weighing 55lbs, plus webbing and a weapon.

Loyalist paramilitaries

The formation of loyalist paramilitary groups dates back to the anti-Irish Home Rule movement in the 1910s. They re-emerged in the mid-1960s from Northern Ireland's Protestant community in response to the civil rights movement and rising nationalism within the Catholic community. The first significant group was the Ulster Volunteer Force, which formed in 1966 and began attacking Catholics. The Ulster Defence Association and its military wing, the Ulster Freedom Fighters, emerged in the early 1970s. For three decades these groups attacked suspected republican paramilitaries, prominent nationalists, critics of loyalism, randomly chosen Catholic civilians, and occasionally each other. The loyalist paramilitaries use the 'Red Hand of Ulster' – the ancient heraldic symbol of the province – as their badge of honour. Although the 'Red Hand' has been used across the sectarian divide, as the most potent symbol of Ulster's identity, it was adopted by unionists and loyalists to signify their resistance to growing Irish nationalism and moves towards a United Ireland.

M16

A 5.56mm, 20-round military-issue rifle.

MacCormick, Donald

MacCormick was a television reporter and presenter at the BBC and ITV between 1967 and his death in 2009.

McGuinness, Martin

A Northern Ireland republican leader who was Deputy First Minister from 2007 until shortly before his death in March 2017. He admitted to having been second-in-command, Derry Brigade IRA at the time of Bloody Sunday in January 1972. But he denied IRA membership from 1974 onwards, although many historians, journalists and contemporaries claim that his membership continued, including holding a place on the IRA's seven-man Army Council.

Mata Hari

A Dutch exotic dancer and courtesan. She was shot as a German spy by a French firing squad in 1917 at the age of thirty-one. She has since become an archetype of the femme fatale.

Mater Hospital

The Mater Infirmorum Hospital is an acute hospital on the Crumlin Road, only a few hundred yards from the Ardoyne. It was established in 1883 and has been serving the people of Belfast ever since.

Mayday

The Mayday Hospital, Thornton Heath was a 600-bed NHS district general hospital with an A&E unit. It is now called Croydon University Hospital.

Maze, the

Her Majesty's Prison Maze was the prison in Northern Ireland used to hold republican and loyalist prisoners during the Troubles. It is located near Lisburn, nine miles south-west of Belfast.

Meehan, Martin

A veteran of the Provisional IRA, Meehan spent a total of eighteen years in prison for various offences. Meehan was born in the Ardoyne and was regarded by its Catholic population as their saviour when under siege in 1970. A volunteer in 3rd Battalion (Ardoyne) Belfast Brigade, he was badly beaten several times while in detention. Claiming he was falsely convicted of the abduction and imprisonment of an alleged informer, he went on hunger strike in March 1980. After sixty days, he was persuaded to give up by Tomás Ó Fiaich, Catholic

Archbishop of Armagh. Meehan was released from prison in 1994 and sat on the national executive of Sinn Féin. He died in 2007 in Belfast.

MI5

Military Intelligence 5, the secret intelligence service responsible for Britain's domestic security.

MI6

Military Intelligence 6, officially the secret service responsible for Britain's foreign intelligence operations.

Milling

Part of P-Company testing. Milling is a boxing challenge where candidates of similar height and build have to attack one another for sixty seconds. It's not a boxing match, but a test of aggression and the ability to withstand a prolonged physical attack.

Millstone grit

The soft yellow sandstone of the Pennines. After being quarried and dressed and made into houses and public buildings, it darkened significantly – because of the pollution of the Industrial Revolution – thus creating the image of 'dark, satanic mills'.

MoD

Ministry of Defence.

Moffie

An Afrikaans insult, meaning 'wuss' or 'wimp', or someone who is effeminate or homosexual.

Monkey jacket

A slim-fitting, tapered zipped jacket. The style was very popular in the 1970s and 1980s.

MP5

A Heckler & Koch 9mm sub-machine gun.

Mugabe, Robert

See *Ian Smith*.

Nairac, Robert

Captain Robert Nairac was a British soldier captured and killed by the IRA in South Armagh in 1977. He was aged twenty-eight at the time. His body was never found. He had served in Northern Ireland as a regular soldier but, after training and selection, returned as a member of 14 Intelligence. Several men were convicted of his murder and confessed to torturing him. They also said that he never revealed his identity even under torture. Nairac was awarded the George Cross in 1979.

OC

Officer Commanding.

OC-SAS

Officer Commanding, SAS.

Ó Fiaich, Cardinal Tomás

Tomás Ó Fiaich (Thomas O'Fee) was Catholic Archbishop of Armagh and Primate of All Ireland until his death in 1990. He had influential links with the republican movement, within which he was much admired, but he strongly condemned violence.

O'Hara, Maureen

Many people regard the red-haired Hollywood legend Maureen O'Hara as the epitome of Irish beauty and fiery temperament. She was born in Dublin in 1920 and went to Hollywood in 1939. She most famously worked with fellow legends actor John Wayne and director John Ford in *Rio Grande*, *The Quiet Man* and *The Wings of Eagles*. She died in 2015 at the age of ninety-five.

Palace Barracks

Palace Barracks, Holywood, County Down, is a large British Army complex near Belfast Airport. It was the headquarters of military intelligence and also of 14 Intelligence, Belfast (East Det) during the Troubles.

P-Company testing

The Parachute Regiment's training regime before recruits can begin parachute training. It involves endurance tests and challenges to test courage and resolve.

Peckinpah, Sam

A leading Hollywood director whose films were notorious for their explicit, choreographed violence. Perhaps his best-known film is the western *The Wild Bunch*, released in 1969, starring William Holden and Robert Ryan. Peckinpah, himself a hard-living, addictive personality, prone to violence, died in 1984.

Pendle witches

Now part of English folklore, the Pendle witches were twelve people from villages around Pendle Hill who were tried for witchcraft at Lancaster Assizes in 1612. All but one, led by 'Old Mother Demdyke', were executed on Gallows Hill, Lancaster.

Pigs

The Humber (British motor vehicle manufacturer) Pig was a four-wheel-drive British Army armoured personnel carrier used extensively in Northern Ireland from the 1970s to the early 1990s, when it was superseded by the six-wheel Alvis Saracen.

Planxty

An Irish folk band from County Kildare, they were part of a significant revival in traditional Irish music in the 1970s and 1980s. The principle members were Christy Moore, Andy Irvine, Dónal Lunny and Liam O'Flynn. *The Woman I Loved So Well* was their fifth album, released in 1980.

Poncho

A military-issue poncho (green or camouflage) is a multi-purpose garment primarily used as a hooded, all-body rainproof protector which, with its hood tied closed, can also be adapted as cover for a bivouac ('basha') or as a groundsheet. *Basha* is Malay for 'shelter'. The SAS brought the word back with them from service during the Malayan Emergency in the 1950s.

Port arms

A position in the manual of arms; the weapon is held diagonally in front of the body with the muzzle pointing upwards to the left.

Powell, Enoch

A distinguished scholar, soldier, linguist and poet, Powell became a prominent British politician who flirted with high office in the Conservative Party before becoming a highly divisive figure in public life. He had forthright views about immigration and protecting what he regarded as the cornerstones of British culture and heritage. He joined the Ulster Unionist Party in 1974 and became MP for the South Down constituency until 1987. Powell died in 1998.

Protestant Ascendancy

A historical term that describes the domination of Ireland by a minority of landowners and the Protestant establishment between the seventeenth century and the early twentieth century.

Red Hand

See *Loyalist paramilitaries*.

Rorke's Drift

In January 1879, during the Anglo-Zulu War, an almost legendary battle took place at Rorke's Drift. The day before the battle, the British suffered a decisive defeat at the Battle of Isandhlwana when a column, 1,800 strong, was attacked by an overwhelming force of Zulus. Less than a third of the column survived. After the battle, a large Zulu *impi* (regiment), at least 3,000 strong, attacked Rorke's Drift, which was manned by only 150 British and colonial troops. The British soldiers were from the 24th Regiment of Foot. Eleven Victoria Crosses were awarded after the battle – an unprecedented number. The Battle of Rorke's Drift became immortalized in modern folklore, in large part because of the success of the 1964 film *Zulu*, directed by Cy Endfield and staring Stanley Baker and Michael Caine (his first film). The opening and closing narration was spoken by Richard Burton.

Royal Ulster Constabulary (RUC)

The police force of Northern Ireland from its inception in 1922 until it was reorganized into the Police Service of Northern Ireland in 2001. The RUC was at the forefront of the confrontations of the Troubles. Although it did attract some Catholic recruits, it was predominantly a Protestant-dominated organization, and accusations of discrimination, bias and collusion with loyalist gangs were widespread and consistent. Nevertheless, it was also praised for its professionalism and bravery in the face of enormous challenges. It was awarded the George Cross in 2000, only the second time the medal has been awarded collectively (the other occasion being the Island of Malta, in 1942). Over 300 RUC officers were killed during the Troubles.

Rupert(s)

A derisory name for army officers, especially those from public-school backgrounds.

RV

A rendezvous point.

S6

The S6 NBC (Nuclear Chemical Biological) Respirator was a protective gas mask. It was developed in the 1950s and in service from the 1960s onwards. It was replaced in 1986 by the S10.

Sands, Bobby

After a fast that lasted sixty-six days, Sands, an IRA prisoner in the Maze prison, became the first hunger striker to die, on 5 May 1981. By the time of his death he had become the MP for Fermanagh and South Tyrone. He was twenty-seven years old.

SB

Special Branch is the name given to the British police units responsible for national security and anti-terrorism work. Initially formed in 1883 to counter the threat from the Fenians (Irish nationalist insurgents), the branch has been renamed in recent years to reflect its role in countering the new terrorist threats of the twenty-first century. For example, the Metropolitan Police unit is now called Counter-Terrorism Command.

Scran

Army term for 'food'. Its origins are with the Royal Navy; the term may have got into army usage through the Royal Marines.

Secretaries of State for Northern Ireland

Name	Party	Dates
Whitelaw, William (Willie)	Conservative	March 1972–November 1973
Pym, Francis	Conservative	November 1973–February 1974
Rees, Merlyn	Labour	March 1974–September 1976
Mason, Roy	Labour	September 1976–May 1979
Atkins, Humphrey	Conservative	May 1979–September 1981
Prior, James (Jim)	Conservative	September 1981–September 1984

Selous Scouts

The Scouts were the special forces unit of the Rhodesian Army during its war against African nationalist guerrilla infiltrators between 1973 and 1980. It was named after the nineteenth-century British explorer and big-game hunter Frederick Courteney Selous. The unit became notorious not only for its effectiveness as a counter-insurgency unit but also for the ruthlessness of its methods, which included assassination, intimidation, torture and extortion. The unit was disbanded when the white-minority government of Rhodesia was succeeded in 1980 by the new, liberation government of Zimbabwe, led by Robert Mugabe.

Semtex

Semtex was developed in the late 1950s in Semtín, a suburb of Par-
dubice, in what is now the Czech Republic. It is a plastic explosive
that was, until recently, difficult to detect and is easily malleable.
Widely used in industry, it was exported to many countries within
the Soviet sphere of influence, particularly Libya, from where it got
into the hands of the IRA in large quantities.

Shankill

An area of West Belfast on either side of the Shankill Road. It is a
predominantly working-class Protestant area, separated from the
Catholic Ardoyne by the Crumlin Road. During the Troubles it was
a hotbed of Protestant paramilitary activity.

Shebeen

An illicit drinking den, where alcohol is sold without a licence and
often without duty being paid. The alcohol may also be stolen or dis-
tilled illegally. The word derives from *sibín*, Irish for 'illicit whiskey'.

Sheffield, HMS

She was a Royal Navy Type 42 guided-missile destroyer. The ship
was hit on 4 May 1982, during the Falklands War, by an Exocet missile fired from a Super Etendard aircraft of the Argentinian Air
Force. She sank six days later. Twenty of her crew died in the attack.

Shergar

The thoroughbred racehorse won the Epsom Derby, the Irish Derby
and the King George VI and Queen Elizabeth Stakes in 1981. He won
the Epsom Derby by ten lengths, a record over its 200-year history. He

was retired to stud in the same year. He was kidnapped in February 1983. The strongest suspects for the kidnap were an IRA gang, but the gang's exploitation of the captured horse was bungled and the police (Garda) investigation was characterized by a catalogue of disasters. No trace of the legendary horse has ever been found. However, despite their continual denials, it is now believed that the IRA leadership ordered the horse's execution when it became clear that its owners were not going to pay the ransom they demanded for its release. Furthermore, it has been reported that the execution was also bungled and that the horse was killed inhumanely in a hail of machine-gun bullets.

Shippon

An Old English term for a cowshed or milking parlour.

Sinn Féin

Established at the beginning of the twentieth century, Sinn Féin – which means 'ourselves', or 'we ourselves' – is the political party of Irish republicanism. It was, and is, active in both Northern Ireland and the Irish Republic. Sinn Féin was the vehicle through which the IRA entered mainstream politics in the 1980s.

Sitrep

US/British Army abbreviation for 'situation report'.

Sitting Bull

Sitting Bull was a leader of the Lakota Sioux during their wars of resistance against the US government. He was shot and killed while being arrested at the Standing Rock Indian Reservation, in South Dakota, in December 1890.

Irish for 'cheers'; strictly speaking, it means 'health'. It is pronounced as (loosely) *slawn-cha*.

Sloane Pony

The popular name for the White Horse pub in Parsons Green, Fulham. It was a renowned gathering place for London's 'Sloane Rangers' – the name given to West London's rich and fashionable young people in the early 1980s, especially the young women.

Smith & Wesson 39

A classic 9mm semi-automatic handgun first introduced by the US arms manufacturer in 1954.

Smith, Ian

White Rhodesian Ian Smith led a white-minority government, which attempted to prevent the country's transition from a British colony to black-majority rule. He made a unilateral declaration of independence (UDI) in 1965. Britain considered military intervention, but Labour Prime Minister Harold Wilson decided to use sanctions instead, a policy which failed. A vicious civil war followed. By 1980, after several attempts at compromise and interim governments, Robert Mugabe, the Marxist leader of the Zimbabwe African National Union (ZANU), became the first democratically elected leader of the new Republic of Zimbabwe.

Special Forces Club

The SFC was established in 1945 by wartime veterans of the Special Operations Executive (SOE), SAS, SBS and various members of the intelligence services. It is a private members' club open to men and women of all ranks who have served in British and international special forces and intelligence units. It is located in Knightsbridge, London.

Spetsnaz

Spetsnaz is an umbrella term that (approximately) translates from Russian as 'Special Purpose Military Units' and refers to Soviet and post-Soviet special forces. Originally it was the armed wing of Soviet military intelligence.

Stirling, Colonel Sir David

From a distinguished Scottish family, Stirling became an heroic figure during the Second World War through the establishment of a unit that ultimately became the Special Air Service Regiment. He was captured in North Africa in 1943 and, after multiple escape attempts, spent the rest of the war imprisoned in Colditz Castle. After the war, he set up various security companies and became entangled with fringe elements on the right of British politics. He was a striking figure at 6ft 5ins, and a heavy gambler and drinker; he was sent down from Cambridge University. He was knighted in 1990 and died two years later at the age of seventy-five.

Stirling Lines

The headquarters of 22nd SAS, in Hereford, named after the founder of the regiment, David Stirling.

Tab/tabbing

Originally 'Tactical Advance to Battle'; now a soldiers' term for long marches.

Taig

An old Gaelic boy's name that means 'poet' or 'philosopher'. Like 'Fenian', it is also used as a derogatory word for Catholics among the Protestant community.

Tan

A derogatory name for a British soldier. It derives from the Black and Tans, a force of temporary constables recruited from British soldiers who had fought in the Great War. The brainchild of the British Secretary of State for War, Winston Churchill, the force was raised in 1919 to support the Royal Irish Constabulary during the Irish War of Independence. Its official title was the Royal Irish Constabulary Special Reserve. The nickname originates from the uniform the men wore: British khaki and rifle green (a very dark green). The Tans became notorious for their acts of brutality against republican activists and civilians alike.

Tanner

In Britain's old imperial money (decimalization was introduced in 1971), a 'tanner' was a colloquial term for a sixpenny piece (6 old pennies) and a 'bob' was a shilling (12 old pennies). There were 20 shillings to £1, thus 40 sixpences and 240 pennies to the pound. In today's decimal money a shilling equates to 5p and a sixpence to 2.5p.

Teddy Hall

The affectionately shortened name for St Edmund Hall, one of Oxford University's oldest colleges.

Thatcher, Margaret

British Prime Minister from 1979 to 1990. Thatcher's leadership still divides opinion. Many see her as Britain's saviour, putting the nation on a firm economic footing after years of government intervention, and an 'iron lady' in foreign policy. Others see her as a right-wing ogre who undermined much of Britain's renowned liberality and sense of the common good.

Theakston

T&R Theakston is a family-owned brewery based in Masham, North Yorkshire. Its most famous beer is Old Peculier – a strong, dark ale revered by real ale aficionados.

Tombstone

Tombstone, Arizona, was the location of the 1881 'Gunfight at the OK Corral', a shootout between 'the Cowboys' (the Clanton brothers, the McLaury brothers and Billy Claiborne) and 'the Marshals' (Wyatt Earp, his brothers Virgil and Morgan, and 'Doc' Holliday). The incident has been immortalized in several books and films.

Troubles, the

The widely used name for the period of conflict and violence in Northern Ireland that began in the late 1960s and, by common consent, ended with the Good Friday Agreement in 1998. Over 3,500 people were killed during the Troubles: over 2,000 by the IRA, and over 1,000 by loyalist paramilitaries.

Twin Towers

French high-wire artist Philippe Petit walked between the Twin Towers of New York's World Trade Center on 7 August 1974. At a height of 1,350 feet, he performed for forty-five minutes, making seven traverses in all. At one point, to the astonishment of the large crowd that gathered to watch him, he performed a little jig on the rope. Petit was arrested, but released without charge after he promised to do a performance for children in Central Park.

Tyke

A colloquial, mildly derogatory name for a Yorkshireman or woman. The Lancashire equivalent is a 'Lanky'.

Ulster Defence Regiment (UDR)

Established in 1970, the UDR was raised through popular appeal and created to ensure the 'defence of life or property in Northern Ireland against armed attack or sabotage'. Initially it had an intake from the Catholic community, but the percentage soon diminished from 18% in 1970 to 3% in 1972. The UDR became mired in controversy and accusations were made that its ranks had been infiltrated by loyalist paramilitaries. The UDR was amalgamated with the Royal Irish Rangers to form the new Royal Irish Regiment in 1992.

Wallace, Colin

Colin Wallace's story is a complex and controversial one. He was a member of the Intelligence Corps in Northern Ireland and part of 14 Intelligence. His speciality was psychological warfare. It seems that he became involved in Operation Clockwork Orange in the 1970s, a covert initiative that tried to discredit the nationalist cause and anyone who supported it. Various journalists, including Paul

Foot, Duncan Campbell and Peter Wright, claim that right-wing elements in MI5 and the military were preparing a coup and that Clockwork Orange was an instrument of that plot. When Wallace refused to continue with Clockwork Orange and made allegations of sexual abuse by senior Protestant politicians at the Kincora Boys' Home, he was dismissed from the army. He was later convicted of the manslaughter of the husband of a female colleague. He served six years in prison, from 1981 to 1987. The conviction was quashed in 1995. Wallace and many who have examined the case claim that he was framed by MI5.

Walther P38

A famous traditional handgun popular with armies and police forces all over the world. A 9mm semi-automatic weapon, it was standard issue in the Wehrmacht (German Army) prior to the Second World War. Thousands of P38s remained in circulation long after the war, especially from Eastern Europe, where huge stocks were captured from defeated German units and arsenals.

Weaver, Sigourney

An American actress who played the central character, Ellen Ripley, in the 1979 science fiction film *Alien*, a box-office hit, directed by Ridley Scott.

Wellesley, Arthur

Arthur Wellesley, 1st Duke of Wellington, was an Anglo-Irish soldier and statesman of great repute. His defeat of Napoleon at the Battle of Waterloo in 1815 secured his place in British history. He was born in Dublin, into a family of the Protestant Ascendancy. He was twice British Prime Minister: from 1828 to 1830, and for a little less than a month in 1834.

White's

White's is a male-only gentlemen's club in St James's, London, probably the most exclusive and elitist of all London's clubs.

William of Orange

William of Orange, the grandson of Charles I, became William III of England in 1689, ruling jointly with his wife, Mary. He is a symbol of Protestant power in Northern Ireland because of his victory over the Catholic forces of James II and the French king Louis XIV at the Battle of the Boyne in 1690.

Woodentops

A derisory name used by plain-clothes officers (and other security personnel) for their uniformed colleagues.

Yomp/yomping

The Royal Marine equivalent of tabbing.

Yorkshire Ripper

The name used by the press for serial killer Peter Sutcliffe, who murdered thirteen women and injured seven more between 1969 and 1980.

Statistics

There is some dispute about the number of people killed during the Troubles between 1969 and 2001, but is around 3,500. It is also worth pointing out that, even in a period of relative peace and calm, there are still deaths and killings that are almost certainly a result of sectarian violence.

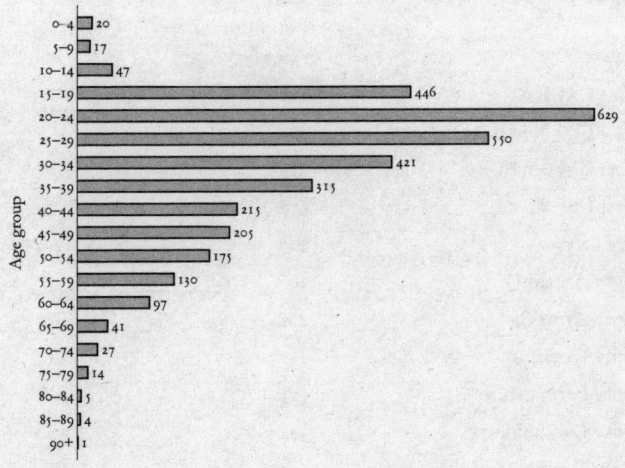

The ages of those who died

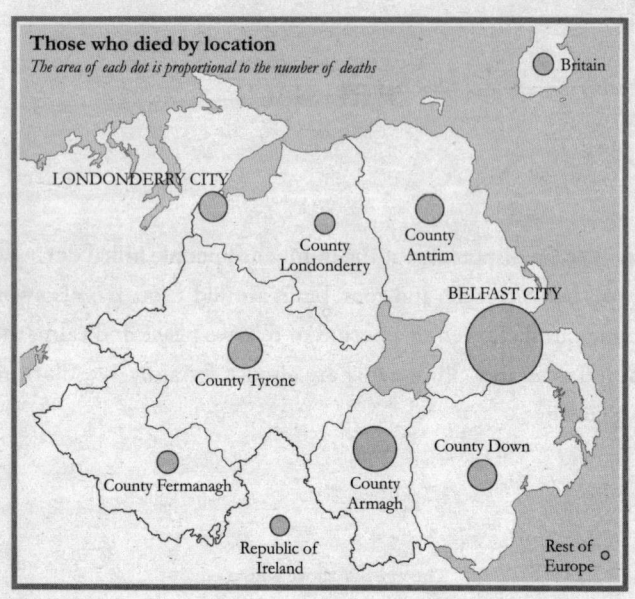

Those who died by location

The area of each dot is proportional to the number of deaths

Britain

LONDONDERRY CITY

County
Londonderry

County
Antrim

BELFAST CITY

County Tyrone

County Down

County Fermanagh

County
Armagh

Republic of
Ireland

Rest of
Europe

Location	Number
Belfast City East	128
Belfast City North	563
Belfast City South	213
Belfast City West	617
Derry City	227
County Antrim	198
County Armagh	468
County Down	235
County Fermanagh	111
County Londonderry	121
County Tyrone	337
Britain	125
Republic of Ireland	105
Rest of Europe	18

Those who died by community

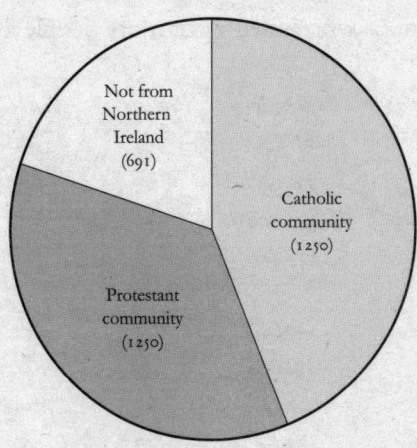

Those who died by their status and the category of group responsible

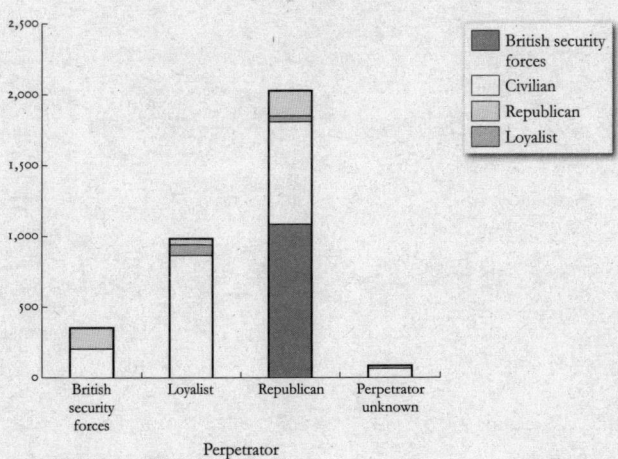

Killings carried out by each group, by community

(Only groups who killed 25 or more people are shown.)

Organization	Total killings	Protestant	Catholic	Not from NI
IRA	1,696 (49%)	790	338	568
UVF	396 (11%)	89	265	42
British Army	299 (9%)	32	258	9
Unknown loyalist	212 (6%)	50	212	7
UFF	149 (4%)	17	132	0
INLA	110 (3%)	55	33	22
UDA	102 (3%)	41	58	3
Unknown	77	27	42	8
RUC	56	9	44	3
Official IRA	51	7	24	20
PAF (loyalist)	37	0	37	0
'Real' IRA	29	11	13	5
Others	117	27	87	3

Maps

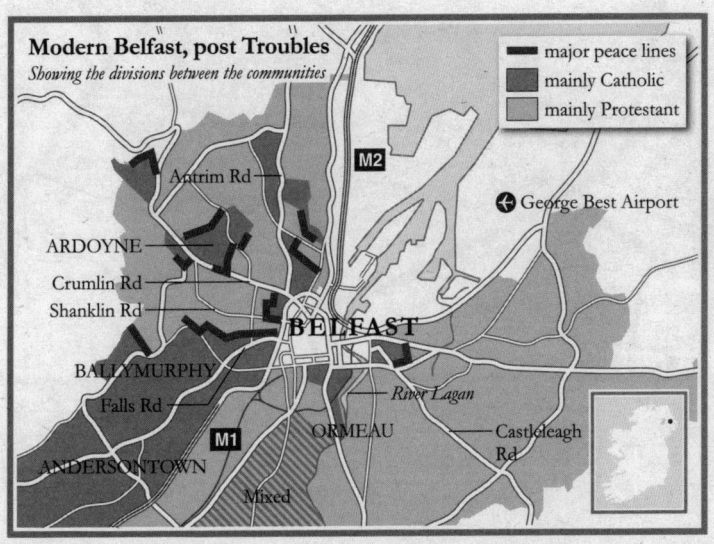

Modern Belfast, post Troubles
Showing the divisions between the communities

- major peace lines
- mainly Catholic
- mainly Protestant

M2

George Best Airport

Antrim Rd

ARDOYNE

Crumlin Rd

Shanklin Rd

BELFAST

BALLYMURPHY

Falls Rd

River Lagan

ORMEAU

Castlereagh
Rd

M1

ANDERSONTOWN

Mixed

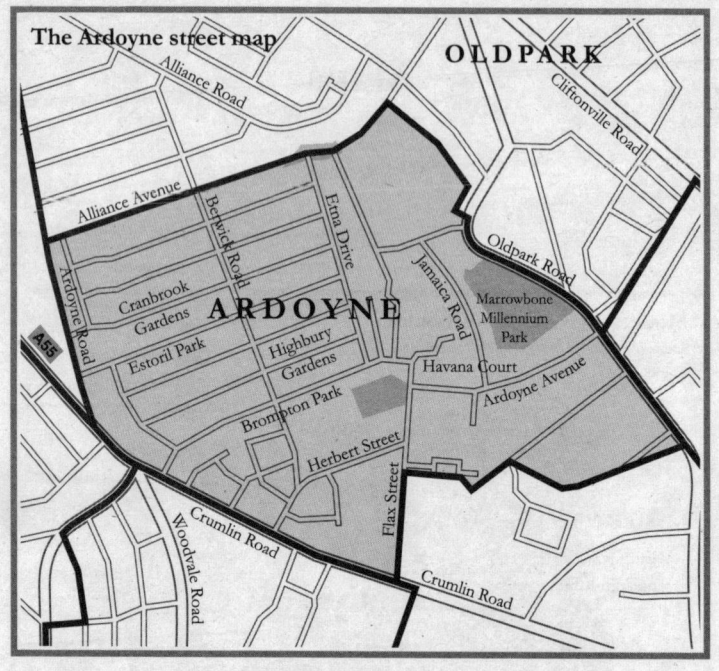

The Ardoyne street map

OLDPARK

Alliance Road

Cliftonville Road

Alliance Avenue

Oldpark Road

Berwick Road

Etna Drive

Ardoyne Road

Cranbrook Gardens

ARDOYNE

Jamaica Road

Marrowbone Millennium Park

Estoril Park

Highbury Gardens

Havana Court

Ardoyne Avenue

A35

Brompton Park

Herbert Street

Flax Street

Crumlin Road

Woodvale Road

Crumlin Road

He just wanted a decent book to read ...

Not too much to ask, is it? It was in 1935 when Allen Lane, Managing Director of Bodley Head Publishers, stood on a platform at Exeter railway station looking for something good to read on his journey back to London. His choice was limited to popular magazines and poor-quality paperbacks – the same choice faced every day by the vast majority of readers, few of whom could afford hardbacks. Lane's disappointment and subsequent anger at the range of books generally available led him to found a company – and change the world.

'We believed in the existence in this country of a vast reading public for intelligent books at a low price, and staked everything on it'
Sir Allen Lane, 1902–1970, founder of Penguin Books

The quality paperback had arrived – and not just in bookshops. Lane was adamant that his Penguins should appear in chain stores and tobacconists, and should cost no more than a packet of cigarettes.

Reading habits (and cigarette prices) have changed since 1935, but Penguin still believes in publishing the best books for everybody to enjoy. We still believe that good design costs no more than bad design, and we still believe that quality books published passionately and responsibly make the world a better place.

So wherever you see the little bird – whether it's on a piece of prize-winning literary fiction or a celebrity autobiography, political tour de force or historical masterpiece, a serial-killer thriller, reference book, world classic or a piece of pure escapism – you can bet that it represents the very best that the genre has to offer.

Whatever you like to read – trust Penguin.

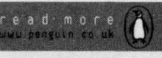